ROMAN POETS OF TH

ANTHONY JAMES BOYLE and JOHN PATRICK SULLIVAN were both educated at St Francis Xavier's College, Liverpool, and Cambridge University but were never present in either institution at the same time. Sullivan was born in 1930, Boyle in 1942. Sullivan taught at Oxford before leaving for the USA; Boyle taught at Cambridge before taking the boat to Australia. Sullivan moved from appointments at the University of Texas at Austin and the State University of New York at Buffalo to his present position as Professor of Classics at the University of California at Santa Barbara. Boyle served twenty years at Monash University, Melbourne, before moving to the USA at the beginning of 1989, where he is Professor of Classics at the University of Southern California, Los Angeles. Both have edited classical literary journals: Sullivan *Arion* and *Arethusa*; Boyle *Ramus*, of which he is still editor. Boyle's publications include *Ancient Pastoral*; *Seneca Tragicus*; *The Chaonian Dove: Studies in the Eclogues, Georgics and Aeneid of Virgil*; *Seneca's Phaedra*; *The Imperial Muse, Vols I and II*. Sullivan's publications include *Critical Essays on Roman Literature: Satire*; *The Satyricon of Petronius: A Literary Study*; *Literature and Politics in the Age of Nero* and *Epigrams of Martial Englished by Divers Hands* (with Peter Whigham). He has also translated and edited Petronius' *Satyricon* and Seneca's *Apocolocyntosis* for Penguin Classics. They live in Santa Barbara, California – but not together.

ROMAN POETS
OF THE EARLY EMPIRE

EDITED
WITH INTRODUCTIONS, NOTES AND GLOSSARY BY
A. J. BOYLE AND J. P. SULLIVAN

PENGUIN BOOKS

PENGUIN BOOKS

Published by the Penguin Group
Penguin Books Ltd, 27 Wrights Lane, London w8 5tz, England
Viking Penguin, a division of Penguin Books USA Inc.
375 Hudson Street, New York, New York 10014, USA
Penguin Books Australia Ltd, Ringwood, Victoria, Australia
Penguin Books Canada Ltd, 10 Alcorn Avenue, Toronto, Ontario, Canada m4v 3b2
Penguin Books (NZ) Ltd, 182–190 Wairau Road, Auckland 10, New Zealand

Penguin Books Ltd, Registered Offices: Harmondsworth, Middlesex, England

First published 1991
1 3 5 7 9 10 8 6 4 2

Printed in England by Clays Ltd, St Ives plc
Set in 10/12 pt Monophoto Bembo

IN MEMORIAM
BETTY RADICE
HUIUS LIBELLI
FAUTRICIS

CONTENTS

CONTENTS

PREFACE

The idea of this volume was originally suggested by the late Betty Radice, although she died before any progress could be made on it. It is to her that it is therefore dedicated. We are grateful to Peter Mayer for his help in executing one of Betty's last legacies to the Penguin Classics series. The hope was that the collection would help fill the gap between Michael Grant's *Latin Literature* and Harold Isbell's *The Last Poets of Imperial Rome*, although it was felt desirable to limit our range essentially to the poetry of the first and second centuries A.D. and to include both familiar and less familiar classical authors.

For some of our primary texts we chose existing and available translations; for most we drew upon the services of trusted literary and scholarly friends. For their collaborative support our thanks. We must also acknowledge our gratitude to other coadjutors: Faye Nennig for her incisive editorial judgement, indispensable stylistic skills and (most of all) her patience; Elizabeth Frech, ever ready to come to our help in times of need; Randall Smith, whose technical expertise was invaluable. On the historical and philological side, William Dominik, John Henderson, Bronwyn Williams, and Marcus Wilson gave generously of their time and advice. More than time was given by James Boyle, Kathy Boyle and Judy Godfrey.

USC, Los Angeles   A. J. Boyle
UCSB, Santa Barbara   J. P. Sullivan
Easter 1990

ACKNOWLEDGEMENTS

Acknowledgements are due to Penguin Books for permission to reprint the translations from Ovid and Juvenal by Peter Green, and from Petronius and Seneca by J. P. Sullivan; to Coronado Press, Kansas, and Richard E. Braun for translations of *Satires* from Persius; to the Ohio University Press and the Southern Illinois University Press for the translations from Martial by J. V. Cunningham and Dorothea Wender; to Timothy d'Arch Smith for those by Brian Hill; to Anvil Press Poetry and Margaret Whigham for those by Peter Whigham; and to Molly Barger, Olive Pitt-Kethley and Anthony Reid for their versions; to New Directions Publishing Corporation for the version of the Emperor Hadrian's address to his soul from *Collected Poems of Stevie Smith*, copyright © 1972 by Stevie Smith; to Ruth Morse and Norman Austin for their translation of *Thebaid* from Statius; to W. G. Shepherd for his version of *Silvae*; to Marcus Wilson for his translations of *Punica* from Silius Italicus and *Latin Anthology* from Seneca; to A. G. Lee for his version of *Eclogues* from Calpurnius Siculus; to Frederic Raphael and Kenneth McLeish for their translation of *Argonautica* from Valerius Flaccus; to Eugene O'Connor for his versions of Phaedrus, Manilius and the *Priapea*; to Cornell University Press for the Jane Wilson Joyce translation of *Civil War* from Lucan.

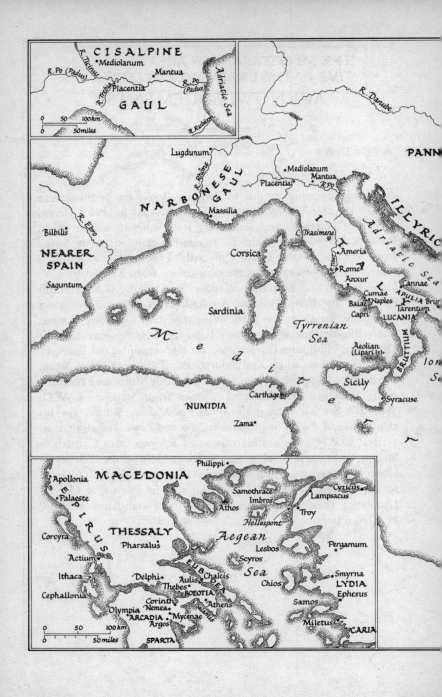

THE MEDITERRANEAN AREA AT THE TIME OF THE EARLY ROMAN EMPIRE

GENERAL INTRODUCTION

Periods of literary history are the convenient inventions of literary historians, who smuggle into them misleading evaluations. More importantly for this collection, how useful would have been the concept of 'Literature of the Silver Age', a term first introduced as late as 1736?[1]

Despite Gibbon's persuasive claim that the Age of the Antonines was the happiest in human history, historians persist in seeing the Augustan Age as a Golden Age of imperial peace and political tranquillity. Success breeds applause, often self-generated: history is the propaganda of the victors. Augustus, that 'cold, calculating terrorist' (Sir Ronald Syme's words), had indeed succeeded in crushing the internecine feuds of the Roman republican oligarchy; he had centralized military power after his own successful *coup d'état*, and despite many reverses, he had instituted, to his own satisfaction at least, rational policies of imperial defence and administrative organization. The occasional follies of his successors, magnified by hostile senatorial annalists, made him look better and better in retrospect.

His lavish but hardly altruistic support of the arts, from architecture to epic, produced impressive monuments of durable marble as well as unageing intellect. 'Augustan' became the paradigm of the classical, the Golden Age – confusingly since our *siglo de oro*,

1. Such blanket divisions serve to muffle the contemporary criticism of Virgil, and Pope's dismissal of *Aeneid* as 'a political puff'. The cool reception of Horace's first three books of *Odes* may be contrasted with Lucan's enthusiasm for Persius, and his pre-eminence as a revolutionary poet in our own Augustan age. The medieval esteem enjoyed by Statius and the enormous European popularity of Martial in the Renaissance and afterwards are often forgotten in the nineteenth-century establishment of the ancient canon.

which produced Shakespeare as well as Cervantes, is separated by a century from the 'Augustan Age' of English literature.

To point to the weakness of such literary terminology is not to deny the great literary merits of the honoured trio of Augustan writers, Virgil, Horace, and Ovid, but merely to undermine some sweeping generalizations and unexamined platitudes. This incidentally explains the title of the present volume, which contains selections from works written in the first century and a half A.D., between the closing years of the emperor Augustus' reign and the death of Hadrian in A.D. 138, whose famous address to his soul concludes the selection.

It is, nevertheless, a frequent criticism of early imperial literature that it is too rhetorical in a period when oratory no longer had the power it had enjoyed under the republic to achieve political goals, since such matters were ultimately decided by the emperor's fiat. Cicero's Catilinarians and Philippics would be inappropriate, indeed unnecessary, under an autocratic regime. The pointed rhetorical style is therefore implicitly criticized as a hangover from its days of glory under Greek democratic or Roman republican institutions. But this is a mistaken view. The literature of the empire is intensely political, indeed ideological, and if the aim of the spoken word was to sway a large audience in the Senate or the assemblies, the aim of the written word was to sway an even larger audience of readers as well as, more immediately, the small influential groups at whom initial publication was aimed. Besides, the need for oratory in the private legal sphere was greater rather than less under the empire, and in actual writing a highly sophisticated narrative and poetic style would be needed to convey the controversial or subversive perspectives of poets, philosophers and historians in such a way as to avoid political retribution. Shrill denunciation is not the only technique in the armoury of rhetoric. The subtleties of the orator, and now the writer, included innuendo, irony, misdirection, omission, and even allegory. As Juan Luis Borgés has said, censorship is good for writers: it forces them to express themselves with ever greater subtlety. And this is not even to take into account the plain oratorical skills needed in a highly litigious society, whose main contribution to legal theory was in the area of private property.

The rhetoric attributed to drama, for instance, is wrongly criticized. The dramatist, whether he be Seneca or Curiatius Maternus, was not handling private themes, but cosmic themes of immediate as well as general import. Reflections on the nature of power or cultural dissolution as conveyed through myth in Seneca's *Trojan Women* might be expressed more directly, and more dangerously, in such historical dramas (*fabulae praetextae*) as the pseudo-Senecan *Octavia* of A.D. 69 and Curiatius Maternus' *Cato* (*c*. A.D. 75?).

The Greek and Roman penchant for the analysis and dissection of how to speak well and persuasively offends somewhat our post-romantic sensibilities, when it comes to poetry and even artistic prose. We cannot envision Shelley or Byron, or Carlyle, pondering the value of an aposiopesis or a synecdoche for a particular line. Pope and Dryden perhaps, but never Coleridge, Keats or Wordsworth. We are familiar with the close analysis of the development of the heroic couplet, but we think fondly that if only Dryden and Pope had liberated themselves from the straitjacket of the antithetical rhyming couplet, true poetry might be visible, the sort of poetry found in the almost inaudible iambic rhythms of Shakespeare and the soaring flights of Walt Whitman and Ezra Pound. But we have to remind ourselves that no *vers* is *libre* for the true craftsman.

To understand this period of Roman poetry, we have to replace the arid and now pejorative idea of 'rhetoric' with the concept of 'wit'. Somehow in the nineteenth century, conceptions changed about the relationship between poetry and rhetoric. Certainly in the mid seventeenth and mid eighteenth centuries in England, poet and critic chided neither Horace for the 'pedestrian' discourse of his satires nor Juvenal for the barbed 'rhetoric' in his. 'Rhetorical' is not an adjective applied, for instance, to the speeches of Cicero: odd, since he, as well as Quintilian, produced texts on the art of oratory. Nor indeed to Livy. But it is difficult to read any evaluation of Tacitus in which the word does not occur. Virgil, a painstaking craftsman who supposedly composed at the rate of a line a day, is similarly too revered to be called 'rhetorical', although his wit, however concealed from us, is surely part of Horace's justification for calling him '*facetus*'. So if the stretched images of Persius and Lucan, their 'conceits', strike us sometimes as far-fetched, it is worth remembering that other ages have thought them well worth the carriage.

For any critical challenge to the spurious and misleading division of Roman literature into Golden and Silver Ages and to the devaluation sometimes implied by the descriptions 'Augustan' and 'post-Augustan', 'classical' and 'post-classical', the work of Ovid, who died four years after Augustus, provides crucial support. Hence his inclusion in these pages.

Ovid, trained for the bar, but preferring poetry, is usually regarded as part of the Golden Age of Roman literature. The adjective 'rhetorical' is somewhat reluctantly applied to him by some critics. The reluctance is due to his date, not the qualities of his poetry. If, however, we see Ovid as among the first of a long line of 'wits', whose popularity with the great English wits, Dryden and Pope, was surpassed only by the popularity of Horace and Juvenal, then we have a radically different critical picture of Roman poetry, as radically different a picture as the revaluation of English poetry represented by those critics who follow the Line of Wit from Donne and Jonson through Dryden, Pope, Churchill, to Hopkins, the early Pound and T. S. Eliot, brushing aside the idols of the market place, Milton, the Romantics, Tennyson, Bridges *et hoc genus omne*. It provides further justification for including his later poetry in this volume. Conventional judgements also will support this decision. One critic has written: 'He was not an Augustan as Horace and Virgil were Augustans: compared with the superbly controlled *Aeneid* the *Metamorphoses* is exuberantly un-classical.'[2]

Still, with a Roman 'classical' tradition now established along-side the Hellenic and Alexandrian traditions that had served to form it, there was a creative urge to experiment as well as emulate. Nor was patronage of literature lacking. Even though Maecenas had become the paradigm of such benefactors, the Julio-Claudians, especially Nero, were generous also and even the Flavians were aware of the social functions of literature, and recognized it in

2. E. J. Kenney, *Oxford Classical Dictionary*, under Ovid.

various competitive ways, the Capitoline, Neapolitan, and Alban contests for example.

In all the major genres, except elegy, where Ovid seemed to have exhausted, not without risk, the autobiographical and personal possibilities, writers of talent, sometimes of genius, emerged, some concerned to develop, others eager to innovate.

Virgil's commanding achievement did nothing to deter emulators. His rewriting of Roman history in the guise of myth perhaps redirected epic talent more towards the historical epic in the case of Silius, who believed that a historical account in verse of Rome's rise to empire would equally exhibit, if not justify, Rome's ways to man. Lucan's revisionist epic, *Civil War*, otherwise known as *Pharsalia*, was explicitly designed to counter the idea, critically explored in Virgil's *Aeneid*, of a principate ordained by fate and crowned by the imperial achievements of Caesar and Augustus. Lucan's political vision transformed Virgil's pessimism about Rome's mission into damning conviction: the dream that had become a nightmare. To strengthen his jeremiad, he jettisoned the comfortable epic machinery of two-dimensional Olympian divinities, following or vainly subverting some dimly discerned destiny, for a grimmer, more Boschian universe of Endorian witches and adamantine fates with a mystical Demiurge somewhere darkly involved.

But even the other cycles of Theban, Cretan, and Athenian myth provided potent symbolism for statements about the human condition and the passions of political power. Although myth might be dismissed as unreal and remote by satirists such as Persius, Martial, and Juvenal, in imaginative hands it could be used to explore the fragility of human existence and the spiritual crises of the human heart. And so Valerius Flaccus and, even more, Papinius Statius took the themes of the Quest for the Golden Fleece and the Seven against Thebes to analyse the nature of leadership, ambition, the vagaries of romantic love and the corruptions of power.

In more compressed form, in an astonishing series of dramas, the younger Seneca, the philosopher turned statesman, who stood for many years on 'the slipper slope of courts' estate', serving and, when possible, guiding the young emperor, Nero, deployed his theatrical talents and breathtaking language to convey his thinking, feeling, admonition, even advice in vivid, histrionic portraits of mythical tyrants, heroes, and heroines, easy enough to transfer mentally from the stage to historical reality. If the dramas were sometimes gory, the age itself was bloody enough not to shudder from them.

The relationship of literature to life was more clearly seen and more stridently proclaimed in the development of that uniquely Roman genre, satire. Here pre-eminently may be seen innovation and accomplishment, first in Persius and then Juvenal. Both stretch the resources of the Latin language to the limit; both are masters of indirection, ambiguity, and irony. Satire is a literary form that makes both its victims and critics uneasy. Is it just an abusive sermon in verse or elaborated prose? Regardless of such doubts, Lucilius and Horace established it as an unmistakable genre, which would have a long history, one strengthened by the highly individual contributions of Persius and Juvenal as well as of that versatile mini-satirist, Martial.

Living in the later second century B.C., Lucilius, protected by powerful political friends, could comment on and castigate freely the political corruption and moral decadence (as he saw it) of his times. Horace flourished in a more perilous and repressive period and found it expedient to adopt the *persona* of the unpretentious and amiable commentator on life, reluctant to libel, but willing to share with the reader his experiences and his Epicurean criticisms of general moral failings and offer some guidance (with traditional illustrations) on the road to contentment.

Similarly debarred under equally authoritarian regimes from forthright criticism of political personages, Persius and Juvenal both grappled with the problem of satirizing social evils without risking retribution or censorship. Each developed his own method of artistic distancing. Persius threw a highly wrought web of complex images, literary allusions and Stoic precepts over his subjects, contemporary moral and literary decadence at the court of Nero and the lack of self-knowledge that automatically vitiated all public and private conduct. Juvenal presented his indictment of a society in blind pursuit of sex and power, gold and glory, through a rapid series of highly graphic and superbly witty illustrations from Greek and Roman political and social history. The proposed remedies of both satirists were traditional, quietist, and hardly radical. But the medium transcended the message and ensured their literary survival into a future that had found more spiritual remedies for the ills they had diagnosed.

The success of the first-century masters in epic, tragedy, and satire should not lead us to overlook the achievements of those who worked in what are often regarded as less prestigious genres. Calpurnius Siculus showed how Virgil's *Eclogues* could be transmuted into contemporary court critique. The didactic mode, now to be measured against the high standards of *Georgics*, showed its continuing viability in that astonishing literary and technical *tour de force*, Manilius' *Astronomica*. The short reflective, descriptive, or anecdotal poem was practised enthusiastically by amateurs but reached its acme in the misnamed *Epigrams* of Martial, whose enormous range of subject matter gives us a better overview of Roman social and literary, even sexual, life than a dozen other authors. His productions, along with Statius' *Silvae*, show how far the art of the literary miniaturist could be taken.

The search for originality and innovation without rejecting *tout court* inherited literary traditions is nowhere seen to greater effect than in two near contemporary ventures into Menippean satire, an old marginal form consisting of a loose *mélange* of prose and verse. The first, from the fertile pen of the younger Seneca, was *Apocolocyntosis*, a short political lampoon ridiculing the political career and the inglorious after-life of the late emperor Claudius to contrast it with the golden promise of the new emperor Nero. The second, more novelistic and more artistic in its ambitions, was Petronius' *Satyricon*, a wandering and digressive narrative that incorporated literary criticism, social satire, and comic characterization with equal zest. (Both could be represented here only by their verse interpolations.)

In short, the common devaluation of Roman literature produced after the deaths of the great Augustan writers is based largely on misapprehension and stock responses, often underpinned by myopic cultural arrogance. It was not cultural aberration that made the European Middle Ages love Statius or Dante choose him as a guide to paradise. Nor was it lack of critical judgement that defined the admiration for Lucan shown by Marlowe, Corneille, Johnson and Shelley. The unmaking and remaking of the epic form which constituted early imperial epic made for tough, difficult verse but verse whose toughness and difficulty were constitutive (in part) of poetic strength, intellectual vigour and political force. It was not a matter of writing better or worse, but of writing differently. Similarly in satire new and different standards were set by Persius and Juvenal, whose work would be as seminal as Horace's for the English classical satire of Dryden and Pope. Literary judgement and textual transmission would choose Seneca the dramaturge, rather than his republican or Augustan predecessors, to ignite the incandescent melodramas of the Elizabethans, Petronius to stimulate the picaresque novels of the Spanish *siglo de oro*, *Lazarillo de Tormes* and *Don Quixote*, and Martial to inspire the European 'epigrams' of the Renaissance and after. 'Classical' and 'post-classical' are not terms of evaluation but indices of literary relationships. Roman post-classical verse of the early imperial period is the product of its own literary history, has its own progeny and needs its own context. This collection of translations and essays is an attempt to provide a basis for its reassessment.

A.J.B., J.P.S.

Further Reading

Ahl, F. M., 'The Rider and the Horse: Politics and Power in Roman Poetry from Horace to Statius', *Aufstieg und Niedergang der römischen Welt* 32.1 (1984) 40–110.

Boyle, A. J. (ed.), *The Imperial Muse: To Juvenal through Ovid* (Berwick, Victoria, 1988).

(ed.), *The Imperial Muse: Flavian Epicist to Claudian* (Berwick, Victoria, 1990).

Sullivan, J. P., *Literature and Politics in the Age of Nero* (Ithaca, N.Y., 1985).

NOTE ON LINE NUMBERS

―――――――

The line numbers appearing in the margins of all translations are those of the original Latin texts. The following translations are essentially line for line: Ovid, *Tristia* Book I; Calpurnius Siculus, *Eclogues*; Seneca, *Trojan Women*; Lucan, *Civil War* Book V; Statius, *Thebaid* Book X and *Silvae*; Silius Italicus, *Punica* Selections.

OVID

INTRODUCTION

In A.D. 8 Ovid was Rome's most distinguished living poet.
Virgil and Horace were long dead and Ovid's poetic achieve-
ment extensive, brilliant and lauded. In the same year he was
banished. In an act virtually unprecedented in Roman history
the empire's major poet was removed by its political leader –
and removed, in part, for his verse. The political leader was the
first emperor, Augustus, sole master of the Roman world since
31 B.C., now an embittered autocrat, frustrated by a long series
of misfortunes – military, financial, dynastic (Pliny, *Natural
History* VII.149f.). He expelled Ovid to a half-Greek city called
Tomis (modern Constanza), situated on the Pontus or Black Sea
in what today is Romania at the extreme edge of the Roman
empire. The effect on the fifty-year-old poet was devastating.
Tomis was the inversion of the Rome he loved: barbarous,
insecure, intemperate of climate, spiritually and culturally barren.
Its inhabitants spoke Getic, Sarmatian, hybrid Greek and no
Latin. For a man such as Ovid separation from friends, society,
the literary world, even his own native tongue constituted a
death sentence. Ovid mentions two reasons for his exile (techni-
cally *relegatio*, 'relegation' – the poet lost neither property nor
civic rights): *carmen*, 'a poem', and *error*, 'a blunder' (*Tristia*
II.207). The 'blunder' or indiscretion is (intentionally) described
obscurely and remains obscure. Ovid claims that he saw some-
thing unwittingly (*Tristia* II.103ff.), and explanations have ranged
from the poet's involvement in the sexual misdemeanours of
Augustus' granddaughter Julia, also banished in A.D. 8, to en-
tanglement in the factional rivalries of the imperial family. The

poem was *Ars Amatoria, The Art of Love*, published much earlier (about 1 B.C.) but now apparently a factor or at least pretext in the banishment itself. The objection to it, according to Ovid's defence especially in *Tristia* II, was its moral subversiveness, its encouragement of sexual immorality ('foul adultery', *obsceni adulterii, Tristia* II.212), at the time of Augustus' attempts to improve the *mores* of the aristocracy. As a consequence, *Ars Amatoria* and, it appears, Ovid's books as a whole were removed from Rome's public libraries. But neither that act nor his own poetry's involvement in the banishment stopped Ovid from writing. Only death would do that. For Ovid poetry not only consoled (*Tristia* I.11.12, IV.10.115ff.). To be alive and to be a poet were the same.

Publius Ovidius Naso was born at Sulmo (modern Sulmona), a town ninety miles east of Rome, on 20 March 43 B.C., one year after the assassination of Julius Caesar and twelve years before Octavian (later called Augustus) defeated Antony at the battle of Actium and ended civil war and the Roman republic. He died at Tomis on the Black Sea in the fourth or fifth year (A.D. 17 or 18) of the reign of Augustus' successor, Tiberius – his sentence of exile unremitted. After his departure from Rome in A.D. 8, evocatively described in *Tristia* I.3, he never saw the city again. He came from a fairly wealthy equestrian family and was destined for a public career, but after holding some minor official posts he jettisoned the political world for that of poetry and art. Although apparently attached in his early years to the literary coterie of the influential statesman Messala Corvinus, who died in the year of Ovid's banishment, the young poet resisted the pressure for public, i.e. political, poetry of the kind associated with the circle of Augustus' administrator Maecenas (exemplified most especially by the later works of Horace), and devoted his talents to what was always to be his prime concern: the human world and its poetization. His early poetry focused not on the imperial grandeur of Rome but on love, sex, friendship, poetry, words, life, on the paradoxes and absurdities of human emotion and human relationships, on emotional distress, and on the female mind – generally approached with wit,

humour, empathy, insight, and a self-conscious, animated literar-
iness (vigorous literary allusion defines all Ovid's works), ex-
pressed in language as technically brilliant as it was poetically
and verbally suggestive. The important works of the first period:
Amores or *Loves*, originally five books of generically playful
'love' poems published about 20 B.C., later reduced to three;
Medea, a tragedy now lost, date uncertain; *Heroides* ('Heroines'),
also of uncertain date, fictive epistles from mythological heroines
to their lovers, the final six being paired letters in which the
woman answers the man; three mock-didactic poems: *Medicam-
ina Faciei* or *On Cosmetics*, date uncertain; *Ars Amatoria* or *The
Art of Love*, three books of parodic, satirical verse purporting to
teach seduction, published about 1 B.C.; *Remedia Amoris* or
Remedies of Love, a mocking sequel to *The Art*, published shortly
afterwards. From A.D. 1 to 8 Ovid was at work on two narrative
poems: *Fasti*, a poem on the Roman calendar (Ovid's only osten-
sible attempt at 'patriotic' verse) of which six books survive and
probably only six were written; and *Metamorphoses*, Ovid's master-
work, an epic poem in fifteen books on change. All Ovid's extant
poetry, including the later verse from exile, was written in elegiac
couplets (dactylic hexameters alternating with dactylic penta-
meters), except *Metamorphoses* which was written entirely in
hexameters, the standard metre for epic. At the time of Ovid's
banishment *Fasti* was incomplete and *Metamorphoses*, if the poet's
protestations are to be believed, required revision before publi-
cation. The latter was published anyway, and indeed seems com-
plete. Ironically it was in *Fasti* and *Metamorphoses* that the poet
came closest in his pre-exilic verse to imperial flattery (at least at the
surface level), concluding his fifteen-book epic with the apotheosis
of Julius Caesar, Augustus' 'divine' father, and a eulogy and pre-
dicted apotheosis of Augustus himself (*Metamorphoses* XV.807ff.;
cf. *Fasti* II.119ff.). It was too little and too late. Perhaps the essential
frivolity of *Fasti* and *Metamorphoses*' indictment of power were
more obvious than the poet intended. At all events, unlike the
fictive creations of Ovid's masterwork, Rome's first emperor was
himself not subject to change.

Ovid reached Tomis in A.D. 9 and immediately sent back to

Rome a volume of eleven short poems composed on the out-
ward journey, the first book of *Tristia* ('Sorrows'). It is an in-
novative, experimental, polyvalent book of verse, the first of a
collection of five books (each composed as a separate entity), in
which the poet articulates the pain and deprivations of exile and
petitions for imperial clemency (for at least amelioration of the
place of exile, if not return to Rome itself). The whole *Tristia*
occupied four years of Ovid's life (A.D. 8–12) and was followed
by four books of *Pontic Epistles*, *Epistulae ex Ponto* (A.D. 12–16,
the first three being published as a unit in A.D. 13). These were
collections of short poems like *Tristia*, dealing with the tribula-
tions of exile but more resigned, even apathetic in tone and more
comprehensive and explicit in the use of epistolary form. (They
even include named addressees – only Augustus and Perilla,
perhaps Ovid's stepdaughter, are named recipients in *Tristia*.)
Such, together with the erudite *tour de force*, a 642-line curse
poem entitled *Ibis* (published about A.D. 11), constitute Ovid's
extant exilic poetry.

It is a remarkable body of verse, virtually unique in the classi-
cal tradition: poetry from exile on exile. The only possible pre-
cedent was the early Greek poet Alcaeus, whom Ovid seems
not to have used. In a sense *Tristia* begins a new genre. Ovid's
readers were devouring the recently published (allegedly un-
revised) narrative epic *Metamorphoses* and awaiting completion of
the narrative *Fasti*. They would have been surprised – but not
disappointed. Ovid's search for the kind of poetry that would
reflect his traumatic situation had led him to break with the
present, to return to the past and to rewrite both. What he did
was complex and merits attention. Firstly, he chose to make
poetry out of his own biographical experience in a way he had
never done before. Secondly, he decided to write in elegiac coup-
lets (represented in the translation as long lines alternating with
short) both because of his past identity with this form (it is the
Ovidian metre *par excellence*) and because of its ancient associa-
tion with death and lamentation, which his employment of it in
Tristia revives. Thirdly, he broke with sustained narrative, return-
ing to the elegiac epistle, a form he had himself developed in

Heroides, to express his own isolation: both *Tristia* and *Pontic Epistles* are in fact epistolary in the strongest sense, viz. communications sent from a distance to readers at Rome. (Not that all individual poems in *Tristia* are overtly epistolary. The use of the form increases as the work progresses. Nearly all are epistolary in Book V.) Fourthly, he took over many of the erotic motifs and language of his earlier work and transformed their function, turning the clichés of the erotic chase to more serious ends. Thus the excluded lover (*exclusus amator*) of Ovid's earlier elegies becomes the banished poet (*relegatus poeta*) of Tomis; the elegiac mistress becomes his wife (I.3.79ff., 6.1ff.); the sufferings, wretchedness, protestations and language of amorous youth, which he had himself so often parodied, become by ironic metamorphosis the actual sounds of Ovid himself. Fifthly, again for intellectual and ironic purposes, he mythologized his own situation – through analogies with his earlier epistolary heroines (e.g. cf. I.1.13f. and *Heroides* III.3) and such epic figures as Ulysses or Aeneas (I.2–I.5, especially I.5.57ff.). In the process his wife became a Penelope or Andromache (I.6.19ff.). Sixthly, through extensive allusion to and rewriting of other poetry, including his own, he not only created an image of himself as poet, but, by showing how his own exile was a construct of experience and of literature recycled and remade (the storm in I.2 is both a real and a literary storm made into a new literary storm), he not only infused his poetry with compelling irony (the storm which Virgil controlled at *Aeneid* I.81ff. and he himself controlled at *Metamorphoses* XI.474ff. now controls him) but signalled the fusion for Ovid of literature and life. The five books of *Tristia* are and are not personal poetry. The *persona* of the poet in the work is a manufactured one, and the work is that most public form of writing, a petition – its addressees are Augustus and the Roman people. But the poetry is grounded in history and Ovid's life in a way that had not occurred before, and its conjunction of literature and experience exemplify that life. More than any representation in marble or gemstone (I.7.1ff.) *Tristia*'s literary construct images both poet and man.

Tristia I is the text chosen. Its image is intricate, particular, distinctive. Written when the sentence of banishment was still fresh and its permanence uncertain, the book occupies a liminal position in Ovid's works. The old wit, verve, irony, wordplay, allusion and rhetorical strategies are still present but subject to a new moral seriousness and a potent thematic design. Though transitional, the collection serves as paradigm of the visual, emotional and intellectual power of the verse from Tomis. The book is constructed from a series of frames: ironic, witty prologue (I.1 – instructions by the poet to his book on how to behave in Rome) and taut, imagistic epilogue (I.11 – the circumstances of the book's composition) frame sharply focused poems on the journey into exile (I.2, 3, 4, 10), which in turn frame poems on friendship (I.5, 8, 9), themselves a frame for the central poems on Ovid's wife (I.6) and masterwork (I.7 – on *Metamorphoses*). Only the inner poems I.5 to I.9 have explicit epistolary form, i.e. are addressed to an (unnamed) individual. A triad of 'public' themes pervades the seemingly diverse topics: exile as spiritual and poetic turbulence or death (on exile as death – I.1.18, 2.72, 4.28, 6.32, 7.39, 8.14, and I.3 *passim*); imperial clemency (e.g. I.1.20, 1.73f., 2.62, 9.25f.); the petition for a reprieve (*passim*). Poetically powerful is the image–theme fusion evident in the use of the storms of the journey as a figure for the turbulence and shipwreck of Ovid's exilic life (e.g. I.1.42f., 5.36, 6.7f., 11.34). The bracketing of the famous account of the departure from Rome (I.3) by the storm poems I.2 and 4 secures early in the book the association between storm and exile. Relevant here is the identification of Augustus, instigator of Ovid's banishment, as the storm-god Jupiter, also secured early in the collection (I.1.69ff.).

The identification is relevant not only to Ovid's 'public' themes. For permeating the book and interacting with its overt statements is a pattern of emphases, motifs, images, juxtapositions and implied propositions which not only articulate more fully the nature of the collision between poetry and political power but intimate the intrinsic superiority of the former and the arbitrariness and cruelty of the latter. The assertions of the emperor's clemency, for example, sit ill with his association with hawk and

wolf (I.1.75ff.); so too with his representation as wrathful
storm-god whose thunderbolts make men quake (e.g. I.1.71ff.,
3.11ff., 4.26, 5.3, 5.75ff., 9.21), especially when placed against the
mildness of the *error* for which Tomis was the punishment (e.g.
I.2.97ff., 3.38, 5.41f.). The irony of Ovid's categorization of his
fate as yet another metamorphosis to add to his masterwork
(I.1.120f.) pointedly underscores his status as victim of arbitrary
divine wrath. Most telling of all in *Tristia* I's statement of the
confrontation between poetry and politics is the book's focus on
poetry itself. The first poem opens with an ironic display of
poetry's – but not the poet's – inherent freedom despite the
'shoddiness' which the political world may impose upon it. And
an aspect of that freedom which the political world cannot
control is dwelt upon in the central poem of the collection
(I.6): poetry's ability to confer immortality, its own deathlessness.
In language designed to recall the poet's own boast in the
final word of his great epic – *vivam*, 'I shall live' (*Metamorphoses*
XV.879; cf. also *Amores* I.15.42) – Ovid gives his wife the
immortality which the political world vainly sought: 'You shall
live (*vives*) through these verses for all time' (*Tristia* I.6.36). Nor
is this the only reference to *Metamorphoses* in *Tristia* I. The *vivere*
motif occurs importantly at I.1.19f., 3.101, 7.25. In I.1 Ovid even
asks for his change of fortune to be 'reckoned one more/among
their [*Metamorphoses'*] bodily changes' (120f.); while I.7 builds
itself out of allusions to *Metamorphoses* even as it portrays the
poet's (and Augustus') failed attempt to destroy the epic. Such
citations join with manifold references to other Ovidian works
(especially *Amores*, *Ars Amatoria* and *Heroides*) to confirm Ovid's
position as the greatest living poet and the unfettered power of
his poetic voice. Yet it is not only Ovidian power at issue. *Tris-
tia* I's rewriting of Catullus (cf. especially Catullus I.1ff. and IV
with *Tristia* I.1.5ff. and I.10), of Horace (cf. especially *Epistle*
I.20 with *Tristia* I.1) and of Virgil (the storm scene of *Aeneid* I
and the departure from Troy in *Aeneid* II are sub-texts of *Tristia*
I.2 and I.3 – Ovid even imitates Virgil's narrative sequence: divine
wrath [Jupiter/Augustus, *Tristia* I.1; Juno, *Aeneid* I], storm, recollec-
tion of departure) as well as of Ovid himself, makes of the three

Augustan poets and their republican predecessor a quartet of irresistible poetic power. It was a power that was to ensure the imperishability of Rome long after its political dominion was as dust.

Tristia I can profitably be seen as the first collection of post-classical Roman verse. It is shaped by and rewrites the works of the great Augustans, Virgil, Horace and Ovid, even as it is written by one of them in a consciously self-reflexive mode. Its use of wit, irony, paradox, hyperbole, epigram, its rhetorical and declamatory structures, its emotionality, literary allusiveness, verbal texture and verbal play foreshadowed the poetic modes to come; while its manipulation of tension between overt panegyric and latent criticism, its 'rhetoric of subversion', became a paradigm of imperial discourse. But it is also a historical document, a 'letter' sent by a figure in history as an attempt to alleviate the pain of exile and reverse the metamorphosis of his own fortune which the political world had brought about. As we know, the attempt failed. As did that of the remaining *Tristia*. But they left to the great century of literature which followed, to the Middle Ages and to the Renaissance a mode of verse, a form of discourse and a model of disaffection (increasingly overt in *Tristia* II–V) and poetic integrity which they never forgot. Even to the casual reader *Tristia* I may speak of exilic death; but its constant pointer is to the truth of *Metamorphoses*' climactic boast and the triumph of the life of the spirit over barbarism.

> Anyone may close my life with the barbarous sword,
> But my fame will survive the dying;
> While Mars' Rome surveys victorious from her hills
> The whole world mastered, I shall be read.

(Tristia III.7.49–52)

A.J.B.

Further Reading

Evans, H. B., *Publica Carmina: Ovid's Books from Exile* (Lincoln and London 1983).

Hinds, S., 'Booking the Return Trip: Ovid and *Tristia* I', *Proceedings of the Cambridge Philological Society* n.s. 31 (1985) 13–32.

Kenney, E. J., 'Ovid', in E. J. Kenney and W. V. Clausen (eds.), *The Cambridge History of Classical Literature II* (Cambridge 1982) 420–57.

Mack, S., *Ovid* (New Haven and London 1988).

Malouf, D., *An Imaginary Life* (London 1978).

TRISTIA

BOOK I

Translated by Peter Green

I.1

Little book – no, I don't begrudge it you – you're off to the City[1]
  without me, going where your only master is banned!
On your way, then – but penny-plain, as befits an exile's
  sad offering, and my present life.
5 For you no purple slip-case (that's a colour
  goes ill with grief), no title-line picked out
in vermilion, no cedar-oiled backing, no white bosses[2]
  to set off those black
edges: leave luckier books to be dressed with such trimmings:
10   never forget my sad estate.
No smoothing off your ends with friable pumice – appear for
  inspection bristly, unkempt.
And don't be embarrassed by blots. Let anyone who sees them
  sense they were due to my tears.
15 Go, book, and bring to the places I loved my greeting –
  let me reach them with what 'feet'[3] I may! –

1. Rome.
2. Bosses or knobs were frequently attached to the end of the stick of wood or ivory round which the papyrus roll or 'paper' was wrapped. There was some-times a 'slip-case' or wrapper to protect the roll. This was often stained red or 'purple'. Cf. below, Statius, *Silvae* IV.9.6ff.
3. The pun on 'feet' (Latin *pes* can mean either 'human foot' or 'metrical foot') is one of the most familiar in Roman poetry.

And if, in the throng, there's one by whom I'm not forgotten,
    who should chance to ask how I am,
tell him I live (*not* 'he's well'!), but emphasize I only
    survive by courtesy of a god.   20
For the rest, keep silent. If people demand more details
    take care not to blab out
any state secrets: a reader, once reminded,
    will recall the charges against me, I'll be condemned
in public, by popular vote. Though such accusations   25
    may wound you, make no defence. A good-for-nothing case
stands beyond any advocacy. Find one who sighs at my exile,
    who can't read *those poems* dry-eyed,
and who prays (but in silence, lest the malicious hear him)
    that Caesar's wrath may abate,   30
my sentence be lightened. Anyone gets my prayers
    for happiness, who prays the gods to bestow
a benison on the unhappy. May his hopes be fulfilled, may ebbing
    Imperial anger give me the chance to die
on my native soil! Yet, book, though you follow   35
    all my instructions, you may yet be dismissed
as falling short of my genius. Any judge must unravel
    not the act alone, but also its context – if
context is what's stressed, then you're in the clear. But poems
    come spun from serenity; my heart   40
is clouded with sudden troubles. Poems demand for the writer
    leisure and solitude: *I'm* tossed by sea and wind,
savaged by winter. Terror chokes off creation. My hapless
    throat cringes every moment in fear
of a sword's edge slicing through it. Your fair-minded critic   45
    will be amazed that I achieve even this much,
will peruse my work with indulgence. Put even Homer
    amid dangers like mine, his genius would fail
when faced with such troubles. Lastly, remember to go
        unbothered
    by public opinion: if you leave a reader cold   50
don't worry – I'm not favoured enough by Fortune
    for you to keep tally on your praise!

While I walked safe still, I yearned for recognition,
    was on fire to make myself a name;
55   but now let it suffice me not to detest the poems,
    the pursuit that proved my undoing: it was my own wit
brought me to exile. So go in my stead, you have licence,
    be my eyes in Rome (dear God, how I wish I could be
my book!) – but don't assume just because you've reached the
    Big City
60   from abroad, you'll be incognito. You may
lack a title: no matter, your style will still betray you;
    dissimulate all you like, it's clear you're mine.
Slip in unnoticed, then: I wouldn't want my poems
    to do you harm. They're not
65   so popular as they were. If you meet someone who refuses
    to read you because you're mine, who thrusts you away,
'Look at the title,' tell him, '*I'm* not Love's Preceptor;
    that work[1] has already paid
the penalty it deserved.' Perhaps you thought I'd send you
70   up the Palatine, bid you climb
to Caesar's home? Too *august*. The site – and its incumbent
    gods – must excuse me, but the bolt that struck my head
came from that citadel. The Beings up there are forgiving
    (shall I ever forget it?), but I still fear the gods
75   who did me harm. A dove once raked, hawk, by your talons
    takes fright at the faintest whirr of wings.
A ewe lamb that's been dragged from the fangs of a hungry
    wolf won't dare to stray far from the fold.
Had Phaethon[2] lived, he'd have steered clear of those horses
80   he once was crazy about, kept out of sky.
What scares *me* is Jove's weaponry, I've been its target:
    whenever there's thunder I'm sure
the lightning's for me. Any Greek who's avoided shipwreck
    off the rocks of Euboea steers clear

---

1. *Ars Amatoria, The Art of Love.*
2. Killed by Jupiter's thunderbolt 'unjustly launched' (*Metamorphoses* II.378). The stories of both Phaethon and Icarus (line 89) are told in Ovid's *Metamorphoses* (II.1ff., VIII. 152ff.).

of those waters thereafter; my small skiff, once beam-ended   85
    by a fierce hurricane, shudders at sailing back
into the eye of the storm. So be watchful, unassuming:
    seek no readers beyond the common sort.
Look at Icarus: flew too high with that rickety plumage,
    gave his name to the Icarian Sea.   90
Should you row, or hoist sail to the breeze? It's hard, at this
        distance,
    to decide: you must improvise as occasion dictates.
Catch him when he's at leisure, when his mood's all mellow,
    when his temper has lost its edge;
find someone to murmur a few words of introduction   95
    and present you (hesitant still, still scared
to approach him): *then* make your bid. On a good morning
    and with better luck than your master's, you might just
get in there and ease my suffering. None but the person
    who himself inflicted my wounds   100
can, like Achilles,[1] heal them. Only take care your helpful
    efforts don't hurt me instead – in my heart
hope runs well behind fear – or rewake that quiescent
    fury, make *you*
an extra occasion of punishment. When you've won admission   105
    to my inner sanctum, and reached your proper domain,
the book-bins, there you'll find your brethren, all in order,
    all worked through and through with the same
vigilant care. Most of these will display their titles
    openly, have a label for all to read;   110
but three[2] you'll find skulking in an obscure corner;
    even so, they teach, something everyone knows,
how to go about loving. Avoid them, or, if you have the courage,
    call them Oedipus or Telegonus.[3]

1. The reference is to Achilles' healing of Telephus, king of Mysia, with the rust of
    the spear he had used to wound him. Ovid uses the story elsewhere: e.g. *Amores*
    II.9.7ff.; *Metamorphoses* XII.112; XIII.171. See also Seneca, *Trojan Women* 215ff.
2. The three books of *The Art of Love*.
3. Famous unwitting parricides. Ovid is suggesting that the three books of *The Art
    of Love* similarly killed their father, himself – and killed him unwittingly. The

115 If you respect your father, don't treat any one of the three
        (though it teach you the way itself) with love.
    There are also fifteen books of *Metamorphoses*, worksheets
        lately saved[1] from my exsequies:
    to them I bid you say that the new face of my fortunes
120   may now be reckoned one more
    among their bodily changes: by sudden transformation
        what was joyful once is made fit matter for tears.
    I meant (if you're curious) to give you still further instructions,
        but I fear I've been holding you up –
125 Besides, little book, if you took all my afterthoughts with you
        your bearer would find you a heavy load.
    It's a long trek: make haste. Meanwhile my habitation
        remains the world's end, a land from my land remote.

I.2

    You gods of sea and sky – what's left me now but prayer? –
        Don't break up our storm-tossed ship:
    Don't, I beseech you, endorse great Caesar's fury! Often
        when one god's hostile another will bring help:
5   Mulciber stood against Troy, on Troy's behalf Apollo;
        Venus was pro-Trojan, Pallas pro-Greek,
    Juno hated Aeneas, had more sympathy for Turnus –
        Yet through Venus' power Aeneas stayed safe.
    Time and again Neptune made savage assaults on prudent
10   Ulysses; time and again
    Minerva deflected her uncle's wrath. Though I lack such heroic
        stature, who says *I* can't get heavenly aid
    when a god's angry with me? But my words are all wasted,
        spindrift stings my lips as I speak, the waves
15 tower up, these fearful storm-winds scatter my message,
        stop my prayers reaching the gods

father whom Telegonus killed was Ulysses, with whom Ovid aligns himself
elsewhere in *Tristia* I (see especially I.5.57ff.).
1. See I.7.17–24.

to whom they're addressed, and (to cause me double trouble)
   are driving both sails and entreaties heaven knows where.
Ah misery! what great mountains of heaving water –
   up, up, about (you'd think) to touch   20
the summit stars: ah, what yawning liquid valleys –
   down, down, about (you'd think) to plumb the black
abyss. Look where I may, there's only sky and water,
   here swollen waves, there menacing clouds: between,
howl a vast ground-bass of winds: the sea-swell cannot   25
   decide which master to obey,
for now from the red east the tempest gathers momentum,
   now veers round from the twilit west,
now blasts with chill fury from the ice-dry pole-star,
   now from the south flings its cold front into the fray.   30
The steersman's at a loss, can't work out when to close-haul her,
   when to run with the wind. His expertise
is foxed by such four-way troubles. We're surely done for,
   no hope of safety. As I speak, a wave
drenches my face. The sea will overwhelm my spirit,   35
   I'll gag down the killing water, all my prayers
frustrated. My loyal wife[1] grieves only for my exile –
   the one misfortune of mine she knows and laments.
She has no idea I'm being tossed around the ocean,
   no idea that I'm wind-whipped, at death's door.   40
What good luck that I didn't allow her to board ship with me –
   that would have meant (poor me!)
enduring a double death. As it is, though *I* perish,
   her freedom from danger guarantees
my half-survival. Ah, see that swift lightning flicker   45
   amid the clouds, hear the crash
shatter the heavens! Those seas now pounding at our timbers
   slam home like artillery-stones in a city wall.

---

1. Ovid's third wife, whose name is unknown. She seems to have been connected
with the household of Paullus Fabius Maximus, addressed in *Pontic Epistles* I.2
and III.3. See also *Tristia* I.3.17ff., I.6.1ff.

Here surges a huge wave, overtopping all waves before it,
50   the proverbial tenth.[1] It's not
death as such that I fear, but this wretched way of dying –
    only spare me shipwreck, and death will come
as a blessing. Whether you're caught by cold steel or natural causes,
    it's something, when dying, to lie on solid ground,
55 to bequeath your remains to your kinsfolk, in expectation
    of a proper tomb, not to be fishes' food.
Even suppose I deserve such an end, I'm not the only
    passenger aboard: why should my
punishment drag down the innocent? You gods in heaven,
60 you sea-green gods of the deep (I implore both groups),
stop your threats, let me lug to its appointed destination
    this life that Caesar's most merciful anger spared!
If you want me to pay the penalty I deserve, remember
    my judge himself has rated my fault as short
65 of a capital sentence: if Caesar had wished me across the Stygian
    lake, he could have dispatched me without *your* aid.
He owns no invidious quantity of my life-blood: what he
    gave he can withdraw again at will.
But you, whom surely – I think – no crime of mine has injured,
70 rest content, I beseech you, with my present woes!
Yet even so, supposing you're all agreed to save my
    wretched life, how can the *me* that's dead
achieve salvation? Give me calm seas, a following
    wind – though you spare me, I'm an exile still.
75 It's not with goods to trade, and in avid pursuit of unbounded
    wealth that I plough the vasty deep;
nor am I now, as once, a student bound for Athens
    or the cities of Asia, sites I saw long ago,
or travelling to far-famed Alexandria to sample
80 the fleshpots of wanton Nile.
The reason I'm begging a wind is – oh, who'd believe it? –
    to sail for Sarmatia: *that*'s the land I seek!

---

1. Especially devastating. Cf. Lucan's novel use of this commonplace at *Civil War*
V.672.

I'm forced to coast up the sinister *rive gauche* of Pontus,
    and still I complain that my voyage from home is so slow.
To see the men of Tomis in their nowhere backwoods   85
    I actually pray for a shorter route!
If you love me, restrain these monstrous billows, use your
    powers to save our ship — but if
I've incurred your hatred, then speed me to my landfall: part of
    my punishment is in its chosen place.   90
Blow, winds! Belly my canvas! Here I have no business —
    why do my sails strive back towards Italy's shore?
Such was not Caesar's purpose: why hold back one who's banished?
    Time for the Pontic shore to glimpse my face.
Such his command. I deserve it. Besides, it's wrong, it's impious   95
    to defend any case *he's* condemned.
Yet if you gods are never deceived by mortal actions
    you must know my fault was no crime:
So if you *do* know, if I was misled by my own error,
    if my mind was not criminal, just inept   100
if (though in minor matters!) I supported his house, accepted
    Augustan public fiat, spoke out
in praise of the Happy Age with him as Leader, offered
    pious incense for Caesar, for all the Caesars — then
if such was my record, gods, then grant me deliverance;   105
    if not, may a mighty wave crash down
and overwhelm me! *Am I wrong? Aren't those heavy storm-clouds*
    beginning to clear? And isn't the sea's wrath
subsiding? No accident: I invoked you on oath: *you* cannot
    be deceived — it's you who are bringing me this aid!   110

I.3

Nagging reminders: the black ghost-melancholy vision
    of my final night in Rome,
the night I abandoned so much I dearly treasured —
    to think of it, even now, starts tears.

5   That day was near dawning on which, by Caesar's fiat,
      I must leave the frontiers of Italy behind.
    I'd lacked time – and inclination – to get things ready,
      long procrastination had numbed my will:
    Too listless to bother with choosing slaves, attendants,
10   the wardrobe, the outfit an exile needs,
    I was dazed, like someone struck by Jove's own lightning
      (had I not been?), who survives, yet remains unsure
    whether he's dead or alive. Sheer force of grief unclouded
      my mind in the end. When my poor wits revived
15   I had one last word with my friends before departure –
      those few friends, out of many, who'd stood firm.
    My wife, my lover, embraced me, outwept my weeping,
      her undeserving cheeks
    rivered with tears. Far away in North Africa, my daughter[1]
20   could know nothing of my fate. From every side,
    wherever you looked, came the sounds of grief and lamentation,
      just like a noisy funeral. The whole house
    mourned at my obsequies – men, women, even children,
      every nook and corner had its tears.
25   If I may gloss the trite with a lofty comparison,
      such was Troy's state when it fell.[2]
    By now all was still, no voices, no barking watchdogs,
      just the Moon on her course aloft in the night sky.
    Gazing at her, and the Capitol – clear now by moonlight,
30   close (but what use?) to my home,
    I cried: 'All you powers who dwell in that neighbour citadel,
      you temples, never more to be viewed
    by me, you high gods of Rome, whom I must now abandon,
      accept my salutation for all time!
35   And although I assume my shield so late, after being wounded,
      yet free this my exile from the burden of hate,

---

1. Ovid's daughter by his second wife. She was already married (*Fasti* VI.219ff.).
2. The poet pictures himself as a second Aeneas, whose departure from the sacked city of Troy is described by Virgil in *Aeneid* II (634ff.).

and tell that *heavenly man* what error beguiled me, let him
    not think my remissness a crime – so that what *you* know
may likewise be discerned by the author of my expulsion:
    with godhead appeased, I cannot be downcast.'   40
Such my prayer to the powers above; my wife's were countless,
    sobs choked each half-spoken word:
she flung herself down, hair loose, before our familial
    shrine, touched the dead-cold hearth with trembling lips,
poured out torrential appeals on behalf of the husband   45
    she mourned in vain. Our little household gods
turned a deaf ear, the Bear wheeled around the pole,
    and ebbing dark left no room
for further delay. What to do? Seductive love of country
    held me back – but this night was decreed my last,   50
tomorrow came exile. The times friends said 'Hurry!' 'Why?'
    I'd ask them.
    'Think to what place you're rushing me – and from where!'
The times I lied, swearing I'd set up an appropriate
    departure-time for my journey! Thrice I tripped
on the threshold, thrice turned back, dragging lethargic   55
    feet, their pace matched to my mood.
Often I'd make my farewells – and then go on talking,
    kiss everyone goodbye all over again,
unconsciously repeat identical instructions, eyes yearning
    back to my loved ones. In the end –   60
'Why make haste?' I exclaimed, 'it's Scythia I'm being sent to,
    it's Rome I must leave: each one a prime excuse
for postponement: my living wife is denied her living
    husband for evermore: dear family, home,
loyal and much-loved companions, bonded in brotherhood   65
    that Theseus might have envied[1] – all
now lost to me. This may well be my final chance to embrace
    them –
    let me make the most of one last extra hour.'

---

1. An allusion to the friendship of Theseus and Pirithous, described at *Metamorphoses*
VIII.303 as 'blessed harmony' (*felix concordia*).

With that I broke off, leaving my speech unfinished,
70   and hugged all my dear ones in turn –
but while I'd been speaking, and amid their tears, the morning
    star (so baneful to me) had risen high
and bright in the heavens. I felt myself ripped asunder
    as though I'd lost a limb; a part of me
75 seemed wrenched from my body. So Mettus must have suffered
    when the horses avenging his treachery tore him in two.
Now my family's clamorous weeping reached its climax,
    sad hands beat naked breasts,
and my wife clung to me at the moment of my departure,
80   making one last agonized tearful plea:
'They can't tear you from me – together,' she cried, 'we'll voyage
    together, I'll follow you into exile, be
an exile's wife. Mine, too, the journey; that frontier station
    has room for me as well: I'll make little weight
85 on the vessel of banishment! While your expulsion's caused by
    the wrath of Caesar, mine springs from loyal love:
this love will be Caesar for me.' Her argument was familiar,
    she'd tried it before, and she only gave it up –
still reluctant – on practical grounds.[1] So I made my exit,
90   dirty, unshaven, hair anyhow – like a corpse
minus the funeral. Grief-stricken, mind whirling-black, she fainted
    (they tell me), fell down half-dead,
and when she came round, hair foul with dust, and staggered
    back to her feet from the cold floor,
95 wept now for herself, and now for hearth and household
    bereft of their lord, cried her lost husband's name
again and again, groaning as though she'd witnessed
    her daughter's corpse, or mine,
on the high-stacked pyre; longed to die, to expunge by dying
100   all awareness – yet through her regard for me
could not perish. Let her live, then, ever to succour
    Ovid's exile, since this is what fate has willed.

1. She remained behind in Rome to safeguard Ovid's interests and property, and to
    work for his recall.

I.4

Dipped now in Ocean, the She–Bear's stellar guardian[1]
    is stirring up stormy seas: yet here am I
constrained, not by my will, to plough the Adriatic,
    bold only out of necessity – and fear.
Ah, misery! Gale-force winds black-ruffle the water,   5
    sand, scoured from the bottom, boils up in waves
that crash, mountain-high, on prow and curving sternpost,
    batter our painted godheads. The hull's
timbers resound to their pounding, wind whines in the rigging,
    the very keel groans at my woe.   10
The steersman's pallor betrays his icy fear: no longer
    does his skill control the ship: he gives her her head,
and just as a weak rider will let fall the ineffectual
    reins on the neck of his stubborn horse,
so not where *he* plans, but where the sea's force takes it,   15
    I see our pilot let the vessel ride,
and now (unless Aeolus[2] issues winds from a fresh quarter)
    I shall be carried where I may not go:
for Illyria's far away now on our port side, while forbidden
    Italy's clear in view: may the wind, I pray,   20
cease striving towards precluded territory, join me
    in obedience to the mighty god!
While I speak – in equal hope and fear of being driven
    back – with what fierce strength the waves
pound at our beam! Enough that Jove is angered at me –   25
    show mercy, you gods of the blue deep,
rescue this weary spirit of mine from a fearful
    death – if one dead already may not die!

---

1. The constellation Arctophylax ('Bear-Guardian'), sometimes called Boötes. Its chief star was Arcturus (also used of the constellation), the rising and setting of which were traditionally associated with storms.
2. God of the winds, who causes the storm which drives Aeneas to Carthage in *Aeneid* I (76ff.).

I.5

Friend, henceforth to be reckoned the foremost among my
    comrades,
    who, above all others, made my fate your own,
who first, I recall, when the bolt struck, dared to support me
    with words of comfort – *carissimo!* – who gave
5   kind counsel, the will to live, when in my wretched
    heart all I yearned for was death – such clues
in lieu of your name must tell you whom I'm addressing,
    and you know, very well, the debt
of friendship I have to discharge. These things will remain
    forever
10   deep-fixed in my very marrow, I'll owe you for my life
in perpetuity, my spirit shall blow away into empty
    wind, desert my bones on the tepid pyre,
before oblivion clouds my mind to your high merits
    and the long day sinks such loyalty out of sight.
15 May the gods go easy with you, grant you a fortune
    in need of no man's aid, and unlike mine!
Yet were this vessel being driven by friendly breezes
    your loyalty might well remain unknown:
Pirithous would never have valued Theseus' friendship
20   so highly had Theseus not gone down
alive to the waters of Styx. Your Furies, unhappy Orestes,
    were what made Pylades the model of true
friendship: had Euryalus not fallen fighting Rutulian
    foes, then Nisus would have no renown.
25 Just as red gold is assayed by fire, so in times of trouble
    loyalty, too, should be tested: while Fortune smiles
serenely on our endeavours, and lends us her assistance,
    all things pursue our undiminished luck;
but the first thunderclap scatters them: no one recognizes
30   the man who just now was enringed
by fair-weather comrades. Time was, I gathered this from ancient
    instances: now my own troubles prove it true.

Of all my friends, only you two or three stay faithful –
    the rest were Fortune's followers, not mine.
The more cause, then, being few, to succour my exhaustion,   35
    to offer this shipwreck of my hopes
a friendly shore! And don't, please, get unduly nervous,
    scared lest such devotion might offend the god:
Caesar has often praised loyalty, even in those who fought him,
    loves faith in his own, approves it in a foe.   40
My case is better: I never fostered armed opposition,
    my exile was earned by mere naïvety.
Be vigilant, then, I beg you, over my misfortunes, see if
    the deity's wrath can in any way be appeased!
To demand my full dossier, though, is asking for more than   45
    circumstances permit. The total sum
of my misfortunes matches the stars that shine in heaven,
    the grains of a dust-storm. Much
that I've suffered defies credibility, and although it
    happened in fact, will not sustain belief.   50
A part, too, should die with me: I only wish my silence
    might guarantee its suppression. If I had
an untiring voice, a more-than-brazen larynx,
    multiple tongues and mouths, not even then
could my words encompass the whole, so far does the subject   55
    outreach my powers. Instead
of the warlord[1] from Ithaca our educated poets
    should write about *my* misadventures: I've undergone
worse troubles than he did. He wandered for years – but only
    on the short haul between Ithaca and Troy;   60
thrust to the Getic shore[2] by Caesar's wrath, I've traversed
    seas lying beneath unknown stars,
whole constellations distant. He had his loyal companions,
    his faithful crew: *my* comrades deserted me
at the time of my banishment. He was making for his homeland,   65
    a cheerful victor: I was driven from mine –

---

1. Ulysses.
2. Tomis, most of the inhabitants of which were of Getic stock.

fugitive, exile, victim. My home was not some Greek island,
   Ithaca, Samos[1] – to leave *them* is no great loss –
but the City that from its seven hills scans the world's orbit,
70   Rome, centre of empire, seat of the gods.
He was physically tough, with great stamina, long-enduring;
   my strength is slight, a gentle man's. He spent
a lifetime under arms, engaged in savage warfare –
   I'm accustomed to quieter pursuits.
75 I was crushed by a god, with no help in my troubles:
   he had that warrior-goddess[2] at his side.
And just as Jove outranks the god of the rough ocean,
   so he suffered Neptune's anger, I bear Jove's.
What's more, the bulk of *his* troubles are fictitious,
80   whereas mine remain anything but myth!
Finally, he got back to the home of his questing, recovered
   the acres he'd sought so long; but I,
unless the injured deity's wrath diminish, am sundered
   for everlasting from my native soil!

I.6

Not so dear was Lyde to the Clarian poet,[3] not so truly
   loved was Bittis by her singer[4] from Cos
as you are deeply entwined, wife, in my heart: you merit
   a less wretched if not a better man.
5   You are the underthrust beam shoring up my ruin:
   if I am anything still, it's all due to you.

1. Samos or Same was the ancient capital of the large island of Cephallenia, next to Ithaca off the west coast of Greece, and was sometimes used, as here, for the whole island.
2. Minerva (Greek Athena).
3. The Greek epic and elegiac poet Antimachus, strictly of Colophon, born about 444 B.C. He celebrated his mistress Lyde in a narrative elegy of the same name.
4. The Greek poet Philetas from the island of Cos, born about 320 B.C. Propertius and Ovid refer to him several times as their model in elegy. Bittis was his mistress.

You're my guard against stripping and despoliation
  by those who went for the timbers of my wreck.
Just as the ravening wolf, bloodthirsty and famine-driven,
  prowls in search of unguarded sheepfolds, just as   10
a hungry vulture will scan the wide horizon
  for corpses still above ground,
so that nobody, bad faith battening on our bitter troubles,
  would (if you'd let him) have seized
my remaining goods. Your courage, those influential   15
  friends – I can never thank them enough – put paid
to his tricks. So accept this tribute from a poor but honest
  witness – if such a witness carries weight:
in probity neither Hector's wife excelled you,
  nor Laodamia, who clove   20
to her husband even in death. If you'd lucked out with Homer 21
  to sing your praises, Penelope's renown   22
would be second to yours, you'd stand first in the honoured roll- 33
    call
  of heroines,[1] pre-eminent for courage and faith –   34
whether this quality's inborn, produced by your own nature,
  devotion that owes nothing to a master's words,
or whether that princely Lady,[2] for years your honoured patron, 25
  has trained you to be a model wife, by long
inurement, assimilation to her own example (if great things
  may properly be compared with small).
Alas, my verses possess but scanty strength, your virtues
  are more than my tongue can proclaim,   30
and the spark of creative vigour I once commanded
  is extinct, killed off by my long   32
misfortunes. Yet insofar as our words of praise have power   35
  you shall live[3] through these verses for all time.

1. There is an important second meaning. 'Heroines' also refers to Ovid's *Heroides*,
   a work in which Penelope literally stands first since her letter to Ulysses begins
   the fictive epistles. Laodamia (line 20) also figures in *Heroides* (XIII).
2. Livia, wife of the emperor Augustus.
3. Latin *vives*. Cf. Ovid's boast at the end of *Metamorphoses* (XV.879): *vivam*, 'I
   shall live'.

I.7

If you're one who keeps a bust made in my likeness,[1]
    strip off the Bacchic ivy from its locks!
Such signs of felicity belong to fortunate poets:
    on my temples a wreath is out of place.
5 This is for you, dear friend: disown me in public, acknowledge
    my words in your heart – you who wear
(and long may you!) my gold-framed image on your finger,
    makeshift memento of an exile's dear
features: perhaps when you look at it you're prompted
10   to muse 'How far from us friend Ovid lies!'
Your devotion's a comfort, yet my poems will furnish
    a larger portrait: read them, such as they are,
those verses[2] that tell of human transformations,
    the work, cut short by its author's unhappy flight,
15 which, like so much else of mine, on my departure
    I sadly consigned to the flames with my own hand.[3]
And just as Althaea (a better sister than mother)
    is said to have cremated her own son
in the guise of a log,[4] so I flung my books, doomed to perish with
    me,
20   my very vitals, upon that raging pyre –
whether through hate of the Muses (who'd wrought my
    downfall)
    or because the opus was still unfinished, still
in rough draft. Several copies, I think, were made: the poem
    was not destroyed outright, remains extant.

1. It was not unusual to own busts of favourite poets, often crowned with ivy (sacred to Bacchus).
2. *Metamorphoses*.
3. Ovid here claims to have done to *Metamorphoses* what Virgil instructed the executors of his will to do to *Aeneid*. Virgil's instructions were disobeyed. *Metamorphoses* was already in 'several copies'.
4. The story is told by Ovid at the (almost) precise centre of his masterwork: *Metamorphoses* VIII.451–514.

And now it's my wish that it live,[1] let it enhance my readers' 25
    far-from-idle leisure, remind them of me –
yet no one will be able to peruse it and keep patience
    who doesn't know that it lacks my final hand:
a job snatched from me half-done, while still on the anvil,
    a draft minus the last touch of the file. 30
What I seek is not praise but pardon, I'm praised in abundance
    if, reader, I contrive to avoid your scorn.
And here are six lines more for you, to be placed in the volume's
    frontispiece (if that honour's what you think they deserve):
'All you who touch these rolls, now orphaned of their father, 35
    grant *them* at least a place
in your City! *He* didn't publish them (that's in their favour):
    they were, in a manner of speaking, snatched
from their master's funeral. So whatever faults this unfinished
    poem reveals, he'd have mended if he could.' 40

I.8

Back from the sea now, back to their sources shall deep rivers
    flow, and the Sun, wheeling his steeds about,
run backward: earth shall bear stars, the plough cleave heaven,
    fire shall give forth water, and water flames,
all things shall move contrary to the laws of nature, 5
    no element in the world shall keep its path,
all that I swore impossible will happen now: there's nothing
    left that one can't believe. This
I prophesy after my betrayal by that person
    who, I'd believed, would aid me in my distress. 10
False friend! Did you consign me to such utter oblivion,
    were you so scared to come near
affliction, that you gave not a look, no crumb of comfort –
    you stone! – to my downfall, did not follow my bier?

1. See I.6.36 and note.

15 Does the sacred and venerable title of friendship
      lie, mere trash, beneath your feet?
    What trouble to visit a comrade crushed by such weighty
      disaster, to help cheer him with kind words,
    and even if you couldn't shed tears at my misfortunes,
20   at least pretend to be sorry, offer a few
    polite clichés, like a stranger – 'What a rotten business' –
      parrot stock phrases, common turns of speech;
    finally, gaze your last, while you could, at those grief-stricken
      features you'll not behold again,
25 hear, and return in kind, the never-to-be-repeated-
      in-a-lifetime word, 'Farewell'?
    Others did this, not close friends, the merest acquaintances,
      their feelings proved by their tears.
    But weren't *you* linked to me by the strong bonds of a lifetime's
30   association and friendship? Hadn't you been
    privy to all my moods, both serious and lighthearted,
      as I was privy to yours?
    Were we merely urban companions? Didn't you travel
      everywhere with me, see the world?
35 Has all this gone for nothing, blown away on the god's wind-
          blasts,
      swallowed by Lethe's waters, forgotten, lost?
    No, you surely weren't born in Rome, that civilized city –
      to which I can never again return –
    but here, by the Black Sea's sinister rocky shoreline,
40   on the wild Scythian or Sarmatian hills,
    heart cradled with veins of flint, an iron seeding
      to stiffen your breast; and she
    who once gave your soft mouth her full and milky udder
      was a tigress – else you'd not
45 be so alienated today from my misfortunes,
      or stand accused by me
    of hardheartedness. But since, to crown these other fated
      troubles, my early days have failed of their hope,
    work hard, now, to ensure that I forget your shortcomings;
50   correct your attitude, win praise where you garnered blame.

I.9

You who are reading this work without malice, may you
    cross life's finishing-line without a spill!
For you, I hope, my prayers may find fulfilment,
    though for me they failed to move the obdurate gods.
So long as your luck holds good, your friends will be legion: 5
    if clouds gather, then you're on your own.
You've seen how pigeons flock to a white dovecote,
    while a dirty habitat attracts no birds;
ants likewise never make for an empty granary,
    and not one friend will come round   10
to visit the bankrupt. As a shadow dogs walkers in sunlight,
    but vanishes when the sun is overcast,
so the inconstant crowd pursues the light of fortune,
    yet as soon as a cloud blocks it, will take off.
May this formulation, I pray, always ring hollow   15
    and false to you: for me
events proved it all too true. Before my house's downfall
    visitors thronged the place, I was *à la mode*
if not ambitious. The first tremor sent them running –
    a prudent mass exit, scared of being caught   20
in the collapsing ruins. Small wonder if men dread lightning,
    since it burns up everything around –
yet friendship that remains constant through tribulations
    wins Caesar's approval, even in a foe
that's earned his hatred. Nor is he prone to anger –   25
    none more restrained than he! – when true
devotion persists in adversity. Even Thoas,
    learning the story of Pylades, we're told,
approved; the unswerving friendship of Patroclus
    for Achilles elicited Hector's praise.   30
When loyal Theseus followed Pirithous down to Hades
    they say that the Dark God[1] shared

---

1. Pluto or Dis, divine ruler of the underworld.

his grief; when Turnus learnt how Euryalus and Nisus
    kept faith,[1] the tears (it's fair to assume)
35 poured down his cheeks. There's trust even among the wretched;
    in a foe it wins praise. Alas, how few are moved
by these words of mine! My present state and fortune
    are such that my tears should know no bounds,
yet my heart, though overwhelmed by grief at its own disaster,
40   has still found serenity in your success.
Long ago, dear friend, I must tell you, I saw this coming
    when the wind in your sails was still the merest breeze;
if moral integrity or a life without a blemish carry
    a price-tag, no man could command
45 a higher figure; if anyone's climbed to prominence
    through the liberal arts, it's you; is there *any* cause
your eloquence can't make good? That's why I told you,
    right from the start, 'My friend, a major stage
awaits your talents.' This I learnt not from thunder
50   on the left, or sheep's guts, or the cry
or flight of a bird: reason's my augury, my prediction
    for the future: thus I divined, thus got
my knowledge. And since it's come true, wholehearted
      congratulations
    to you (as well as to me!)
55 that your talents have not remained hidden – though I wish my
      own had,
    and in blackest darkness: best if no light had shone
on my creations! And just as your eloquence has been aided
    by serious arts, so an Art[2] of another kind
hurt *me*. But my life's well-known to you – the author's
60   own morals had no truck with these 'arts';
you know that this poem was written for fun, a product
    of my youth: not a good joke, but a joke.

---

1. The allusion is to the ill-fated attempt of the Trojan warrior Nisus to save his
young friend Euryalus when he is captured by the Italians in *Aeneid* IX (367–
449). Both are killed. As Trojans, they were enemies of the Italian Turnus.
2. *The Art of Love.*

Thus though my offence can't be camouflaged or defended,
    at least it has some excuse. So, as far as you can,
excuse it: don't desert your friend's cause; so may you   65
    ever advance as well as you've begun!

I.10

I have (may I always keep!) blonde Minerva's[1] protection: my
    vessel
    bears her painted casque, borrows her name.
Under sail she runs well with the slightest breeze; her rowers
    speed her along when there's need for oars.[2]
Not content with outstripping any companion vessel   5
    she'll somehow contrive to overhaul any craft
that's set out before her: no storms will spring her timbers,
    she'll ride tall waves like a flat calm;
first met at Cenchreae, harbour of Corinth; since then
    the faithful guide and companion of my flight,   10
kept safe by the power of Pallas through countless hazards,
    across endless gale-swept seas. Safe still —
I pray! may she thread vast Pontus' entrance-channel
    and enter the waters of the Getic shore.
But as soon as she'd brought me into Aeolian Helle's seaway,[3]   15
    setting course for the long haul through the narrows, then
we swung away westward, leaving Hector's city,
    and made harbour at Imbros. Thence
with a light following breeze our wearied vessel
    rode over to Samothrace,   20
from where it's a short haul to Tempyra on the Thracian
    coast, and a parting of the ways between

---

1. Goddess of the arts and protector of Ulysses, with whom Ovid often associates himself in *Tristia* I (see especially I.5.57ff.).
2. These and several of the following lines recall Catullus' poem on his yacht, Poem IV. Not accidentally Catullus' yacht came from the Pontus or Black Sea area.
3. The Hellespont, now called the Dardanelles.

master and ship: I planned an overland journey
    through Thrace, while she was to sail back
25   into Hellespontine waters, coasting along the Troad,
    past Lampsacus, home of the country god
Priapus, through the straits between Sestos and Abydos –
    scene of not-quite-virgin Helle's fatal flight –
to Cyzicus in the Propontis, barely linked to the mainland,
30   Cyzicus, Thracian colony of renown,
and so to Byzantium, guarding the jaws of Pontus,[1]
    great gateway between twin seas.
May she win past all these, I pray, and with a strong following
    south wind wing her way through the Clashing Rocks,
35   skirt Thynias' bay, set course by Apollo's city
    under Anchialus' lofty walls, and thence
sail on past the ports of Mesembria and Odeson,
    and that citadel named
for the wine-god, and the hilltop where Megarian exiles
40   (we're told) made their home from home:[2]
cruising thence may she safely reach the Milesian foundation[3]
    to which I'm consigned by the wrath
of an injured god. If she makes it, I'll sacrifice to Minerva
    a lamb for services rendered: I can't afford
45   anything larger. You, too, twin brother-gods of this island,
    sons of Tyndareus,[4] watch over our separate paths
with propitious power (one craft is to thread the Symplegades,
    the other's for Thracian waters). Make the winds,
though we're bound for diverse destinations, favour
50   this vessel and that alike!

1. The strait of the Bosphorus, linking the 'twin seas' of the Propontis or Sea of
Marmora and the Pontus or Black Sea.
2. The places mentioned in lines 35–40 were on the west coast of the Black Sea
south of Tomis.
3. Tomis, founded by colonists from the Greek city of Miletus on the coast of Asia
Minor.
4. Castor and Pollux, the heavenly 'twins' (*gemini*) and patron deities of sailors.
Worshipped by the people of Samothrace ('this island', 45).

I.11

Every letter you've read in this whole book was written
    during the anxious days
of my journey: scribbling lines in mid-Adriatic
    while December froze the blood,
or after we'd passed the twin gulfs of the Isthmus[1]   5
    and transferred to another ship,
still verse-making amid the Aegean's savage clamour
    (a sight, I fancy, that shook the Cyclades).
In fact, I'm surprised myself that in all that upheaval
    of spirit and sea inspiration never flagged.   10
How to label such an obsession? Shocked stupor? Madness?
    No matter: by this one care all cares are relieved.
Time and again I was tossed by wintry tempests
    and darkly menacing sea;
time and again the day grew black with storm-clouds,   15
    torrents of wind-lashed rain;
time and again we shipped water; yet my shaky
    hand still kept writing verses – of a sort.
Now winds whistle once more through the taut rigging,
    and massy-high rears up each hollow wave: 20
the very steersman, hands raised high to heaven,
    his art forgotten, turns to prayer for aid.
Wherever I look, there's nothing but death's image –
    death, that my split mind fears
and, fearing, prays for. Should I come safe to harbour   25
    terror lurks there too: more hazards on dry land
than from the cruel sea. Both men and deep entrap me,
    sword and wave twin my fear:
sword, I'm afraid, hopes to let my blood for booty,
    wave wants the title of my death. Away   30
on our left lies a barbarous coast, inured to rapine,
    stalked ever by bloodshed, murder, war –

1. Of Corinth.

the agitation of these wintry waves is nothing
    to the turbulence in my breast.
35 All the more cause for indulgence, generous reader,
    if these lines fall short — as they do —
of your hopes: they were not written, as formerly, in my garden,
    while I lounged on a favourite day-bed, but at sea,
in wintry light, rough-tossed by filthy weather, spindrift
40   spattering the paper as I write.
Rough winter battles me, indignant at my presumption
    in ignoring its fierce threats, still scribbling away.
Let the storm have its will of the man — but let storm and poem
    reach their end, I pray, each at the same time!

CALPURNIUS SICULUS

INTRODUCTION

Calpurnius has been and is an enigma. Other than what may be (cautiously) inferred from his seven eclogues, nothing is known about him. Even his approximate date is disputed. Some have recently argued for a Severan dating (early third century A.D.); most are unconvinced. The evidence that Calpurnius was a poet of the fifties A.D. whose pastorals were a poetic response to Nero's Rome is overwhelming. There seem pointed references in his poems to the comet of A.D. 54 (*Eclogue* I.77–81: see Seneca, *Natural Questions* VII.17.2; Suetonius, *Claudius* 46; Pliny, *Natural History* II.92), to Nero's speech on behalf of the inhabitants of Ilium in A.D. 53 (*Eclogue* I.45: see Tacitus, *Annals* XII.58), to the wooden amphitheatre built by Nero on the Campus Martius in A.D. 57 (*Eclogue* VII.23ff.: see Tacitus, *Annals* XIII.31; Suetonius, *Nero* 12), as well as more general allusions to the events of the early part of Nero's principate. Furthermore, Calpurnius' poetic strategies, especially his rewriting of Virgil, accord fully with the tenor of the Neronian renaissance. Indeed some have identified Calpurnius with a certain Calpurnius Statura listed in the *Life of Persius* as one of the satirist's friends from childhood. This Calpurnius died while still a young man and before Persius' own death in A.D. 62. Such identifications are necessarily conjectural. But at least this identification fits the available data and receives some support from the fact that, like Persius, the author of the Calpurnian eclogues is no uncritical admirer of the last and most disappointing of the Julio-Claudian emperors.

Calpurnius' book of seven eclogues, presented here in its entirety, is structured in a precise, almost fastidious fashion. Two overtly political eclogues (I and VII), concerned with issues and events of Neronian Rome, encompass the collection; a third political eclogue (IV) – a contest poem and the longest poem in the book – provides its core. The intervening eclogues are non-political, but they too are positioned to enhance the symmetry of the book. The first and last non-political eclogues (II and VI) are contest poems, while the inner non-political pastorals pit dialogue (III) against monologue (V) and frame the central contest poem, the political *Eclogue* IV. The arrangement obviously derives from the 'failed' symmetry of Virgil's *Eclogues*, which it self-consciously 'refines'.

The political thrust of the collection also derives from Virgil, who made of pastoral not only a fully formed genre but a political critique. Calpurnius exploits the generic expectations which his predecessor had developed, from whom, however, he differs in both rustic realism ('sun-burnt faces', 'bonnets', 'legs . . . scratched by brambles', etc.) and historical specificity. As regards the latter, Calpurnius not only refers to identifiable historical events (see above), but is more direct and concrete in his statement of what constitutes political improvement (e.g., safety for senators, proper magistrates: I.6off.) and more precise in some of his political imagery (e.g. I.69ff.). He also uses the standard political imagery and motifs of his predecessor, especially the image of the 'golden age' and the motif of the 'divine', 'youthful' ruler, employed by Virgil with (self-consciously optimistic) reference to late republican/Augustan Rome and by Calpurnius with reference to the principate of Nero, who was himself heralded in contemporary literature as a new Augustus (e.g. Seneca, *Apocolocyntosis* 4, 9f., 23f.; *On Clemency* I.1.5, I.8.11; see also Suetonius, *Nero* 10.1, and note the play on 'august' and 'Augustan' at *Eclogues* I.94 and IV.86, 91) and as a future, if not actual, god (see Lucan, *Civil War* I.33ff.). Calpurnius' displayed attitude to this golden age is more overtly pessimistic than the comparable attitude in Virgil's *Eclogues*. It accords more with the adamantine pessimism of *Aeneid*. For, though Calpurnius' political eclogues appear to eulogize Nero's golden age, what they in fact present is the gradual corruption of a pastoral figure and pastoral values by the urban world of Rome, politics and power. The pastoral figure concerned is Corydon, who appears only in the three political eclogues, which are clearly arranged (and in this too there is a development of something in Virgil: witness the treatment of Gallus in *Eclogues* VI and X) to form a psychologically significant dramatic sequence. What this sequence depicts is Corydon's movement from (*Eclogue* I) naïve awareness of the new golden age about to be inaugurated by the young divinity, i.e. Nero, at Rome, through (IV) a desire to compose political encomia and receive appropriate rewards, into (VII) total subjection to and adulation of the glittering world of power, in which the pastoral world is rejected and imitations of nature are preferred to nature itself. It is a movement from innocence to corruption, from truth to falsehood, from nature to glowing artifice.

The collection is richly allusive. There are references throughout the seven eclogues to the pastoral and literary tradition which Calpurnius reshapes, especially to Theocritus, Virgil, Horace, and Ovid. Allusions to and rewritings of Virgil are the most numerous and thematically the most important. Faunus' prophecy of the imminent golden age at I.33ff. reshapes aspects of Virgil's so-called 'Messianic' *Eclogue* IV. Such reshaping often has critical bite. The ending of Calpurnius' fourth eclogue (IV.152–6), for example, rewrites the opening of Virgil's sixth eclogue (VI.3–5), transforming a promulgation of poetic intent into a request for property. *Eclogue* VII rewrites Virgil's first and second eclogues developing and intensifying their qualified pessimism. At least the Corydon of Virgil's second eclogue, though affected negatively by the urban world to which his lover has fled, still affirms pastoral values, even if the possiblity of their realization in Corydon's life has now been rendered doubtful. Calpurnius' Corydon rejects the pastoral world absolutely, and by his rejection signals not only the unimpedable corruption exerted by city on country but the death of the pastoral vision in Nero's Rome. Nor perhaps simply the pastoral vision. Marked allusions to Virgil as poetic model in *Eclogue* IV (62–77, 160–63) – especially the climactic allusion to the whole Virgilian *œuvre* (162f.) – suggest that what is perhaps involved in Corydon's failure is the failure of the Roman literary and cultural tradition itself.

The non-political eclogues (II, III, V, VI) seem positioned to effect (among other things) a thematic counterpoint with the political poems. Images of the pastoral world, ideal and non-ideal, are generated for the purposes of contrast with and comparison to the urban context. Like the political eclogues they manifest a directness and a realism in the presentation of the rural world and abound in homely details of country and country-dweller. Calpurnian pastoral in fact takes much from Virgil's more realistic depiction of agricultural life in *Georgics* (and also of course from the elegiac tradition, especially Ovid). To Virgil's *Georgics* the 'didactic' pastoral, *Eclogue* V, is particularly indebted. The non-political eclogues too are individually most carefully structured. The amoebaean contest of *Eclogue* II, for example, reveals a more precise verbal and ideational strophic correspondence than is to be found in Virgil's contest poems. The tone of these eclogues varies considerably. The second is light and playful, the third at times bitter, even vengeful, as well as self-pitying; the fifth is virtually didactic monotone, the sixth emotional and rancorous. This variation in tone has point. The non-political poems display a development from harmony to discord which reflects upon, and is parallel to, the gradual corruption of Corydon in the political poems. The harmony of the singers, Astacus and Idas, in *Eclogue* II dissolves by *Eclogue* VI into the acerbic malevolence of the potential singers, Astylus and Lycidas, whose inability to control their own malice, hatred and rage aborts the possibility of both song and judgement. Though *Eclogues* III and V remind the reader of the theoretical power, including didactic power, of song, *Eclogue* VI presents the pastoral singer as a rough-hewn bumpkin who has little understanding of the values implicit in the pastoral tradition and its vision. This inability of Astylus and Lycidas to sing prefigures the total capitulation in *Eclogue* VII of Corydon, the first actual singer in Virgil's *Eclogues*, to the glittering artifice of Nero's golden Rome.

A.J.B.

Further Reading

Davis, P. J., 'Structure and Meaning in the *Eclogues* of Calpurnius Siculus', in A. J. Boyle (ed.), *The Imperial Muse: To Juvenal through Ovid* (Berwick, Victoria, 1988) 32–54.

Keene, C. H. (ed.), *The Eclogues of Calpurnius and Nemesianus* (London 1887, repr. Hildesheim 1969).

Korzeniewski, D. (ed.), *Hirtengedichte aus Neronischer Zeit* I (Darmstadt 1971).

Leach, E. W., 'Corydon Revisited: An Interpretation of the Political Eclogues of Calpurnius Siculus', *Ramus* 2 (1973) 53–97.

'Neronian Pastoral and the World of Power', in A. J. Boyle (ed.), *Ancient Pastoral* (Berwick, Victoria, 1975) 122–48.

ECLOGUES

Translated by Guy Lee

Eclogue I

CORYDON

Not yet does parting summer gentle the Sun's steeds
Although the presses thrust hard down on soaking clusters
And the must frothing up with a hoarse whisper seethes.
Look Ornytus – you see how the cows we mind for father
5   Have spread out their soft flanks beneath the shaggy broom?
Why shouldn't we take shelter too in nearby shade?
Why merely shield our sun-burnt faces under bonnets?

ORNYTUS

Sooner the grove here, brother Corydon. Let's make
For Father Faunus'[1] covert where the pine-trees mass
10   Their slender hair and raise heads towards the raging sun
Where the beech-tree screens water bubbling from its roots
And tangles light and shade among its random boughs.

CORYDON

Wherever you call I follow, Ornytus; for my
Leuce by saying No to embraces and night's joys
15   Allows me access to horned Faunus' holy place.
Out with your reeds then and the songs you've stored away.

---

1. A native Italian god of field, flock and tillage, who features in Virgil's *Aeneid*
(VII.81ff.) as a divine prophet of Rome's future.

My pan-pipe will not fail you, which resourceful Ladon
Lately put together for me of seasoned reed.

ORNYTUS

Together now we are sheltering in the shade we sought. –
But what is this inscription on the sacred beech   20
Not long ago incised with hasty pruning hook?
Do you see how every letter still preserves its green
Edges without yet gaping open and drying out?

CORYDON

Ornytus, take a closer look. You can more quickly
Run over the lines carved high up into the bark,   25
For father largely gave you length of limb enough
And mother no less generously tall stature.

ORNYTUS

No shepherd and no traveller in doggerel
Sings this but the God himself. No cattle ballad here;
No mountain yodelling separates the sacred lines.   30

CORYDON

You speak of marvels. But make haste and with attentive
Eye forthwith read through the inspired song for us.

ORNYTUS

'Guardian of fell and forest, son of heaven, I Faunus
Sing this future for the world and choose to carve
My sacred tree with glad verses revealing Fate.   35
Rejoice, O above all, you woodland tenantry,
Rejoice, you people of mine. Though keeper unconcerned
Should let his whole herd go astray, and though at night
Shepherd should fail to close the cote with ashwood hurdle,
Yet shall the robber practise no deceit against   40
The fold or drive away cattle with loosened halter.
The Golden Age with carefree peace is born again
And there returns to earth at last, from dust and dirt

Rescued, kind Themis.[1] Happy days the young man[2] brings
45   Who won the case for his maternal Julii.
While as God he rules the world, impious Bellona
Shall yield, hands tied behind her back, and robbed of weapons
Shall sink demented teeth deep into her own flesh
And having lately filled the world with civil strife
50   Shall make war on herself. Now Rome shall mourn for no
Philippi,[3] as her own prisoner celebrate no Triumphs.
All wars shall be interned in Tartarean dungeon,
Hiding their heads in darkness, terrified of light.
Fair Peace, white-robed, shall come – no longer seeming fair
55   As often in the past when, free of open war,
With foreign foes defeated, still with brigand force
And silent steel she propagated public strife.
Clemency bids each fault of Peace's counterfeit
Away, begone! and shatters those demented swords.
60   No death-condemned procession of Senators in chains
Shall weary the executioner, nor crowded jail
Compel the Hapless Curia to count a few Fathers.
Full quiet will be there, a stranger to drawn steel,
Bringing to Latium a second reign of Saturn,[4]
65   A second reign of Numa, who first taught soldiers drunk
With blood, still fired by Romulus' campaigns, the work
Of peace – who first commanded weapons to be silent
And trumpets to ring out in sacred rites, not wars.
No longer buying the form of insubstantial honour
70   Shall consul be content to gain meaningless rods[5]

1. The goddess of justice, who was driven from earth by the moral decadence that ended the Golden Age.
2. Nero. The reference is to his speech on behalf of the inhabitants of Ilium in A.D. 53: see Tacitus, *Annals* XII.58.
3. The site of the battle between Caesarian and republican forces in 42 B.C. and the archetype of 'civil' slaughter.
4. i.e. a second Golden Age. Virgil refers to Augustus, the first emperor, in similar terms (*Aeneid* VI.791–4).
5. The *fasces*, bundles of rods and axes carried before the highest magistrates as symbols of their legal power to punish and execute.

And vain tribunal, but with laws restored full justice
Shall come back and a better God shall give the Forum
Its old look and tradition, banishing bad times.
Let every race rejoice, whether in sunken South
Far down or in vertical North it dwells, or whether   75
It lies to East or West or swelters in the Tropics.
You see how this the twentieth night shines now in sky
Unclouded and reveals a comet radiant[1]
With peaceful light? How clear and full it gleams, harmless –
Its torch not showering either pole with blood-red flame,   80
As often happens, or glittering with blazing gore?
It was not of old, when, after Caesar's murder,[2]
It burdened wretched citizens with fatal wars.
Surely a very God in his strong arms takes over
The massive weight of Roman power, so steadily   85
That neither thunder crashes at the world's transfer
Nor will Rome deify the dead as they deserve
Until the rising star look back upon the setting.'

CORYDON

For long now, Ornytus, like one divinely inspired
I have been shaken, feeling terror mixed with joy.   90
But let us worship vocal Faunus for his goodness.

ORNYTUS

Let us recite the verses which the God himself
Gives us to sing, and play a tune on slender oat.
Meliboeus will maybe bring these things to ears august.

---

1. An allusion to the comet of A.D. 54 which was taken to have heralded the death of Claudius (13 October) and the ascent of Nero.
2. A comet appeared in the summer of 44 B.C., following the assassination of Julius Caesar. See Virgil, *Georgics* I.487ff. for a description of the celestial phenomena associated with Caesar's death.

Eclogue II

Chaste Crocale by two boys, Astacus and Idas,
Idas the woolly flock's lord, Astacus the garden's,
Had long been loved, both beautiful and not ill-matched
At singing. These, when sultry summer scorched the ground,
5 By chance meet at a cool spring and beneath the same
Elms and get ready to compete in sweet singing
And for a stake. Agreed that if defeated one
Should forfeit seven fleeces, the other his garden produce;
And a great match it was, with Thyrsis as the judge.
10 Present: all kind of cattle, all kind of wild beasts
And all whose migrant wings beat upon lofty air.
There gathered all who pasture under shady holm-oak
Slow sheep, and Father Faunus and the two-horned Satyrs.
Dry-foot the Wood-Nymphs came, the Water-Nymphs wet-foot,
15 And the fast-flowing rivers arrested their onrush.
East winds ceased aggression against trembling leaves
And made a profound silence over all the hills.
Everything rested. Bulls trod down unnoticed pasture
And even the daedal bee during the competition
20 Ventured to disregard the nectar-bearing flowers.
And now in ancient shade Thyrsis had sat him down
Between them, saying, 'My boys, if I'm judge, I request
No wagering. Let it be recompense enough
If victory bring praise and defeat dishonour.
25 But now, the better to decide whose turn it is
To sing, each raise his hand three times in a game of *morra*.'[1]
Their fingers quickly settling it, Idas begins.

IDAS

Silvanus loves *me*, gives me a ready oaten pipe
And binds my temples with a garland of pitch-pine.

---

1. A game in which two players put up a number of fingers and each tries to guess
the total.

When I was still little, he sang me no light song: 30
'For you a light pipe grows already, of slanting reed.'

ASTACUS

For me, though, Flora paints my hair with pale green grass
And ripening Pomona plays under the trees.
'Here,' said the Water-Nymphs, 'here, boy, are springs for you.
Now you can channel them to feed the watered garden.'   35

IDAS

Pales' self teaches me flock-care, how a white ewe's
Black mate affects the fleece of each lamb born to them,
Which cannot imitate the look of either parent
But testifies to both by its ambiguous colour.

ASTACUS

No less adaptable by my skill the tree bears   40
Exotic foliage and non-indigenous fruit.
My skill now crosses pears with apples, now compels
Engrafted peaches to displace unripened plums.

IDAS

I like to prune wild olive and the tender willow
And take them to the lambs, that they may learn to crop   45
Leafage and nibble back the grass with their first bites,
Lest after weaning they should miss their wandering dams.

ASTACUS

But when I'm setting yellow roots in the dry ground,
I drench the nursery-bed with water from the spring,
Soaking it thoroughly, lest drooping from the change   50
Of soil the plantlets miss their earlier moisture.

IDAS

O if some God brought Crocale here, then he on earth
And he in heaven for me would be the only King.

I'd set apart a grove and say, 'Beneath these trees
55   A presence dwells. Keep out (it's holy ground) you wicked!'

ASTACUS

We burn for Crocale. If any God should hear
My prayers, for him alone, where jewelled fountain sends
Green waters and with trembling stream runs past the lilies,
A beech-tree I would plant among vine-tendrilled elms.

IDAS

60   Never look down on cottages and shepherds' huts.
Yes, Idas is a yokel, but not a savage too.
Often a ram-lamb quivers on my smoking peat,
Often a ewe-lamb falls, vowed at her feast to Pales.

ASTACUS

We also to the Lares of our orchard like
65   To offer first-fruits and cake-figures to Priapus,
And we give dewy honeycombs and liquid honey,
No less welcome than if a he-goat stained the altar.

IDAS

We feed a thousand ewe-lambs that bleat beneath the udder
And as many Tarentine ewes give me their fleeces.
70   Snow-white cheese is pressed by me the whole year through;
Come, Crocale – your guerdon shall be all this year's.

ASTACUS

He who would count how many apples underneath
Our trees I gather will sooner count the grains of sand.
We always harvest greens – in summer and midwinter;
75   Come, Crocale – my garden shall be all yours.

IDAS

Although parched soil is shrivelling up the withered grass,
You can still take away buckets of curdled milk.

Fleeces we'll give when the first sunny weather comes,
After the warm Kalends, when sheep-shearing begins.

ASTACUS

But we, whom also scorching summer months reward,   80
Will give you a thousand Chian figs with smiling skins
And just as many chestnuts when December suns
Burst open the green prickly husks of the ripe nuts.

IDAS

I don't look ugly, do I, or prematurely old?
I'm not deceived, poor wretch, when touching my soft cheeks? 85
Or ignorant when I detect first flowering's
Traces? My fingers really do feel wispy down?

ASTACUS

Whenever I see myself in a clear pool I always
Like what I see. Indeed my face so wears the flower
Of youth, as I have often noticed on the tree   90
The waxy quinces shine beneath their fine-spun wool.

IDAS

Love calls for song, nor does the pan-pipe yield to Love.
But look, day flies and the evening star calls back twilight.
You, Daphnis and Alphesiboeus, drive home the flocks.

ASTACUS

Now leaves are rustling, now the trees drown our singing.   95
Go over, Dorylas, and open the full channel
And let the thirsty garden have water at last.

They had hardly finished when old Thyrsis gave this verdict:
'Be equal and so live in harmony, for you
Share both alike good looks and song and love and youth.'   100

Eclogue III

IOLLAS

Lycidas, in this valley have you maybe seen
A heifer of mine? She likes to run after your bulls,
And now it's almost two hours I've been looking for her
But still no sign. My legs have long been suffering
5 From butcher's-broom and I've put up with them being scratched
By brambles, but despite the bloodshed I've got nowhere.

LYCIDAS

I've not been watching. I've no time. I burn, Iollas,
Burn desperately. Ungrateful Phyllis has left me
For a new lover – Mopsus – after all my gifts!

IOLLAS

10 O woman's fickler than the winds. So that's your Phyllis.
Yet, I remember, every time you went away
She'd swear that even honey without you seemed sour.

LYCIDAS

I'll deal with this more deeply when you've time, Iollas.
Now make for the willows there and turn left under the elms.
15 For when the meadows are too hot our bull loves resting
There and lays his great bulk down in the cool shade
And with his dewlaps ruminates the morning grass.

IOLLAS

Though rebuffed, Lycidas, I will not go away.
Tityrus, make for the said willows on your own
20 And if you find her there catch her and thrash her hard
And drive her here, but come back, mind, with a broken stick.
Well now, Lycidas, say what big quarrel brought
The hurt. What God has come between you and your love?

LYCIDAS

Happy with Phyllis only, as you know, Iollas,
I spurned Callirhoë's offer, though she brought a dowry.   25
And then she starts to make a wax-joined pipe with Mopsus
And to sing beneath the holm-oak, squired by the boy.
When I saw this, I own, I felt such fire inside
That I could take no more. Instantly I ripped off
Both her tunics and attacked her naked breasts.   30
She went to Alcippe in a rage saying, 'I've left you,
Wicked Lycidas. Your Phyllis shall love Mopsus.'
Now she is staying with Alcippe, and oh I'm scared
I shan't be admitted. But more than to have Phyllis back
I long for her to fall out with that puffing Mopsus.   35

IOLLAS

Your quarrel was your doing. You must be the first
To hold your beaten hands up. One should humour girls
Even when they're in the wrong. If sending word will help,
As messenger I'll make her hear despite her anger.

LYCIDAS

I've long been practising a song to disarm Phyllis.   40
Perhaps by hearing verses she can be brought round,
For she has always praised my poetry to the skies.

IOLLAS

Then sing, for I shall carve your words on cherry bark
And take the song away incised on the red rind.

LYCIDAS

Your now wan Lycidas sends you, Phyllis, these prayers,   45
This song which he's composing in the bitter night,
Weeping the while and ruining his sleepless eyes:

No thrush grows thinner, when the olives have been stripped,
No hare, when gleaners gather the last of the grapes,

50   Than haggard Lycidas drifting without his Phyllis.
     Ah, without you lilies look black to wretched me,
     Fountains are tasteless, wine turns bitter as I drink.
     But if you come, lilies grow dazzling white again,
     Fountains regain their taste and wines are sweet to drink.
55   I am that Lycidas whose singing, so you said,
     Could make you happy, whom you'd often give sweet kisses,
     Whose tunes you would not hesitate to interrupt
     And sought his lips while they were traversing the reeds.
     Ah, grief! And have you fallen now for Mopsus' gravel
60   Voice and feeble song and squealing wild oat pipe?
     Think, Phyllis, whom you follow and whom fly. They say
     I'm handsomer than he, and so you'd swear to me.
     I'm also richer. He can barely feed as many
     Kids as there are bulls of ours at the evening count.
65   Why tell you what you know? You're well aware, best Phyllis,
     How many are the heifers milked into my pails
     And how many have offspring tugging at their udders.
     But since you've gone I never weave of osier willow
     A slender frail or turn milk into quivering curd.
70   But, Phyllis, if you're still afraid of cruel assault,
     Look, I surrender. Tame my hands with twisted withies,
     If you so wish, and tough vine-stems behind my back,
     As Tityrus tied up the wicked wrists of nighthawk
     Mopsus and strung him up, the thief, in mid-sheepfold.
75   Take them, don't hesitate; they've each earned punishment.
     Yet these have often, these same hands, laid in your lap
     A ring-dove, often too a frightened leveret
     Whose mother I have snared. Through me the earliest lilies
     Would come your way and the earliest roses. Bees had hardly
80   Tasted the flowers again, and you were crowned with garlands.
     Maybe that liar boasts to you of golden gifts,
     Who's said to gather deadly lupins in the dusk
     Of dawn and boil down his broad beans for lack of bread,
     Who thinks he's lucky, truly fortune's favourite,
85   Whenever he grinds up cheap barley in his hand-mill.
     But if a shameful love (which God forbid!) reject

My entreaties, in my misery, I'll hang a noose
From the ilex there which first did violence to our love.
But first I'll carve this couplet on that wicked tree:
'Shepherds, beware of ever trusting fickle girls.   90
Mopsus has Phyllis, the end of time has Lycidas.'
Well now, Iollas – if you ever help the wretched,
Take this and plead with Phyllis in melodious song.
I'll stand aloof myself, concealed by the spike-rushes,
Or hiding closer behind the nearby garden hedge.   95

IOLLAS

We'll go, and she'll come back, unless the signs deceive me.
Good Tityrus has given me, ah, a lucky omen.
Returning, look, successful, with my heifer found.

Eclogue IV

MELIBOEUS

Why, Corydon, the silence and that frequent frown?
Why sit in an unusual place, beneath this plane-tree
By which a noisy brook chatters? You like the moist
Bank? And the nearby river's breath freshens the day?

CORYDON

For long, O Meliboeus, I have been pondering songs   5
Not of the woodland note but such as can proclaim
A golden age and celebrate the God himself[1]
Who governs nations and cities and toga'd peace.

MELIBOEUS

Sweet is your music nor does contrary Apollo
Despise you, young man, but great Rome's divinities   10
Are fit for no such ballad as Menalcas' sheepfold.

---

1. Nero.

CORYDON

Such as it is, although it smacks of the backwoods
To sharp ears and is famous only in our village,
Still my uncouthness, if not for the polished art
Of song, at least wins credit for its dedication.
15 Beneath this same rock which the mighty pine-tree shades
My brother Amyntas practises the same as I,
Whose time of life brings our two birthdays close together.

MELIBOEUS

Do you no longer stop the boy from joining reeds
20 And ties of fragrant wax, whom often you've forbidden
With fatherly concern to play on the light hemlock?
Corydon, more than once I've heard you saying this:
'Break your reeds, boy, and turn your back on empty Muses.
Instead go gather beechnuts and red cornel-cherries;
25 Drive flocks to milking-pails and loudly through the town
Cart milk for sale. Whatever will your pipe bring in
To ward off hunger? Certainly there's no one hums
My songs but windy echoes among yonder crags.'

CORYDON

I did say that, Meliboeus, I own, but long ago.
30 Now times are different and we have a different God.
Hope smiles more. If I gather no wild strawberries
Or blackberries nor solace hunger with green mallow,
It's thanks to you. Your kindness feeds us on good grain.
In pity for our small means and teachable youth
35 You stop us breaking our long fast on winter beechnuts.
Yes, Meliboeus, thanks to you we've no complaints.
Thanks to you we lie back well-fed in safe shade,
Enjoying Amaryllis' woods. Recently but for you
We should have set eyes, Meliboeus, on earth's furthest
40 Shores, on Geryon's furthest pastureland, exposed
To savage Moors where mighty Baetis, we are told,
With his clear current beats upon far western beaches.

I'd surely now be lodging cheap at the world's end –
Ah, grief! – and as a hired hand with Iberian flocks
Whistling uselessly on a pipe of seven reeds.   45
No one among the thornbrakes there would care at all
For my Muse. Perhaps even God himself would never lend me
A ready ear to hear, I fancy, the far-distant
Lengthy murmur of my prayers at the world's end.
But if no better tune has claim upon your ears   50
Or other songs than ours perhaps attract you more,
May today's page of verse be polished by your file?
Not only have the Gods commissioned you to warn
Farmers of coming winds and what manner of day
The golden sun will bring, but you often compose   55
Sweet songs and now the Muse honours you with Bacchic
Ivy, then fair Apollo shadows you with laurel.[1]
So, if you can forgive my nervousness, I'll try
Perhaps those reeds which skilled Iollas yesterday
Gave me and said, 'This pan-pipe can propitiate   60
Wild bulls and play the sweetest tunes to our Faunus.
Tityrus[2] owned it, who was first among these hills
To sing a modulated tune on Hybla's oat.'

MELIBOEUS

By striving to be Tityrus you're aiming high,
Corydon. He was a sacred bard who could on oaten   65
Pipe outsound the lyre, at whose music wild beasts
Would fawn and frisk, whom migrant oaks would halt to hear,
And every time he sang the Naiad would bestrew
With red acanthus and comb out his tangled hair.

CORYDON

Yes, Meliboeus, he's a god. But nor will Phoebus   70
Perhaps reject me. Do you please be kind and listen,
For well I know Apollo never ignores you.

1. Bacchus and Apollo were the chief gods of poetry. Ivy (sacred to Bacchus) and
   laurel (sacred to Apollo) were used for honorific poetic wreaths.
2. The reference is to Virgil.

MELIBOEUS

Then please begin; I'm with you. But be careful that
No high-pitched pipe of fragile boxwood blows the notes
75 It's used to voicing for you when you praise Alexis.
These, rather, are the reeds to go for. Finger now
The tenor pipes that sang woods worthy of a consul.[1]
Begin and don't wait. Look, here comes your brother Amyntas.
He shall sing second, alternating with your verses.
80 Lead on the song at once and lead it back in turn,
And you shall go first, Corydon; Amyntas, next.

CORYDON

With Jove he should begin, whoever sings of heaven,
Whoever shoulders Atlantean Olympus' weight.
But me let him whose present godhead rules our world,
85 Whose youthful vigour brings us everlasting peace,
Prosper with happy smile upon his august lips.

AMYNTAS

Let Caesar, accompanied by eloquent Apollo,
Also bless me and condescend to approach the hills,
That Phoebus loves and Jupiter himself protects,
90 Where fruits the laurel, destined witness of repeated
Augustan triumphs,[2] and the laurel's neighbour grows.

CORYDON

Even he who tempers North and South with fire and ice,
Our parent, Jupiter himself, to whom you now
Stand second, Caesar, often briefly lays aside
95 His bolt to visit Cretan fields and in green grot
Reclining hears Curetes sing from Dicte's woods.

---

1. An allusion to Virgil's 'Messianic' eclogue, *Eclogue* IV (line 3).
2. Of Nero, the new 'Augustus'.

AMYNTAS

D'you see how the green woods on hearing Caesar's name
Fall silent? I remember, though a storm was blowing,
A grove as suddenly grew quiet, its branches stilled,
And I said, 'It's a God has driven east winds away,'   100
And all at once Parrhasian reeds were piping loud.

CORYDON

D'you see how tender lambs suddenly frisk about,
How the ewes' teats are heavier with plenteous milk,
And, although lately sheared, their fleeces overflow?
This I remember seeing once before in this   105
Valley and the sheepmasters said Pales had come.

AMYNTAS

Certainly all the earth and every race adores him.
Gods' favourite he, whom thus the arbutus silently
Reveres, at mention of whose name insensate earth
Grows warm and blossoms, and when he's invoked the wood   110
Thickens its fragrant leaves and spellbound trees re-bud.

CORYDON

Soon as the world experienced his majesty,
From once deceiving furrows a more fertile crop
Luxuriated and at last in their plump pods
Beans barely rattled nor was harvest choked untimely   115
By harmful darnel or grew pale with idle oats.

AMYNTAS

No longer does the ditcher fear to wield the offending
Mattock but can use the gold he happens to find.
Nor is the ploughman, turning soil today, afraid
His share may clink against an inconvenient ingot,   120
But openly drives forward, ploughing ever deeper.

CORYDON

By his permission farmers can dedicate to Ceres
The first corn-ears and sprinkle Bromius with new wine;
The naked wine-treader can jump on the burst grapes,
125 And thronging villagers applaud their good master,
Who holds impressive games at the open Compita.[1]

AMYNTAS

There's peace by his permission on my hills, and thanks
To him, look, no one stops me if I like to sing
Or foot the slow grass thrice, and I can play for dances
130 And I can keep my songs in writing on green bark,
And snarling trumpets no more deafen our reed-pipes.

CORYDON

More carefree, thanks to Caesar's godhead, even Lycean
Pan can live in woods again, Faunus lie back
Carefree in shady pleasance; in untroubled pools
135 Naiads can bathe and without treading in human blood
Fleet Oreads can race dry-foot over the fells.

AMYNTAS

Pray, Gods, only recall this young man whom you've sent
(I can't be wrong) from heaven after a long, long life;
Or else unmake his mortal garment, granting him
140 Celestial threads of everlasting metal; let him
Be God yet not exchange the Palatine for heaven.

CORYDON

You too, O Caesar, whether you come as Jove himself
In altered form or hide some deity in feigned
And mortal guise (for God you are), rule this world, pray,

---

1. At the *compita* or 'cross-roads' an annual festival was held in honour of the Lares or tutelar deities.

Pray rule its folk for ever, holding cheap your love   145
Of Heaven, as father cherishing the peace you brought.

MELIBOEUS

I used to think the woodland Gods had granted you
Up-country ballads, suitable for coarser ears,
But what you've just performed on well-matched oat pipes, has
So limpid and so sweet a fall I'd not prefer   150
The nectar that Pelignian bees are used to sipping.[1]

CORYDON

O what songs, Meliboeus, running in well-rounded
Verse, would resound for me if I ever should home
Among these hills, if I ever should have the luck
To see fields of my own. Too often envious   155
Poverty pulls my ear and tells me, 'Mind your sheepfold.'
But if you think them after all not negligible
Then, Meliboeus, take my songs to God, for you
Can enter the inner shrine of Palatine Phoebus.[2]
Then you will be to me like him[3] who brought sweet-singing   160
Tityrus from the woods into the queen of cities,
Showed him the Gods and said, 'Tityrus, scrap the sheepfold,
And we'll sing, first, the countryside and, later, arms.'[4]

AMYNTAS

If only fairer fortune looked upon my labours
And God himself would favour my deserving youth!   165
But meanwhile we shall sacrifice a tender kid
And cook besides the courses of a makeshift dinner.

MELIBOEUS

Now lead your sheep down to the river. Summer shrills
And sun moves shorter shadows closer to our feet.

1. i.e. the poetry of Ovid, born in the Pelignian town of Sulmo.
2. The imperial palace on the Palatine near the temple of Apollo built by Augustus.
3. Maecenas, 'patron' of Virgil.
4. The three Virgilian poems, *Eclogues*, *Georgics*, and *Aeneid*, are here alluded to.

Eclogue V

Old Micon, once, and Canthus, Micon's foster-child,
Were sheltering from fierce sun beneath a spreading holm-oak,
When the old man, to advise his youthful foster-child,
With trembling lips voiced falteringly such words as these:

5 'The she-goats you see wandering among thorn-bushes
And tearing off the grey-white shoots with frisky bite,
Canthus my boy, the flocks – look! – that have left the hill
And you observe are cropping grass on the open plain,
These your old father gives you in your young days. Take them
10 And tend them. Certainly you now can sweat at work,
Can now employ your active youth on my behalf.
You see that now my time of life brings on a thousand
Complaints and stooping old age needs a stick to lean on.
But you must learn the rules by which to manage she-goats
15 That love the thickets and lambs that better stay in soft
Meadows.
             'In new spring, when the birds begin again
To chirrup and returning swallows daub their nests,
You'll move the whole flock forthwith from its winter fold.
For then a better forest puts forth vernal buds
20 And starts to build up once again the summer's shade;
Then crops grow and the year is born again in green,
Then Venus and the ardour of hot love spark off
And the salacious flock accepts the leaping he-goats.
But don't send out the herds to pasturage before
25 Propitiating Pales. Make a hearth of living
Turf and with salted meal invoke the place's Genius,
Faunus and Lares. Stain the knife warm with a victim,
But also, while she lives, parade her round the folds.
Without delay you'll then give sheep the plains, and goats
30 The thorns, at sunrise, soon as he begins to climb
Above yon hill and warms the course of day's first hour.
But if you've time, while sun is loosening the morning

Frosts, let swollen udders froth into your milk-pails.
Fill with the morning flow and in the morning likewise
Make cheese of what the sunset hour's milking yields.   35
But spare the brood-ewes. A quick profit is not worth it
If cheese for sale plays havoc among snow-white lambs;
For you must care for the new brood with special love.
And don't be ashamed, when visiting the sheepfolds late,
To carry on your shoulders any ewe that lies   40
Helpless from recent lambing, and in your parent bosom
Her trembling children, not yet able to stand up.
You will not look for grass far distant from the stalls,
Nor for their nourishment in woodland too remote,
While Jove's vicissitudes bring springtime to an end.   45
For Spring cannot be trusted; sometimes with clear brow
It smiles invitingly, sometimes it brings black storms
Of rain and with its floods sweeps off the wretched lambs.

'But when, in time, long days bring on the thirsty heat
And sky is no more changeable at God's caprice,   50
Then trust flocks to the woods, then look for grasses further
Afield. But send them out before daylight. Moist air
Makes sweeter food, whenever, East winds flown away,
The chilly pasturage is touched by dew at night
And in the morning drops are glistening on the grass.   55
But soon as the shrill-tongued cicadas scold the grove,
Drive all the flocks to water and thereafter stop them
Ranging the grassy plain, but let some ancient oak
Shelter them meanwhile underneath its spreading shade.
Then, when the ninth hour starts to cool off, as the sun   60
Goes down, and it seems now the time for a late lunch,
Pasture the flocks again, leaving the dim-lit grove,
And do not pen them in the summer fold until
Birds in their lightweight nests begin to think of catching
Sleep and twitter plaintively from trembling throats.   65

'But when the time arrives to take off the ripe wool
And tie the juicy fleeces up with slender rush

And cut the he-goats' manes and evil-smelling beards,
Yet first divide the flock, and after marking them
70 Pen the same coats together, so as not to mix
Long wool with short, or fine with coarse, or white with black.
But when a sheep without her covering shows you ribs
Stripped bare, look closely, lest the skin be harmed
By sharp shears or a boil should enclose silent pus
75 Beneath a hidden sore, which, if it be not broken
With iron, ah, infection from a brittle ulcer
Will gnaw at the poor body and cause its bones to rot.
I recommend foresight: take living sulphur with you,
A head of sea squill, and strong-smelling bitumen
80 To bring first aid to wounds; and don't lack Bruttian pitch.
Remember, if a back is scratched, to smear on liquid
Pitch ointment. Also cook a lump of quicksilver
With honey in a cauldron, and viscous bitumen,
To mark the sheep with your name, for the owner's mark,
85 Read on the shoulder, saves you from prolonged disputes.
Now too, when fields are parched, when earth is overheated,
When marsh, cracked open and with all its mud dried up,
Swelters and sun reduces feeble grass to dust,
It pays to kindle yellow galbanum inside
90 The pens and purify your huts with hartshorn smoke.
That smell puts evil snakes off. You'll see for yourself
How serpent's menaces collapse. None can unsheathe
Her crooked fangs but feebly and with useless mouth
Droops and falls flat, disarmed, her poison powerless.

95 'Come now, consider how you best may cope with nearby
Wintertime. When vineyards open up their rows
And carefree watchmen bear away the gathered grapes,
Start cutting back with hook the grove and its live leaves.
It's now you need lightly to strip the tender shoots,
100 To stock your winter foliage now, while it is moist
And green, before South winds shake down the trembling shade.
You'll find it practical to bring this out from your
Warm hayloft when year's end has shut your beasts indoors.

Here you must press on, here our work returns in season,
Active perseverance and pastoral manliness.   105
Don't hesitate to mix dry branches with new-cut
And to provide fresh sap, lest parching winter threaten
Its storms and with excessive frost and driven snow
Should wish to bow the grove and bind its leaves together.
Despite this you'll cut back smooth ivy or soft willow   110
Down in the valley. Canthus, you must offset your
Flock's thirst with green food. Hoarded dry stuff, though piled up
In heaps however huge, does them no good at all
If they are lacking shoots swollen with liquid sap,
Which have a vital element in their full pith.   115
Above all, strew the frozen ground with straw and fallen
Leaves, lest penetrating *rigor* burn their body
And devastate the beasts with internal disease.

'I'd like indeed to remember more, for more remains.
But now late daylight fades, and now, with sun in flight,   120
The cold Night-bringer pushes summer hours away.'

Eclogue VI

ASTYLUS

You're too late, Lycidas. Nyctilus and boy Alcon
Have just ended a singing-match beneath these boughs
With me as judge and for a stake. Nyctilus bet
Kids with their mother-goat, Alcon Leaena's puppy
And swore to his pedigree, but swept the board as winner.   5

LYCIDAS

That untrained Alcon beat Nyctilus at singing
I'll credit, Astylus, if crows can beat goldfinches
And hooting owls defeat the tuneful nightingale.

ASTYLUS

I'll give up Petale, the one whom now I pine for,
10 If Nyctilus comes any nearer him in trained
Skill on the pipes or singing than he does in looks.

LYCIDAS

Ah, now I understand. You had to judge, and one
Came pale and bristlier-bearded than a porcupine,
The other fair and fresher than a hairless egg,
With laughing eyes and locks that imitated gold,
15 Whose name could be Apollo – if only he'd not sing.

ASTYLUS

Oh, Lycidas, if you had any skill in song
You too could recognize that Alcon deserved praise.

LYCIDAS

Then, as you're no match even for me, you rascal, will you
20 (Judge though you may have been) take on my pipes with yours?
Will you compete? And if you like Alcon can umpire.

ASTYLUS

Could *you* beat anyone? Or would anyone deign
To have a match with you, who struggle to blurt out
A meagre trickle of vocal strains and stuttering words?

LYCIDAS

25 Keep lying, rascal. For you can't hurl true insults
At me, although Lycotas can at you – in plenty.
But there's no need to waste more time in useless wrangling.
Look, there's Mnasyllus. He'll be a judge (if you can face him)
Not taken in, you rascal, by conceited words.

ASTYLUS

30 I'd sooner, I confess, go off condemned unheard
Than, using half my voice's range, compete with you.

Still, not to let you get away with it, d'you see
The stag that's resting over there among white lilies?
Though he's my Petale's darling, take him if you win.
He's used to yoke and bridle, answers to his name   35
Trustfully and presents a modest muzzle at table.
You see how wide his branching antlers spread and how
Beneath them from his slender neck there hangs a chain?
You see too how his forehead, clasped by a snow-white halter,
Gleams and on his back the girth which goes right round   40
His belly has alternate glass beads on each side?
His tines and branchy temples are entwined by soft
Close-fitting roses and upon his neck there floats
A collar with red-gold tongue, in which is set a pendant
Boar's tusk, to decorate his breast with its white crescent.   45
This, as you see, Mnasyllus, is the stake I'm pledged
To forfeit, so he knows he's not beaten without one.

LYCIDAS

He thinks I'm terrified, Mnasyllus, by his offer!
See how I'm scared. I have, as you both know, a most
Uncommon breed of mare. Of their blood I will stake   50
Swift Petasos, who, having left his dam, has now
Begun to crop grasses with tender teeth. His back
Sits well; light-necked he tosses a proud head
And his well-rounded hooves are cased in narrow horn,
Those hooves on which he gallops over the green field   55
And merely brushes without bending the frail stems.
By the forest Gods, I swear, if beaten, to give him.

MNASYLLUS

I have the time and I'll enjoy your songs.
So, if you like, compete and I'll be judge. Look, there,
Ahead, beneath the ilex, Muses have made a couch.   60

ASTYLUS

But lest the nearby river's sound should trouble us
Let's leave the grasses and the running ripple's bank.

For water under scooped-out tufa answers me
Raucously and the noisy current's gravel grates.

LYCIDAS

65 Please let us seek the cave and nearby crag instead,
The crag from which green moss hangs down a dripping fleece,
And, like a scooped-out carapace, the shell-shaped roof
Stands over rocks that curve into a hollow arch.

MNASYLLUS

We're in the cave – with silence in exchange for noise.
70 If you would like to sit, the tufa, look, will seat us;
If to recline, green grass is better than a rug.
Now stop your bickering and let me hear the songs.
I'd like you to take turns and sing of tender love.
Praise Phyllis, Lycidas, and you, Astylus, Petale.

LYCIDAS

75 Now you have just to listen to us, please, Mnasyllus,
As you are said to have heard this fellow and Acanthis
Not long ago as judge in the Thalean wood.

ASTYLUS

I really can't keep quiet when that fellow riles me.
I'm furious, Mnasyllus. He's asking for a row.
80 Since that's his wish, let him recite or listen. Truly
I shall be pleased enough to watch Lycidas tremble
And pale at hearing his faults publicized before you.

LYCIDAS

It was at me, I suppose, that neighbour Stimicon and
Friend Aegon in these bushes quietly laughed, for wanting
85 To imitate a man's kisses with young Mopsus.

ASTYLUS

I'm no match for Mnasyllus. If only he weren't here
I'd make sure you saw no one uglier than yourself.

MNASYLLUS

Why d'you both rage so? Where's this madness taking you?
If you're prepared to sing in turn – but no, I'll not
Be referee. Some other judge can settle this.   90
And look, there's Micon coming – neighbour Iollas too.
They can take on the task of ending your dispute.

Eclogue VII

LYCOTAS

You've been in Rome a long time, Corydon. It must
Be twenty nights now since our woods began to miss you
And the oxen waited sadly for your yodelling.

CORYDON

Dear, dull Lycotas, more set than the toughest axle,
Who'd sooner watch old beech-trees than the modern shows   5
That our young God is giving in the big arena!

LYCOTAS

I wondered what your reason was for staying so long,
Why your pan-pipe defaulted in the silent woods
And only Stimicon sang, who, in your sad absence,
Won from us the pale ivy crown and tender kid.   10
For while you stayed away Thyrsis purged the sheepfolds
And told the young men to compete on the shrill hemlock.

CORYDON

Let Stimicon unbeaten carry off rich prizes,
Let him not only enjoy the kid that he's received,
Let him win all the sheepfolds Thyrsis purifies,   15
He'll never equal my joy. And if anyone
Should give me all the herds in the Lucanian forest
They would delight me less than what I saw in Rome.

LYCIDAS

Then tell me, Corydon, tell me. Don't be mean, despising
20 Your audience. I promise to find your words as sweet
As is your singing when at sacrifice you call
On either fertile Pales or pastoral Apollo.

CORYDON

We saw an amphitheatre[1] rise on interwoven
Beams skyward, nearly as high as the Tarpeian summit,
25 And measuring the steps and gently inclined slopes
We came to those seats where the crowded common sort
Wearing dark garments watch among the women's places.
For all the free space lying under the open sky
Is thronged with either knights or tribunes wearing white.
30 Just as the valley here is shaped like a huge O
And bending laterally, with sloping woods all round,
Curves its concavity amidst unbroken hills,
So there the sand's wide curve encloses level ground
And the oval in the middle is bounded by twin structures.
35 How can I tell you now what we ourselves could hardly
Take in, even partially? The brilliance everywhere
So dazzled that I stood transfixed and open-mouthed,
Amazed at everything, still ignorant of fine details.
At that point an old man who happened to be sitting
40 Next to me on the left said, 'Countryman, no wonder
You're staggered by such splendour, being unused to gold
And knowing only squalid buildings – huts and hovels.
Why even I, doddering now, white-headed and grown old
In Rome, am still amazed at everything; indeed
45 Whatever we have seen in former years seems cheap
And we despise the shows we attended in the past.'
The jewelled 'Belt', look, and the Arcade with its gold-leaf,
Look, vie in brilliance; and where, at the arena's edge,

---

1. Most plausibly taken to refer to the wooden amphitheatre built by Nero on the
Campus Martius in A.D. 57: Tacitus, *Annals* XIII.31; Suetonius, *Nero* 12.

The marble podium provides the nearest seats,
Fine ivory's inlaid on wooden bars, joined up,   50
To form a slippery cylinder which with sudden spin
On smooth well-rounded axle thwarts the claws placed on it
And throws the beasts off. There were shining golden-knotted
Nets too, projecting on whole tusks above the sand,
Tusks of the same size, and believe me, in good faith,   55
Lycotas, every tusk was longer than our plough.
How cover everything? I saw all kinds of wild beasts,
Here snow-white Arctic hares and wild boars that had horns,
And here the elk that's rare even in its native forests.
We saw bulls also – some had ugly humps above   60
Their shoulders and no neck, while others on their crests
Tossed shaggy manes and from their chins grew matted beards
And their dewlaps were stiff, covered with twitching bristles.
Nor was it only monsters of the wild forest
We had the luck to look at. I watched sea-calves and bears   65
Fighting, and that unsightly beast known, even so,
By the name of horse, a native of the famous river
Which waters the crops along its banks with a spring flood.
Oh how excited we all were to see the arena's
Floor splitting apart and from the gaping hole   70
Wild beasts emerging, and from the same cavity
Golden arbutus often grew in a saffron shower.

LYCIDAS

O lucky Corydon, still free from doddering
Old age. O lucky that it pleased a kindly God
To root your early years in this generation!   75
Now if chance granted you a near view of our reverend
Power and you could note, close to, his face and bearing,
Then tell me, Corydon, tell me, what Gods look like.

CORYDON

If only I had not been wearing country clothes!
Then I'd have seen my Power close to. But shabbiness   80
And black-clad poverty and clasp with crooked pin

Prevented me. Somehow, though, I'd a distant sight
Of him, and thought, unless my eyes made fun of me,
Mars and Apollo both were there in that one face.

PERSIUS

INTRODUCTION

Of all the early imperial poets Aulus Persius Flaccus, because of his
complex imagery and language rather than because of any ob-
scurity in his thought, requires an effort of the literary imagination.
Born of a wealthy Etruscan family, he died in A.D. 62 at the early
age of twenty-seven, but he left behind him a highly admired
volume of six satires, consisting of less than 600 lines, which
retained an honoured place in medieval and Renaissance times.

The uniquely Roman genre of hexametric satire had been firmly
established by the politically active and fearless Gaius Lucilius
(d. 102 B.C.), who used the loose and hospitable form for autobiogra-
phical reflections, casual moral comment, and political invective.
Horace, who produced his satires (*Sermones*) largely between 36
and 30 B.C., added structure and unobtrusive polish to this de-
ceptively casual format. To convey his witty criticism of society
and human passions, he adopted the satiric mask (or *persona*) of an
amiable, experienced *homme moyen sensuel*, who avoided philo-
sophical fanaticism in favour of a mildly epicurean common sense.

Persius looked to both of his predecessors for his models, but
donned the *persona* of a young eager devotee of Stoicism, who had
no illusions about himself or the rest of mankind, except perhaps
for his beloved teacher, the Stoic author, Annaeus Cornutus. But
it was not as a moralist, although Stoic principles of virtue and
happiness are easy enough to distil from his writings, but as a
master of imagery, allusion, and phrase that he captured the admira-
tion of his contemporaries, not least Lucan, and of posterity alike.

For the modern reader the problem is that Persius' highly or-
iginal style, with its striking, often eccentric images and turns of

phrase, and its knotty 'conceits', reminiscent of no poet more than John Donne, is hard to reproduce in English. It plays off, and often frustrates, the linguistic expectations of the audience, adapting ingeniously familiar phrases of Horace and other poets for novel effects and contexts, syncopating, heightening, and revivifying familiar poetic images and tropes. (See, for example, in the opening of *Satire* V, the elaboration of the motif of the hundred voices traditionally called for by a poet to express an important theme.)

The subtlety of his poetic technique drew upon him eventually the understandable charges of obscurity or immaturity. And yet the topics of each satire are plain enough: an attack on the Neronian literary situation, on the sort of writing that comes neither from the heart nor the head, and Persius' perhaps hopeless programme of reform (I); reflections to a friend on the vanity of corrupt human wishes (II); admonitions to himself on how to live and how not to live (III); a dialogue between Socrates and Alcibiades on the importance – and difficulty – of self-knowledge (IV); an affectionate tribute to Cornutus, in which he recalls how the Stoic taught him what should be his goals in life and the nature of true freedom, which is to be found in the soul and not in circumstances (V); and, finally, a letter to a fellow poet on the proper use of prosperity (VI).

For all the simplicity of his themes, Persius became an uneasy and unaccountable figure in the development of Roman satire. And yet if obscurity and compression are the main charges against him, one might surely have expected some greater sympathetic consideration and understanding for him in the century which has paid such critical homage to Donne, Hopkins, and even Propertius and which has made T. S. Eliot and Wallace Stevens into modern classics.

The questions to be first asked are these: What is it in Persius that makes the modern generation of readers of ancient poetry find him so alien? Is it that the understanding and appreciation of his satire can result only from a profound and inward feeling for the Latin language, something progressively harder to attain these days? Or is it that a certain critical evaluation of his poetry has been so widely and unthinkingly disseminated that he can only be saved by the desperate rescue operation of the sort certain recent critics have embarked upon? Or is our correct appreciation hampered by the assumptions we make about satire in general and Roman satire in particular, most notably that we are dealing with moralists in verse, whose message, however, may be marred by obscurity or eccentricity or (in Juvenal's case) by insincerity and hyperbole? One has to insist against this view that a verse satire is a poem or a set of poems written on moral or aesthetic subjects. Such poems may be personal or objective, ironic or vindictive, successful or unsuccessful. They may even have extrinsic aims – to make money, express personal spleen, or reform society – just as love poems are sometimes intended to persuade someone to go to bed. All this may be interesting, but is rarely relevant. What has to be avoided is the downgrading of verse satire into some form of *non-poetry*, into sermonizing or pamphleteering, where non-literary criteria, generally moral, may be introduced to judge this bastard genre. Most of all, we must not listen to ancient critics on the subject of satire, neither to the grammarians nor to the poets themselves, as one critic does in speaking of 'Persius, who considered himself a poet as well as a satirist'. Horace's facetious denial that satire is poetry (*sermoni propriora*) is just analogous to the elegists' use of the term *lusus* or Martial's references to his *nugae*. All such disclaimers are merely conventional bows to the traditionally high status epic enjoyed with ancient critics, despite sporadic revolts against its dominance by satirists and epigrammatists, and despite the vast stretches of bad writing for which it was responsible.

The evidence that Persius was a poet, not just a stuttering moralist, was there, of course, all the time, whether we look to his feeling for tradition in his admiration of Lucilius and his subtle imitations of Horace or to his keen critique of contemporary literary decadence and flatulent Alexandrianism in the first satire. However modest or ironic the tone, Persius is speaking of *poetry* when he says in his prologue, echoing more than one Augustan poet:

> I can't recall my lips were baptized in the hack's fountain;
> I've not napped a single dream on the Muses' double mountain;

I can't explain how I became a poet so suddenly.
To those whose busts give marble suck to imitation ivy,
I leave the privilege of pale draughts, the Heliconian strain.
I come to the bardic festival, but, only half a swain,
I bring an uninspired song, my own exclusively.
Who could have taught the Cockatoo his glib command of Greek?
Who prompted our own Italian Magpie to try to speak?
None but that patron of genius and Artistic Director
Belly, whose imitative craft can say what sense might never.
When the crafty cage of cash gapes with show of gold caress,
Then listen to our poet Crow and Magpie poetess;
You'd think they had inspired their song with Pegasus's nectar.

(trans. Richard E. Braun)

The prologue (or epilogue) is an important guide; it tells us that Persius' aim is writing *poetry*, but poetry of a different kind from that attacked in the first satire. The very first line contains the suggestive 'hack's fountain' (*fonte caballino*), an ironic touch which simultaneously derides the grand style, mythological conventions and traditional invocations – each picked to pieces at greater length in the first satire and the opening of the fifth.

   Persius is hardly trying to reform the world or Neronian society – the selectness of his anticipated audience ensures that. He is rather setting himself up in competition with Lucilius and Horace as a practitioner of what turned out to be one of the most vital and long-lived of Roman literary genres. The interesting problems are how Persius conceived of his task and what is the nature of his achievement, once we see that his success is not to be reckoned by his effectiveness as a missionary or a revivalist; that is, by the persuasiveness of his moral lessons. Horace had clearly succeeded in reducing a fairly free form, free in terms of both subject and language, into a smooth conversational musing, and the best an-alogy here is Pope's 'translations' of Donne. The form could, of course, have a tight structure when desired and it admitted, accord-ing to the implicit laws of the genre, a good deal of colloquial and obscene language – and those who see Persius as a Stoic saint should not underrate the strong element of obscenity Persius allows into his verse: 'Are you swishing your arse, Romulus?' (an, Romule, ceves?, I.87). But to imagine that Persius could not have followed Horace in his conversational smoothness is to do him an injustice.

Persius is rather trying to do what the metaphysical poets, such as Donne and Cowley, were trying to do: to produce (in Dr Johnson's words) 'a combination of dissimilar images, or discovery of occult resemblances in things apparently unlike', the connection of literature and sex, or morality and food, for instance. Persius claims to be skilled in the striking juxtaposition of words (iunctura callidus acri, V.14), which is close to Johnson's description of metaphysical wit, in which 'The most heterogeneous ideas are yoked by violence together; nature and art are ransacked for illustrations, comparisons, and allusions . . . ' It is then in his unique metaphysical style and in his imagery that much of his merit lies, provided we also comprehend the texture of his language, that is to say the careful allusiveness, the subtle literary echoes of Horace, Lucretius, Lucilius, Ennius, and even others, poets who are no longer extant. These are set against the background of the verba togae (V.14), the ordinary educated Roman speech, which, in different ways and within different limits, was accepted by Lucilius and Horace as the standard medium of satura. Persius, however, instead of accepting the smooth, polished version of the sermo pedestris that Horace generally employed in his Sermones and Epistulae, harks back to the freer, rougher, and more anomalous diction of Lucilius; he is trying to present a contemporary equivalent of Lucilius' 'improvisations' in a careful amalgam of archaisms, vulgarisms, literary allusions, the clipped affectation of real dialogue, and the homely, or sometimes outré, language of the household and the harbour. Behind this is something exquisitely subtle, a self-conscious poetic and satiric attitude that expresses itself through a certain way of writing, through a refined irony which shows itself in delicate linguistic ways, in a sensitivity to how language is used in other contexts, and then heightening it to produce a sometimes contrary or subversive effect. So magniloquence can be made to criticize magniloquence, vulgarity to criticize vulgarity, and poeticism to criticize poeticizing.

It is for these qualities and complexities that Persius has been valued in the past, before they were mistaken for obfuscation, and it is these qualities which present such a challenge to the translator, which we believe has been successfully faced in our selections.

J.P.S.

Further Reading

Bramble, J. C., *Persius and the Programmatic Satire: A Study in Form and Imagery* (Cambridge 1974).

Braun, Richard Emil, *Persius: Satires* (Lawrence, Kansas, 1984). Translated with an introduction and notes.

Clausen, W. V. (ed.), *A Persi Flacci Saturarum Liber* (Oxford 1956).

Connor, Peter, 'The Satires of Persius: A Stretch of the Imagination', in A. J. Boyle (ed.), *The Imperial Muse: To Juvenal through Ovid* (Berwick, Victoria, 1988) 55–77.

Lee, Guy (trans.), *The Satires of Persius* (Liverpool 1987). Introduction and commentary by William Barr.

Morford, Mark, *Persius* (Boston 1984).

Nisbet, R. G. M., 'Persius', in J. P. Sullivan (ed.), *Critical Essays on Roman Literature: Satire* (London 1963) 39–71.

SATIRES

SELECTIONS

Translated by Richard Emil Braun

Satire I

O human cares! How much in man's affairs
is immaterial . . .[1]
        'Who's going to read that?'
Are you talking to me? Lord, no one. 'No one?'
A couple. Maybe none. 'Disgusting. Too sad.'
How so? If Polydamas and the Daughters
of the Trojan Confederation prefer   5
Attius Labeo[2] to me, what am I
supposed to do? Join them? It's just a game.
Every time the muddled crowds of Rome
make light of something, do you march up and slap
the misbehaving hand of the dial
of their scale? No: you look inside, not out.
You test yourself, not them; because in Rome
        everyone . . .
I wish I could say it. We should say it, too,
considering the grey hairs, our lives' sour style,
and all we've done, since we left our nuts and jug,   10
to take on the elder smack of no nonsense
        disciplinarians.
We have a natural duty to speak out.

---

1. A quotation from Lucilius.
2. A contemporary and very literal translator of Homer's *Iliad* and *Odyssey*.

When I consider that . . .
Sorry. I won't say it. What should I do?
I've got a tough vein of malice in me
                    that comes out in giggles.
We lock ourselves in rooms and write: measure,
or free of foot, something so great it makes
lungs, however lavish of the living breath,
wheeze. It is understood that you will read
this product publicly: combed, fresh laundered, white,
wearing a carnelian – decked out, in fact,
as though it were your birthday – on a lofty
rostrum, in a flowing recitativo,
from nimble, liquid gullet, and rolling
over the audience an orgastic eye.
Soon, you can see enormous Toms and Dicks
off good behaviour: their voices fog over,
they begin to flutter as the chant enters
via their backsides and their insides are tweaked
                    by twitching verses.
Why you, old-timer? Why gather dainties
for these others' ears? You're fed up to the skin
yourself, with catering, and fit to burst.

'But what does a man work towards? Why go to school?
Skill is like yeast: useless unless it rises.
An inborn talent is a wild fig:
it needs to come out, and your heart explodes.'

So that's what your pale years of stern devotion
amount to! Knowledge is nothing to you
if no one knows you know it.
                    'No, yet it's nice
to have fingers point at you and hear tongues say
"That's him." And don't claim having a hundred
curly-headed schoolboys take you down
from dictation carries no weight with you.'

Posterity?
Look: here's a banquet. Well fed, Romulus'   30
posterity is busy drinking. They ask:
'And what has divine poesy to tell us?'
Somebody in a hyacinthine stole
utters hesitantly, down his nose,
something that's been kept around a bit long –
a 'Phyllis', an 'Hypsipyle',[1] Tales to Make
You Cry from the Earlier Roman Poets.
He tries to let them flow clear, but the words catch
and stumble on his tender little palate.   35
The host renders approval. Doesn't that gladden
the poet's ash? Isn't the stone that crushes
his bones lighter today? The guests are praiseful.
What luck for his cinders! Won't violets grow
                    from the ghostly mound today?

'Go on, laugh,' he says, 'you can't resist hooking us   40
on your nose. Don't tell me anyone turns down
the chance of earning popularity.
Whoever utters poems worth preserving
hopes to leave them fearless of fish or spice.'

Whoever you – debator I've created –
are, Sir, no: when I write, if some competent   45
piece comes out, and one could well come out
(a Rare Bird), then, no, I'm not afraid of praise.
I still have nerves. I'm not a pachyderm.
But your idea, that 'Bravo' is the right goal
and 'Fine' our ultimate aim, I must turn down;
because if you poke through all of this 'fine work',
there's nothing you won't find inside, including:
                    that hellebore addict
Attius' incorrigible *Iliad*;[2]   50

1. Mythological heroines of sentimental love poetry, such as Ovid's Heroides.
2. See note 2, page 75.

all the epigrams crude notables dictate
(products of undigested delicacies);

                    anything, in fact,
written on expensive furniture.
Now you, Sir, you have skill — at presenting
hot sow-teat dinners. You have knowledge, too:
if a crony shivers, you know enough

                    to give him a smooth, old coat.
But when you tell your cronies 'I love truth,'
55   then say to them 'Tell me the truth about
myself,' how can they? I can tell you. Shall I?
You've grown a fat pot, Baldy, standing half
a yard in front of you, but even so

                    you go on playing games.

O Janus, no stork clacks, no nimble hands
mimic white ears, and no tongue imitates
60   a Southern bitch's thirst behind Your back!

You, though, albeit of patrician blood,
are assigned, for life, a head with — by God's rule —
a blind back side; so you, O mortal man,
must turn, and meet posterior mockery.

                    'That's what you say.
What the public says, is "Now at long last
poems flow along pliantly metrical,
so smooth that the most picky fingernail
runs over where the parts fit. Today's poet
65   has the skill to line up verses just as though
he had a cord and rouge[1] and one eye closed.
And no matter what he needs to speak up on —
manners, abuses, or, say, regal lunches —
the Muse supplies him with great material."'

---

1. Builder's implements for levelling.

Look, here we go
teaching people to report (now, today!)
the feelings of Heroes, when what they're used to
is playing Greek word-games. They aren't craftsmen
enough to represent woods or praise farmlands –   70
well fed place of baskets, braziers, pigs,
the hay-smudge at the Festival of Pales;[1]
home ground of Remus and of you, Quintius,[2]
grinding the cusp down smooth in the furrow:
All in a flutter, your wife invested you
in the state robe of Dictator of Rome.
Your team of oxen stood as witnesses.
A solemn lictor hauled your plough back home. –
Bravo! That's poet's work. But listen here: 75

'There's nobody today likely to take
much time over the varicose volumes
Of Bacchic Accius, or Pacuvius
with his verrucose *Antiope*,[3] quote:
Worries are the pillars of her heart of woe.'

When you see fathers
(your Public, squinting with short-sightedness)
pouring advice like that in their boys' ears,
you needn't search further for the origin   80
of this modern cracknel of language, rendered
bloodless if not fat-free, now on every tongue,
or for the source of your own falls from good form
that make the smooth-legged horse-warriors hop
in their chairs when you recite.

---

1. A country festival (21 April) in honour of livestock; bonfires were part of the ritual.
2. Quinctius (less strictly 'Quintius') Cincinnatus was appointed dictator in 458 B.C. After rescuing Rome, he went straight back to his farm.
3. *Antiope*, like Pacuvius' play, *Bacchae*, also alluded to here, represents archaic drama and diction. The line quoted contains a couple of rare or obsolete words, which some moderns were imitating.

Perils swoop
at your grey old head; but you can't repel them:
instead, you hope for tepid compliments
on your propriety of form – unashamed
as Pedius. 'You're a thief,' they tell him.
85   What does Pedius do? He weighs the charges
on the smooth-shaved balance of antithesis.
He bribes the jurors with a presentation
of poetic tropes. They praise him: 'Fine work!'
Fine? For a high-bred Roman to wave his tail?
Do Romulus' posterity's posteriors
swish these days? Am I more likely to be moved
to produce a penny for a shipwrecked
outcast if he sings a song to me?
Sing, as well as cart a portrait of himself
adrift on a broken timber? If you want
90   to bend me to your grief, cry; but don't prepare
your tears the night before.

'But these days numbers are raw no longer.
Form has come, and a closer fit. Poets
have learned to lock up a line like "Attis
of Berecynthus", and "Dolphin spreading
a crack in Nereus' deep blue", and like
95   "Short-cut a rib from lengthy Apennine".'[1]

And why not *Arms and the man*,[2]
as long as you're at it? At least I find
the 'arms' – froth padding and fat cork puttees –
adequate; but the 'man' is an antique twig,
cooked down until the bark's too big for it.
If that's your heroic style, what do you have

1. Modern metrics and strained poeticisms; perhaps those in fashion at Nero's court.
2. The opening of Virgil's *Aeneid*.

that's tender and little and meant to be heard
         with head hung lax?

'"Mimallonean droning brims o'er the horrid horns.
The Bassarid, about to lift a lofty calf's clasped   100
head off, and the Maenad, mad to twine around a lynx
a berry-clad ivy bough, twice each 'Euhoë' cries;
and Echo resurrects two pairs of twins of sound."'

Would anybody slobber forth such stuff
if there were still a vein of our forefathers'
balls alive in us? Maenads! Attises!   105
It's backless, it's sideless; it swims to the top
and soaks the lips soft with tasteless nonsense.
No smack there of desk-tops smitten or nails
         munched to the knuckles.

'Why rasp truth's teeth on tender little ears? Please –
watch out. The doorways of the Noble could well
freeze shut on you, with your bitching and growling
         and talking down your nose.'

All right. As far as I can care, from now on   110
everything's fine. Bravo! Well done! Wonderful!
But as for you, all you've done is to declare
an interdict, impose a veto, cry,
'Let none bestink this spot.' . . . like a janitor
who posts a portrait of a pair of snakes
then says, 'Children, this is a holy place.
        Go piss out there.'[1]
             Good-bye.
Lucilius attacked his Rome – bit Lupus,   115
bit Mucius, and broke a molar on them.
Flaccus, wise to the world, would make his friend laugh
as he probed him and felt out what was wrong;

---

1. Such warning notices were common around sacred places.

let into the heart, he had fun there.
He was a veteran at poking his snout out
and hanging the public from it; while I . . .
can't I even give a quiet growl?
Not even if it is my sacred duty?
In secret? Not even in a hole? Nowhere?
All the same, I should. I will. I'll bury it
in this little book. What I've seen, I've seen:
EVERYONE HAS ASS'S EARS.
                                    There it is,
covered over: my private laugh, a nothing
which I wouldn't sell you for the . . . not for
                any *Iliad*.
All you who are inspired by the fearless
Cratinus; you that turn pale when Eupolis,
or the Old Man, the greatest of the Three,[1]
grows angry — consider what follows, too:
you could well hear things cooked down even denser.
Ears which they have steamed may boil for me.
I don't need readers who make fun of Greeks'
squeaky boots; men ready to call a man
with one eye One Eye;[2] a local bureaucrat
who thinks he's in Society, head aloft
because he broke irregular half pints;
somebody enabled by worldly wisdom
to laugh at numbers and tables and proofs,
and capable of being much amused
when a tough street-walker jerks a Cynic's beard.
To them, I recommend the Police Reports,
mornings, and after lunch, a Musical.

120

125

130

1. Cratinus, Eupolis and Aristophanes were the three most famous and fearless
   representatives of fifth-century Athenian Old Comedy.
2. A possible reference to a work of Nero's.

Satire V

From the earliest poets, the fashion stands
of praying for ninety-nine more voices.
We hope for a hundred mouths, a hundred tongues
to sing . . . a tragedy, say, for an actor
to present through a drawn forever down
and open mouth; or, say, a history:
the Parthian dragoon, dragging the lance-head
from his wounded crotch . . .

                            'What's the point of this
for you? The pile of poetic morsels   5
you serve up is not so sturdy as to need
a hundred gullets to get it out or down.
Men who plan great utterances: they can try
some potshots among Heliconian clouds.
They'll hit the jackpot, if Procne boils it
for them, or Thyestes; and Glycon can keep
coming pot luck as usual, equipped
with his deadpan wit and unfailing good taste.
But you're not setting limits on the winds
in a wheezing bag while ore cooks, are you?   10
You aren't growing hoarse from hushed mumbling
of dismembered monologue in grim crow-clucks.
It's not your purpose to puff up your cheeks
to the point of rupture, to produce a pop.
No. You imitate the words of the well-dressed
civilian; these, with veteran skill, you fit
together, sharp edges joined, into new shapes.
You use reasonable wind, enough to smooth
your jaws' corners, when you rasp at behaviour
such as turns men pale. In poetic fashion,   15
you pin down wrong: sport for a gentleman!
                This is your proper fare.
Leave behind you, Persius, the festal board

of beauteous Mycenean Majesties
                    head, feet, and all.
Taste the lunches of the proletariat.'

Me? You know me better. Have I ever worked
at swelling pages with solemnities
20   that change smoke into substance? That's just a game.
Today, my utterance is private, meant
                    solely for you.
The spirit of my song lends me courage
to open my heart for you to poke through.
It will be good, once and for all to show,
                    delightful friend Cornutus,
how large a portion of my soul is yours.
(But please be sceptical: give me a shove;
distinguish the solid-sounding plaster
25   from the rattling panels of self-portraiture.)
This is the only reason, this is why,
                    if I but durst,
I'd turn down one and pray for a hundred throats:
to pour forth in clear speech the winding depth
of the folds of my chest where I keep you pinned;
to unseal the stock of my insides' feelings
too secret, still, for tongue to tell in toto.
30   When my Protector, proud in bands of purple,
abandoned me to early terrors; after
my amulet became a dangling gift
to the bare-legged Lar;¹ when bright white garb
and my cronies' coaxing made all downtown
a place to scatter glances and never blink;
and when the winding way wandered where life
35   is an unknown that drags the fluttering will
onto trails that branch off, I put myself,
                    Cornutus, under you.

1. On officially entering manhood, the Roman male dedicated his protective
   amulet to the household gods, often depicted as dancing youths.

You pick me up, tender in my little years.
You enfold me in your Socratic arms.
The artful try-square you put to my bent
morals fools me, makes me straighten out.
Limited by the pressure of reason,
my windy spirits struggle to surrender.
Under your craftsman's thumb, I take on form.   40
Yes, and it was with you that I used up
long spells of sun – as I recall – and gathered
the early fruits of the night in feasting.
Sharing both as one the common task,
together at the modest board we'd rest:
we'd keep a serious cask going, and let
                    serious matters go.
Let no doubt stand: a firm pact binds us both.   45
From one star, our days are drawn in harmony.
Maybe the Birth Sprite (that tight clutcher of truth)
hung our lives from Libra's level scale;
or, say, the Natal Hour distributed
the faithfully attuned pair's destinies
between the concordant twins of Gemini.
Since, together, we break grim Saturn against
our Jupiter, the fact stands firm: some star   50
directs the symphony of our two souls.

There are a thousand aspects to mankind's
motley ways. Everyone has the will to live
                    by a different hope.
Here's a man in the land where the sun is fresh
replacing Italian goods with wrinkled
pepper and pale cumin seeds; here's one   55
who'd rather lie swelling with fluid sleep;
another goes all out for sports; one gets
cooked down at dice; and one goes to pieces
                    over a love affair.
Just so: and when the stony gout has broken
their knuckles – twigs on an antique tree – then

they groan for foggy days they tramped across
60 and fatuous bog-lights followed (too late!)
and life left behind.
                            What's good for you, though,
is growing pale nights-long over your papers,
                    preparing to serve, by day,
as the Young People's Horticulturist,
purging their barren ears and planting the seed
of Cleanthes.
                    Children (yes, and elders!),
here's the grove to pick: for your aspirations,
an exact goal; and provisions for the road
65   that turns you weak and grey.
'I can begin tomorrow just as well.'
Then do, tomorrow.
                            'What? You're giving me
one day? Sure you're not being too generous?'
Yes, I'm sure. Already when the new day dawns,
we've used up yesterday's tomorrow. Look:
new tomorrows keep the years moving,
and always stay a bit ahead of them.
It's much the same as though you were a tyre
trying to catch another tyre turning
70 near you on a single frame: you never will,
because your wheel is running behind it
to begin with, stuck on the back axle.

            We need freedom:
Freedom, not what goes by the name, and means
only that someone transferred from the Slave List
to the Register of the Indigent
deserves to be the undisputed master
of a food-ticket's worth of scabrous grits.
The seed of truth has rotted in them who think
75 one turn around[1] can make a citizen.

1. A part of the ceremony of emancipation.

Here's Dama: ostler; value, not a nickel;
has that typical, bad-wine squint; steals feed,
and covers up the deceit by mixing thin.
His master turns this same man like a top.
Around he goes, and out comes 'Marcus Dama'.
Wild! How about a cash loan? You wouldn't
refuse, if Marcus covers it, would you?
Marcus is the judge. Are you turning pale?   80
Marcus said it: you'd better believe it!
Marcus, witness my signature . . .

        Pure freedom.
    We get it with our caps.[1]

'Well, isn't someone who can lead the life
he chooses free? I'm free to live as I please.
Therefore, I'm as free a man as Brutus.'
Your reasoning (at this juncture, a Stoic,
ears munched clean by vinegar, avers)
is deceptive. I accept your premise.   85
Just delete 'I'm free to' and 'as I please'.

'The Praetor dubbed me with his wand.[2] I marched off.
I'm my own man. Why can't I do whatever
my wants command that's not against the law?'   90

You want to know why? Unwrinkle your snout,
and drop that look of angry mockery.
Listen and learn, and let me jerk Granny's
antique assumptions from your huffing lungs.
A Praetor's functions never have included
conferring subtle senses of duty
upon fools, or, when life rips full career,
the skill to hold their lane: you'd engineer

---

1. i.e. the caps donned by freedmen to symbolize their new status, a fashion
 picked up by the French Revolution.
2. An alternative ceremony for emancipation from slavery.

95 a carter's competence at the virginals
more readily! Reason blocks you, takes you
aside in private, and gabs in your ear:
'No one is free to do as he pleases
                    when he's sure to do it wrong.'
Statute and Nature both contain the rule
that an interdict on action be maintained –
as a duty, both public and humane –
for ignorance and disability.
100 Do you prepare a purgative solution
                    of hellebore
without knowing at exactly what point
on the dial to halt the hand of the scale?
Medicine's intrinsic law's veto
prevents you. If a ploughman, who never heard
of the morning star, tossed off his mud-boots
and prayed for a ship's command, Melicertes
would yell, 'The sense of shame is sunk ashore!'
                    How about you?
Has the art of thinking right conferred on you
a straight-legged life-stance? Are you a veteran
105 at distinguishing truth from appearance,
in case, below the gold, brass chimes deception?
Have you marked your goals and models, first, with chalk,
next, your dangers and disgusts with charcoal?
Kept your hopes within reason? Set limits
to home and farm? Are you your friends' delight?
110 Can you tighten up on the meal sack now,
and now let it go lax? Pass by a penny
pinned down in mud, and not be forced to gulp
the overflow of your mercurial mouth?
                    When you can say
'I have achieved, and I maintain all that,'
then it's proven. So be it! You are free . . .
as you are sensible; free by the favour
of Jupiter no less than by the Praetor's.
115 But if, though just a bit ago you flocked

together with us, you've retained your old spots;
or if you're wearing sheep's clothing to hide
a sour grape; if so, I've given you
enough rope. Reason won't stop blocking you.
Jut out a finger – there's no slighter job –
you spoil even that. No matter what grade
of spice you burn, your prayer won't be answered.   120
Not half an ounce of right thinking can stick
inside a fool; the two don't mix: it's God's
and Nature's law. Bathyllus couldn't keep
three steps of his *Rustic Ballet* in measure
if he were really and strictly a farmer.

'I'm a free man.'
             Where do you find your data?
'Free', when you're subject to so many things?
Do you know no master beyond the man
who let you go with the waft of a wand?   125
'Boy, go fetch Crispinus' scrapers for him.
He's at the Baths.' – When a master makes sounds
like those – 'What you waiting for? You playing
games with me, boy?' – it's clear-cut slavery.
It doesn't shove. It doesn't enter you
to make your muscles move. It stays external,
sharp as hacked rock, quick as a bitter word.
             But when the masters
are born inside you, in sore spots of your heart,
then do you come out unharmed? No, no more   130
than he, when whip and boss-fear start him moving
to fetch those scrapers.
             Morning: stubbornly,
you snore. 'Hey,' says Greed, 'get up!' You refuse.
But Greed maintains the pressure: 'Get up now!'
I can't.
      'Get up.'
             In order to do what?
'Do what? You need to be told? All right. Go East:

135 bring ocean perch, beaver musk, heavy flax,
and ebony and spice and myrrh and slick silks.
Be first to load the fresh pepper, and first back:
don't stop to water the camels! Get a loan.
Take an oath.'
              But Jupiter will hear it.
'Too bad, buddy. Want to stay a pot-licker,
keep this up. You'll scrape rock, if you aim to live
on good terms with Jupiter.'
                          By this time,
you're bustling bare-legged, arranging hides
140 and barrels on your crew's backs. Quick, to the ship!
And nothing could keep you from ripping across
the sea on a desolate mass of timber,
if Sloth didn't artfully divert you
to a quiet corner first, and warn you:
'Sick, sick! Where are you rushing to? What do
you want? Has that choleric libido
bloated and inflamed your torso so badly
145 that a pot of hemlock couldn't cool it off?
You, hop across the sea? Lean on a pillar
of twisted hemp? Have dinner off a thwart
beside a squat keg that pants the bouquet
of ruined rosso and stale tar in your face?
What are you after? Here, you've always nursed
your cash along within reason: five per cent.
Oh, but now you're going to push it, are you,
150 sweat out eleven? What for? Give in! Live!
Gather delights! Your life is all you have,
then all you are is an ash and a ghost
and a story. Live with death in mind. Time runs:
it's going while we stand and talk about it.'

Well, what's the matter with you? You're being split
155 by a pair of opposed hooks. Which way to go?
Twin ties force you now to wander off from,
now to submit to each of two masters.

Suppose you can stand up against an order
one of these times; and when pressure is maintained,
refuse, for once, to yield. Don't say, 'At last
I've snapped my chains!' You're just like the bitch: she strained,
ripped out the knot; but all the same, as she runs
away, she is trailing a lengthy section of
               chain from her neck.   160

Davus, ready! I command you to believe
what I tell you! I'm pondering putting
an end to my past sorrows . . .
                  (Chaerestratus,
mumbling a thumbnail raw, is the speaker.)
I'm just a stumbling-block before my family's
sober steps, fallen from their peak of good form.
I can't go on this way, breaking the hulk
of my estate on rumbling reefs of a scandal!
My father's freight lies at the sordid portal,
at Chrysis' door, slimy with brine of tears,   165
where, an addict of drunken song, holding
my spent and cold flambeau, I sulk . . . no more,
no more!
       'Bravo, my boy, you've got good sense!
Kill a she-lamb for the Gods: They're sure your
watchful shepherds.'
              But, Davus, do you figure,
when I leave her, she'll cry?
                'Don't play games, my boy.
She'll give you hell with the old red slipper
to teach you better than to try to flutter
or nibble the narrowing net. Right now,   170
you're wild and violent. Yet if she calls,
right away you'll say, "Well, what should I do?
Go marching back to her? Not even now
that she summons me with voluntary vows,
prayers, and promises?" No, not even now!
Stay out the way you came out: in one piece,

and with a particle of self-respect left.'

Here it is, here's
the very thing we're looking for; here, not
175   in the incompetent straw the lictor wafts.[1]

Is a flattered man, drawn open-mouthed along
by ambition (Ambition, laundered proper
white, and checked with chalk), is he a master
or slave? Stay up all night! Serve up such a pile
of chickpeas for the public to scramble for,
that they'll be able to recall your lavish
Festival of Flora when they're old men
dozing in the sun some day. Isn't that nice?
No?
          You're free?
                    And yet, when Herod Day comes,[2]
180   and violet-laden lamps arranged in greasy
windows puke fat fog, and the tuna swims
in a red plate that his tail hugs, and wine bloats
the trusty, white jars of the Faithful Few,
                    quietly you move your lips;
you turn pale at the Sabbath of the Skinned.
185   Then, black ghosts are manifest, and the perils
of the exploded egg swoop. Then, those great
Gallinaceans[3] (who don't crow, are natives
of no Gallican nation, and can't gallant),
and the sistrum-waving, one-eyed priestess
poke gasifying Gods inside you, unless,
that their words may be fulfilled, at dawn you taste,
                    thrice, a head of garlic . . .

1. Another feature of an emancipation ceremony.
2. A reference to the Jewish Sabbath. The Jews and the worshippers of Cybele and
   Isis are here prime illustrations of religious superstition.
3. Persius' wordplay centres on *gallus gallinaceus* (a cock) and on Gallus (a castrated
   priest of the Mother Goddess).

Speak like this among the vein-strung Centurions,
straight off, enormous Harry gives a thick laugh   190
and bids ninety-nine dimes for a hundred Greeks.

Satire VI

Has Sabine winter brought you to your fireside,
Bassus? By now, the lyre strings have come alive
to your stiff pick. And a wonderful workman
you are, who have made it your aim to align
the rough blocks of our antique speech in metre
and tune the Latin harp's manly racket,
keeping the fun of being young moving
to honoured rhythm, as you, the exception,   5
        growing old, play.
I, in the meantime, am wintering beside
my warm sea, Liguria, where enormous
shore cliffs' corners stand exposed while the coast
        withdraws in a deep hollow:
Learn Moon Harbour, men: 'tis worth your time,[1]
as Ennius commanded from the heart
after he snored himself awake from being   10
Quintus, alias Homer, former peacock,
ex-Pythagoras.
        Down here, I don't care
what the mob plans, and what the south wind, that makes
the herds infertile, is preparing; don't care
if my neighbour's field's far corner is fatter
and richer than my own. However much wealth
my born inferiors gain, I shall go on   15
refusing to shrivel in senile gloom,

---

1. A quotation from Ennius' Satires.

dine without oil and, when a bottle's stale,
to probe the seal with a paranoid snout.[1]

Someone else might rattle on quite differently . . .
(Even twins diverge, their Guardian Spirit
being bow-legged.) . . . as, for instance, the man
who wets his greens on his birthdays only,
and even then only with brine,[2] of which –
wise as he is to worldly ways – he buys
one cupful, if the cup comes with it free.
There follows the aspersion of the tray
                    with sacred pepper . . .
Quite different, was one youngster with spirit
aspiring to grandeur, who chewed clean through
his fortune . . .
                    I too like spending, and intend
to spend
        as much of the reasonable heap
I have as reality asks for.
                    I'm not
so splendid as to serve my freedmen flatfish,
and not so artful as to sex a thrush,
slobbering over the subtle aftertaste.

Eat all you reap, if the harvest is your own.
Mill the whole grist: it's not your duty not to!
Why worry? Harrow! A new crop juts its shoots.

                    But duty calls:
Timber snapped, a friend is clutching rock.
He has nothing. All his goods, his muffled hopes,
have been deposited at sea. He lies
on the coast alone except for enormous

20

25

---

1. In case the slaves had been at it.
2. As a cheap substitute for olive oil.

Gods off the poop and ribs ripped from the hull
which ducks come greeting. Now's the time to break   30
a bit of your live turf off and be your friend's
patron. He has nothing. Make sure he needn't
wander off carting a portrait of himself
        on a deep-blue board.[1]

'Suppose you help him. What about your heir?
He'll be angry. He'll neglect your funeral
banquet because you bobbed the property.
And he'll be capable of putting your bones
in the pot in an un-aromatic
condition, not minding if the cinnamon's
scent is muffled or, say, the cassia   35
is spoiled with cherry bark.
                 "Shrink my fortune?
Well, I fixed you. Yes, Bestius gives those Greek chefs
their comeuppance. Let me quote: *That's how it goes,*
since this contemporary, castrated,
senseless tastelessness arrived in Rome
along with cargoes of pepper and dates;
since then, even your mowers and your stookers
have started pouring thick, spice-flavoured grease
in their porridge. I tell you, it's all wrong."   40

Yet, as you say, why worry? When your ashes
go in the pot, you'll be beyond all that.'

        Now you, my heir –
whoever you will be, you'll be my heir –
let me divert you to a quiet corner,
away from the crowd a bit. Now listen,
        my dear fellow:

---

1. Shipwrecked sailors, when begging, carried round a depiction of their cata-
strophe.

Caesar has sent a laurel. Didn't know that,
did you? Total Victory in Germany!
45   They're poking the cold ashes off the altars.
Caesonia's accepting bids on contracts[1]
for armour for the doors, robes for the kings,
sallow, shag cloaks for the common captives,
and chariots and enormous Father Rhines.
Therefore, I'm offering a hundred pairs
to the Gods and our Leader's Guardian Spirit
because of his exceptional achievements.
Veto me? Just try. Woe unto you, unless
you wink at this. Also, I'm lavishing
50   oil and pasties on our paltry populace.
Or will you stop me? Tell me, clear and loud.
'I reject the bequest,' you say. 'The estate
               has been well nigh filet'd.'
Come on! None of my paternal aunts is left;
none of my uncles' or my father's uncles'
daughters. My maternal aunt was sterile,
and now she's dead. Nothing surviving out
          of Granny, either.
55   Even so, all I need do is march straight
to Bovillae, up the Hill of Virbius,
and there, willing and waiting, is Manius,
my new heir.
          'Some random stranger sprung
from the land?'
             Not quite . . . If you ask me who
my great-great Grandad was, I won't be prompt,
but I will name him: it's within my means.
Go back one, back one more: by now, we've found
a 'son of the land'. And, by the dignified
rules of genealogy, this Manius

1. Caligula's wife is in charge of his planned triumph over the Germans, represented
    by the images of the river Rhine. Persius' financing of a hundred pairs of
    gladiators for combat in the amphitheatre would be generous.

comes out as a near connection of one
or another of my own mother's mother's
   mother's brothers.   60

This is my last lap. Why pray for the torch
before I catch up with you?
      Consider me
Mercury, come to you in person, as He
does in His portraits. But this visitation
is actual. Would you rather shake your head,
or be glad with what I leave you?
        'The total
is lacking something.'
       Yes, thanks to me, it shrank.
    But all there is –
whatever it will be, it's all there is –
is all for you, and for you to thank me for.
So, *run from wondering* [1]   65
where the legacy Tadius willed me
once upon a time is now. Quit giving me
dictations like: 'Invest the family fortune,
and its wages will come marching home. But dip
into capital, what's left?'
     Left?
       Anoint them,
boy, quick, thicker! grease those cabbages!
It's a holiday.
     I'll cook me no nettles,
smoked hog jowl, sow brain and split ear, so that,   70
some day, your swollen grandson, when he's fed well
off the vitals of a goose, can answer
the throbbing and sobs of that blasé vein
on his rambling crotch by making the seed-sac
of an authentic patrician dame sop
his piss. Or should I be left transparent

---

1. A quotation from Horace, *Odes* I.9.13 (on the theme of *carpe diem*).

as an unwoven warp so he can wobble
the adipose caul of his priest-size belly?

75   Be sure you make a profit
when you sell your soul.
                    Do some artful trading.
Poke through every corner of the cosmos.
See to it that no dealer up on the stiff
scaffold is a more outstanding clapper
of firm, fat Cappadocian captives. Increase
your money twofold . . .
                    'I've creased it till the folds
have wrinkles: three times, four times, ten. A fellow
able to fix the point where I could stop
80   could find a true ending to Chrysippus's Heap!'[1]

---

1. *Sorites* is a salami-type method of argumentation: as, for example, when does a heap of stone cease to be a heap in the process of subtraction? How many hairs does one have to lose to qualify as 'bald'?

SENECA

INTRODUCTION

Lucius Annaeus Seneca was born about 1 B.C. at Cordova in southern Spain. In A.D. 65 at a villa outside Rome he killed himself on instructions from the emperor Nero, whose tutor and chief minister he had been. Undoubtedly the most brilliant literary figure of his day, he was also its most complex and most enigmatic. Orator, Stoic philosopher, essayist, epistolary, natural scientist, satirist, poet, tragedian, statesman, financier, courtier, sycophant – Seneca has rarely drawn from history the complexity of response which his life and works demand. Few of us have stared into the face of a Caligula or experienced the paralysing nightmare of a tyrant's court. Seneca had. His tragedies are product and index of an age of moral and cultural crisis. Their style is the style of shock.

There are eight extant Senecan tragedies. Four are masterworks: *Phaedra*, *Medea*, *Thyestes* and *Trojan Women*. Each of them reveals why Seneca so deeply influenced Renaissance drama: psychological insight, vivid and powerful verse, highly effective staging, and an intellectually demanding conceptual framework. Each is a profound witness of its age. In dramatic conventions exploited, literary and rhetorical modes adopted, themes and issues addressed, Senecan tragedy mirrors the spectacular, histrionic and self-consuming world of late Julio-Claudian Rome. A world defined by political repression, moral lethargy, and the hollowness of societal and linguistic forms, a world which screamed its aesthetic structures, imaging itself through painting, sculpture, architecture and literature in increasingly hyperbolic forms. A world which felt the onset of its own dissolution.

Did we of all mankind seem worthy
To be crushed by the disjointed
Universe? With us has the final
Age come? O we're creatures of bitter
Fate, whether we wretches destroyed
The sun or banished it.

(*Thyestes* 875–81)

The major themes of Senecan tragedy – death, dissolution, civilization, the fragility of social, religious and linguistic forms – reflect this dying age.

Trojan Women is our play. Its spare and rhetorical style, its concentric, asyndetic structure, its psychological and thematic focus mark the work's genesis in late Julio-Claudian Rome. Among its major concerns: human power, human impotence, human knowledge, human delusion, language, fate, death, compassion, freedom and captivity, history's determined and dissolving cycle. The themes of death and dissolution pervade and unite the play – from Hecuba's opening presentation of the dissolution of her kingdom and the death of her children, her husband and her world to the bitter, quasi-erotic summoning of death with which she almost closes the drama (1171–5). Imagery and motifs of dust, ashes, smoke, loosing, tearing, ravaging, scattering, dismembering, bursting, collapsing, sustain the play's preoccupation with death and dissolution. So too the dramatic action itself. The main body of the drama – Acts II, III, IV and V – concerns itself with the tearing of a child from its mother (Astyanax from Andromache, Polyxena from Hecuba – their deaths are required if the Greek fleet is to sail) and the dissolving of the bond that ties mother to life.

The play's preoccupation with dissolution is apparent too in the choral odes. The chorus of Trojan women enter the play to find Hecuba locked in grief and their joint lamentation for the death of Troy, its chief warrior, Hector, and its king, Priam, realizes itself in imagery of dissolution and dismemberment, in dust, ashes, the untying of hair, the opening of dresses, the rending of flesh – in Priam's headless trunk on the beach. The chorus' nudity itself dissolves earlier values. Later odes focus even more sharply on dissolution. The second choral ode presents death as personal dissolution absolute: 'it kills the body, spares not the soul' (401f.). The third and fourth odes focus on social dissolution – the scattering of Trojan women through every part of Greece, the dissolving of their union and their land.

Especially important in the play is the presentation of the conceptual and linguistic dissolution that attends the death of a culture. Categories, linguistic and behavioural forms, devised to order and control the world, dissolve. The mother of children is the mother of corpses; the king of kings is the slave of fate; the free and victorious are as helpless as the conquered and captive; the marriage-breaker is a marriage-broker. Rites and rituals manifest the same contradictions. A dirge is a laudation; a wedding is a funeral; a sacrifice is a bloody murder. The forms of civilization are employed to implement barbarism, and ironically they accord with nature's laws: Polyxena's death is the setting of a sun (1139–42). Death itself in the tragedy is the ultimate unresolved contradiction. To the chorus and perhaps to Polyxena it is annihilation; to Andromache, Hecuba, perhaps Astyanax, it is freedom and Elysian bliss. Notably, as elsewhere in Senecan tragedy – and in Seneca's own life – it is at death that human greatness shines, as Astyanax and Polyxena show.

On the issue of human power the play is unambiguous. From Hecuba's prologue onwards it is dramatized as illusion. What happens in the play is what 'fate demands'; and what 'fate demands' (see especially 360–70) is the repetition of history. Again virgin-sacrifice ends the delay of the Greek fleet; again Achilles' wrath claims a girl-prize; again marriage inaugurates death and slaughter. But fate also demands the death of Astyanax. History's cycle realizes itself with augmented devastation.

The play's form and mode mirror its contents. History's cycle is reflected in the formal circles of the play. Hecuba begins and ends the drama, and within the dramatic circle formed by Acts I and V is another circle formed by Acts II and IV, concerned with Polyxena and her sacrificial wedding. At the centre of the two circles is Act III, itself structured concentrically to complete a triad of circles. Concentricity is the principle too structuring Acts II through to V, transforming the separate fates of Astyanax and Polyxena into a closed dramatic unit. This imprisonment of form binds the allusions to the past into an imprisonment of events. The circle too is one of texts. As the dramatic events of *Trojan Women* recycle earlier events, Seneca's play recycles earlier plays. It rewrites and recycles many texts – most obviously, Sophocles' *Polyxena*, Euripides' *Hecuba*, *Trojan Women* and *Iphigenia in Aulis*, Accius' *Astyanax*, Catullus' *Peleus and Thetis*, Virgil's *Aeneid*, Ovid's *Metamorphoses*, Seneca's own *Agamemnon* – making of *Trojan Women* itself a self-conscious, multi-allusive text, which engages in a constant and pervasive counterpoint with the dramatic and poetic tradition. Seneca's rewriting of earlier texts, i.e. the play's palimpsestic mode, is model of a central theme: the rewriting and recycling of history. Seneca's drama differs from all the works it rewrites; but the pattern of the tragic myth, like the pattern of history, remains constant. Like the past, the myth changes to remain the same. Seneca's *Trojan Women* is not merely palimpsestic; it images a palimpsestic world.

The world imagined is not only that of the play. Late Julio-Claudian Rome was itself a palimpsestic world, one dominated by the forms of a past which it attempted to re-*present*. According to Suetonius (*Nero* 10.1) Nero proclaimed his intention of modelling his reign on that of the dynasty's founder, Augustus; but what he succeeded in doing was to recycle the tyranny of his predecessors together with the political, social, religious and legal forms of the Roman world emptied of their substance. Relevant to *Trojan Women* is that Nero actively sought to sustain the image of Rome as Troy reborn. He participated in the Trojan Games of A.D. 47 (Tacitus, *Annals* XI.11); he delivered an oration on behalf of the contemporary city of Ilium (*Annals*, XII.58) 'setting out the origins of the Roman people in Troy, Aeneas the founder of the Julian house'; he wrote an epic on the fall of Troy, *Troica*, which his detractors claim he sang during the great fire of Rome in A.D. 64. Like Seneca's tragedy, late Julio-Claudian Rome was self-conscious palimpsest.

It was also self-conscious theatre. Indeed in Tacitus' brilliant account of Nero's reign (*Annals* XIII–XVI) acting is presented as the emblematic metaphor of the age. Nero's own appearances on the stage served sharply to focus the political and social imperatives of role-playing in a theatricalized world, where citizens mourned what they welcomed (*Annals* XVI.7), applauded what they grieved (XIV.15), offered thanksgivings for monstrous murder (XIV.59, 64), and celebrated triumphs for national humiliation (XV.18) or horrendous and impious sin (XIV.12f.). The overt theatricality of *Trojan Women* reflects this theatricalized world. The play features extensive scenes of role-playing, in which characters play actors before other characters as audience: Andromache before Ulysses, Ulysses before Andromache, Helen before the Trojan women. And in the final act the metaphor of the theatre pervades the whole of the reported action. The cultural dissolution of Seneca's *Trojan Women* dramatizes the 'form and pressure' of an age. It was a dramatization which presaged history. Three years after Seneca killed himself at Nero's command, history's cycle dissolved Nero's world. The Julio-Claudian dynasty came to an end as abrupt as that of the royal house of Troy.

A.J.B.

Further Reading

Boyle, A. J., 'Senecan Tragedy: Twelve Propositions,' in A. J. Boyle (ed.), *The Imperial Muse: To Juvenal through Ovid* (Berwick, Victoria, 1988) 78–101.

(ed.), *Seneca's Troades* (Leeds 1992).

Fantham, E., *Seneca's Troades: A Literary Commentary* (Princeton 1982).

Lawall, G., 'Death and Perspective in Seneca's *Troades*', *Classical Journal* 77 (1982) 244–52.

Wilson, M., 'The Tragic Mode Of Seneca's *Troades*', in A. J. Boyle (ed.), *Seneca Tragicus* (Berwick, Victoria, 1983) 27–60.

TROJAN WOMEN

Translated by A. J. Boyle

DRAMATIS PERSONAE

Trojans

HECUBA, queen of Troy, widow of Priam and mother of
    Hector
ANDROMACHE, widow of Hector and mother of Astyanax
OLD MAN, servant of Andromache
ASTYANAX, son of Andromache and Hector
POLYXENA (*non-speaking*), daughter of Hecuba
CHORUS of Trojan Women

Greeks

TALTHYBIUS, herald of the Greek army
PYRRHUS, son of Achilles
AGAMEMNON, leader of the Greek expedition
CALCHAS, priest of the Greek army
ULYSSES, king of Ithaca and strategist of Troy's fall
HELEN, wife of the Greek king Menelaus and consort of
    Hecuba's son Paris
MESSENGER
SOLDIERS and ATTENDANTS (*non-speaking*)

SCENE

The scene is set in and around Troy after the night of the Greek sack of the city.

TIME

The play begins in the early morning, possibly at dawn.

ACT I

(*Enter Hecuba among the ruins of Troy*)

HECUBA

Whoever trusts power and plays potent lord
In princely court unafraid of fickle gods
Lending a credulous heart to happiness
Look on me . . . and on you, Troy. Fortune brings
5   No greater proof of the fragile basis
Of pride. The pillar of mighty Asia
Lies toppled, glorious masterwork of gods.
For her defence men[1] came who drink icy
Tanais as it spreads its seven mouths,
10   Men[2] too who first capture the reborn day
Mingling tepid Tigris with the crimson sea,
Even she[3] who borders the nomad Scyths
And pounds Pontic shore with her manless hordes . . .
Yet Troy fell before steel; Pergamum lies crushed.
15   See the walls' high glory heaped in ruins,
Our homes gutted. Fire now circles the palace,
Everywhere smoke rises from Assaracus' house.
No flame forestalls the victor's greedy hands:
Troy's ravaged as she burns, and the sky hides
20   In billowing smoke. As if choked by dense cloud
The black day grows foul with Ilium's ash.
The victor stands . . . wrath unglutted; his eyes
Measure stubborn Ilium. Now the savage
Forgives the ten years. He shudders at Troy's fall.
25   He sees her defeated but can't believe
Her defeat. Plunderers seize the Dardan spoils;

---

1. Thracians under King Rhesus.
2. 'Ethiopians' under King Memnon, son of Aurora the dawn-goddess. The 'crimson sea' is the Persian Gulf.
3. The Amazon, Penthesilea.

A thousand ships cannot contain the booty.
   I call to witness heaven's hostile will,
My country's ashes and you, Phrygia's lord,[1]
Whom all Troy covers buried by your realm,   30
And you[2] . . . now dead . . . whose strength made Ilium stand,
And you, the great flocks of all my children,
Less mighty shades: every reverse we've borne,
Every evil raging Phoebas[3] foretold
With frenzied speech in which the god banned belief   35
I Hecuba . . . pregnant . . . foresaw,[4] and spoke
My fear, vain prophet before Cassandra.
No cunning Ithacan nor that Ithacan's
Night-friend[5] made you flame; nor that liar Sinon.
This fire is mine; you are lit by my brand.   40
    Why weep for a city fallen and gone?
You cling to life, old woman. Remember,
Wretch, recent griefs. Troy's now an ancient wrong.
I saw . . . most foul sin . . . the killing of a king,
At the altars (which magnified the crime),   45
When savage Aeacius[6] full-armed twisted
The king's hair in his left hand, jerked the head back
And buried his evil blade in the great gash.
The sword thrust hilt-deep. Though Priam received it
Gladly, it came out dry from the old man's throat.   50
Who could not be turned from brutal slaughter
By a man pressuring life's final stage,
By divine witnesses and a fallen realm's

1. Priam.
2. Hector.
3. Cassandra, prophetess inspired by Phoebus Apollo but never believed (because she rejected Apollo's love).
4. Hecuba, when pregnant with Paris, had a dream in which she gave birth to a firebrand – a warning that the child she was carrying would destroy the city.
5. Diomedes, who together with Ulysses ('the Ithacan') captured the supernatural horses of Rhesus and the Palladium, with both of which Troy's fate was associated.
6. Pyrrhus, son of Achilles, whose butchery of Priam is described in detail in Virgil's *Aeneid* (II.533ff.).

Once holy place? Father of many kings,
Priam lies untombed, lacks funeral flames
While Troy burns . . . Yet the gods are not content.

(*Enter the Chorus*)

Right now an urn picks masters for Priam's daughters
And his sons' wives. I'll follow, a vile prize.
Someone claims Hector's rights, another wants
Helenus' bride, another Antenor's:
And there's one, Cassandra, who seeks your bed.
My lot is feared; alone I terrorize Greeks.

  Do your tears flag? My band of prisoners,
Beat your breasts and shriek your lamentations,
Hold requiem for Troy. The sounds of fateful
Ida have long been due, that cursed judge's[1] home.

CHORUS

No raw crowd new to tears
You ask to weep. For unbroken
Years we've sobbed, since Phrygian guest
Touched Greek Amyclae[2] and mother
Cybele's sacred pine
  Cut the sea.
Ten times Mount Ida paled with snow,
Ten times we stripped her for our dead,
Ten harvests Sigean reapers
Cut trembling on the plains:
No day lacked lamentation,
New reasons furnished tears.
On with the lament: raise, queen,
Your suffering hand. This vile crowd

1. Hecuba's son Paris, reared by shepherds on Mt Ida near Troy. He was appointed to judge a beauty contest between the goddesses Juno, Minerva and Venus and he awarded the prize to Venus, who had promised him the most beautiful woman in the world (Helen) as a reward. Paris then went to Sparta and abducted Helen to Troy.

2. Helen's home in Sparta. The 'Phrygian guest' is Paris.

Will follow its mistress. We are
   Not untrained to weep.

HECUBA

Faithful companions of my fall,
   Untie your hair.
Let it flow round mourning necks   85
Defiled by Troy's tepid dust.
   Fill your hands –   102
This even we can take from Troy.   103
Expose your arms in readiness;
Open dresses, bind their folds,
Bare bodies to the womb.
What marriage veils your breasts,   90
   Captive shame?
Tie loosened skirts with shawls;
Free frenzied hands for scourging blows
Of grief . . . That's how, how you should look.
I recognize a Trojan band.   95
Let the old grief return.
Surpass your standard tears.
   This is Hector's dirge.

CHORUS

We have all untied our hair
   Torn for many deaths;
It falls free of its knot.   100
Faces streak with warm ash;   101
Dresses drop from bare shoulders   104
Gathering round our thighs;   105
Naked breasts demand our blows.
Now, grief, now release your power.
Let Rhoetean shores ring with grief
And that cave-haunting niggard
Echo no more send back   110
   Final words
But all the tears of Troy

For sea and sky to hear.
    Rage hands.
Bruise breasts with savage blows.
115   Standard grief does not suffice.
    This is Hector's dirge.

HECUBA

For you I strike these arms,
For you strike bloodied shoulders,
For you fists pound this head,
120   For you my breasts are ripped
By mother's hands. Let the scars
I made at your funeral burst,
The blood flow and gush in streams.
Pillar of the nation, our fate's
125   Delay, shield of tired Troy
And her wall, for ten years
Your shoulders buttressed Troy.
With you she fell: Hector's final
Day and the nation's were one.
130   Change the lament.
Shed your tears for Priam.
    Hector has enough.

CHORUS

Lord of Phrygia, take this lament,
Take tears for second loss, old sir.
Nothing happened but once
135   In your reign.[1] Twice Greek steel shattered
Dardan walls; twice Hercules'
Quiver emptied.[2] Hecuba's sons,

---

1. Hercules had earlier taken the city, when Priam was a child. See below, line 719ff.
2. The bow of Hercules, inherited by Philoctetes, was an important instrument of Troy's second fall (as of the first). Without it the city could not have been captured. Paris was slain by an arrow from the bow.

That princely flock, lie buried;
You, father, complete the cortège,
A victim hacked for mighty Jove,   140
Headless weight on Sigeum's beach.

HECUBA

Turn your tears elsewhere, women
Of Troy. My Priam's death deserves
No pity. All proclaim:
'Blest is Priam.' He walks free   145
To the ghosts below, never
To bear Greek yoke on conquered neck.
He sees no twin Atridae
Nor Ulysses the liar,
And will grace no spoils of Argive   150
Triumph, neck trophy-bowed.
Sceptred hands will not be pinned
Behind him, nor will he follow
Agamemnon's chariot, hands
Bound in gold, a spectacle   155
    For wide Mycenae.

CHORUS

'Blest is Priam,' we all proclaim:
Dying took his kingdom with him.
Now he roams safe shadows
In Elysium's grove and blest
Seeks Hector among the good.   160
Blest is Priam, blest is he
Who dying in war takes all things
    With him . . . consumed.

                                        (*Exit Hecuba*)

ACT II

(Enter Talthybius)

Talthybius, Chorus

TALTHYBIUS

O the long delay in port the Danai
165   Always face if they seek war[1] or their home.

CHORUS-LEADER

Tell us what causes delay for the ships . . .
And Danai. What god blocks the voyage back?

TALTHYBIUS

Fear grips my mind; my body shakes with horror.
Portents too hideous for truth . . . hard to believe . . .
170   I've seen, myself seen. Titan touched the high peaks
170a   With his morning rays, day had conquered night,
When suddenly from its blind depths earth roared,
Bellowed, convulsed and dragged up its hidden folds.
The tree-tops shook; the towering forest
And sacred grove thundered with a mighty crash.
175   Rocks tumbled from Ida's fractured ridges.
Not only earth trembled; ocean too felt
Lord Achilles[2] near and stilled its waters.
Then the cleft valley reveals vast caverns
And gaping Erebus provides a way
180   Upwards through earth's rift and raises the tomb.
A huge ghost flashed out – of Thessaly's chief,[3]
Looking as when in practice for your fate,

---

1. Talthybius alludes to the earlier delay experienced by the Greeks ('Danai') at Aulis, when they were about to set sail for Troy. On that occasion the delay was ended by the 'wedding' and sacrifice of Agamemnon's daughter, Iphigenia.
2. 'Lord' Achilles, because his mother Thetis was a goddess of the sea.
3. Achilles, from Phthia in Thessaly.

Troy, he defeated Thracian arms or killed
That gleaming white-haired young son of Neptune;[1]
Or when in battle-rage between the lines   185
He body-blocked the streams and the tardy
Xanthus' bloody flow wandered course adrift;
Or when he stood proud victor in his chariot
Plying the reins and dragged Hector . . . and Troy.
The sound of his anger filled the whole shore: 190
'Go, skulks, go, and scavenge the prizes owed
To my hands. Untie your ungrateful ships
To sail on my seas. Greece paid no small price
For Achilles' wrath;[2] again she'll pay greatly.
Let Polyxena be bride of my ashes,   195
Sacrificed by Pyrrhus to water my tomb.'
He spoke and shattered the day with deep night.
He sank and made for Dis, sealing the huge chasm
As earth closed. The ocean lies motionless
And tranquil. The menacing winds subside.   200
A calm sea gently murmurs. From the deep
A Triton chorus sang a wedding hymn.

                                        (*Exeunt*)

(*Enter Pyrrhus, Agamemnon and Calchas. The scene is the Greek camp.
Soldiers and Attendants are present*)

Pyrrhus, Agamemnon, Calchas

PYRRHUS

In high spirits you spread your sails for home
And forgot Achilles, whose hand alone
Shattered Troy. What delay Troy gained by his death   205
Was simply hesitation where to fall.
Even if you wanted and hurried to grant
What's asked, you are too late; by now all our chiefs
Have claimed their prize. What lesser reward fits

1. Cycnus.
2. Achilles' earlier wrath and attendant withdrawal from the war caused many
   Greek deaths. It was the subject of Homer's *Iliad*.

210 His great valour? Or was that man's merit slight
Who, when ordered to shun war and spend a long
Old age idly and surpass the senile
Pylian[1] in years, stripped off his mother's trick[2]
And lying dress and proved his manhood in arms.
215 Reckless Telephus,[3] whose unfriendly realm
Barred Achilles' access to fierce Mysia,
First stained my father's raw hand with regal blood
And felt the same hand strong and merciful.
Thebes[4] fell; Eetion defeated saw
220 His kingdom lost; little Lyrnesos perched
On its high ridge fell to the same disaster.
The land now renowned for Briseis' capture
And that source of royal strife, Chryse,[5] lie low,
And famed Tenedos and fertile Scyros,
225 Whose luxuriant pastures feed the herds of Thrace,
And Lesbos, sundering the Aegean sea,
And Phoebus' love, Cilla. What of the lands lapped
By Caycus' waters swelling with spring floods?
    This havoc of nations, this holocaust,
230 These cities razed as by a hurricane,
For other men would be fame's pinnacle;
For Achilles . . . his journey. My father
Arrived waging great wars in practice for war.
Forget his other deeds, wouldn't Hector alone
235 Have been enough? My father conquered Troy,
You sacked it. It gives me pleasure to pursue

1. Nestor, king of Pylos, renowned for his longevity.
2. Achilles' mother disguised him as a girl at the court of King Lycomedes on the island of Scyros, that he might avoid war and live to a great old age.
3. King of Mysia, wounded by Achilles and later healed with the rust of Achilles' spear. See Ovid, *Tristia* I.1.99ff.
4. Not the mainland Greek city but one near Troy, ruled by Eetion, father of Andromache. Most of the places which follow are situated in, or off the coast of, the Troad.
5. Home of Chryseis, the girl whose possession by Agamemnon generated the famous 'strife' between himself and Achilles, which resulted in the latter's withdrawal from the war.

Great father's famed heroics and brilliant deeds.
Hector lay dead killed before his father's eyes,
Memnon before his uncle's; his grieving
Mother[1] brought in the doleful day ashen-faced.   240
The victor shuddered at what his action meant;
Achilles learnt that even goddess' sons die.
Then the savage Amazon fell, our last fear.
You owe Achilles by his deserts a girl
From Mycenae or Argos if he asked.   245
Still unsure? Pity's now the vogue and you think
It brutal to sacrifice Priam's daughter
To Peleus' son? You father killed your daughter[2]
For Helen. What I claim has precedent.

AGAMEMNON

Ungoverned passion is a fault of youth.   250
Some are ravaged by manhood's early lust,
Pyrrhus by his father's. I tolerated
Proud Aeacides'[3] fierce temper and threats:
Great patience is required of great power.

    Why spatter a great leader's honoured ghost   255
With grisly slaughter? You need first to learn
The limits of victory and defeat.
Violent rule has never lasted long,
Controlled it endures; the higher fortune
Has raised and exalted human power,   260
The more her favourites should check themselves,
Shiver at changing circumstance and fear
Too generous gods. Victory has taught me
Greatness falls at a touch. Does Troy make us
Arrogant and brutal? We Danai stand   265
From where she fell. I admit that sometimes
I've misused my power and been too proud.
But that same spirit has now been broken

---

1. Aurora, the dawn-goddess. Memnon's 'uncle' was Priam.
2. Iphigenia.
3. Achilles, grandson of Aeacus.

By what elsewhere is its cause, fortune's favour.
270 You, Priam, make *me* proud . . . and terrified.
Am I now to think kingship but a name
Coated with false glitter, a head adorned
With a hollow band? A moment's chance takes them –
Even without a thousand ships or ten years.
275 Not everyone finds fortune so reluctant.
I must confess (forgive me for saying this,
Land of Argos) I wanted the Phrygians
Broken and conquered; but sacked, razed to the ground,
This I would have stopped. But wrath, a seething
280 Enemy and victory loosed on the night
Cannot be curbed. Anything that might be thought
Shameful or brutal was the work of anger
And darkness, when passion inflames itself,
And the teeming sword made lustful by blood's
285 Taste. What parts of Troy survive her ruin
Shall stand. We've exacted punishment enough . . .
And more. That a virgin princess should die
Presented to a tomb to water its ashes
And men call this dreadful murder 'marriage',
290 I shall not allow. All blame falls back on me:
The power to ban crime, unused, commands crime.

PYRRHUS

Then will Achilles' ghost gain no reward?

AGAMEMNON

It will. The whole world will sing his praises,
And lands unknown will hear his mighty name.
295 But if pouring blood upon his ashes helps,
Let's slit the fleshy necks of a Phrygian herd
And shed blood which no mother needs to mourn.
What rite's this? Since when is human life offered
To the human dead? Shield your father from scorn
300 And hate. You demand not honour but vengeance.

PYRRHUS

You are so puffed up when success exalts
Your spirit, then all panic when fear sounds,
Despot of kings. Is your heart now inflamed
With a sudden passion or a new lust?[1]
Are you alone to keep taking our spoils?   305
With this hand I'll give Achilles his victim.
If you refuse and hold her back, I'll give
A greater gift . . . worthy of Pyrrhus. Too long
Has my hand been starved of kingly slaughter;
Priam claims his peer.   310

AGAMEMNON
                    I do not deny
It is Pyrrhus' greatest glory in the war
That Priam lies hacked by his savage sword,
His father's suppliant.[2]

PYRRHUS
                    My father's suppliants
And enemies I learnt were the same. Yet Priam
Pleaded in person. You, panic-stricken,   315
Too scared to ask, gave your pleas to Ajax
And the Ithacan and skulked fearing your foe.[3]

AGAMEMNON

But your father, I suppose, felt no fear
When in the midst of Greek slaughter and charred ships

---

1. Pyrrhus alludes to Agamemnon's insistence on taking Achilles' war-prize, the young woman Briseis, in compensation for the loss of his own, Chryseis.
2. In *Iliad* XXIV (468ff.) Priam successfully supplicated Achilles for the return of the body of his son Hector. The incident is referred to again at line 325ff. below.
3. The incident referred to is narrated in *Iliad* IX (114ff.), where Agamemnon sends Ajax, Ulysses and Phoenix to ask Achilles to return to the fighting. Achilles is playing his lyre (see lines 321 and 323) when the embassy arrives.

320   He dallied, careless of war and of arms,
And plucked his tuneful lyre with delicate pick.

PYRRHUS

It was then great Hector despised your arms
But feared Achilles' songs. Amid great terror
A profound peace lay on Thessaly's ships.

AGAMEMNON

325   And indeed to that same Thessaly's ships
Profound peace returned . . . for Hector's father.

PYRRHUS

Only a king profound will spare a king.

AGAMEMNON

Then why was your hand raised to kill a king?

PYRRHUS

It's often mercy to grant death – not life.

AGAMEMNON

330   It's now mercy to seek virgins for tombs?

PYRRHUS

So you now think virgin-sacrifice a sin?[1]

AGAMEMNON

To place country above children fits a king.

PYRRHUS

No law spares captives or checks their punishment.

1. Another reference to Agamemnon's sacrifice of his own virgin daughter, Iphigenia.

AGAMEMNON

If no law forbids it, shame forbids it.

PYRRHUS

The victor can do whatever he please.   335

AGAMEMNON

He who can do much should please himself least.

PYRRHUS

You dare say that to these men, crushed by ten years
Of tyranny – till Pyrrhus released their yoke.

AGAMEMNON

Scyros[1] breeds this pride?

PYRRHUS

                            Free from brothers' sin.[2]

AGAMEMNON

Hemmed in by waves . . .   340

PYRRHUS

                            Of my kinsman the sea.
I know Atreus' and Thyestes' noble line.

AGAMEMNON

You furtive embryo of virgin rape,
Got by Achilles before he was man.

1. Pyrrhus' birthplace. He was Achilles' bastard son by Deidamia, daughter of the
   king of Scyros. See lines 342–3 below.
2. The sin of Agamemnon's father Atreus and the latter's brother Thyestes. Atreus
   killed and cooked his brother's sons and fed them to him at the ensuing banquet.
   This 'sin' forms the subject of Seneca's *Thyestes*.

PYRRHUS

By that Achilles whose lineage rules
345　　The world and covers each divine kingdom:
Thetis the sea, Aeacus the dead, Jove the sky.

AGAMEMNON

By that Achilles whom Paris' hand laid low.[1]

PYRRHUS

Whom no god dared to challenge face to face.

AGAMEMNON

I could check your words and tame your spirit
350　　With pain. But my sword shows mercy even
To captives. Better to call Calchas over,
The gods' spokesman. If fate demands it, I'll pay.

(Calchas comes forward)

　　You who broke the bonds of the Pelasgian fleet
And war's delay,[2] whose art unseals the sky,
355　　For whom entrails' secrets, the crack of heaven
And the trailing star with long paths of fire
Provide the signs of fate, whose responses
Ever cost me dear: declare what the god
Commands, Calchas, and with your counsel . . . rule.

CALCHAS

360　　Fate grants Danaans passage at the usual price:
　A virgin must be sacrificed on the tomb
Of Thessaly's chief – but dressed like a bride
In Thessaly, Ionia or Mycenae.

---

1. Achilles was fatally wounded in his heel by Paris with an arrow guided by Apollo. See Virgil, *Aeneid* VI.56ff.; Ovid *Metamorphoses* XII.597ff.
2. It was Calchas who ten years previously divined that only the sacrifice of Agamemnon's daughter would break the delay of the Greek fleet at Aulis and enable the expedition against Troy to commence.

Pyrrhus is to hand his father his wife.
She will thus be duly wed. This cause alone   365
Does not detain our ships: more noble blood,
Polyxena, than your blood is required.
Whom fate demands must fall from beetling tower –
Priam's grandson, Hector's son – to his death.
Then let the fleet's thousand sails fill the sea.   370

                                                        (Exeunt)

(Enter the Chorus. The scene is before Hector's tomb.)

CHORUS

Is it truth or a mind-drugging myth
That a ghost survives the buried corpse
When the wife has sealed her husband's eyes,
The final day blotted out the sun,
And the dismal urn confined the dust?   375
Is it useless to hand death our souls,
But must the wretched keep on living?
Or do we die whole, no part of us
Persist when breath has fled and spirit
Mingling with mists vanishes in air   380
And the flamed torch touches naked flesh?

All that sees the rising sun, all that
Sees it set, all that's washed by Ocean's
Ebbing tide and feels its blue return,
Time will snatch up with Pegasus' speed.   385

Fast as the twelve stars fly on the winds,
Fast as the star-king spins the rolling
Ages, fast as Hecate hurtles
Her chariot down its slanting course,
We seek our fated end; who has touched   390
The lake[1] sacred to gods no longer
Exists at all. As smoke from hot fires

---

1. The Styx, by which the gods swore their 'greatest and most dread oath'.

Fades, staining the air for a moment,
As pregnant clouds we ourselves have seen
395 Yield to arctic Boreas' assault,
The spirit which directs us dissolves.

After death is nothing; death itself
Is nothing, swift race's final post.
Let greed lose hope, anxiety fear.
400 Time's greed and chaos devour us.

Death is indivisible: it kills
The body, spares not the soul. Taenarus,
The pitiless king's[1] realm, Cerberus –
Threshold guardian of no easy gate,
405 These are hollow rumours, empty words,
Myth that resembles an anxious dream.
Wish to know where you lie after death?
  Where the unborn are.

ACT III

(*Enter Andromache, Old Man and Astyanax*)

Andromache, Old Man, Astyanax

ANDROMACHE

Wailing band of Phrygians, why tear your hair,
410 Beat sorrowing breasts and drench cheeks with floods
Of sobs? Our sufferings must be trivial
If tears suffice. For you Ilium fell just now,
For me long ago, when that brutal chariot
Ravaged my limbs and Pelian axle[2]
415 Screamed aloud shuddering beneath Hector's weight.
That day crushed and killed me. I now endure
Events numb and stiff with pain, impervious.

1. Dis or Pluto, ruler of the dead.
2. Of Achilles' chariot, as it dragged the dead Hector round the walls of Troy.

I'd escape the Danai and follow my spouse
Now, if he (*points to Astyanax*)
     didn't hold me. He tames my pride
And prevents my death. He compels me still   420
To importune the gods. He prolongs my pain.
He's robbed me of suffering's finest fruit:
Fear of nothing. All chance of happiness
Is snatched away, horrors can still reach us.
Fear is its most painful when hope is dead.   425

            (*Exit the Chorus*)

OLD MAN

What sudden fear has stirred your deep distress?

ANDROMACHE

From great evil a greater rises up.
The fate of falling Troy is not yet finished.

OLD MAN

What new disasters could god find for us?

ANDROMACHE

The bolts of deep Styx and its darkest caves   430
Are unlocked, and to keep the conquered fearful
Enemies long buried rise from hell's pit.
Are Danai alone allowed the journey back?
No, death is impartial. That terror shocks
And alarms all Phrygia; my mind is filled   435
With private fear from a dreadful night's dream.

OLD MAN

What visions oppress you? Tell me your fears.

ANDROMACHE

Gentle night had almost passed two watches,
The seven stars had turned the shining wain,[1]

---

1. The constellation known as the Wain, Plough or Big Dipper; also called the
'Great Bear', *Ursa Maior*.

440 A rare peace at last visited my distress
And a brief sleep stole over weary cheeks –
If the stupor of a dazed mind is sleep;
When suddenly Hector stood before my eyes –
Not as he looked when he stormed the Argives
445 And attacked Greek ships with Ida's torches,
Nor when he rained slaughter on the Danaans
Raging and wore the false Achilles' true spoils.[1]
Gone was the face that shone with beams of fire;
It was weary and downcast, tear-ravaged
450 Like mine, and half-hidden by matted hair.
Yet what joy to see him! He shook his head.
'Wake from this sleep,' he says, 'and save our son,
My faithful wife. Hide him; it's our only hope.
Forget your tears. Do you weep for Troy's fall?
455 I wish she were razed utterly. Hurry, take
Where you can the tiny seedling of our house.'
Freezing fear and shivering threw off my sleep.
My frightened eyes scanned this way and that distressed.
Forgetting our son I searched for Hector.
460 His delusive ghost slipped through my embrace.
    O my son, true child of your great father,
Sole hope of Phrygia and our shattered house,
Progeny of ancient blood too famous,
Too like your father. These very features
465 My dear Hector had. He walked as you do,
Bore himself as you do, held strong hands . . . like this,
Shoulders high . . . like this, tossing his head sternly
To spread streaming hair from his fierce brow . . . like this.
    O my son, too late for Phrygia, for mother
470 Too soon, will that time come and blessed day
When you Troy's champion and avenger

1. The armour of Achilles, which Patroclus, the 'false Achilles', wore when Hector killed him, taking the armour as spoils. The incident is narrated in *Iliad* XVI.783ff.

Set up Pergamum restored, bring her scattered
People home and return to our country
And the Phrygians their name. But knowing my fate
I fear such mighty prayers. Enough for captives   475
That we live. O what place will not betray
My fear, in what shelter shall I hide you?
Our citadel secure in wealth and its walls
Divine,[1] world-famed and weighted with envy,
Is now deepest dust. All was razed by fire.   480
From that vast city not enough survives
Even to hide a child. Where can I choose?
There is my dear husband's great tomb, sacred,
Feared by our foes, which his father constructed
Of massive size, lavishly, no miser king   485
In grief. I'd best entrust him to his father . . .
Icy sweat soaks all my limbs; I tremble
In distress at the omen of this death-place.

OLD MAN

One cause has saved many from destruction:
Belief in their death.   490

ANDROMACHE

                No real hope remains.
He is crushed by a huge weight, his high birth.

OLD MAN

To avoid betrayal, have no witnesses.

ANDROMACHE

If our enemies search?

OLD MAN

                Died in the city's fall.

---

1. The fortifications of Laomedon's Troy were built by Apollo and Neptune.

ANDROMACHE

What good's concealment if he will be caught?

OLD MAN

495   The victor's fierce impulses are his first.

ANDROMACHE

What if he is afraid to stay concealed?

OLD MAN

The oppressed seize any help, the safe choose.

ANDROMACHE

What place, what remote and pathless region
Will hold you safe? Who'll help us in our fear?
500   Who will protect us? Now shield, as always,
Hector, your kin. Guard your loving wife's secret;
Receive him, dear ashes, that he may live.
Approach the tomb, my son. Do you shrink back,
Spurn base refuge? I recognize your breeding:
505   You're ashamed of fear. Forget your noble pride
And former spirit; behave as chance dictates.
See what army remains: a tomb, a boy,
A captive. We must yield to misfortune.
Be bold, enter your father's sacred place
510   Of burial. If fate helps the oppressed,
You have safety; if fate denies you life,
You have a grave.

(*Exit Astyanax into Hector's tomb*

OLD MAN

            The vaults protect their charge.
To stop your own fear from exposing him,
Step back from here and hold yourself apart.

ANDROMACHE

Proximity of danger reduces fear.   515
But, if you advise it, let us withdraw.

OLD MAN

Silence for a moment; stop your laments.
Cephallenia's cursed chief[1] approaches.
                                      (*Enter Ulysses with Soldiers*)

ANDROMACHE

Gape, earth, and you, my husband, rip land apart
Down to the bottommost caves and bury   520
My treasure in the deepest womb of Styx.
Ulysses is here – with hesitant step
And expression. His mind weaves some cunning trick.

Ulysses, Andromache

ULYSSES

The servant of a harsh lot requests
That, though these words are spoken by my mouth,   525
Of all the Greeks and chiefs, whom Hector's child
Keeps from their long-sought homes: him fate demands.
Precarious peace's troubled faith will
Always plague Danaans, always fear from behind   530
Will make them look back, unable to disarm,
While your son gives heart to conquered Phrygians,
Andromache: so teaches augur Calchas.
And without augur Calchas' voice, Hector
Said as much. Even his seedling I dread.   535
Seeds of noble birth rise to match their source.
The tiny adjunct of a mighty herd,
Before his first horns have yet pierced the skin,

---

1. Ulysses.

Suddenly with neck high and beetling brow
540 Leads his father's herd, commands the cattle.
The tender sapling sprung from a hacked trunk
Soon grows to be level with its mother
Giving earth shade and leafage to the sky.
The neglected ashes of a great fire
545 Regain their force. Grief is no impartial
Judge of things. But, if you reflect on it,
You'll forgive the fact that a soldier,
An old man after ten winters, ten harvests,
Fears wars and new disasters and a Troy
550 Not truly dead. One great thing daunts the Danai,
A future Hector: free the Greeks from fear.
This cause alone keeps our ships on the beach;
This stops the fleet. Don't think me cruel for seeking
Hector's son commanded by the lot. I'd have
555 Sought Orestes. Accept what the victor bore.[1]

ANDROMACHE

O that you were in your mother's arms, my son,
Or that I knew what chance stole and keeps you
From me, or what place . . . O not if my breast
Had been pierced with hostile spears and my hands
560 Bound with biting chains, not if scorching fire
Enfolded my body, would I have shed
A mother's duty. My son, what place now,
What fortune holds you? Do you wander the fields
Lost? Or has our country's vast conflagration
565 Consumed you? Did the savage victor sport
With your blood? Or mauled by some monstrous beast
Do you now feed the birds of Ida . . . dead?

ULYSSES

Drop this pretence. You won't find it easy
To fool Ulysses. I've beaten mothers' schemes,

1. Again the sacrifice of Iphigenia is alluded to.

Goddesses' too.[1] Forget your futile ploy.   570
Where's your son?

ANDROMACHE

    Where's Hector? Where's all the Phrygians?
Where's Priam? You seek the one; I seek the world.

ULYSSES

You'll be forced to say what you won't freely speak.

ANDROMACHE

She's safe, who's able, ought and wants to die.

ULYSSES

Approaching death exorcizes proud words.   575

ANDROMACHE

If you would force Andromache through fear,
Ulysses, threaten life: death is my prayer.

ULYSSES

Whips, fire, death, torture – their pain will compel
You against your will to scream what you hide;
It'll root out your heart's deep buried secrets.   580
Necessity is more powerful than love.

ANDROMACHE

Bring on your flames, your wounds and evil pain's
Fiendish arts, and hunger and savage thirst
And every kind of affliction, and iron
Thrust into flesh and a blind prison's filth,   585
Whatever a wrathful victor dares . . . in fear.

---

1. It was Ulysses who foiled Thetis' attempt to hide her son Achilles on Scyros, disguised as a girl. See Ovid, *Metamorphoses* XIII.162ff.

ULYSSES

Vain loyalty – to hide what soon you'll show.

ANDROMACHE

A mother with mettle admits no fear.

ULYSSES

This very love in which you proudly persist
590 Tells the Danai to think of their small sons.
After such weary warfare, after ten years,
I'd fear Calchas' fright less, fearing for myself.
But you nurture wars for Telemachus.

ANDROMACHE

I hate, Ulysses, to give the Danai joy.
595 Yet I must. Confess the sorrow you hide, grief.
Gloat, sons of Atreus. You . . . take the Pelasgi,
As usual, good news: Hector's child is dead.

ULYSSES

What proof do you give Danaans that this is true?

ANDROMACHE

So may I receive the most a victor
600 Can threaten, and fate free me with an early
And easy death and bury me on my soil,
So may ancestral earth press Hector gently,
As my son lacks the light. He lies with dead men.
Entombed he has received the dues of death.

ULYSSES

605 The fates are fulfilled, Hector's seed is gone,
Peace assured – this I'll gladly tell the Danai.
(Aside) What's this, Ulysses? The Danai will trust you.
But you trust . . . a mother? Would any mother
Lie and not fear omens of frightful death?

130

Omens are feared when nothing worse is feared.   610
She had pledged her faith by swearing an oath.
If she swears falsely, what worse can she fear?
Summon now your guile, my soul, now tricks, deceits,
Now all Ulysses; truth is never lost.
Examine the mother. She mourns, weeps, groans,   615
But paces her anxious steps up and down
And strains her troubled ears to pick up sounds.
She's more afraid than grieving. We need our wits.
(*Aloud*) Most times it's right to console a parent's grief,
But you, poor wretch, are lucky to have no son.   620
A savage death awaited him, hurled headlong
From the only tower those ruined walls still have.

ANDROMACHE

(*Aside*) Life seeps from my limbs. They quiver, give way.
My blood congeals, bound fast by freezing ice.

ULYSSES

(*Aside*) She trembled. This, this is where I must probe.   625
Fear unmasked the mother. I'll double that fear.
(*Aloud*) Go, go, men! Quickly! A mother's trick hides
Our enemy, the Pelasgians' last blight.
Wherever he hides, root him out, bring him here!
    Good work! He's caught! Quick, hurry, drag him here –   630
(*To Andromache*)
Why look back and tremble? Surely he's now dead.

ANDROMACHE

I wish it were fear. My fright's just habit.
The mind unlearns late what it has long learned.

ULYSSES

Because the boy has forestalled the lustral rite
Due to the walls and can't follow the prophet –   635
Snatched by a better fate – Calchas declares
That the ships may be cleansed for their return

If scattered Hector's dust placates the waves
And his whole tomb is levelled to the ground.
640   Now, since the boy escaped his due of death,
I must lay hands upon this sacred place.

ANDROMACHE

(*Aside*) What can I do? Dual fear splits my mind –
Between my son and my dear husband's dust.
Which cause will win? I call ungentle gods
645   To witness and true gods, my husband's ghost,
That nothing, Hector, pleases in my son
But you. Let him live to re-create your
Features.
                Will your ash be flung from the tomb
And sunk? I let your bones be torn and scattered
650   Across endless sea? Better he should die.
     Can you, mother, see him led to monstrous
Murder? See him on the high battlements
Come wheeling down? I can, I will, I'll bear it,
If my dead Hector does not suffer abuse
655   At the victor's hands.
                          But the child can feel
His punishment. Death keeps his father safe.
Why waver? Decide whom you'll snatch from vengeance.
Ingratiate, you hesitate? There's your Hector –
No! Both are Hector. Here's life and feeling,
660   Destined perhaps to avenge his father's death.
Both cannot be spared. What then can be done?
From two, my soul, save the one Danaans dread.

ULYSSES

I'll fulfil the response. I'll smash the whole tomb.

ANDROMACHE

The one you sold us?[1]

1. The reference is to the ransom paid to Achilles by Priam for Hector's body. Hence in lines 665ff. Andromache invokes Achilles' 'pledge'.

ULYSSES

I'll drag this sepulchre
From its high mound.   665

ANDROMACHE

I invoke heaven's pledge
And the pledge of Achilles: Pyrrhus, protect
Your father's gift.

ULYSSES

This tomb will soon cover
The whole plain.

ANDROMACHE

This one crime the Danai
Left undared. You've desecrated temples,
Even friendly gods;[1] your rage ignored graves.   670
I'll fight. I'll pit bare hands against armed men.
Anger will give me strength. Like a ferocious
Amazon felling Argive troops or god-struck
Maenad, thyrsus-armed, terrifying forests
With frantic step, her mind gone, giving wounds   675
And feeling none – I shall attack. I'll fall
Defending this tomb, allied to its dust.

ULYSSES

(*To Soldiers*)
Why do you stop? Does a female's tearful
Outburst move you, her futile rage? Quick! Obey
Your orders.   680

---

1. The temple of Minerva, supporter of the Greeks, was violated by the theft of the
   Palladium (in which Ulysses was involved – see line 39 above and note) and by
   the rape of Cassandra and her abduction from the shrine by Ajax son of Oileus.

ANDROMACHE

Me, me strike first with your steel . . .
They drive me back. O pity! Break fate's chains,
Heave the earth, Hector. Your ghost is enough
To tame Ulysses – there, clashing his arms,
Hurling firebrands – see, Danaans, Hector?
685   Only I see him?

ULYSSES

I'll smash every stone.

AROMACHE

(*Aside*) What are you doing? One collapse kills son
And husband, mother. Perhaps prayer can placate
Danaans. The tomb's huge weight will break the one
I buried at once. Let the poor wretch die
690   Anywhere rather than father crush son
And son smother his sire.
(*Aloud*)   I fall to your knees,
A suppliant, Ulysses, and at your feet
I stretch the hand that no man's feet have known.
Pity a mother. Receive my prayers of love
695   With kindness and patience. As the gods raised
You higher, tread more gently on the fallen.
Gifts to the wretched are gifts to fortune.
So may you return to a chaste wife's bed
And Laertes prolong his years to see
700   You home; so may your young son welcome you,
Exceed your prayers in his blessed nature,
Surpass his grandsire's age and father's mind.
Pity a mother. The only solace
In my distress is him.

ULYSSES

Show your son. Then plead.

ANDROMACHE

Come from your hiding-place,   705
A poor mother's piteous secret.   (*Enter Astyanax*)
Here, Ulysses, here's the terror
Of a thousand ships.
(*To Astyanax*)   Arms outstretched
Kneel suppliant at your master's feet;
Worship him; accept without shame   710
Fortune's dictates to the wretched.
Forget royal ancestors
And the great old king's domain
World-famed; banish Hector;
Play captive and on bended knee,   715
If death is still unreal,
Copy your mother's tears.

(*To Ulysses*)
Once before Troy witnessed tears
Of a boy-king; tiny Priam
Transformed fierce Alcides'[1] threats.   720
That ferocious man whose vast
Strength made all beasts cower,
Who smashed the doors of Dis
And found the blind way back,
Fell to tears from a tiny foe.   725
'Take up the reins,' he said; 'be king.
Sit high on your father's throne.
Wield sceptre with truer faith.'

1. Hercules, descendant of Alceus. The story referred to here concerned Hercules'
   earlier sack of Troy in revenge for the breach of faith by Laomedon, Priam's
   father. See above, line 134ff.

So that conqueror treated captives.
730 Learn Hercules' gentle wrath.
Or do his arms alone please you?[1]
At your feet lies a suppliant
Great as the other, and begs life.
Troy's crown let fortune take
735   Where it will.

ULYSSES

This mother's stricken mourning truly moves me,
But the Pelasgian mothers move me more.
For to them the boy's growth would bring great grief.

ANDROMACHE

This . . . this ruin of a city turned to dust –
740 Will he revive it? These hands rebuild Troy?
Troy has no hope, if she has hopes like these.
Troy's devastation is not such that we
Can still be feared. His father inspire him . . .
Dragged in dust? Once Troy fell his father
745 Would have lost that pride which great disaster breaks.
If you wish to punish (what worse can you want?),
Set the yoke of serfdom on his noble neck.
Enslave him. Can royalty be refused this?

ULYSSES

Calchas, not Ulysses, refuses it.

ANDROMACHE

750 Genecist of deceit, craftsman of evil,
Whose courage in battle made no man fall,
But whose evil mind's guile and cunning killed
The Pelasgi too.[2] Do you blame the seer

---

1. It was Ulysses who arranged for Philoctetes and the bow of Hercules, upon
   which the fall of the city depended, to be brought back to Troy.
2. Ulysses contrived the death of Palamedes, the innocent son of Nauplius, king of
   Euboea.

And guiltless gods? This crime is from your heart.
Nocturnal soldier,[1] brave to kill a child,   755
Now you dare to act alone and in daylight.

ULYSSES

Ulysses' courage the Danai know well,
The Phrygians too well. I've no time to waste
The day with futile words. The fleet weighs anchor.

ANDROMACHE

Grant me a brief delay to pay my son   760
A mother's final office and to sate
Grief's desire with a last embrace.

ULYSSES

                    Pity
I wish I could show you. But all I can give
I will: time and a delay. Fill your heart
With the tears you wish: weeping lightens grief.   765

ANDROMACHE

O sweet pledge, O glory of a fallen house
And Troy's final death, O Danaan dread,
O mother's futile hope – mad, I wished for you
Your father's battle fame and the years
Of your grandsire's prime. God ignored our prayers.   770
You shall not wield Ilium's sceptre potent
In your kingly court, nor give the world its laws
Bringing conquered nations beneath your yoke.
You'll rout no Greeks, drag no Pyrrhus in dust,
Hold no tiny weapons in tender hand   775
Boldly chasing wide-scattered beasts through broad
Woodlands. On the appointed lustral day

1. A reference to Ulysses' night expedition with Diomedes described in *Iliad* X.

You'll renew no Trojan Game's[1] holy rites
Princely child at the head of swift squadrons;
780   At the altars you'll make no fast and nimble
Step, as the curved horn booms in stirring rhythms,
Honouring barbaric temples with ancient dance.
O form of death more grim than death itself.
Our walls will see a sight more piteous
785   Than great Hector's murder.

ULYSSES

                   Mother, stop your tears.
Great grief creates no limit for itself.

ANDROMACHE

My sobs, Ulysses, beg a small delay.
Allow a few tears more that my hand may close
His eyes while he lives.
                You die – yet so small,
790   But already feared. Your Troy awaits you.
Go, walk in freedom, find Trojans who are free.

ASTYANAX

Pity me, mother.

ANDROMACHE

             Why cling to my breast
And vainly clutch your mother's helpless hands?
A young calf when it hears the lion's roar
795   Cowers timidly against its mother;
The savage lion hurls the mother aside,
Grips the tiny prey in its massive jaws,
Snaps it and takes it: so our enemy

---

1. The *lusus Troiae*, a Roman institution originating according to tradition at Troy. It was essentially a series of equestrian manoeuvres performed by young patricians and was used by the Julio-Claudian emperors to draw public attention to their heirs. Nero participated in the Trojan Games held by Claudius in A.D. 47 (Tacitus, *Annals* XI.11). See also Virgil, *Aeneid* V.545ff.

Will tear you from my breast. Receive now, child,
My kisses and weeping and mangled hair,   800
Race to your father filled with me. Take him
Your mother's brief complaint: 'If the dead feel
Former affections and flames do not kill love,
Can you let Andromache serve a Greek man,
Cruel Hector? Do you lie dull, inert?   805
Achilles returned.'
                            Once more take my hair,
Take my tears, sole relics of my husband's
Piteous death. Take kisses to deliver
To your father. Leave your mother this cloak
To comfort her. It was touched by my tomb   810
And the dead I love. If his dust lurks here,
My lips will find it.

ULYSSES

                    There's no end to her tears.
Remove at once the Argive fleet's delay.

                                                            (*Exeunt*)

(*Enter the Chorus. The scene is Troy away from Hector's tomb*)

CHORUS

            What home awaits us prisoners?
            Thessaly's hills or Tempe's shade,   815
            Or Phthia's tested breeding ground
            For heroes,[1] or rugged Trachis
            Rich in its crop of warlike beasts?
            Or Iolcos, the vast sea's mistress?
            Broad Crete of the hundred cities,   820
            Tiny Gortyn, barren Tricce,
            Mothone sparkling with gentle

---

1. Because Achilles was born there. Most of the places mentioned in this opening
   section were in north-east Greece, especially Thessaly.

Streams shadowed by Mount Oeta's woods,
Which twice dispatched the deadly bow[1]
825   To level Troy?

Or Olenos sparsely peopled,
Pleuron the goddess virgin's[2] hate,
Troezen curved on the broad sea's gulf,
Prothous' proud realm of Pelion,
830   Third stepping stone to heaven,[3] where
Chiron lay stretched in mountain cave,
Tutor to a boy already
Vicious,[4] and struck the ringing chords
To whet the vast wrath even then
835   With songs of war?

Perhaps marble-veined Carystos,
Or Chalchis on the wild sea's edge
Where Euripus ever surges?
Or Calydnae's easy harbour,
840   Gonoessa always windy,
Enispe awed by Boreas?
Peparethos off Athens' coast,
Or Eleusis proud of silent rites?[5]
Or Salamis home of Ajax,
845   Calydon famed for savage boar,
Or the lands slow Titaressos
Floods before flowing down to hell?
Bessa, Scarphe, senile Pylos,

1. Of Hercules, see lines 136–7 above. Hercules died on Mt Oeta on the border of Aetolia and Thessaly.
2. Diana, who hated towns of Aetolia because of an offence by its king Oeneus. The enraged Diana sent against the Aetolians (see line 845) the Calydonian boar.
3. Mt Ossa was placed on Mt Olympus and Mt Pelion on Mt Ossa by the giant sons of Aloeus, Otus and Ephialtes, in their attempt to climb from earth to heaven. See Statius, *Thebaid* X.849ff.
4. Another reference to Achilles. Chiron the centaur was his tutor.
5. The famous mysteries celebrated in honour of Ceres (Demeter) and Proserpina (Persephone) at Eleusis, north-west of Athens.

Pharis, Jove's Pisa, or garland-
Glorious[1] Elis? 850

Let the grim squall blow us wretches
Where it will – for any land's gift,
If Sparta, plague of Troy and Greece,
Be distant, and Argos distant,
And savage Pelops' Mycenae, 855
Small Zacynthos, tiny Neritos,
And guilty Ithaca's lying rocks.[2]

(*Enter Hecuba, Andromache and Polyxena*)
What fate, what master awaits you,
Hecuba, where will he lead you
As spectacle? In whose realm to die? 860
(*The Chorus remain on stage*)

ACT IV

(*Enter Helen with an Attendant carrying bridal clothes*)

Helen, Andromache, Hecuba, Polyxena [*silent*]

HELEN

(*Aside*) Every marriage fraught with death and sorrow
Merits Helen's blessing. Even in their ruin
I'm forced to harm the Phrygians. I'm ordered
To report Pyrrhus' false marriage and provide 865
Greek jewellery and dress. By my deceit
Paris' sister will be caught, by my skill killed.
Make her deceived: far easier for her, I think.

1. Because it was associated with Olympia, where the games were held in honour
 of Olympian Jupiter. Elis was both the district in the north-west Peloponnese in
 which Olympia was situated and a city in its vicinity.
2. The places named in this final section were associated with Helen (Sparta),
 Agamemnon (Argos and Mycenae) and Ulysses (especially Ithaca).

Ideal death is to die without death's fear.
870 Why delay your orders? Compelled crime returns
The guilt to its author.
(*Aloud*)   Noble virgin
Of Dardanus' house, a kinder god at last
Looks on the afflicted and prepares to dower
You with fruitful marriage – with a union
875 Neither pristine Troy nor Priam could offer.
The great glory of the Pelasgian race
Seeks you for the holy rites of wedlock.
His wide realm spreads over Thessaly's plain.
Great Tethys and all the sea-deities
880 And the swollen deep's tranquil goddess, Thetis,
Will call you theirs. Pyrrhus' bride will be called
Daughter by Peleus, daughter by Nereus.
Remove these filthy clothes, don festive ones,
Unlearn captivity. Smooth your unkempt hair
885 And allow expert hands to part it neatly.
This fall perhaps will place you on a higher
Throne. Captivity profited many.

ANDROMACHE

This was the one grief we shattered Phrygians lacked –
Bliss. All around flattened Pergamum burns.
890 What wedding day! Or would anyone dare
Refuse? Who would hesitate to marry
On Helen's advice? You plague, holocaust, blight
Of both nations – see this graveyard of heroes
And the naked bones lying all over
895 The plain unburied. Your nuptials strewed them.
For you spurted Asia's blood, spurted Europe's,
As you viewed duelling husbands – indifferent,
Unsure of your wish. Go, prepare the wedding.
Who needs torches or the ritual brand?
900 Who needs fire? *Troy* lights this novel marriage.
Celebrate Pyrrhus' wedding, women of Troy.
Celebrate it well. Beat your breasts and sob.

HELEN

Though great grief lacks reason and refuses
To be swayed and sometimes hates the partners
Of its own sorrow, I can still defend   905
My case before a hostile judge – for I
Have suffered more. Andromache mourns Hector,
Hecuba Priam; only Helen must shed
Secret tears – for Paris. It's hard, odious, grim
To suffer slavery? I've long borne this yoke,   910
Ten years a captive. Is Ilium sacked,
Her gods toppled? It's hard to lose one's country,
Harder to fear it. Companionship eases
Your distress; at me victor *and* vanquished rage.
Which slave-woman each man would take has long   915
Remained unknown; my master took me at once
Without the lot. Was I the cause of war
And Troy's calamity? Consider it true
If a Spartan ship cut through your waters.
But if I was the raped spoils of Phrygian ships,   920
A victorious goddess' gift to her judge,[1]
Then pardon the spoils. For my case will have
An angry judge: Menelaus' decision
Awaits. Now stop grieving for a moment,
Andromache, prevail on her . . . I can scarce   925
Hold my tears.

ANDROMACHE

                    Helen weeps our great distress.
But yet why does she weep? Tell us what tricks,
What crimes the Ithacan weaves. Must the girl
Be hurled from Ida's peaks? Dropped from the soaring
Citadel's high crag? Pitched into the vast sea   930
Down sheer-sided cliffs which tall Sigeum lifts
For the spectacle of its shallow bays?

1. An allusion to the 'judgement of Paris'. See line 66 above and note.

Speak, tell us what your treacherous face hides.
Anything's better than Pyrrhus as Priam's
935 Son-in-law – and Hecuba's. Tell us, reveal
The pain you plan. Spare our disaster one thing:
Deception. You see women prepared to die.

HELEN

I wish the gods' spokesman would command me too
To burst with the sword this hateful light's delay,
940 Or die before Achilles' grave by Pyrrhus'
Raging hand, the companion of your fate,
My poor Polyxena, whose surrender
And sacrifice before his dust Achilles
Commands for a wedding in Elysium's fields.

(Polyxena tries on the bridal robes)

ANDROMACHE

945 Look! Her great heart rejoices to hear her death.
She reaches for the glowing apparel
Of royal robes, she lets her hair be combed.
She counted marriage as death; she counts death
As marriage. *(Hecuba faints)*
  Poor mother's stunned to hear this grief.
950 Her mind's lost its grip. Rise up, lift your heart,
Poor woman, strengthen your failing spirit.
How thin the thread from which her frail life hangs.
The slightest touch makes Hecuba happy.
She breathes and lives. Death flees the wretched first.

HECUBA

955 Achilles still lives to scourge the Phrygians?
Still renews war? O feeble hand of Paris![1]
Even his dust and tomb thirst for our blood.
Just now a happy crowd circled my side.

---

1. Whose arrow killed Achilles. See line 347 above and note.

I grew tired sharing all my mother's kisses
With that great flock. Now she alone remains,   960
My prayer, companion, grief's comfort and peace.
She is Hecuba's whole brood; her voice alone
Now calls out 'mother'. Harsh and barren life
Come slip away, now spare me at long last
This single funeral.   965
           Weeping floods her cheeks,
A sudden shower falls from her conquered face.
Be glad, rejoice, daughter. How Cassandra
And Andromache would crave your marriage.

ANDROMACHE

Weep for us, Hecuba, us, us, Hecuba,
Whom the tossed fleet will scatter here and there.   970
She will be covered by her home's dear earth.

HELEN

You'll envy her more when you know your lot.

ANDROMACHE

Is part of my punishment unknown to me?

HELEN

The urn has allotted captives their masters.

ANDROMACHE

Whose slave am I? Say it. Who's my master?   975

HELEN

The Scyros boy[1] won you with the first lot.

ANDROMACHE

Happy Cassandra, whom frenzy and Phoebus
Exempt from the lot.

1. Pyrrhus.

HELEN

Great lord of kings[1] has her.

HECUBA

Does anyone want Hecuba called his?

HELEN

980 You're the reluctant Ithacan's short-lived prize.

HECUBA

What reckless, harsh and brutal arbiter
Of this unjust urn gave royalty to royalty?
What malignant god assigns captives like this?
What cruel and callous judge cannot choose
985 Masters for the oppressed, bestows unjust fates
Like a savage? Who weds Achilles' armour[2]
To Hector's mother?
                              Ulysses summons me.
Now I seem conquered, now captive, now crushed
By all disaster. The master shames me,
990 Not slavery. Shall he who won Achilles' spoils
Have Hector's too? That sterile land enclosed
By savage straits does not contain my tomb.
On, on, Ulysses, no delay. I follow
My master; my fate will follow me. Ocean
995 Will have no tranquil calm, sea will rage with winds;
And wars will follow and fire, my pain and Priam's.
Until they come, this is your punishment:
I have consumed your lot, plundered your prize.

                              (*Enter Pyrrhus with Soldiers*)

But here comes Pyrrhus with that urgent stride
1000 And grim face. What's stopping you, Pyrrhus? Come

---

1. Agamemnon.
2. Ulysses is here identified with the armour of Achilles, which he was awarded after Achilles' death.

Open my breast with the sword and unite
Achilles' in-laws.[1] Strike, old man's butcher;
This blood suits you.
> (*Exeunt Pyrrhus and Soldiers with Polyxena*)
>> Drag the prisoner away.
Defile the gods above with dismal murder.
Defile the dead. What should I curse? I pray   1005
For seas to match these rites and for the whole
Pelasgian fleet, its thousand ships, to suffer
The curse I'll make on my ship inside it.
> (*Exeunt Helen and Attendant.*
> *Hecuba, Andromache and the Chorus remain*)

CHORUS

It's sweet to grieve when nations grieve,
Sweet when a people rings with cries.   1010
Mourning and tears sting more gently
When a thronging crowd joins the sobs.
Ever, ever grief is spiteful,
Glad when many suffer its fate
And punishment's not exclusive.   1015
To bear the lot that all endure
    None refuse.

Erase the happy: none will think
Himself wretched. Remove the gold-
Encrusted rich, remove fertile   1020
Fields ploughed by a hundred oxen,
The poor man's crushed spirit will rise.
Comparison creates misery.

It's sweet in vast devastation
To see no man with joyful face.   1025
But he moans and bewails his fate
Who cuts through waves in lonely ship
And falls naked into harbour.

---

1. Priam and Hecuba, parents of Achilles' 'bride'.

Chance and tempest cause less distress
1030 To one who sees a thousand ships
Engulfed in the same sea and shores
Strewn with wrecks, as the breakers heave
And Corus bars the sea's return.
Phrixus lamented Helle's fall,[1]
1035 When the flock's gold-fleeced leader bore
Brother and sister on its bright
Back and cast its burden into
Mid-ocean. Pyrrha and her man[2]
Checked their complaints, when they saw sea,
1040 When they saw nothing but the sea,
Sole relics of mankind on earth.

The fleet will dissolve our union,
Will scatter our tears as it drives,
When trumpet blasts bid crews spread sail
1045 And the winds and speeding oars grip
The deep, and the shoreline retreats.
What will we wretches feel as all
Land shrinks and ocean looms large
And Ida's summit fades away?
1050 Son will tell mother, and mother
Tell son, showing where Troy now lies,
Pointing to it in the distance:
'There is Ilium, where smoke snakes
High to heaven and clouds hang foul.'
1055 So the Trojans will know their land.

1. She fell into the Hellespont (named after her) from the back of the golden ram which was carrying her and her brother Phrixus to 'safety', away from the wrath of their stepmother Ino.
2. Deucalion. He and his wife Pyrrha were the only survivors of the great flood sent by Jupiter.

ACT V

(*Enter a Messenger*)

Messenger, Hecuba, Andromache

MESSENGER

O brutal fate, savage, pitiful, cruel.
What crime as bestial, as ugly has Mars
Witnessed in ten years? Whose news shall I groan
First? Your loss — or rather yours, old lady?

HECUBA

Whatever loss you weep, you'll weep for mine.   1060
Each feels their own disaster, I feel all.
All death is mine; all grief is Hecuba's.

MESSENGER

The virgin is sacrificed. The boy hurled
From the walls. Each died with a noble heart.

ANDROMACHE

Recount their deaths in order and describe   1065
This double crime. Great sorrow loves to dwell
On all its agonies. Speak, relate all.

MESSENGER

There is one great tower still left from Troy.
Priam knew it well. From its battlements
Sitting there on high he controlled the war   1070
And ordered the lines. On this tower he held
His grandson in his arms; as Hector drove
Fear-routed Danai with sword and fire
The old man showed the boy his father's battles.
This once famous tower and pride of the walls,   1075
Now a savage crag, is circled by a milling

Crowd of chiefs and people. The whole host left
The ships and assemble. A distant hill
Gives some a clear view of the open space,
1080   A tall cliff others: on its top the crowd
Stood poised on tiptoe straining for a view.
Some climb pine-trees, some laurels, some beeches;
The whole forest shivers with hanging men.
One chooses the edge of a beetling rock,
1085   Others burden half-burnt roofs or stonework
Jutting from fallen walls and – most horrible! –
A callous spectator sits on Hector's tomb.
      Through this densely packed space the Ithacan
Proudly strides – his hand drags the little one,
1090   Priam's grandson. Without hesitation
The boy mounts the high walls. As he stood there
On the tower's height, he gazed about him
With defiance – like the tiny young cub
Of some massive beast who's not yet able
1095   To rage with its fangs, but still it bristles,
Tries toothless bites and swells in spirit.
So the boy, gripped by his enemy's hand,
With his proud ferocity stirred the mob,
The chiefs, even Ulysses. The boy doesn't weep;
1100   All weep for him. And as Ulysses speaks
The priest's words and prayers and calls savage gods
To the rites, of his own will the boy leapt
Right into Priam's kingdom.

ANDROMACHE

What Colchian, what Scythian nomad
1105   Ever did this, or what Caspian sea's
Lawless tribe dared it? Brutal Busiris
Never spattered his altars with child's blood.
Diomedes never gave his herds small limbs
To feast on . . . Who will cover your body
1110   And consign it to the tomb?

MESSENGER

What body
Survived that steep place? His heavy fall smashed
And scattered the bones. That bright form's features,
That face, those noble traces of his sire,
Were pulped by the body's weight dropped to earth.
The neck unhinged as he struck the flint rock. 1115
His head split and the brain squeezed out. He lies
A shapeless corpse.

ANDROMACHE

Then he's like his father still.

MESSENGER

When the boy fell sheer from the lofty walls
And the Achaean crowd wept their own sin,
The same people turned to another crime 1120
And Achilles' tomb. The tomb's far side is lashed
By the soft waves of Rhoeteum's waters;
Its near side faces a plain where a high
Vale's gentle slopes enclose a central space
And rise like a theatre. The thronging mass 1125
Filled the whole shore. Some think this death dissolves
The fleet's delay. Others are glad to have
The foe's seedling pruned. Most of the fickle mob
Hate the crime and watch it. The Trojans too
Attend their own funeral. Quaking with fear 1130
They view the final act of Troy's collapse.
　Suddenly torches advance like a wedding
And Tyndaris[1] as bride's attendant, head
Bowed in grief. 'Such be Hermione's[2] wedding!'
The Phrygians pray; 'So like this restore 1135
Vile Helen to her husband!' Terror holds

1. Helen, daughter of Tyndareus.
2. Daughter of Helen and Menelaus.

And stuns both peoples. Polyxena keeps
Her eyes lowered in shame but her cheeks glow,
And her last beauty shines more than ever
1140   Like that sweeter light of Phoebus which comes
As he sets, when stars resume their station
And doubtful day succumbs to night's approach.
The whole crowd is numbed – mankind admires more
What's doomed. Some respond to beauty's glory,
1145   Some to tender youth, some to life's shifting course.
All respond to a brave heart meeting death.
She walks before Pyrrhus. All souls tremble,
Marvel and pity. As soon as she'd reached
The steep mound's summit and the youth stood there
1150   Raised up on the top of his father's tomb,
The heroic girl boldly kept her ground.
She faces the blow with grim ferocity.
Her courageous spirit strikes every heart –
And there's a new portent: Pyrrhus slow to kill.
1155   As his hand buried the thrust blade hilt-deep,
She embraced death and a sudden spurt of blood
Burst through the huge gash. Not even in death
Does courage fail her. To crush Achilles
With earth she fell forward with angry force.
1160   Both sides wept. But the Phrygians uttered
Timid sobs, the victor sobs more loudly.
Thus the rite's ritual. The spilled gore didn't stay
Or float on the surface. At once the grave
Savagely sucked all her blood and drank it.

HECUBA

1165   Go, go, Danai, head home now all is safe.
Fleet, spread your sails and cut those longed-for seas
Free from fear. The virgin and boy have died.
The war is done.
                Where can I take my old tears
And spit out death's delay? Should I weep for
1170   Daughter or grandson, husband or country,

The world or myself?
                    Death, my only prayer,
You visit with violence virgins and babes,
Savage in your speed. You fear and shun me
Alone. I chased you that whole night amid swords
And spears and torches. You fled your lover.   1175
No foe or devastation, no fire consumed
My limbs. Yet how near I stood to Priam.

MESSENGER

Proceed towards the sea, prisoners, quickly.
Now sails unfurl on the ships. The fleet moves.

(Exeunt)

LUCAN

INTRODUCTION

Lucan dismembered epic. His subject-matter demanded it. The topic was the dismemberment of Rome by the civil wars fought a century earlier (49–45 B.C.) between the armies of Julius Caesar and those of the Roman Senate (led by Pompey and Cato). For Lucan this was the turning-point of history: whence the triumph of Caesarism, the tyranny of the principate and the death of Roman liberty. His *Civil War* survives in an appropriately truncated form. Nine and a half books of epic text take the 'story' from Caesar's crossing of the Rubicon in 49 B.C. (Book I) through his defeat of Pompey at the battle of Pharsalus in 48 B.C. (Book VII) to his occupation of Pharos in Egypt in 47 B.C., when the poem abruptly breaks off at X.546. The nine and a half books are a work of post-classical revolutionary brilliance. They systematically unmake the Roman epic tradition by inverting in manner and matter its canonic text. As *Aeneid* narrated the growth of a culture (Rome), its ideologies, its history against a backdrop of divine discord and support, *Civil War* banishes the gods, sings cultural disintegration and refuses to narrate.

> Wars worse than civil we sing, waged on Emathia's plains;
> Justice given over to crime; a powerful people,
> its conquering swordhand turned into its own flesh;
> kindred front lines; and, after tyranny's pact had shattered,
> all the staggering world's forces locked in a struggle,
> rivals in evil; standards charging belligerent fellow-
> standards; duelling Eagles, and javelin menacing javelin.
> *What frenzy was this, O citizens? what unleashing of steel?*
> *Did it please you to show the races that hate us a Latin bloodbath?*

> *While arrogant Babylon stood, yet to be stripped of Ausonian*
> *trophies; while Crassus strayed, his ghost unavenged,*
> *was it your pleasure to wage wars that could yield no Triumphs?*

(*Civil War* I.1–12; trans. Joyce)

Lucan's poem is neither narrative nor descriptive epic; it is perform-ance epic – a curse, a lamentation, an expression of cultural pain. It is a linguistic re-enactment of the death-throes of pre-imperial Rome, of *romanitas* and *libertas* (which to Lucan's Cato are iden-tical: *Civil War* II.302f.). It is a poetic re-presentation of civil war's disintegration of social and moral order, cultural values, freedom and language. Extraordinary content is mirrored in extraordinary form: discontinuous narrative, constant poetic intervention and apostrophe, descriptive set-pieces, verbal lists, declamatory structure, epigram, hyperbole, paradox, the summoning of reader into text, prosaic language and discordant rhythm, negative formulation, 'scientific' precision, fluent moralization, an armoury of rhetorical techniques and strategies – everywhere passion, force, vehemence. The dissolution of human and political tissue that paradoxically 'constitutes' civil war seeks expression in a dissolved epic style.

Civil War is an epic whose subject is beyond narration and description. Virgil called his 'Iliadic' *Aeneid* (Books VII–XII) a 'greater work' (*maius opus, Aeneid* VII.45); Lucan explodes this statement by naming his text a 'work without end' (*opus immensum*, I.68). His *Civil War* loathes its own story and seeks constantly to interrupt it, reshaping epic mimesis into a performance for voices. The poet-narrator continually intervenes, addressing the reader, addressing his own created characters, addressing himself, tearing epic form apart and its assumptions of historical and cultural con-tinuities. Product of a rhetorical age, the work has often been misread as incompetent narrative – witness Quintilian's dismissal of Lucan as 'a more suitable model for orators than poets' (*Institutio Oratoria* X.1.90). But the 'rhetorical moment' with its moral im-plications is not simply a disruptive unit of composition in *Civil War* but a major force in its unmaking of the epic tradition and re-presentation of cultural collapse. At the heart of Rome's dis-integration the poem reveals a struggle for and with language of which the poem itself is part. Hence the textual focus on the fight to name ('consuls', 'magistrates', 'senators', 'kings', 'justice', 'law'), on the gap between Pompey and his name, the 'Great', *Magnus*, on the steady movement of 'Caesar' towards synonymity with 'Power'; hence too the self-conscious and self-reflexive demonstration of the inadequacy of inherited linguistic, rhetorical and literary forms to encompass the dissolving agony of civil war. A dismembered style for a dismembered world. A failed performance for a world of failed performers.

Some of these performers were Stoics. One was Lucan's uncle, the tragedian, philosopher and statesman, Seneca. Another was the Stoic philosopher and Lucan's teacher, Annaeus Cornutus, with whom the satirist Persius also studied. They and others (especially the Stoics publicly opposed to Nero) seem to have influenced some of the central concerns of the work, especially its focus on 'freedom' and on 'fate', and some of its historical portraiture, most noticeably, its portrait of Cato. But it would be a mistake to regard *Civil War* as a Stoic tract. Neither the work's despairing concept of 'fate' nor its complex presentation of Caesar would have been acceptable to conventional Stoicism. There were other performers too who influenced the poem – non-Stoic ones. None less Stoic or more influential than the epic's contemporary target, the emperor Nero, two years Lucan's senior and throughout most of Lucan's short but abundant creative life an admirer, intimate, even 'friend'. For Lucan's life was lived at the centre of the power he curses.

Marcus Annaeus Lucanus was born at Cordova on 3 November A.D. 39 into the politically important and cultivated family of the Annaei. He came to Rome at an early age, where he received the standard liberal education, excelling especially in rhetoric, and studied philosophy (together with Persius) under the Stoic Annaeus Cornutus, who was possibly a freedman of the family. Through the influence of Seneca, his uncle, he gained access (after Seneca's return from exile in A.D. 49) to imperial circles. In the late fifties and early sixties A.D. he was a major figure in Nero's literary coterie and received from the emperor several favours, including a quaestorship before the legal age (probably taken up in December A.D. 62) and an augurate. His poetic output was prolific. Apart from

the nine and a half books of *Civil War*, fragments survive of an
Iliacon, a *Catachthonion*, an *Orpheus* and *Epigrams*, which seem to
reflect the Alexandrianizing tendency of Nero's group, and he is
credited too with several other works which survive only in titles.
Among the latter are ten books of *Silvae* (or 'Impromptu Pieces' –
see the Introduction to Statius, below), a eulogy of Nero, which
Lucan performed at the Neronia of A.D. 60, and a poem *On the
Burning of the City* (*De Incendio Urbis*), which accused Nero of
causing the disastrous fire at Rome in A.D. 64 (Statius, *Silvae* II.7.60–
62). The latter was written after a serious rift had developed between
Lucan and the emperor (probably in late A.D. 64), which resulted in
Nero prohibiting Lucan from reciting his poetry or appearing in the
law-courts. The ban was probably political in motivation and, again
probably, stemmed at least in part from the anti-imperial thrust of
Lucan's *Civil War*, the first three books of which – including the
famous ironic panegyric of Nero (I.33–66) – were written and
published/recited in the early sixties. The ban ensured that no further
books were openly available during what little remained of the
poet's life. After the ban Lucan seems to have committed himself
to the removal of Nero, becoming (according to Suetonius' *Vita*)
the standard-bearer for the Pisonian conspiracy to assassinate Nero
in A.D. 65. Lucan attempted to unmake history, as his text unmade
epic form. In the event history unmade the poet and itself. In
April A.D. 65, after the Pisonian conspiracy had been detected,
Lucan committed suicide. He was twenty-five years of age. Three
years later Nero killed himself and civil wars returned – but not
the republic of pre-imperial Rome.

Lucan's *Civil War* is in no sense a politically marginal work.
Like Seneca's *Trojan Women* it was written by one at the heart of
Roman force. It is as much a call to revolution as it is a curse upon
a past revolution; as Nero's reaction showed, it was an exercise in
political power. Book V is one of Lucan's most carefully structured
performances. The beginning and end of the book (1–64, 722–815)
set public against private world; they focus on Pompey and his
name – *Magnus*, 'the Great' – and their relationship to *ROMA*,
'Rome', and its verbal and cultural inversion *AMOR*, 'Love'. The
centre of the book, its thematic core, presents a juxtaposition of

vatic power, the power of the prophet (and poet), and historical power, the power of Caesar. The narrative mode, as elsewhere in the epic, is interrupted throughout. Significantly Book V's gladiatorial pair (V.3) do not meet. The book is a competition of voices: the epic poet's voice, senatorial voices, the Sibyl's voice, rebel voices, Caesar's voice quelling mutinous troups and violent nature, the boatman's voice, Pompey's voice of *AMOR*, 'Love', Cornelia's voice of pain. Especially important is the implied analogy between the prophetess, Phemonoe, and the epic poet himself. Allusions in Book V to the poet's statement of his own inspiration by Caesar (Nero) in the proem to Book I (I.63–7) exhibit the Sibyl and Lucan as 'seers' (*vates*) driven by frenzy and pain to tell the truth. Phemonoe endures Apollo; Lucan Apollo's surrogate, Nero. To tell the truth is to tell of destiny and death (*fatum*); the reward: vatic death and silence. Against them Lucan sets death-dealing Caesar, whose voice quells other voices, even the voice of nature. His voice is that of power and tyranny, as the poet's voice is that of freedom. Throughout the epic in fact the major antithesis is not Pompey and Caesar, nor even the Senate or Cato and Caesar, but Caesar and *libertas*; they are in the language of Book VII 'the eternally matched pair' (VII.696). And to prevent the enemy of *libertas* from receiving the charisma of heroism which his historical success and the narrative of his exploits would confer, Lucan not only continually breaks that narrative but uses his own unmaking of Virgil to define Caesar's aheroic nature. Unlike Aeneas in Virgil's storm scene (*Aeneid* I.81ff.) to which Book V refers (see also *Odyssey* V.291ff.), Caesar is undismayed by the prospect of dying ingloriously (*Civil War* V.668–71). He is not interested in glory, but in power – the power that comes from the ability to generate fear. If that survives he is content. Ironically this obsession with power, even as it defines Caesar as the antithesis of Rome's heroes, makes him in one sense Rome's paradigm; for Rome in Greek, *Rhômê*, means precisely 'Power'. Significantly Book V's other failed Aeneases – Appius Claudius, whose deluded and fatal encounter with the Sibyl (64–236) is modelled on Aeneas' 'successful' one in *Aeneid* VI (42–155), and Pompey, whose capitulation to *AMOR* (722ff.) marks both an inversion of inherited models (especially Aeneas) and a 'literal' inversion of *ROMA* itself – have no such relationship to Rome. They serve only to underscore the epic's central paradox: the enemy of Rome and absolute antithesis of its values is its paradigm; the defender of Rome is 'a great name's shadow' (of Pompey at I.135). Civil war not only dissolves human tissue but, as Caesar continues the work that will make his own name and that of Rome/*Rhômê* synonymous, it dissolves the language, culture and values of pre-imperial Rome.

Lucan had no direct successors, although his influence on post-Neronian epicists, especially Statius, was profound. His dismembering epic was product of a unique sensibility at a precise moment of cultural pain. A sensibility that unmade the epic tradition, as its possessor tried to unmake history and the world.

ANALYSIS OF *CIVIL WAR* V

(The poet's interventions are in italics.)

1–64 THE SENATE IN EPIRUS: In the last days of 49 B.C. the retiring consuls call a meeting of the (exiled) Roman Senate in Epirus in north-west Greece (1–11). *The poet interjects (11–14)*. Lentulus proposes that the command of the war be given to Pompey (15–47). Pompey is appointed leader and the allies are rewarded (47–57). *The poet addresses Ptolemy and curses him (57–64)*.

64–236 THE DELPHIC ORACLE: The republican senator, Appius Claudius, goes to consult the Delphic oracle (64–70). Description and origin of the oracle (71–85). *The poet speculates about the oracle's divine source (86–96)*. Further description of the oracle: the heavy cost of divine inspiration (97–120). The reluctant Delphic priestess, Phemonoe, is seized (120–30). She attempts to deter Appius (130–40); subject to force, she feigns prophecy (141–57). After further pressure Phemonoe subjects herself to the full onslaught of prophetic inspiration (*at the climax of which the poet addresses Apollo:* 173–7) and prophesies (157–97). *Impassioned address by the poet to Apollo and the Delphic tripod asking why the empire's fate was not revealed (198–208)*. The Delphic priestess collapses (208–24). *The poet addresses Appius Claudius pointing up his delusions (224–36)*.

237–373 CAESAR QUELLS A MUTINY (at Placentia): Background to the mutiny; its causes (237–60). The soldiers voice their complaints (261–96). *The poet intervenes sarcastically in support of the rebels* (297–9). Caesar responds immediately (300–309). *The poet upbraids Caesar* (310–16). Caesar harangues the troops (316–64), who yield (364–73).

374–460 PLACENTIA TO EPIRUS: Caesar orders the army to Brundisium, and heads for Rome, where he is elected consul (374–84). *The poet comments bitterly on the election* (385–402). Caesar reaches Brundisium, finds the fleet delayed (403–11) and commands immediate departure (412–23). The fleet sails: at first becalmed, it eventually arrives at Palaeste in Epirus (424–60).

461–721 CAESAR QUELLS A STORM: Description of the site of the adjacent camps of Caesar and Pompey (461–9). *The poet comments sarcastically and addresses Pompey* (469–75). Caesar reproaches Antony for lagging behind (476–97). Having decided to recross the Adriatic at night, Caesar approaches the hut of Amyclas, a poor boatman (497–527). *The poet praises the carefree existence of the poor* (527–31). Dialogue between Caesar and Amyclas, who agrees to sail despite adverse weather-signs (531–59). A storm begins to rise (560–67). When Amyclas urges return (568–76), Caesar dismisses the storm's threats (577–93). An unprecedented storm rages, threatening cosmic collapse (593–653). Caesar shows contempt for the storm: his greatness cannot be diminished (653–71). A miraculous tenth wave drives Caesar to land (672–7). His soldiers remonstrate with him on his return (678–702). Antony crosses from Italy with the rest of Caesar's troops (703–21).

722–815 POMPEY AND CORNELIA: Pompey resolves to send his wife, Cornelia, to Lesbos (722–7). *The poet addresses Pompey, lamenting his subservience to love* (727–31). After delaying, Pompey – in bed with Cornelia – reveals his decision (731–59). Cornelia's passionate and reproachful reply (759–90). Her grief-stricken departure (790–805). *The poet addresses Cornelia* (805–8). Cornelia's torment (808–15).

A.J.B.

Further Reading

Ahl, F. M., *Lucan: An Introduction* (Ithaca, N.Y., 1976).

Barratt, P. (ed.), *M. Annaei: Lucani Belli Civilis Liber V* (Amsterdam 1979).

Bramble, J., 'Lucan' in E. J. Kenney and W. V. Clausen (eds.), *The Cambridge History of Classical Literature* II (Cambridge 1982) 533–57.

Henderson, J., 'Lucan/The Word at War', in A. J. Boyle (ed.), *The Imperial Muse: To Juvenal through Ovid* (Berwick, Victoria, 1988) 122–64.

Housman, A. E. (ed.), *M. Annaei Lucani Belli Civilis, Libri X* (4th edn Oxford 1958).

Sullivan, J. P., *Literature and Politics in the Age of Nero* (Ithaca, N.Y., 1985).

CIVIL WAR

―――――――

BOOK V

Translated by Jane Wilson Joyce

Thus, by turns, the leaders suffered the wounds of war.
In the Macedonians' land, mingling bad luck with good,
Fortune detained her gladiators.

                          Winter had already strewn
Haemus with snow, the Pleiades had slipped from the icy sky,
5   and the day[1] drew near that grants the calendar new names,
the first feast day of Janus, who leads the seasons in.

While the last days of their dwindling term yet remained,
the two Consuls[2] summoned to Greek Epirus[3] the Fathers[4]
scattered by wartime duties. Outlandish and squalid chambers
10 received the Roman elders; the Curia heard matters
of State business, a guest beneath a foreign roof.

(*And who would call those Axes, those Rods[5] unsheathed in accord
with the law, a camp? That reverend body taught the nations
it was not Magnus' party, Magnus was part of it.*)

15 As soon as silence had laid hold of the gloomy assembly,
Lentulus, raised high on his dais, addressed them:

---

1. 1 January 48 B.C.
2. Marcellus and Lentulus, consuls of 49 B.C.
3. A province of north-west Greece, now part of Albania.
4. Members of the Roman Senate.
5. The reference is to the *fasces*, bundles of rods and axes carried before Roman
   magistrates as a symbol of their legal power to scourge and execute.

'If you have in your hearts the sternness befitting your Latin
birth and noble bloodlines, ignore what land we meet in,
ignore how far off we sit from the roofs of our captured
City! Do but regard the pomp of your gathering!   20
Commanders-elect of the world! realize this one fact – no
puzzle to kingdoms and peoples: Fathers, *we are* the Senate!
For whether beneath the icy Wain of the Arctic Bear,
or in the zone where tropical air, sticky with heat-haze,
allows neither nights nor days to grow over-long –   25
wherever Fortune leads, the State follows *us*, Power
escorts *us*. When Gallic torches set our Tarpeian
meeting-house ablaze[1] and Camillus moved to Veii,
that was Rome. Never has this body lost its rights
by changing its site. Caesar has possession of sorrowing   30
halls and vacant houses, the silenced laws and the Forum,
closed for this grim holiday: *that* Curia sees
only those Fathers it banished when Rome teemed with Romans;
all who were not cast out from our august body are here.
Unaware of evil and lulled as we were by long-lived peace,   35
war's first frenzy dispersed us: but now the body politic
is reassembled.

                    'See how the Gods Above make up
Hesperia's weight with the whole world's strength! Our enemy[2]
        lies
drowned in Illyrian waves; on Libya's scorching plains,
Curio fell, that mainstay of Caesar's Senate.   40
Hoist your standards, general! hasten destiny's course!
Show the Gods your good hope, and may Fortune bestow upon
        you
mettle to equal that our cause bestowed when we fled
the foe!

1. A reference to the burning of the Capitol ('our Tarpeian meeting-house') by the
   Gauls. *c.* 386 B.C. In Livy's account (V. 39 ff.) Rome – but not the Capitol – is
   burned.
2. Vulteius and his Gauls. Their demise and that of Curio were described in Book
   IV.

'The year has run out, our term draws to a close;
45   but you, whose authority never comes to an end,
consider the common good, Fathers: command Magnus
to be the leader.'

               With joyful shouts the Senate hailed
his name and charged the Great Man with the nation's fate
and their own.

             Then, to kings and meritorious peoples
50   commendations were given: Rhodes, queen of the seas
and home of Apollo, was honoured, as were the untamed troops[1]
of icy Taygetus; Athens of ancient fame was praised;
and for Massilia's sake, Phocis, her mother city, was freed.

Next they commended Sadalas, brave Cotys, and Deiotarus,
55   faithful ally; also King Rhascypolis, Lord
of the Frozen Coast;[2] and Libya, by the Senate's decree,
must bow to Juba's sceptre. And oh, irony of Fate!
you, too – the man most worthy to rule a faithless race –
you, Ptolemy,[3] Fortune's shame and the God's disgrace, *you*
60   they permit to crown your curls and crush them with Alexander's
diadem! The boy takes up a sword his people will rue,
and oh, that only the people had! The throne of Lagus
was made a gift; with it came Magnus' throat. The sister
was robbed of her realm, the father–in–law of his crime.[4]

                          At last,
65   assembly adjourned, the group took up arms. While peoples
and leaders made ready – their chances unsure and their lot in
        doubt – one

1. Laconians from the mountain range west of Sparta.
2. Thrace. Of the other allies Cotys and his son Sadalas are also from Thrace and
   Deiotarus from Galatia.
3. Ptolemy XIII, aged about thirteen at the time of the civil war, whose men
   assassinate Pompey in Book VIII.
4. Cleopatra and Julius Caesar ('father–in–law' alludes to his previous relationship to
   Pompey, the 'son–in–law') are meant. Ptolemy had expelled his sister Cleopatra,
   with whom he had been appointed joint ruler, from Egypt.

man alone feared to face the War-god's hazardous
game: Appius[1] wheedled the Gods Above to reveal to him
the final result, unbarring what had for many a year
been bolted shut – oracular Phoebus' Delphic shrine.   70

★

From Hesperia's pale as distant as from the Dawn's,[2]
Parnassus rakes the air with double peaks, holy
mount of Phoebus and Bromius where, for godheads
    commingled,
Theban Bacchants return for their Delphic triennial festival.

When the Flood washed over the lands, only this crag   75
stood clear, a bold mark dividing sea from stars.
And even you, Parnassus, lapped by those wide waters,
could scarce uphold your crown. As it was, one peak lay hid.

An avenger came this way, one whose mother was banished
though unborn twins weighted her belly:[3] Paean, with shafts   80
still green, pierced Python, when Themis had tenure of tripod and
    realm.

Paean, seeing how the Earth's enormous chasms
breathed forth divine truth, how the soil exhaled loquacious
vapours, enshrined himself in the sacred caves; brooding
over the sanctum, he there became prophetic Apollo.   85

Which of the Gods Above lies hidden here? What deity,
forced from ethereal realms, deigns to dwell in viewless caverns?
A God of heaven earthbound? Which one endures this,
keeping all secrets of ever-flowing Time, telling the world
its future, ready to show Himself to our race,   90
to suffer the touch of man? A God mighty and strong,
one who sings us our fate? or, if with His song He bids it,
one who creates it?

1. Appius Claudius Pulcher, Roman governor of Greece during the civil war. His
   consultation of the Delphic Oracle seems to be historical. He had been augur in
   63 B.C. and was interested in the supernatural.
2. Delphi was thought to be the 'navel' or geographic centre of the world.
3. Leto, pregnant by Jupiter with Apollo and Diana.

Perhaps, planted in the world to rule,
holding the globe aloft and poised in the void space,
95 *a large part of the Whole, of Jove,[1] escapes through Cirrha's*
caves and is there inhaled, though knit to the heavenly Thunderer.

When this divine essence has filled a virgin's bosom,
battering the human soul, it roars and bursts from the prophet's
lips: picture how, with heaving flames, the Sicilian peak
100 inundates Etna; how struggling Typho,[2] pinned by Inarime's
ageless mass, makes the stones of Campania steam.

Though his shrine is open to all and to none denied, this
godhead alone still avoids the poison of human
frenzy: there, no wicked prayers take shape in wordless
105 whispers, for He, singing things fixed, that none can alter,
forbids mortals to plead. Kindly to honest men, He has
often provided a site when a whole city emigrates,
as He did for Tyre;[3] He has helped to dispel the menace of war,
as the Sea of Salamis remembers;[4] has eased the woe
110 of barren land – shown how to end it; has rolled away
fever-laden air.

No greater gift of the Gods
is lost to our generation: the Delphic shrine has fallen
silent,[5] now that kings have come to fear the future
and forbidden the Gods Above to speak.

But the vatic sisters
115 of Cirrha feel no grief that their voice is stopped – they rejoice

1. The reference here is to the Stoic doctrine of the 'world soul' (*anima mundi*).
2. A hundred-headed monster, quelled by Jupiter with a thunderbolt and imprisoned beneath a volcano (normally Mt Etna in Sicily: here the volcanic island of Inarime off the Campanian coast). The monster's fiery breath caused the volcano to erupt.
3. Either a reference to the founding of Thebes by Cadmus or to general Delphic advice to Tyre, which suffered many earthquakes, to found colonies.
4. The Athenians, encouraged by the Delphic Oracle, defeated the Persians at the battle of Salamis in 480 B.C.
5. The oracles of Apollo, Jupiter and Ammon were all obsolescent by the end of the republic.

that the temple is closed. For, once God enters the breast,
premature death is the price for grace received – or else
its reward; for indeed, at the sting and flood of that frenzy,
the human frame falls to pieces, and the God's hammer-strokes
shatter delicate souls.   120

        And thus, the tripod[1] so long
unshaken, the vast mountain-top's silence were troubled at last
when Appius came to pry into Hesperia's ultimate
doom. When ordered to open the venerable shrine and usher
the trembling prophetess in before the Gods, the priest
who stood at the door seized Phemonoë,[2] straying, aimless   125
and happy, near the Castalian Springs and woodland groves;
he forced her to break the doors of the temple open.

The threshold filled her with dread; fearing to stand there, the
      Phoebas
plans with futile guile to frighten the leader, to blunt
his passion to know the future. She says: 130

                'Roman! What
brazen desire for truth afflicts you? The chasm is mute;
Parnassos, hushed, has smothered its God. Perhaps, the spirit
has deserted these channels and sought a subsidiary duct
leading to trackless wilds. Perhaps, when the barbarous torch[3]
      seared
Python, ashes sifted into the measureless caves   135
and clogged Phoebus' path. Perhaps, Cirrha is silent
by the Gods' will, and it is enough that the long-lived Sibyl's
mystic riddles,[4] entrusted to Rome, spell out the future.
Perhaps, accustomed to drive the wicked out of His shrine,
Paean finds none in our time for whom He would unseal His lips.'   140

1. On which the Delphic priestess sat.
2. The name connotes 'Prophetic Mind'. It was said to have been the name of the
   first Pythia or Delphic priestess (also called the 'Phoebas' at line 128).
3. A reference to the burning of the Delphic temple by the Gauls in 278 B.C.
4. The Sibylline books guarded by a special priestly college at Rome and consulted
   only at the direction of the Senate.

The virgin's ruse was blatant; her very fear made him
credit the deities denied. So then the knotted fillet
bound the curls at her temples, and long hair fell down her back;
the white brow-band was plaited with sprigs of Phocian laurel.
145   Dragging her up to the doorway, though she lagged and hung
      back,
the priest shoved her inside. Dreading the oracular shrine
of inmost sanctum, she halted just by the entrance and,
feigning the God within her quiet breast, delivered
a speech of her own contrivance. No mutter of babbled
150   words bespoke a mind on fire with sacred frenzy.
The lies she spun for the leader would do less harm to him
than to Phoebus' tripod and good repute. Words that failed
to erupt with a quavering wail, a voice insufficient to fill
the echoing cavern's vault, no prickling scalp, no upraised
155   hair dislodging the laurel, temple thresholds unshaken,
the grove at rest – all betrayed her reluctance to yield
to Phoebus.

               Appius noticed the motionless tripod; raging, he
   cried:

'Not only will I punish you as you deserve, blasphemer –
the Gods you ape will, too, unless you enter the cave
160   and, when asked about the tremendous trials of the trembling
      world,
cease to speak on your own.'

                  Thoroughly frightened at last, the
   virgin
rushed to the tripod and, as she drew near the vast chasm,
halted; in her unpractised breast gathered a power divine
which fumes from the rock, still unexhausted centuries later,
165   wafted up to the prophetess. Finally, Paean mastered
her Cirrhan heart: never before so potent, he forced
his way into the Phoebas' marrow and thrust out her previous
thoughts, commanding the human to yield to him with her whole
heart. Wild as any Bacchant, she raced round the cave, her body
170   possessed, shaking the God's fillets and laurel wreaths

from her bristling hair; whirled across the wide floor of the
    temple,
head jerking from side to side; overturned the tripod
that stood in her wavering path. She blazed up – a bonfire –
under the weight of your wrath, Phoebus. Nor is it the lash
alone you ply, raking her belly with spurs and flames: 175
she must take the curb as well – you do not permit
your prophet to tell all she knows.

                              Time rolled into one
conglomerate, whole aeons loaded her pitiful breast,
the endless chain of events was revealed, the entire future
floundered into the light; destinies wrestled, contending for   180
her voice. Nothing was missing – not the first day of the world
nor the last, not Ocean's sweep nor a tally of grains of sand.
As once in her Euboean retreat,[1] the Sibyl of Cumae,
resenting the fact that her frenzy was slave to so many
nations, culled with her disdainful hand from a welter   185
of destinies just the Roman ones, so Phemonoë, brimming
with Phoebus, laboured long till she found *you*, Appius, come
to consult the veiled God of Castalia's land – a diligent
search amid many important fates to uncover yours!

That done, a rabid jabber poured from her foaming lips,   190
then groans and loud babblings as she gasped to draw
breath, doleful howls and wailing filled the vast caverns;
and then, when the virgin was mastered, the sound of her voice
    saying:

'You escape the war's cataclysmic menace, you have
no part in this mighty struggle, Roman; you alone   195
will rest in peace in a deep fold of Euboea's coast.'

Apollo choked off her other words and gagged her mouth.

1. A reference to the founding of Cumae by settlers from Euboea and Aeolis.
Overt mention of 'the Sibyl of Cumae' (line 183) draws attention to the famous
Sibylline episode of Virgil's *Aeneid* (VI.42–155), to which Lucan alludes through-
out this Delphic section (64–236).

Tripod, custodian of destiny! mysteries of the universe!
and you, Paean, Prince of Truth, from whom the Gods
200 *Above have concealed not one day of the future – why*
do you fear to disclose the final throes of the Empire's collapse,
leaders slain and the deaths of kings, all nations drowned
in Hesperia's blood? Have the gods not yet resolved
on a crime so dire? Does the planets' indecision whether
205 *to have Pompey's head suspend the whole of destiny?*
or is your silence meant to ensure that Fortune achieves
deeds with a righteous sword – ambition punished, tyranny
met once more by a vengeful Brutus?[1]

Now the priestess
flings herself at the doors – they yield; spurred on, she leaps
210 from the temple; frenzy keeps pace, for her speech is not done;
the God stays with her, she has not bucked him off. Her wild
eyes rolling, she plays the random beam of her glance all across
the sky. Her face is now fearful, now dark with menace:
her expression never stills; fiery flushes stain
215 her brow and bruised cheeks; hers is not the pallor of fear –
it inspires fear. Nor do her wearied heartbeats subside, but,
as the swollen sea complains after the North Wind's hoarse
blustering, so her mute breath whistles and shakes the seer.

While she returned to common light from the holy brilliance
220 which bathed her visions, a spell of darkness overcame her.
Paean infused her marrow with fluid from Stygian Lethe,
to flush out the God's secrets. At length, the truth fled
from her heart, and the future returned to the tripod of Phoebus;
barely restored, she sank down.

But the nearness of death holds no
225 terrors for you, Appius, beguiled by your riddling oracle!

---

1. The assassination of Julius Caesar in 44 B.C. by (among others) Marcus Iunius
   Brutus was often coupled with the legendary expulsion of the last king of
   Rome, Tarquinius Superbus, by Lucius Iunius Brutus almost five centuries ear-
   lier.

With the rule of the world unsettled, you found a home
in Euboean Chalcis, carried away by vain delusions!
You idiot! not to notice the clangour of war, to avoid
the whole world's misfortunes – which of the Gods has power
to grant you this but Death? You will dwell in seclusion   230
on Euboea's coast, hidden away in a funeral monument
there where an arm of the sea is crushed between rocky Carystos
and Rhamnus, which worships the deity[1] hostile to arrogance;
trapped in this cleft, the tide boils up in a swirl of waters,
and Euripus' unpredictable currents sweep the ships   235
of Chalcis out to a port unfriendly to fleets – to Aulis.[2]

★

Meanwhile, Caesar was returning from mastered Spain
ready to move his victorious eagles into a new world,
when the Gods nearly diverted his destiny's mighty stream
away from prosperity:[3] unsubdued by the War-god,   240
the general feared that, within the tents of his own camp,
the success of his crimes would unravel, since troops loyal through
          all
his campaigns, glutted at last with bloodshed, came near to
          deserting
their leader – either because, for a little while, the bugles'
dismal blare having stopped and the sword grown cold in its   245
          sheath
had repulsed the Furies of war; or else because the soldiers,
seeking greater rewards, had spurned both cause and leader,
putting their already guilt-stained swords up for sale once more.
No other struggle made it so painfully clear to Caesar
that the peak from which he surveyed the world was not stable –   250
it shook: he was standing atop a teetering pedestal.
An amputee with all limbs missing, almost reduced

1. Nemesis.
2. There seems to be a reference here to the delay at Aulis of the Greek Trojan
   expedition led by Agamemnon, which was ended by the sacrifice of his daughter.
3. The revolt described here by Lucan took place at Placentia in north Italy (see
   Dio, XLI.26ff.). Lucan does not mention the location.

to his own blade, the man who was dragging the nations to war
learnt that swords, once drawn, belong to soldiers, not generals.
255 Grumbling was no longer timid, anger was not kept hidden
in locked hearts, for what often curbs wavering allegiance –
each man fearing the fellows he himself frightens, each man
thinking that he alone is galled by his officers' unfairness –
this motive checked them no more. Indeed, being a mob made
        them
260 bold, melting their fears. Wrongs that thousands commit go
        unpunished!
They poured out threats:

                              'Caesar, give us leave to withdraw
from the frenzy of crime! You ransack land and sea for steel
to slash our throats, ready to pour out our humble lives
against any foe you can find: Gaul snatched some of us
265 from you; Spain, with its hard campaigns, carried off others;
some lie dead in Hesperia – throughout the world, while you
conquer, your army dies.'

                              'Why delight that you spilled our blood
in Arctic lands where the Rhone and the Rhine were enslaved?'

'In return for all these campaigns, you have given me civil war!'

270 'When we drove out the Senate and captured our nation's capital,
which of the men, which of the Gods did you let us plunder?
We go from crime to crime, our hands and swords reeking –
poor as saints! What goal do you seek with our weapons?
What is enough if Rome is too little?'

                                  'See how grey
275 our hair is, how weak our hands – look at our wasted muscles!
Zest for living fades – we have eaten our days up with warfare.
Send us away to die – old men!'

                              'Oh, what outrageous requests!'

'Grant that we not fling dying limbs across some hard
rampart; grant that no helmet cage our departing soul;

spare us the vain search for a hand to close our eyes at death;   280
give us the lap of a weeping wife, the assurance of a pyre
prepared for our corpse; let our old age end in disease;
let Caesar's men meet some fate other than sword-blades!'

'Why try to deceive us, as if we were blind to the horrors
you train us to meet? Are we the only men in the war   285
who do not know which crime will bring us the highest pay?
All our wars have been wasted, if *he* has not yet learnt
that our hands stop at nothing! Not sworn oath, not bonds of law
forbid that bold attempt. On the banks of the Rhine, Caesar
was leader; here, he is soldier. Crime stains all the same hue.'   290

'Besides, with an ingrate judging our merits, our courage
is wasted: anything we achieve is dubbed "good luck".
He should know that we are his fate!'

                                'You expect the Gods'
total compliance; but because your soldiers are angry, Caesar,
there will be peace!'

                      This said, the whole camp began to run   295
amok; they howled for their leader, and rage was on every face.
Let their will be done, O Gods! Since Duty and Good Faith
have failed us, since all we have left is trust in wicked ways,
mutiny must bring about the end of civil war!

What other leaders would that mob have left unafraid?   300
But Caesar was used to risking his fate on a razor's edge,
staking his fortune on the longest odds; he came out
to meet them, laughing – he did not wait till their anger
cooled, but strode into their midst to test their frenzy's force.

To them he would not have refused cities and temples to sack –   305
not even Tarpeian Jove's shrine;[1] senators' mothers and daughters
would have met with unspeakable fates. Clearly, he longed to be
    begged
licence for mayhem, longed for the War-god's spoils to be prized.
He only feared his berserk soldiers' return to their senses.

      1. The great Temple of Jupiter on the Capitol in Rome.

310 *Does it not shame you, Caesar, to gloat alone – your soldiers*
already condemn this war! Shall they, sooner than you, grow
sick of bloodshed! Shall the rule of steel chafe them while you
overturn Right and Wrong at will! Learn to relax and endure
power without weapons, let yourself set a limit on evil!
315 *Savage! why harry, why rail at men no longer compliant?*
Civil war eludes you!

                    He took his stand on a platform
of stacked sods, his jaw set; he deserved their fear, being
unafraid himself. Anger prompted the words he spoke:
'You raged at me in my absence just now, with scowls and fists,
320 soldiers! Here you have my chest – bared and ready for stabbing!
Plant your swords here and run if you want an end to war! –
Unmasked! rebels so faint of heart you dare not do
anything, an army intent only on running away,
exhausted by your undefeated leader's success!

325 Get out! leave the war to me, and me to my destiny!
These weapons will find hands, and once I am rid of *you*,
Fortune will give me replacements – a hero for each idle spear.
If Magnus, fleeing, has in his train Hesperia's
tribes and a mighty fleet, will Victory not bring me
330 a host – men who will merely scoop up the spoils of a war
already settled; who, once they have snatched the fruits of your
labour, will march, unscathed, beside my laurel-decked chariot?
You – a despicable huddle of bloodless old men, Roman
civilians by then – will join the crowds watching my Triumph!

335 'Do you imagine the loss occasioned by your desertion
will hinder Caesar's career? It is as if the rivers
should all threaten to withhold the waters they merge with the
        sea:
if they stopped flowing, would sea-level fall? No, no more
than it rises with their influx. Do you really believe
340 yours was the weight that tipped my scales? The God's concern
will never sink so low that the Fates will remark your death
or health: such trifles bob in the wake of a few great men –
men to whom mortals owe their existence.

Terror of Spanish
and Arctic worlds while you soldiered under my name:
were Pompey your leader, you would surely flee; in Caesar's   345
service, Labienus[1] was brave; now, a vile defector,
he roams on sea and land with the leader he chose over me.

'Your allegiance will not mean more to me if you should fight
neither for nor against me; anyone leaving my standards
who then fails to offer his weapons to Pompey's faction   350
wants no part of me! Surely, the Gods have this camp
in Their care – it is Their will that I not engage in battles
so momentous unless my current troops are replaced.
Phew! what a load Fortune hoists from these shoulders, long since
weary of the weight. She helps me unarm swordsmen who grasp   355
at everything – men for whom the world is not enough!
At last I shall wage this war to suit myself!

'Quit my camp!
Hand over our standards to *real* men, you cowardly citizens!

'But a few of you, those who fired this frenzy – you stay:
not for Caesar, but for punishment. Faces in the dirt!   360
stretch out your necks and disloyal heads for execution!
And you raw recruits, by whose unaided strength the camp
will now stand, observe these punishments and learn how to
     strike,
learn how to die.'

His voice, savage with menace, made
the feckless mob cringe; one man – yet a vast army,   365
able to strip him of power, feared him as though he controlled
their swords and could stir a soldier's steel against his will!

As for Caesar, he trembled lest his crimes be denied
weapons and hands. Their passivity surpassed the savage
leader's hopes – they yielded not only their swords but their   370
     throats.

1. Caesar's right-hand man in the Gallic campaign who joined Pompey in 49 B.C.

Between minds steeped in evil there is no stronger bond
than to kill and be killed. By the force of their grim agreement,
calm was restored; the men returned, appeased by their
    punishment.

★

He ordered his army to march nine days and reach Brindisi,[1]
375 commandeering all the boats remote Otranto
and ancient Taranto and Lecce's sequestered coastline harboured,
those berthed at the Bay of Salpi and hill-topped Siponto
where, in Apulia, wooded Gargano rucks Ausonia's
shore, assailed by Dalmatia's northern, Calabria's southern
380 gales as it juts out into the waves of the Adriatic.
Safe without his soldiers, he headed towards Rome – his
    frightened
but well-schooled slave, even when he wore the toga. Of course,
the Dictator[2] gave way to the will of the People and took
the highest office: as Consul, he made the Calendar glad.[3]

385 *(Oh, yes! that age was the first to fashion the lying
titles that we have for so long lavished on our masters!)*

That no lawful use of the sword should elude him, Caesar
desired to mix Ausonia's Axes with his blades,
added the Rods[4] to his eagles and, seizing the empty
390 name of legal power, stamped the grim times with a fitting
mark: for what Consul's name would better mark the year
of Pharsalus? The Campus[5] staged a solemn election
and, though the people were not admitted, their votes were sorted,
roll was called, and the urn was given a half-hearted shake.

1. Brindisi, ancient Brundisium, was the major port of Calabria in the heel of Italy.
   The coastal places mentioned here were in Calabria or Apulia – all within a
   hundred and fifty miles of Brindisi.
2. The 'Dictatorship' was a Roman constitutional magistracy, to which an in-
   dividual might be appointed in times of national crisis.
3. By having his name included in the *fasti consulares* or 'consular calendar', a
   register of the higher magistrates at Rome.
4. A reference to the *fasces* again, the rods and axes which represented the consul's
   legal power.
5. The Campus Martius at Rome.

It was forbidden to watch the sky; augurs were deaf to thunder,   395
birds were declared propitious – even an owl on the left!

From that day forward the once venerable power of Law
withered and wasted; but, lest the period go in need of a name,
a Consul a month marks the age off into eras.

None the less, the divinity enthroned on Trojan Alba,[1]   400
who – since Latium's defeat – has not deserved solemn rites,
watched the night bloom with fires ending the Latin Festival.

★

Caesar sped away from Rome and crossed the fields
which idle Apulians had ceased to hoe and left to the weeds;
faster than Heaven's fires or a tigress with young,   405
he reached the Minoan[2] rooftops ranged round the curve
of Brindisi's harbour and found its waters closed by gales
and blizzards, his fleet cowering beneath winter's star.
The leader was disgusted: the moment to wind up the war
was seeping away in sluggish postponements, and he was detained   410
in port till men Fortune disdained should judge the sea safe!
He filled their unseamanlike souls with confidence thus:

'Once winter's gusts have laid hold of heaven and ocean,
their grasp is fiercer than that of winds which rainy Spring,
with treacherous inconstancy, bars from blowing steadily.   415
We need not trace the coastline's every crook and curve
but, with North Wind alone at our backs, can cut through the
            waves.
I pray that a norther will make the topmost masthead dip,
will swoop down raging, and blow us across to the Greek city
walls – lest Pompey's men from all the shore of Phaeacia[3]   420
should dash their oars and overtake our flapping sails.
Snap the hawsers that hold our lucky prows in check –
too long have we wasted storm-clouds and savage waves!'

1. Jupiter Latiaris, who failed to defend Latium from Aeneas and the Trojans.
2. A reference to the tradition that Brindisi was founded by Cretan exiles (see *Civil War* II.610ff.).
3. Corcyra, with which the Homeric Phaeacia was identified. The reference seems to be to the general area of Corcyra, Dyrrhachium and Apollonia.

The first stars appeared in the sky as Phoebus sank
425   beneath the waves, and the Moon had made shadows of her own,
when the ships cast off together. Halyards shook out
sails full length; hauling the yardend back, keeping the sheet
to port, sailors angled the canvas; hoisting topsails
on high, they collected any breezes going to waste.

430   Wayward air had scarcely begun to stir the sails,
making them belly a little, when they collapsed, flapping
against the mainmast; land had fallen astern when the same
breeze that had carried them out dropped, unable to follow.
The ocean surface was dead calm; bound by a vast lassitude,
435   more lethargic than stagnant marsh pools, the waves flattened.
Like this, freezing the Scythian waves, the stalled Bosporus
halts: Black frost dams the Danube, checking its rush to the main:
the measureless ocean is sheeted with ice; what boats the waves
catch, they crumple – nor does a horseman shatter this water
440   where no ship can sail; an invisible surf roars underfoot
as Bessian nomads' cartwheels rut the Sea of Azov.
The ocean's calm is savage, its depths sullen, its pools
of water standing listless – as if the flat expanse,
deserted by vital force, had come to a halt; forgetting
445   its ancient rhythms, the sea failed to ebb and flow,
to shiver with ripples, to shimmer with moonbeams.
The vessels lay exposed to innumerable dangers:
on the one hand, hostile craft ready to row across the sluggish
waters; on the other – a grave threat for men besieged
450   by an ocean becalmed – famine. Unusual fear invented
unusual prayers: enormous waves and gale-force winds
were prayed for – if only the water would shake off its marshlike
torpor and be an ocean! Clouds . . .? a threatening wave . . .?
No, not one; sky and ocean are dull and slack; all hope
455   of shipwreck is lost.

               But when night had been chased away,
day rose, its radiance streaked with clouds; slowly it stirred
the ocean depths. Ceraunia rushed towards the sailors.

Then the ships began to gather speed; the flat sea
curled astern of the fleet – which, with favourable wind and tide,
came to anchor, jabbing the flukes in Palaeste's sands.   460

★

First to see the rivals pitch adjacent camps was
the land defined by the curved banks of the boisterous Genusus
and gentler Hapsus. Boats can sail on the Hapsus, thanks
to a lake which it imperceptibly drains with its mild current.
But snows thawed now by sun, now by rain make Genusus   465
rush headlong. Neither tires itself with flowing for miles –
the coast is close, and neither knows much of the land.

In this place, Fortune matched up two names whose fame
was widespread. The wretched world's hopes were raised: might
        not
the leaders, parted by only a narrow strip of valley,   470
reject this manifest horror? Each can see the other's
face and hear his voice – and oh, Magnus, the father-in-law
you loved so long never saw you nearer but once
after the ties of unlucky blood were broken – two infants
born and buried[1] – and that once was on Egypt's sands!   475

In Caesar's mind a frantic drumbeat – start the war!
But his partisans forced him to suffer delay of his crime:
commander of all the troops left behind, bold Antony
even then was plotting an Actium for the civil war.[2]

Again and again did Caesar summon the laggard with threats   480
and pleas:

            'Antony! cause of the world's many troubles!
why hinder Fate and Gods Above? All else my quickness
has done, but, in a war that has whirled from one success

1. Caesar's daughter and Pompey's wife, Julia, died during childbirth in 54 B.C.
   The child only survived its mother by a few days. Julia's first pregnancy ended
   in a miscarriage.
2. Actium was the site of the naval battle of 31 B.C. in which Mark Antony and
   Cleopatra fought Caesar's heir, Octavian – and were defeated.

to the next, Fortune demands the finishing touch from *you*. No
485 Libya, split by Sidra's shoals, parts us with treacherous tides!
Would I entrust your weapons to uncharted waters
or draw you into unknown perils? Coward! Caesar
bids you come, not go! I myself led the way
through the thick of our foes; I struck the sands of a hostile power!
490 You fear my camp?

     'I resent losing my hour of destiny –
but I see I am wasting my prayers on wind and wave.
Don't restrain those eager to cross the hazardous sea!
If I know my lads at all, no threat of shipwreck
will keep them from joining Caesar's force!

       'Now I must launch
495 a bitter reproach: we have divided the world unfairly –
Caesar and all the Senate together hold Epirus,
while you are Ausonia's sole master!'

       With three and four such
appeals, Caesar roused Antony; seeing he still delayed,
believing himself neglectful of Heaven and not the reverse,
500 Caesar dared – of his own will – to risk in dangerous
darkness the crossing that scared the men he led. Experience
told him the reckless succeed if God so inclines. He hoped,
in a flimsy skiff, to surmount waves a navy would dread!

Drowsy night had eased the wearisome cares of war –
505 a brief lull for the wretched, whose less exiled destinies
greeted sleep with open arms. Soon the camp fell silent,
and soon, too, the third hour[1] had roused the second watch.
Stepping cautiously through the profound silence, Caesar
attempts what slaves would scarcely dare – he deserts everyone;
510 Fortune alone is allowed to join him.

      As he walked out
of the tent-ground, he sprang over the sprawled limbs of his sleeping

---

1. The end of the first of four night-watches, each occupying three 'hours', the
 time from sundown to sunrise being divided into twelve such 'hours'.

sentries, cursing under his breath because he had fooled them;
he traced the curving shore and found in the shallow waves,
tied with a rope to a jagged rock, a little rowboat.
The Captain and master of this vessel lived   515
not far from there in a snug cabin – not framed of wood
but wattled with hollow rushes and cane from the marsh,
its seaward side sheltered by an upturned dinghy.
Caesar pounded on the door two or three times, making
the roof rattle.   520
        Amyclas[1] sprang up at once from his soft
bed of seaweed and cried:

            'Now who – ? does a shipwrecked sailor
seek my roof? or someone Fortune has driven to my hut
in search of help?'

        So saying, he pulled a length of rope
out from the depths of a pile of still-smouldering wood-ash
and blew on its tiny spark till he had stirred up a flame,   525
unconcerned for his safety – he knew that even in civil
war, huts are not looted.

       Oh, the security and ease
of a poor man's life and meagre hearth! How little account
we take of the Gods' blessings! What temple, what high-walled town
could claim as much – to have felt no thrill of terror   530
at the rap of Caesar's knuckles?

        When the door was unlatched,
the leader said:

        'Expect your modest prayers to be met –
and more! enlarge your hopes, young man! If you follow orders

---

1. The generous reception of the great by the humble has a long literary tradition
to which this episode alludes. Eumaeus' reception of Odysseus (Homer, *Odyssey*
XIV.1ff.), Evander's reception of Aeneas (Virgil, *Aeneid* VIII.362ff.), Baucis' and
Philemon's reception of Jupiter and Mercury (Ovid, *Metamorphoses* VIII.624ff.)
are among the precedents which Lucan rewrites. His Amyclas figure was much
admired in the Middle Ages.

and take me to Hesperia, you need no longer depend
535   solely on boat and brawn, only to end up impoverished.
Don't hesitate to entrust your fate to a God willing
to pour sudden riches into your meagre coffers!'

Thus he spoke: wrapped in a commoner's cloak, he still could
not learn to mimic plain speech.

                    Amyclas the pauper, then:
540   'Many things prevent me from trusting the sea tonight:
the Sun drew no crimson clouds down into the sea;
he produced asymmetrical rays – with divergent light,
half of Phoebus called up the South Wind, half the North.
Then, too, his disk dimmed at the centre; fainting, he faded,
545   his feeble glow allowing our eyes to gaze straight at him.

'And the Moon rose not with a luminous, slender horn,
nor with clear-cut hollows scooped from the middle of her disk;
nor did she draw her tips out fine with horn upright; but,
signalling gales, she blushed; then, paling, displayed cheeks turned
550   sallow, as her sad face began passing behind a cloud.

'More than this, the tossing trees and surf's pounding
dismay me – also the dolphin's confused lunges at the waves;
the way the loon delights in dry land; that the heron
has dared soar aloft, trusting to his ungainly pinions;
555   that, splashing his head in the brine like a bird in a downpour,
the crow paces along the shore with unsteady gait.

'But, if critical moments in great affairs make this demand,
I'll not refuse a helping hand. I will either reach
the shores you want, or else sea and storm will prevent me.'

560   Such were his words; casting off, he spread his sails to winds
at whose blasts not only did meteors swerve and fall
through the upper air, leaving a trail of spangled furrows
behind, but even the stars which stand still, pinned to the heights
of heaven, seem to shiver. A black shudder inked
565   the ocean's skin; a protracted heave, roll upon roll,
and a menacing wave boiled over; unsure of the next gust,

the sea's ugly surface announced the advent of tempests.[1]

Then the pitching dinghy's pilot spoke:

'See what savagery
the sea is brewing! West winds or south – which it intends
is unclear; shifting seas buffet our stern from every side.   570
Clouds and sky say south but, if we judge by the ocean's
growls, north-westerly gales will sweep the main. Such
    turbulence!
Neither ship nor shipwrecked will reach Hesperia's strand.
Our sole hope is to cancel the crossing, abandon our course,
and turn back. Let me make for the shore with my battered   575
boat, lest our nearest landfall still prove all too far.'

Confident every danger will make way for *him*, Caesar
    replied:

'Dismiss the ocean's threats and spread your sails
to the raging wind! If you spurn Italy at Heaven's behest,
then seek it at *mine*! Your only real excuse for fear is   580
ignorance of your passenger – a man the Gods never
fail, a man who justly rails at Fortune only
when she but answers his prayer.

'Slam through the thick of these
    squalls!
Have no fear – I will protect you! This trouble concerns
sky and sea – not our vessel. Weighted with Caesar, she will   585
find she is saved from the waves by her cargo. Nor will the
    winds'
fierce rage be allowed to last long – your boat will deliver
the waves! Don't move your helm! spread sail and flee the
    nearby
shore! Believe that you can reach the Calabrian harbour,
since no other land will be able to offer a refuge   590

---

1. The storm was a literary, especially epic topos from Homer (*Odyssey* V.291ff.)
   onwards. See Ovid, *Tristia* I.2 and 4, and – most relevantly for the episode – the
   storm Aeneas experiences at Virgil, *Aeneid* I.81ff.

to us and our ship. You lack the skill to interpret this vast
turmoil: what Fortune seeks with this tumult of wind and wave
is how she may grant me a favour.'

He said no more:
a rapacious whirlwind smashed the boat and tore away
595 her tattered rigging, sent sails soaring above the slender
mast; the alderwood hull creaked, its joints cracking.

And now, dangers roused from around the world came rushing:
first Corus, North-Westerly Wind, shook the Atlantic brine
from his hair, making the waters seethe; soon, at his urging, surf
600 was raging, trying to heave all its waves to the clifftops.

Glacial Boreas blocked his path and beat back the sea,
till the water hung, doubtful which wind to obey.

And now,
the frenzy of Scythia's North-East Wind prevailed; he whipped up
the waves and made shallows of sands concealed fathoms below.
605 Boreas still could not sweep the sea to the rocks, but broke
his own surge on waves Corus had roused, and the churning
waters
continued to brawl, even after the Winds had withdrawn.
East Wind never ceased his blustering; South Wind, black
with rainstorms, never slept in Aeolus' stony prison –
610 or so I believe; rushing forth from their usual haunts,
each defended his native region with wild typhoons –
and thus we still have an ocean.

People say separate
waters were mixed by the squalls – Tyrrhenian Sea met Aegean,
Ionia's Gulf heard the wandering Adriatic roar.
615 That day saw mountains submerged the sea had endlessly pounded
in vain. What crags and crests the conquered Earth toppled
into the abyss! No shore gave rise to waves of such
magnitude: they came from some other region, rolling
in from the Great Sea; the stream that wreathes the world's rim
620 sent these monstrous breakers.

So, too, Olympus' Ruler
turned his brother's trident against the human race, that time
when lightning flagged;[1] dry land succumbed to the second realm[2]
as seas rolled in over nations; Tethys refused to endure
any shoreline – horizon was all the limit she wished.
Like this would the ocean's mighty mass have risen again,   625
had not Heaven's Ruler weighted the waves with clouds.

A night that was not of Heaven's making fell: sky vanished,
choked with lichenous dusk from ghostly abodes, sagging, pregnant
with tempests; within the clouds, the waves were doused with rain.
Light – even flickering light – died; bolts of lightning did not   630
flash – rather, the storm-packed air split apart in darkness.
Then the domes of the Gods Above rocked, as the highest skies
thundered; the celestial framework was jarred, its joints strained,
Nature was terrified of Chaos – it seemed the elements
had burst their concordant bonds, and Night was back again,   635
blending ghosts with Gods – and Their one hope of surviving
the cosmic downfall was that They had not yet perished.

Shuddering on wave-crests, the sailors saw a wall of salt-water
high as the distance a man can see, looking down on the mild
ocean from Leucas' peak;[3] but when, once again, the swelling   640
waves opened their jaws, the mast scarcely cleared the surface.
Clouds were scraped by their sails, ocean-floor by their keel,
for the sea, where it sank, did not conceal the sands;
all had been sucked into billows, each ripple part of the surge.

These terrors surpassed the baffled helmsman's nautical skills: 645
which wave should he dive through, which evade? The ocean's
     discord
aided the wretches, for no one surge could capsize their craft

---

1. The reference is to the great flood sent by Jupiter to punish the human race.
   Deucalion and Pyrrha alone survived.
2. The 'second realm' is the sea.
3. The south-west promontory of the island of Leucas in the Ionian Sea is a sheer
   cliff rising to a height of two thousand feet.

in face of another – one heels her over, its opposite
rights her; likewise, with all winds blowing, the boat bobs right
    side up.
650 Not the low-lying shoals of Saso, not Thessaly's
jagged rock-bound coast, not the wicked coves of Ambracia's
shore did these sailors fear: it was craggy Ceraunia's peaks
they dreaded!

            At length, believing the danger worthy of his
destiny, Caesar cried:

                  'How much trouble is it for Gods
655 to capsize me? Here I sit in a little rowboat,
and They attack with a tidal wave! If the sea has been given
the glory of my death, and I am barred from the battlefield
I will accept whatever death you Deities give me
without a tremor; though this day, hastened by Fate,
660 breaks off a brilliant career, I have done great deeds enough –
mastered the Arctic tribes, intimidated and quelled
armed rebels, seen Magnus second after me at Rome;
at the People's command, I claimed the Rods denied by battle;
my record will not lack a single Roman office.
665 Yet none but you Fortuna, who alone are privy
to my secret prayers, will know that, though I go down to the
    shades
of Styx loaded with titles – Dictator and Consul both –
I die a commoner. No need for a funeral for me,
O Gods Above: keep my battered body here
670 amidst the waves, let me want for tomb and pyre – provided
I am always feared, awaited by every land.'

Such was his prayer when – wondrous strange! – a decuman
    wave[1]
lifted him up with his leaky boat – not hurling him back
onto the high heap of water, but catching him up
675 and, where a narrow strand was free from sharp-edged stones,

---

1. The 'tenth wave' was supposed to be devastating. See Ovid, *Tristia* I.2.50.

setting him down on dry land. The instant his foot touched the soil,
all realms, all cities were his once more – and his fortune, too!

But next morning, Caesar's return to his camp and companions,
unlike his secret departure, failed to evade detection.
A weeping throng of his men swirled around the leader,   680
reproaching him with groans and not unwelcome wails:

'Hard man! where did your reckless daring take you, Caesar?'

'Yes, and in what peril you placed our worthless souls, when you
          gave
reluctant squalls the chance to tear you limb from limb?'

'When the life and safety of so many nations depend   685
upon your life, when most of the world has chosen you
for its head, it is cruel to court death!'

                              'Has none of your comrades
earned the right *not* to live on, a survivor, after
your demise?'

                    'While the sea was clutching at you, our bodies
wallowed in hoggish sleep – oh! the shame!'   690

                                        'Your reason for
          seeking
Hesperia was this – it seemed heartless to send anyone
out on a sea so wild? When a man has run out of luck,
then he dives into dubious risks, into ventures rife
with danger; but for one who has the world within reach
to grant the sea such a chance – !'   695

                         'Why tax the Gods' patience?
Is enough of the favour and aid you have from Fortune left
to win the war, now that she's tossed you up on our strand?
Is this what you want from the Gods – to be, not world ruler,
not master of mankind, but a lucky shipwrecked sailor?'
During this outburst of questions, night dispersed and the day,   700
serenely sunny, took command, while the sea, exhausted,
calmed its swollen waves with the winds' acquiescence.

And so, when the leaders in Italy saw the ocean
fatigued by storms, and a north wind rising high and steady,
705 one that could counter the water's force, they weighed anchor.
The wind, and hands trained to steer in close formation,
kept the prows level at first; all across the wide sea,
like marching soldiers, the fleet lined up and moved as one.

But cruel Night stole from the sailors their measure of wind,
710 their sails' uniform progress, disrupting the navy's array.

Think how cranes, at winter's urging, depart the frozen
Strymon, bound for the banks of the Nile. The flight begins:
prompted by instinct, the birds form various characters;
presently, when an updraft thrums in their outstretched wings,
715 they cluster, a jumble of random bunches; the alphabet
fractures and fades, in a scatter of feathered wing-beats.

But, as soon as daylight returned, a stiff breeze,
stirred by Phoebus' rising, leaned into their sails.
Despite their efforts, they shot past Elisso's shore
720 but fetched up at Nymphaeum; North Wind had veered to the
      south
making the unprotected harbour a sudden haven.

★

Now that all Caesar's troops had been assembled in full,
Magnus, seeing the final crisis of grim War must soon
march on his camp, determined to set aside the burden
725 of keeping his wife safe and to hide you away, Cornelia,
on Lesbos,[1] at far remove from the savage clash and clamour
of battle.
          Ah me, how rightful Passion lords it over
level heads — even yours, Magnus! Your love made you
cautious, afraid of fighting; the one thing you meant to snatch
730 *from under Fate's blow — where the world and Rome's destiny stood —*
was your wife.

1. The largest of the islands off the coast of Asia Minor. Mytilene (see line 786) was
its capital.

Words failed him, though his mind was made up
long ago; he chose, while shoving aside what must come,
to yield to sweet delay and steal time from the Fates.

Night was just ending, and drowsy sleep had been pushed back
when, holding her husband close, Cornelia stroked his care-   735
laden chest, seeking his tender kisses. He turned away.

Tears pour down his cheeks! Amazed, sorely troubled – his pain
was unsuspected – she dared not question a weeping Magnus.
Groaning, he said:

'You are not sweeter to me than life *now*
when life is vile, but sweeter than my season of joy . . .   740
A sad day has come, wife, and I have deferred too long –
and not long enough. All Caesar's troops are ready to fight.
We must give way; Lesbos will keep you safe from the shadows
of war. – *Do not beseech me!* I have already said 'No'
to myself.   745

'You will suffer no long separation from me:
the end will tumble headlong, ruin rushes apace,
summits topple. To hear of Magnus' perils suffices.
Your love has deceived me if you can bear to watch
civil war.

'The truth is, now that war is upon us,
it shames me that I have spent carefree nights with my wife   750
and, while bugles are jarring the wretched world, have risen
from your bed. I fear sending Pompey off to civil
warfare without some loss of his own to make him sad.

'Meanwhile, hide yourself and, safer than nations, safer than
any king, keep far away: thus your husband's fortune   755
may fail to crush you with all its weight.

'If the Gods should wreck
our forces, let the best part of Magnus remain,
and, if the Fates and a bloody conqueror press me hard,
let me have a place I would want to run to!'

The frail woman
760 barely withstood such grief; her senses fled her stunned breast.
At last, her voice found strength to frame these sad reproaches:
'I have no complaints of our marriage, Magnus, to lodge
against Fates and Gods: death does not break off our love
nor the dismal pyre's final brand; no, by a frequent and all
765 too common lot, I lose my husband through divorce!
Our foe draws near: by all means, break the pledge of our wedding-
torch and delight your kinsman!

'Oh, Magnus, is this how you
regard our troth? Do you think that I need protection more
than you? Do our lives no longer hang by the same thread?
770 Are you ordering me to leave, to bare my head – cruel man! –
to the lightning-bolts of world destruction? Does your chance
of happiness, even as you pray for it, seem to have died?

'Should I spurn being a slave to villains and, choosing suicide,
follow you to the Dead: until the sad news strikes
775 shores far removed, I will be living still, your survivor.
Besides, how cruel to train me for doom, to coach me
to bear such sorrow! Forgive me for speaking out – my fear is
I could endure it.

'But if prayers avail and the Gods
hear me, the last to learn the outcome will be your wife.
780 Soon, when you have won, the cliffs will increase my anxiety,
and the ship which will bring such glad tidings will make me
afraid;
nor will hearing accounts of your victory ease my dread
since, cast ashore in a lonely spot, I could be captured
even as Caesar flees. The coast will gain notoriety
785 from a great name's exile; once Magnus' wife is put there,
who could fail to know of her Mytilenean hideaway?

'This is my last prayer: if your arms are vanquished, leaving you
no course safer than flight, then, when you put to sea,
steer your luckless craft anywhere but here – they will look

for you on my shores.'   790

                    With these words, she sprang up,
deserting their bed, distracted, wanting no delay
to postpone her torment. She does not soothe her sorrowing
Magnus, wind her sweet arms around him, or cling to his neck;
their last chance to taste the fruits of their long love perished,
they pitched headlong into private grief, and, as they parted,   795
neither could bear to say 'Farewell.' In all their life,
no other day was so sad, for their remaining losses
they bore with hearts trouble had already toughened and dulled.
She fainted, unhappy woman; her slaves' hands caught, then
carried her out to the shore where she flung herself down,   800
     clutching
the very sand until, at last, she was put on board,
more unhappy than when she left Hesperia's ports
and her homeland, chased away by savage Caesar's troops.
Faithful consort of Magnus, she ventured forth alone, left
the leader, fled from her Pompey.   805

                    What a night you had next,
sleepless one! In your widow's lonely bed for the first time,
the silence seemed chilly and strange, your body exposed
without your husband close by.

                    How often, sunk in sleep,
she wound her mistaken arms around his empty pillow
and, her flight forgotten, groped in the dark for her husband!   810
For, despite the flame searing her flesh to its speechless marrow,
she did not like to lie spread-eagled across their couch:
she saved his side of the bed. She feared she had lost him –
her Pompey.

                    But the Gods had no such glad day planned.
The hour drew near that would give the poor woman Magnus.[1]   815

---

1. In *Civil War* Book VIII Pompey, defeated at Pharsalus, escapes to his wife on
   Lesbos, only to sail with her to Egypt and his death.

MARTIAL

INTRODUCTION

Marcus Valerius Martialis was born in Bílbilis, in northern Aragón, around A.D. 40. He was one of the many writers who came to Rome in Neronian times to take advantage of the rewarding literary climate there. Unfortunately his friends in the Senecan family fell into disfavour around the time of his arrival in A.D. 64 and he had to wait until the opening of the Colosseum in A.D. 80 by the emperor Titus to become a literary success with his first volume of epigrams, *De Spectaculis* (*On the Games*). After that he issued fourteen volumes of miscellaneous short poems roughly every two years until his death in A.D. 103 in his home town, to which he had retired, somewhat disappointed, a few years earlier. Much of his work however was circulated informally among his large circle of distinguished patrons, many of the occasional poems being addressed to them.

As may be seen from IV.49 and X.4, his poetic programme was revolutionary. Beneath a mock-modest affectation of non-seriousness, he aimed at subverting the traditionally respected genres of epic and tragedy in favour of the short lyric and the witty epigram. His claims for his own popularity with contemporary readers indicate a measure of success. His later reputation has varied enormously, reaching its peak in the European Renaissance and in England in the sixteenth and seventeenth centuries. His lack of esteem in Victorian and later times was due to the large number of flattering poems directed to his patrons and the high proportion of obscene material in his verses, which has always constituted a stumbling block for moralistic and aesthetic critics. (He himself defended this element in his work on grounds of realism, 'social significance', and by analogy with fertility and apotropaic ritual.)

His main poetic talent was for 'wit' (in its broadest sense), which accounts both for the gnomic concision of his quotable reflections on life, society, and human foibles and for the vivid, concrete imagery in his descriptions of people and places.

Strong claims have been made for his superiority as a thoughtful Epicurean commentator on friendship and the Happy Life – his poem on this subject (X.47) being perhaps the most frequently translated short poem in literature – or as a writer of poignant memorial poems on dead friends and servants, but his *forte* was surely the satiric epigram. His accomplishment here inspired his friend Juvenal and a host of English imitators in the Elizabethan and Jacobean periods, not least Ben Jonson and Robert Herrick.

The picture of the world of Rome that Martial offers us is remarkable for its *pointilliste* detail, but the satirical lens he directs on it has a conservative focus. Martial's vision of his society, a society based on imperialist expansion and a slave economy, is hierarchical and he does not question its underpinnings. At the summit is the present emperor, whoever he may be. Good (or apparently beneficent) emperors are to be praised (Augustus, Titus, Domitian, Nerva, Trajan) and the bad rulers are to be damned (Nero and, after his death, Domitian). Next are the senatorial and equestrian classes, who, if they fulfil their proper functions in terms of military achievements and generous patronage towards their clients, not least their literary *protégés*, must be duly honoured. If however they fall into such vices as avarice, stinginess, extrava- gance, or effeminate sexual perversions, they must be castigated. Upstart rich freedmen must not ape their betters or cross social boundaries. And, from the other side, upper-class ladies must not violate the engendered social codes by adultery, by liaisons with slaves (V.17; VII.14) or by even more disreputable activities, which usurp the sexual privileges of the active Roman male, who may of course take sexual advantage, in a manly way, of prostitutes and slaves, both male and female. If these know their proper place (cf. III.65; IV.7; XI.26; XI.39), they will be properly complimented.

Martial, however, like his fellow satirists, describes a world where these social barriers have crumbled. And the veneer of hypocrisy and pretence which overlays the countless moral, sexual, and civic transgressions of aristocrats of both sexes, philosophers, miscreant oldsters, social climbers and impudent slaves stimulates still further his mordant and obscene wit. The poet professes to be shocked and he tries to shock his audience in return.

To secure these calculated effects Martial has at his disposal a wide variety of metres, an inward grasp of the Graeco-Roman literary tradition, not least of satire and invective, a keen eye for disreputable resemblances and analogies, and, in general, a superb command of the Latin language and its armoury of rhetorical and poetic techniques. (His fondness for puns and *double entendre* are, of course, not as much now to the readers' taste as they once were.)

We are left then an impressive body of work of enormous range from the lyric and elegiac to the satiric and pornographic, from which emerges a well-defined and critical personality (or *persona*) moving confidently in a fully realized, if sometimes sombre, world, which alternately fascinates and disquiets.

The problem for the modern reader is how to explain, and so appreciate, the reasons for the enormous popularity and influence that Martial enjoyed in the Renaissance and the seventeenth century among European poets and critics. Humour and wit are his most obvious characteristics, but these are not easily transmitted to later generations whose taste for jokes and in particular amusing verbal play will differ radically from that of Romans in the early empire. And of course there is more to this great Spanish poet than those qualities. Besides the marmoreal and serious poems on death and friendship, there is also the brilliant imagery so admired by Lord Macaulay as well as the imaginative conceits borrowed and stolen by the Elizabethan masters of the epigram such as Sir John Harington and Ben Jonson, not to mention the French poets of the Pléiade and such Spanish wits as Baltasar Gracián and Francisco Quevedo in the *siglo de oro*.

A clue to his fascination for later writers may be found in the younger Pliny's obituary written on learning of the poet's recent death around A.D. 104. Pliny wrote: 'I hear that Valerius Martial is dead and I am very distressed. He was a man of great talent, sharpness and perception. His poems show a high degree of wit and sarcasm (*sal, fe*) and, equally, a desire to please (*candour*).' The ambiguity Pliny notices in Martial's work is certainly there and accounts for the intriguing juxtaposition of extravagant praise for his patrons and savage satire on the institution of patronage itself; of lavish compliments to selected high-class Roman matrons and obscene disparagement of the female sex in general.

Humour and wit, however, have long been recognized, well before Freud pointed it out, as the classic verbal modes for expressing disguised, and even unconscious, hostility. No one played better on the humorous inconsistencies and pretentious folly generated by social hypocrisy than Martial, all the while taking his audience into his confidence and disarming all outraged reaction by his deferential apologies to the reader and the modest stance of the poor, but intermittently independent, poet.

This ambivalence in his work in general has led, in more recent eras, to serious misjudgements about his *œuvre*: these range from tepid and selective praise to moral vilification and even censorship. But literary periods which have relished the double edge of wit and serio-comic comments on society and sexuality have been more than ready to give Martial his due.

J.P.S.

Further Reading

Lindsay, W. M., *M. Val. Martialis Epigrammata* (Oxford 1929).

Ker, W. C. A., *Martial, Epigrams* (Loeb Classical Library, Cambridge, Mass., and London 1968).

Sullivan, J. P., 'Martial', in A. J. Boyle (ed.), *The Imperial Muse: To Juvenal through Ovid* (Berwick, Victoria, 1988) 177–91.

and Peter Whigham (eds.), *Epigrams of Martial Englished by Divers Hands* (Berkeley 1987).

EPIGRAMS

SELECTIONS

Translated by Various Hands

I.1

He unto whom thou art so partial,
O reader, is the well-known Martial,
The epigrammatist: while living,
Give him the fame thou wouldst be giving
5 So shall he hear, and feel, and know it:
Post–obits rarely reach a poet.

GEORGE GORDON, LORD BYRON

I.35

Cornelius sighs . . . the lines I write
Are such no dominie would recite:
They are not 'prim' . . . but epigrams,
As men for wives, no pleasure can
5 Procure without what makes a man.
You'd have me write a Hymen hymn
Nor use the words for hymning him?
We clothe ourselves at Flora's feast,[1]
In chaste stole let whores go dressed?
10 One rule for witty songs like these:
They may not, without prurience, please.

1. A licentious holiday (28 April–3 May). See note 1, page 350.

Then stifle primness, I must ask;
Take not my toys and jests to task.
Nor bowdlerize my pretty verses —
Than Priapic Gallus naught there's worse is.   15
                    PETER WHIGHAM

I.57

My taste in women, *Flaccus*? Give me one
Neither too slow nor yet too quick to bed.
For me, the middle sort: I've not the will
To be Love's Martyr — nor his Glutton either.
                    PETER WHIGHAM

II.5

Believe me, sir, I'd like to spend whole days,
    Yes, and whole evenings in your company,
But the two miles between your house and mine
    Are four miles when I go there and come back.
You're seldom home, and when you are deny it,   5
    Engrossed with business or with yourself.
Now, I don't mind the two mile trip to see you;
    What I do mind is going four to not to.
                    J. V. CUNNINGHAM

II.8

The breath of balm from foreign branches pressed;
    The effluence that falling saffron brings;
The scent of apples ripening in a chest;
    Or the rich foliage of a field in Spring;

5   Imperial silken robes from Palatine;
      Or amber, warming in a virgin's hand;
The far-off smell of spilt Falernian wine;
      A bee-loud garden in Sicilian land;

Odour, which spice and altar-incense send;
10   Or wreath of flowerets from a rich brow drawn;
Why speak of these? Words fail. Their perfect blend
      Resemble my boy's kiss at early dawn.

You ask his name? Only to kiss him? Well!
You swear as much? Sabinus, I won't tell!

                  ANTHONY REID

II.59

Look round: You see a little supper room;
But from my window, lo! great Caesar's tomb!
And the great dead themselves, with jovial breath,
Bid you be merry and remember death.

            ROBERT LOUIS STEVENSON

II.89

Gaurus, you have a fault for which
I freely pardon you:
You love to drink too much, too late;
That vice was Cato's too.
I'll even praise your scribbling
Verses, instead of prose,
With NO help from the Muses, for
That fault was Cicero's.
5   You vomit: so did Antony,

You squander: records *may* show
Apicius as your model – now,
Who led you to fellatio?
DOROTHEA WENDER

II.90

O chief director of the growing race,
Of Rome the glory and of Rome the grace,
Me, O Quintilian, may you not forgive
Though, far from labour, I make haste to live?
Some burn to gather wealth, lay hands on rule,   5
Or with white statues fill the atrium full.
The talking hearth, the rafters swart with smoke,
Live fountains and rough grass, my love invokes:
A sturdy slave: a not too learned wife:
Nights filled with slumber, and a quiet life.   10
ROBERT LOUIS STEVENSON

III.43

You were a swan, you're now a crow.
Laetinus, why deceive us so,
With borrowed plumage trying?
The Queen of Shades will surely know
When she strips off your mask below –
In Death there's no more dyeing.
OLIVE PITT-KETHLEY

III.65

They smell of *Corycian* saffron, of a
girl's tooth biting a fresh apple,

Of first bunches of white grapes and sheep-cropped
5   grass and myrtle leaves and chafed amber.
They're in the herb harvest. They're in the flame
    golden with myrrh. Earth smells of them
In summer after rain, and jewellery
    reeking of expensive heads.
Your kisses, my cold jewel, smell thus. How would
10   they smell if love had warmed their giving?

                    PETER WHIGHAM

IV.7

Why, Hyllus, do you deny to me today
What you so freely gave just yesterday?
Last night you were a soft and yielding youth;
Today you greet me with a sullen mouth.
You've grown a bristly beard and manly hairs?
What lingering night could last so many years?
5 You're joking, Hyllus! Tell me how you can
Turn yesterday's boy today into a man.

                    MOLLIE BARGER

IV.22

After her wedding-night, the nymph,
    avoiding what she seeks (her husband's touch),
Runs to the bright concealments
    of her pool. But water (like glass) betrays
The hidden woman. *Cleopatra*
    glitters through her cloak of water. So
5 Ornamental flowers, in glass
    or crystal, shroud themselves in the same cheat-
ing clearness. I joined her there. I
    tore up water kisses. Transparent
Crystal robbed us of the rest.

                    PETER WHIGHAM

IV.49

Who deem epigrams mere trifles,
  Flaccus, know not epigram.
He trifles who describes the meal
  wild *Tereus*, rude *Thyestes* ate,
The *Cretan Glider* moulting wax, [1]   5
  the one-eyed shepherd herding sheep.[2]
Foreign to my verse the tragic sock,[3]
  its turgid, ranting rhetoric.
'Men praise – esteem – revere these works.'
  True: them they praise . . . while reading me.   10

PETER WHIGHAM

IV.56

You want me to call you *generous*
  Because you shower gold
On widows, and send costly gifts
  To none but the very old?
There's nothing quite so nasty
  Or so sordidly unpleasant
As what you do and what you say
  When you call a snare a 'present'.
The treacherous hook is 'generous'   5
  To the greedy fishes, too;

1. Icarus.
2. Polyphemus.
3. The elevated boots worn by the actors in tragedy.

Trappers lay bait for stupid beasts –
 They're generous just like you.
You want to learn the meaning of
 True generosity?
I'll teach you about pure largesse:
 Just send your gifts to me!
DOROTHEA WENDER

IV.69

You serve the best wine always, my dear sir,
 And yet they say your wines are not so good.
They say you are four times a widower.
 They say . . . A drink? I don't believe I would.
J. V. CUNNINGHAM

V.10

Why is it modern books are little read,
And no one's famous till he's safely dead?
It must be envy, Regulus, when men praise
Old authors more than new. Thus, nowadays
Pompey's old Walk is sorely missed by us,[1]
Our elders love that 'temple' of Catulus.
Great Homer was a laugh to his own age,
Few praised Menander's glories on the stage,
Rome still reads Ennius – Virgil's left alone,
Ovid is only by Corinna known.
Then be content, my books, to be slow-paced;
Death before glory means – no need for haste.
OLIVE PITT-KETHLEY

1. Pompey's colonnade was built around 55 B.C.

V.17

For rank, descent and title famed,
  To gentry Gellia showed her hauteur;
She'd wed only a duke, she claimed –
  But then she ran off with a porter.

J. P. SULLIVAN

V.20

Were lives of ease, dear Namesake,[1] ours
We'd so dispose our carefree days,
Life should be for living, free from
Anterooms of dominant men,
From forum pressures, legal strains,   5
From portrait galleries of the great;
For us, the boulevards . . . bookstores . . .
Esplanades . . . shade and *Tiberside* . . .
Portici . . . baths cold and thermal.
There we'd linger, there we'd labour.   10
Now, twin lives are not their own.
Our good suns flee and disappear,
Debited, as they die, to us.

Who hesitates that's learned to live?

PETER WHIGHAM

V.34

Fronto, Father, Flaccilla, Mother, extend
  your protection from the Stygian shadows.

---

1. The poem is addressed to his friend, Julius Martialis.

The small *Erotion* (my household Iris)
    has changed my house for yours. See that the hell-
hound's[1] horrid jaws don't scare her, who was no
      more than six years old (less six days) on the
Winter day she died. She'll play beside you
    gossiping about me in child's language.
Weigh lightly on her small bones, gentle earth,
    as she, when living, lightly trod on you.
PETER WHIGHAM

V.58

You say, *Postumus*, you'll live 'tomorrow'.
    Postumus, tell me, when comes 'tomorrow'?
Is't far that 'morrow'? Where? In what place found?
    – Not lurking 'mid *Armenians, Parthians*?
Their 'morrows' now wear *Priam's, Nestor's* years.
    At what cost, tell me, is that 'morrow' bought?
'Tomorrow'? – *Postumus*, today's too late.
    The wise man, *Postumus*, lived yesterday.
PETER WHIGHAM

VI.82

He scanned me closely, Rufus, just as
Slaves by trainers are e'er purchased –
Sizing me up with eye and thumb.
Then: 'Are you Martial, you the one
Whose lewd wit delights all ears
Excepting those a Dutchman wears?'
A faint smile, an inclination,
Acknowledging the imputation.

1. Cerberus.

'Why then,' he said, 'the shabby clothes?'
'It's how a shabby poet goes.'   10
To shield me, where your poet goes,
Send, Rufus, some not shabby clothes.
                              PETER WHIGHAM

VII.14

Aulus, my girlfriend's in a dreadful plight:
She's lost her plaything, her supreme delight;
No trivial thing, like Lesbia's sorry fix,
Losing that sparrow she'd taught naughty tricks;[1]
Nor like Ianthis,[2] mourning her dead dove   5
(Read Stella) which performed such feats of love.
My girl is not upset by mundane matters;
It's not for nothing that her heart's in tatters.
She's lost a boy of twice-six years. The clinch is:
He had a penis nearing thrice-six inches.   10
                              ANTHONY REID

VII.47

Pre-eminent among scholars,
    whose accents speak of earlier days,
Sura is ours again (Fate smiles!) recalled
    with *Lethe's* waters all-but sipped . . .
Our prayers lacked hope, resignedly   5
    we wept, and tears were tears of loss:
Dis (odium to avoid) restored
    the unravelled distaff to the Fates.

---

1. An allusion to Catullus' famous poem on Lesbia's grief for her dead sparrow.
2. Ianthis was Stella's nickname for his mistress (and later wife) Violentilla.

Knowing the grief your false death caused,
    you've reaped, posthumously, your own fame.
Live snatched from death; seize fleet delight;
    waste not one day of life won back.
PETER WHIGHAM

IX.8

You gave Bithynicus thousands yearly; still
He left you not a penny in his will.
But don't be sad; you really score —
You needn't send him money any more.
J. P. SULLIVAN

IX.76

This was the young Camonus; this his face,
This each lithe limb.
Not twice ten years in ever-changing race
Could alter him,
Save that the manlier his beauty shone,
Until old Time
Looked on him enviously and wished him gone
Still in his prime.
Cruel, to cut the thread of his young years
Not fully spun!
Cruel, to draw a parent's fruitless tears
For youth undone!
But, lest this portrait be his only shrine,
Here on my page
A sweeter picture shall be drawn to shine
With his image.
BRIAN HILL

X.2

Slipshod writing, premature publication,
    brought Book X back for pumice work.
Much you'll recognize that's been refashioned;
    more that's new: smile, Reader, equally
On each – Reader, Patron, willed to me by *Rome*   5
    saying: 'No greater gift! Through him
You'll flee neglectful *Lethe's* stagnant flood –
    the better part of you'll survive.
Wild-fig rives the marble, heedless muleteers
    deride the busted steeds of bronze.   10
But verse no decrease knows, time adds to verse,
    deathless alone of monuments.'

                    PETER WHIGHAM

X.4

Read of *Thyestes*, *Oedipus*, dark suns,
    of *Scyllas*, *Medeas* – you read of freaks.
Hylas' rape . . .? *Attis* . . .? *Parthenopaeus* . . .?
    Endymion's dreams changed your life? The *Cretan*
Glider moulting feathers[1] . . .? *Hermaphroditus*? –   5
    averse to advances of *Salmacian* fount . . .
Why waste time on fantasy annals? Rather
    read my books, where Life cries: 'This is me!'
No *Centaurs* here; you'll meet no *Gorgons*, *Harpies*.
    My page tastes of man. Yet you're incurious   10
To view your morals, view yourself. Best stick
    to *Callimachus* – the mythic *Origins*.

                    PETER WHIGHAM

1. Icarus.

X.32

This portrait which I treasure so
Is Marcus painted long ago
When he was young and gay and fair,
Who now is old with silvered hair.

5   Would that the artist's brush could bind
In paint the beauties of his mind,
For then, I swear, the world today
No rarer picture could display.

BRIAN HILL

X.42

Irresolute the down upon your cheek,
    soft so sunlight or a breath of wind must
Bear it off. *Cydonian* quinces under
    a young girl's fingers lose their feathery bloom
5   And gleam. Five hard kisses, *Dindymus*, I
    press on you. Bearded from your lips mine come.

PETER WHIGHAM

X.47

My carefree Namesake,[1] this the art
Shall lead thee to life's happier part:

1. Julius Martialis.

A competence inherited, not won,
Productive acres and a constant home;

No courts, few formal days, your mind stable,   5
A native vigour in a healthy frame;

A tact in candour, friendships on a par,
Convivial courtesies, a plain table;

A night, not drunken, yet shall banish care,
A bed, not frigid, yet not one of shame;   10
A sleep that makes the dark hours shorter:

Prefer your state and hanker for none other,
Nor fear, nor seek to meet, your final hour.
                              PETER WHIGHAM

X.53

Rome, I am Scorpus, foremost in the race,
The short-lived darling of the populace;
Fate heard the long list of my victories told –
And cut me off thinking I must be old.
                              BRIAN HILL

X.61

Underneath this greedy stone,
Lies little sweet Erotion;
Whom the fates, with hearts as cold,
Nipt away at six years old.
Thou, whoever thou mayst be,
That hast this small field after me,
Let the yearly rites be paid
To her little slender shade;

So shall no disease or jar
Hurt thy house, or chill thy Lar;
But this tomb here be alone,
The only melancholy stone.

LEIGH HUNT

X.65

Since you, Charmenion, come from Corinth
    And I from quite another
Part of the world, from Tagus, tell me
    Why do you call me 'brother'?

You're Greek – my ancestors were Celts
    And Spaniards. Do we share
Some physical resemblances?
    Well, you have oily hair,

In ringlets – my stiff Spanish locks
    Are obstinately straight;
I'm shaggy-legged and bristle-cheeked –
    Daily you depilate

Your silky skin. Your voice is light;
    You lisp in a charming way –
My daughter strikes a stronger note.
    Enough! I'll simply say:

We're less alike than eagles and doves,
    Or lions and does, so Mister
Don't you call me 'brother', or
    I'll have to call you 'sister'.

DOROTHEA WENDER

X.66

Did he have eyes and, if so, did he look,
The fool who made fair Theopompus cook?
Could any man be mad enough to mar
Such lovely hair with kitchen soot and char?
What boy can take your place, and look divine   5
Pouring with graceful hand Falernian wine?
If perfect beauty was for this decreed,
Jove would have made a cook of Ganymede.

ANTHONY REID

XI.13

Traveller on the Flaminian Way,
Pause a little here, and stay
On this monument your eyes —
Here the actor, Paris, lies,
Delight of Rome, the wit of Nile,
All joy, all art, all grace, all style,
Of all the Roman theatre chief,   5
Its former joy and now its grief;
Nor for him only shed your tear —
Love and Desire lie with him here.

OLIVE PITT-KETHLEY

XI.16

Let every prudish reader use his feet
And bugger off — I write for the elite.
My verses gambol with Priapic verve
As dancing harlots' patter starts a nerve.

Though stern as Curius or like Fabricius,
5   Your prick will stiffen and grow vicious.
Girls, growing wet – even the chastest folk –
Will read each naughty word and dirty joke.
Lucretia blushes, throws away my book.
10   Her husband goes. She takes another look.

ANTHONY REID

XI.21

Lydia is as wide and slack
As a bronze horse's cul-de-sac,
Or sounding hoop with copper rings,
Or board from which an athlete springs,
Or swollen shoe from muddy puddle,
5   Or net of thrushes in a huddle,
Or awning that won't stay outspread,
In Pompey's theatre, overhead,
Or bracelet that, at every cough,
From a consumptive poof slips off,
French cushion, where the stuffing leaks,
Poor Breton's knackered, baggy breeks,
10   Foul pelican-crop, Ravenna-bred!
Now there's a rumour – he who said
I had her in the fish-pond joked;
It was the pond itself I poked.

OLIVE PITT-KETHLEY

XI.26

Cure of my unquietness
    object of my sighs,
Than whom within my arms
    none now dearer lies,

Yield kisses of *Falernian*,
   shared lip yield to lip
that from the reeking goblet
   Venus forth shall slip,   5
Then not *Jove* nor *Ganymede*
   shall, as we, enjoy
Themselves my sweetest cock-
   tail shaking wine-cup boy.
PETER WHIGHAM

XI.39

You rocked my cradle, Charidemus, once,
And played the guardian to the schoolboy dunce,
But now my barber's towel's black with beard;
By tender lips are my rough kisses feared.
But to you I've never grown up: just another one   5
Of the slaves in the fear-ridden household you run.
You allow me no licence for women or for sport:
You do what you like – I must do what I ought.
You chide and you spy, you sigh and complain;
Your anger keeps eyeing that juvenile cane.   10
If I smell of perfume, or dress up for a show,
You protest that my father would never act so.
With twitching brow, you count the cups I pour,
As though each drop came from your private store.
No more of it, ex-slave! You carp – I'll rage!   15
My mistress will tell you – I've now come of age.
J. P. SULLIVAN

XI.104

Out of the house or be the wife I want:
Numa's moral code was never mine.

I spin out dinner with a string of toasts,
    you leave us early, glum on mineral water.
5 You like the bed-light off, I like it on:
    I get my rocks off with a lamp watching.
You'd have it partly dressed – in bra and slip:
    naked, no girl lies nude enough for me.
I ask for kisses soft as *Venus'* doves,
10   your peck is like the family kiss at breakfast.
You will not stoop to stir with mouth or finger
    but come to bed as you would go to church.

When *Hector's* wife makes use of *Hector's* horse,
    the *Phrygian* slaves jack-off behind the door.
15 *Odysseus* snores, but chaste *Penelope*
    learnt long ago to use her hand at night.
You jib at sodomy, yet *Cornelia*,
    Portia and *Julia* served their husbands thus
20 (and *Juno, Jove*, before young *Ganymede*,
    the sweet *Dardanian* cocktail-shaker came).
Hug your propriety. You have my leave –
    be Lucrèce *to the world by day*,
    but Lais *in the night to me*.
                PETER WHIGHAM

XII.18

While unquiet, *Juvenal*, you haunt
The shrill *Subura* or loiter
On *Dian's Aventine* . . . while your
5 Damp toga flaps round great men's doors . . .
While you grow worn with mounting now
The big, the little *Caelian* – I
These winters late, revisiting my
Bilbilis (replete with gold and iron)
10 Have been accepted . . . countrified.

Here lazily are trips (sweet chores)
To *Platea, Boterdus*. (Ah,
These *Celtiberian* vocables!)
. . . Indulging in inordinate
Amounts of sleep – past nine or ten –
That's paying myself back, in full,   15
For thirty years of lack of it.
Togas are unheard of . . . a quilt
From some disused sedan will serve.
Rising, I've a log fire greet me,
Fed handsomely from neighbouring oak.   20
My maid drapes it with cooking pots.
The hunting boy comes in – he's one
Some bosky dell would set you lusting.
My steward gives the houseboys food,
Pleads: May he wear his long locks shorter?   25
These my aids to living, aids to death.

PETER WHIGHAM

XII.34

Just half our three score years and ten
I mind me, *Julius*, spent with thee,
The bitter and blessèd blent –
The bless'd preponderant.

          Count here,
There, the parti-coloured pebbles:[1]   5
White beats the black!

          If sorrow's ruth
Thou'dst void, her heart-bite parry,
Caution in comradeship be thine: 10
Less sorrow, as less joy, thou'lt know.

PETER WHIGHAM

---

1. Romans marked lucky and unlucky days with white and black pebbles or counters.

XII.61

Ligurra's fearful I'll contrive
Some pungent piece, some sprightly ditty
And longs to be considered worth it.
Longings baseless! Baseless fears!
5   The *Libyan* lion paws the *Libyan* bull
But does not bat the butterfly.
What people write of you you'll find
In dismal dives where sodden poets
10 Scrawl their rhymes on toilet walls.
Your forehead shan't disgrace my brand.

                    PETER WHIGHAM

STATIUS

INTRODUCTION

Publius Papinius Statius grew up in a highly cultured Graeco-Roman environment. His father was the owner and headmaster of a successful school in Greek-speaking Naples, where Statius was born about A.D. 45 and returned to die in A.D. 96. The school placed a particular emphasis on Greek literature and the father was himself a noted 'Greek' poet, who won prizes at the Pythian, Nemean and Isthmian games. Statius was presumably bilingual. From the mid-sixties onwards much of Statius' life was spent in Rome, where the young poet would have experienced the bloody political and social convolutions of the civil wars of A.D. 68/69, when within approximately eighteen months the Roman world endured five successive emperors, Nero, Galba, Otho, Vitellius, and finally Vespasian, founder of the (short-lived) Flavian dynasty. The final phase of the war formed the subject of one of his father's poems (see *Silvae*, V.3.197–206). By the time of the last Flavian emperor, Domitian (A.D. 81–96), Statius was one of the capital's leading literary figures; the popularity of his recitations is attested even by the enemies of epic (Juvenal, *Satire* VII.82–6). Some of Statius' success has been attributed to his sycophancy towards Domitian, apparently eulogized in several works (e.g. *Thebaid* I.16ff., *Silvae* IV.2). But as in Lucan's encomium on Nero (*Civil War* I.33ff.), fulsome imperial flattery clothes ironic, even mordant verse. All Statius' surviving works are relatively late. His major work, *Thebaid*, an epic in twelve books, took twelve years to write and was published in A.D. 91 or 92. The first three books of *Silvae* or 'Impromptu Pieces' were published in A.D. 94 and the fourth in the following year. He also left behind an unfinished epic, *Achilleid*, and a fifth book of *Silvae*, published posthumously.

Thebaid is a dark, brooding, pessimistic poem. Modelling itself overtly on the Virgilian canon of mythological narrative epic, it expresses a vision as politically pointed as that of its Augustan predecessor, and as despairing as that of Lucan. Its subject is the conflict between the sons of Oedipus over the throne of Thebes, which embroils the cities of Argos and Thebes in a devastating, mutually destructive war. After the demise of Oedipus the throne of Thebes falls to his sons, Eteocles and Polyneices, who agree to rule in alternate years. When after the first year Eteocles refuses to yield power to Polyneices, the latter, who has married into the royal house of Argos, receives the help of the Argive king Adrastus and his people to take the throne by force. The ensuing war between brothers, the most famous ancient mythic paradigm of civil war, had been treated extensively in Graeco-Roman tragedy and epic and had recently been used by Lucan with explicit reference to Rome (*Civil War* I.550ff., IV.559ff.). The second half of *Thebaid*, Books VII-XII, focuses entirely on this 'civil' war – a war which, as the poem makes clear even in its opening lines, raises issues of both universal and contemporary (Roman) import (see especially I.15–22, 150–62, and the programmatic recall of Lucan in the epic's first two words). And *Thebaid*'s presentation of these issues is not designed to comfort. For the epic's account of the war, its preceding events, its aftermath, articulates a world characterized by malevolence and injustice both human and divine, by blood, death, suffering and the naked lust for power – power which the poem defines as, and restricts to, the ability to inflict death. Human limitation and pain are plangently underscored, so too the ever widening spiral of causality that transforms bystander into victim and innocent observers into active participants in bloody war. Two things especially stand out: the abuse of monarchal power and the inability of the human species to resist the impulse to kill. Or rather one thing. For the abuse of monarchal power by figures such as Eteocles in *Thebaid* II and III (relevance to Domitianic Rome is here almost overt) is presented as *exemplum* of the same ungovernable instinct evident in the orgiastic butchery of the seer Thiodamas in Book X. *Thebaid* X in fact, which deals with the last part of the fighting before the issue is settled by a personal duel between the brothers, is almost unrelieved in its concentration on blood, suffering and human futility. Particularly prominent is the malevolence of the gods, who arrange for the slaughter of the sleeping Thebans (Juno: X.80–346) and even provide light to assist the killing (X.282ff.), or deceive the naïve and courageous (X.661ff.) into thinking their death will end the carnage. One of Book X's most telling touches is that it commences with Jupiter's lack of pity and ambiguous sadness (X.2f.) and concludes with his laughter before he hurls the fatal bolt (X.907). Against divine laughter is set a mother's piercing cry (X.792–826), that points up the futility of youth's self-sacrifice, even as it arraigns the cruelty of gods. Dark reflection of continuing Roman realities, *Thebaid*'s mythic narrative numbs.

Of course Jupiter was the great divinity of Rome's so-called 'national epic', *Aeneid*, which, like Lucan's *Civil War* (lauded in *Silvae* II.7), serves as a sub-text throughout the poem. In the epilogue to *Thebaid* XII (816–17) Statius is quite explicit about following in Virgil's footsteps and nowhere is this clearer than in Book X, which features a sustained example of creative allusion, the Hopleus and Dymas episode of 347–448. Here the pointed reference at the conclusion of the episode (X.445–8) to Virgil's Euryalus and Nisus (*Aeneid* IX.314–449) not only signals the historicity of the issues with which *Thebaid* deals and their specific relevance to Rome, but directs the reader to attend to similarities and differences in the two episodes and in their implied world-view (in Virgil Euryalus and Nisus kill and are killed, in Statius Hopleus and Dymas do not kill but are killed anyway; those who do kill, Thiodamas and others, return victorious to the Argive camp). For *Thebaid*'s self-conscious projection of itself as Virgilian palimpsest is as much critique of Virgil as acknowledgement of indebtedness. *Thebaid*'s world is more brutal and more horrific than that of *Aeneid*. The former's baroque, theatrical, mannerist, luxuriant, at times hyperbolic style (often contemned) entexts the nightmare of its different world – and age. Bizarre, grotesque slaughter (e.g. X.296–325, 515–18, 554f.) and the theatrics of transfiguration in death (X.921ff.) speak directly to a society that made of death – both within and outside the gladiatorial arena – a form of theatre.

A brief description of the content of *Thebaid* X may be useful. The book opens as night falls and warriors on both sides leave the bloodied battlefield and its burden of weapons, horses and corpses (1–10). Exhorted by their king, Eteocles, the Thebans besiege the Argive camp (11–48). The scene switches to Argos, where the women of the city request the goddess Juno's aid in the destruction of Thebes (49–70). Juno responds by sending Iris to the cave of the god Sleep to solicit his assistance, which he promptly gives by descending onto the battlefield and overcoming the besieging Theban force (71–159). The Argive seer Thiodamas incites his comrades to attack the sleeping Thebans and avenge the death of the former seer of the army, Amphiaraus, who visited Thiodamas in a dream (160–218). Thirty are chosen to perform the butchery and with Juno's help Thiodamas, Agylleus, Actor and others kill the sleeping soldiers (219–346). The Argive warriors, Hopleus and Dymas, rescue the unburied bodies of their respective kings but are killed in the process (347–448). The Argives advance on Thebes and attack (449–551). Panic, fear and grief break out in the city; the blind seer Tiresias is approached, who prophesies victory with the death of 'the last-born of the brood of dragon's teeth', viz. Menoeceus, Creon's son (552–627). Valour descends and, disguised as Tiresias' daughter Manto, exhorts Menoeceus to perform the fatal act, from which his father Creon fails to dissuade him (628–737). The Argive warrior Capaneus begins a devastating attack upon Thebes (738–55). Menoeceus commits suicide; his mother laments (756–826). Capaneus increases his assault upon the city, overcomes all Theban resistance and challenges the gods. Transfixed by Jupiter's thunderbolt he blazes to his death (827–936).

Silvae seems a different world. Personal, urbane, witty, at times ludic, the five books of 'Impromptu Pieces' set themselves on the surface a predominantly epideictic task and exploit a wide variety of literary genres and forms in its realization. Included in the selection here are a *eucharistikon* or 'Thank You' poem (IV.2) apparently glorifying the emperor Domitian, an *epicedion* or 'Lamentation' (V.3) in memory of Statius' father, a descriptive (I.6) and a bantering (IV.9) poem in hendecasyllabics reminiscent of Catullus and Martial, and the famous 'sonnet' to Sleep (V.4). IV.2,

V.3, V.4 were written in dactylic hexameters, the metre of *Thebaid* and the most common metre of *Silvae*. The poem in memory of his father (V.3) is an important document of literary history and provides invaluable details concerning the life and career of a 'Greek' professional poet in the middle of the first century A.D. It is the longest poem in the five books and one of the best and most carefully structured – its strength of thinking and feeling a function of its evocative, controlled detail and stringent form. Similarly punctilious in its descriptive detail but also deft in its control of nuance and hyperbole – and more complex in the demands it makes of its readers – is the encomium on Domitian (IV.2), a text that has been seriously misread. Many still find evidence in this poem for the conventional view of Statius as imperial bootlicker. The poem is in fact a paradigm of ironic eulogy. From Virgil onwards imperial panegyric was a necessary and complex discourse more often defined by latent, critical irony than self-seeking adulation: the mode of double-speak in an age of tyranny. The poet who indicted the abuse of monarchal power in *Thebaid* was under no illusions about Domitian.

A.J.B.

Further Reading

Ahl, F. M., 'Statius' *Thebaid*: A Reconsideration', *Aufstieg und Niedergang der römischen Welt* 32.5 (1986) 2803–912.

Boyle, A. J. (ed.), *The Imperial Muse: Flavian Epicist to Claudian* (Berwick, Victoria, 1990). Essays on Statius and Flavian epic by W. J. Dominik, P. Hardie, D. E. Hill, and D. McGuire.

Hardie, A., *Statius and the Silvae* (Liverpool 1983).

Marastoni, A. (ed.), *P. Papini Stati Silvae* (Leipzig 1961).

Vessey, D., *Statius and the Thebaid* (Cambridge 1973).

Williams, R. D. (ed.), *P. Papini Stati Thebaidos Liber Decimus* (Leiden 1972).

THEBAID

BOOK X

Translated by Norman Austin and Ruth Morse

Damp night overwhelmed Phoebus at the western gates,
sped by Jove, who pitied neither Pelasgian camp
nor Theban forces, though saddened by so much waste
by the sword of their allies and the undeserving.
On the outstretched plain, fouled with huge amounts of blood,

5 they leave behind weapons, horses, abandoned limbs,
the pyre-deprived corpses of those who moved so proudly.
Then, with tattered flags, the inglorious, weakened rout
withdraw their lines; and gates too narrow for the crowds
as they left for battle, gape wide at their return.

10 Though both sides grieve equally, yet Thebes takes comfort
that four Argive bands wander leaderless:[1]
like ships deprived of helmsmen through huge seas,
alderwood governed by god, chance, and the tempest.
So the Tyrian spirit bursts out of their own walls

15 to follow their enemies' flight, lest by good fortune
they regain Mycenae; the password gives the message
to the sentries changing guard. To lead the night strike
are Meges (by lot) and Lycus (by his own will).
To the troops come arms, food, and fire; the king[2] urges them:

20 'Conquerors of the Argives, dawn is not far off
and the dark which saved the terrified will not last.
Keep your spirits and your hearts worthy of the gods

---

1. The reference is to the deaths of Amphiaraus (VII.794ff.), Tydeus (VIII.716ff.),
   Hippomedon (IX.446ff.) and Parthenopaeus (IX.841ff.). See below, lines 24–8.
2. Eteocles.

222

who favour you. Argos has lost all its glory
with its leadership: into avenging Tartarus   25
has sunk Tydeus; Death marvels at the untouched seer;[1]
Ismenos' stream swells with Hippomedon's rich spoils;
Parthenopaeus we exclude for shame from the count.
The prize is in our grasp, these proud war captains are gone,
gone the crests of the seven leaders of war bands.   30
What have we to fear in the madness of battle?
Adrastus' age? worse, my brother's youth? Capaneus?[2]
So go, surround the besieged with vigilant flames.
Fear nothing from the enemy, whose booty and wealth
are already yours.' Exhorting the fierce Thebans,   35
he fills with pleasure at recounting their past battles.
Just as they are (their limbs still caked with dust, blood, and
         sweat)
they retrace their steps; scarcely pausing to speak,
or embrace, or clasp the hands of their fellows,
they shake them off. Then sharing out front, rear, and flank,   40
curving completely around the ramparts, they ring them
with hostile fires. So ravening wolves form a pack
at dusk; from the whole countryside long starvation
has leaned them, then opened their mouths with reckless daring.
Already pressing the sheepfold, frustrated hope   45
at the frightened bleats and smell of fat twists their jaws.
They manage only to break their claws and bruise their chests
against the strong stakes, grinding dry teeth on the gates.
Meanwhile, in distant Argos, women gather,
suppliant at the threshold of the temple,   50
prostrate before ancestral altars, imploring
sceptre-bearing Juno[3] for aid and their men's return,
and they press their faces to the painted doors
and cold stones, and teach small children to bend in prayer.

---

1. Amphiaraus, augur and seer of the army, swallowed by the earth at the end of
   Book VII.
2. Adrastus, Polyneices and Capaneus combine with the four lost leaders to make
   up the famous 'Seven'.
3. Patron deity of Argos.

55   Day is laid to rest with prayers, fresh night brings its cares,
the vigilant altars are heaped high with flames.
Their gift is a robe of marvellous fabric –
no barren woman, none parted from her husband
helped make it; the garment, brought in a basket,

60   cannot be rejected by the chaste goddess;
embroidered with purple, its patterns blaze with gold:
she herself was there, about to wed the Thunderer,
innocent, she timidly sets sisterhood aside;
her eyes lowered, she lightly kisses youthful Jove,

65   trusting, not yet outraged by infidelity.
The Argives clothe the holy ivory statue,
then these mothers petition with tears and complaints:
'Queen of starry heaven, look at the citadel
of the sacrilegious Cadmean whore,[1] her defiant

70   tomb – destroy them with another thunderbolt!'
What can she do, knowing Fate opposes her Argives,
and Jove against them? Yet she would not have great gifts
and prayers be in vain. Then Fortune brings the chance
of powerful help. From the sky above she sees

75   the gates tight shut, the ramparts kept by watchful guards;
stung by goads of rage, she shakes the sacred diadem
from her mane of hair, no less angry than when
she blazed alone in heaven at the doubled night
when Jove made Alcmene Hercules' mother.

80   She plans to destroy the Thebans, entangling them
in the sweet timelessness of sleep. She sends Iris
to put on her rainbow, and tells her the whole task.
The shining goddess obeys and descends to earth,
suspended high by the arch as she leaves heaven.

85   West above night's cloudy couch, and the other
Ethiopia,[2] lies a still forest, opaque
to starlight; below hollow cliffs a gloomy cave
opens deep into the mountain. Here, lazily,

1. Semele, daughter of Cadmus, the founder of Thebes, and mother of the god
Bacchus by Jupiter, the fire of whose thunderbolt killed her.
2. The western Ethiopia (as against that of the south-east).

Nature set the palace and safe home of idle Sleep.
Shady Rest and slow Forgetfulness guard the door   90
and torpid Languor never stirs his face to wake.
In the porch Inaction and Silence sit mute, their wings
tightly folded; they repel rough winds from the roofs,
stop the branches swaying and the birds' coo and beat.
Though all other shores are clamorous, here no sea sounds   95
nor thunder; even the river breaks near the cave
down rocks and boulders, soundless from the valley.
Here the herds are black, whole flocks are recumbent,
new buds wither, and the earth's breath droops the grass.
Flame-smith Mulciber decorated the inside: 100
a thousand pictures of the god, here Pleasure clings,
garlanded, there Sleep's companion, Toil, nods off,
there Bacchus, there Cupid, son of Mars, shares his couch.
Hidden deeper in the dwelling, he lies with Death –
but nobody sees this miserable vision.   105
Such are the pictures. The god lies under dewy vaults,
somnolent, drugged by pillows stuffed with flowers;
rugs breathe scent; under his supine body, cushions
are warm; dark vapour rises from his open mouth;
one hand pushes curls off his forehead, the other   110
releases his forgotten chalice. Attending him
stand the countless faces of errant Dreams: true, false,
mingled together, like waters seething with flames.
Night's dark mob cling to ceiling and doorpost, they lie
on the ground. A pale and feeble glow surrounds   115
the palace, flickering lights welcome early sleep,
even their flames fall back and are extinguished.

  Down through the Caerulean sped the rich-hued goddess.
Radiant woods and shady valleys smile upon
the goddess, and smitten with her glowing beams,   120
the house awakens; except the god himself –
not her shining, neither sound nor voice arouse him.
He slept on until all the Thaumantian's splendour
shot deep and penetrated his unmoving eyes.
The golden maker of storm-clouds began to speak: 125

'Sleep, gentlest of all gods, Juno exhorts you: bind
the Sidonian leaders, and fierce Cadmus' people
who watch the Argive camp in ceaseless vigil;
swollen with the day's victory, they resist your power.
130 Answer this urgent prayer – it is rare to be able
to satisfy Jove and keep Juno on your side.'
While she spoke her right hand beat on his sleepy breast
lest he ignore her; she pressed him again and again.
He accepted her commands, his nodding unchanged,
135 and Iris, heavy-eyed from his dark cave, left him
and raised her radiance, dulled by so much rain.

      He, too, bestirred his winged step and windswept forehead,
and filled his swirling cloak with chilly dark sky.
Floating through air on his silent course, from far
140 he brought drowsiness to loom over Theban fields.
At his breath birds and beasts, wild or tame, stretch on the
            ground,
wherever his flight passes, in the furthest regions,
the seas sink down limp from the rocks, sluggish clouds cling,
the topmost crests of the forests droop, and even
145 many stars slip from the loosened grasp of the sky.
The battlefield first sensed the god by a sudden fog;
numberless voices and noises of men hush,
and then he bears down with his damp wings on the camp;
pitch-black shadow darker than ever, he comes there.
150 The soldiers' eyes wander, their heads grow heavier,
in mid-conversation words are left unfinished.
Soon they let both their gleaming shields and brutal spears
fall from their hands and their tired heads droop on their chests.
Now all is silent. Horses themselves refuse to stand,
155 even the fires are extinguished to sudden ash.
But Sleep brings no such rest to the fearful Argives.
The night-wandering god's sweet force keeps his mists away
from the adjacent camp where they all stand to arms,
furious at the shameful night, the arrogant guards.
160   Now, suddenly, horror seizes Thiodamas,
the gods press him to frenzy, in fear and tumult

reveal what must happen – whether the urge begins
with Saturn's daughter[1] or good Apollo to his priest.
He leaps into their midst, frightening to see and hear,
scarcely bearing the god, his frail mind unable   165
to contain him: the torments which gush from his stark mad face
distend and drain his cheeks, trembling with throbbing blood.
His eyes dart here and there, the garlands twisted
in his hair shake loose and beat against his neck.
Thus the Idean Mother[2] pulls from her horrid shrine   170
a bloodstained Phrygian, making him disregard
his arms all slashed with knives. He thrashes holy pine-brands
on his chest, shakes his bloody hair, outrunning
his wounds. The countryside and the gory cult-tree
quiver, astonished lions rear her chariot high.   175

He enters the inner council room, sacred home
of the standards, where Adrastus desperately
ponders the sickening sequence of disasters.
Newly promoted captains surround him, each post
filled by the next successor to the slain great kings,   180
not joyful, but grieving to have been raised so high.
So when in mid-voyage a ship loses her helmsman,
the guardian of the decks or the sea-cutting prow
takes the empty tiller, but the ship hesitates,
her tackle slow to follow – she will not assent   185
to obey a lesser master. The prophet spoke,
and so stimulated the fearful Argives,
'Commanders, I bring weighty orders from the gods
and awful warnings. These words come not from my own heart,
but his whose fillets I wear,[3] his whom I serve   190
as your trust obliged me, and as he consented.
This night portends an act of splendid deception.
Divine auguries invite us, courage calls us,

---

1. Juno.
2. Cybele, the great mother-goddess of Asia Minor.
3. Thiodamas refers to Amphiaraus, whom he has succeeded as Argive seer and
   priest.

and Fortune demands valour. Sleep has stupefied
195 the Theban army. It is time to avenge dead kings
and the day's grief. Take up your arms and go smash down
the hindering gates. They will light our comrades' pyres,
bury our friends. Today, while our strength was repulsed
and as we were beaten back – by the tripods I swear,
200 by the strange fate of my lord, so suddenly lost –
the birds I watched beat round me were favourable.
Now my belief is secure. For now Amphiaraus
rose again from the chasm and came to me –
just as he was, only his team marked by the depths.
205 These are not meaningless dreams – I was not asleep –
I speak of portents revealed. He spoke: "Unworthy!
Will you permit the idle sons of Inachus
to waste such a great night? Give back my Parnassus
garlands, and give back my gods. Did I teach you
210 heaven's secret ways and wandering flights? Come on, then,
at least, avenge me with the sword!" He seemed to lift
his spear, to force me with his chariot to these doors.
Act now, use the gods' favour – no killing hand-to-hand
but while they sleep – here is the chance to destroy them.
215 Who will go? None reluctant, only those who seek fame
while the Fates allow it. See again the birds of night –
favourable! I'll go, and even if none of you
follow, I'll go alone! He shakes his reins, and comes!'
    Shouting so, he disrupted the quiet night. They went,
220 as if one god inspired them all, the leaders
burning for his enterprise to unite their luck.
On his orders three groups of ten, the flower
of the bands, were chosen, while around him indignant
youths objected to staying in camp in idle
225 cowardice. Demanding the chance, calling high birth,
high deeds, their own, their men's, shouting for lots to be drawn,
they make Adrastus exult amid the disasters.
So on Mt Pholoe the breeder of fleet horses
rejoices to see the fecund spring renew his herd:
230 some leap up the steepest slopes, some swim swift rivers,

while others race their parents. Then his mind ponders
which should be broken gently to bear the yoke,
which have strong backs, which were born for battle cries,
and which will grow to win the palm of Elis.
The long-lived leader of the Argives thought this way,   235
and rose to the task: 'Where have you appeared from at last,
you gods who return so late to broken Argos?
Is this the courage in the face of disaster
whose spirit survives in us despite adversity?
I praise your nobility, young men, and rejoice   240
in this great scheme: but in covert action a crowd
cannot be secret enough to spring a hidden trap.
Keep up your spirits until the avenging day,
when we will all take arms openly against them.'
At length the young men quieten and reign their spirits in,   245
as if he were father Aeolus, in command
of his cave's tumult, forcing a boulder across
the door to restrain winds which already seek the sea.

   The seer takes Agylleus, son of Hercules,
who boasted he was as strong, as well as Actor,   250
equally skilled in speech, to lead the groups of ten,
who would have terrified Thebes in open combat.
Because he shares this novel martial deception
he removes the sacred wreath,[1] Apollo's insignia,
entrusting his brow's glory to the aged leader,   255
and puts on Polyneices' welcome gift of armour.
Wild Capaneus invests Actor with his great sword –
not stooping himself to take part in deception
even to follow the gods against the enemy.
Agylleus takes the weapons of fierce Nomius,   260
since in the dark Hercules' bow gives no advantage.
Then, lest loud groans from the camp's bronze gates betray them,
they leap from the ramparts' projecting battlements.
Ahead of them numberless prey lie on the ground
as if already dead, transfixed by many swords.   265

---

1. The laurel wreath sacred to Apollo, god of seers.

'Go, comrades, where the pleasure of unending killing
leads – I beg you, be worthy of the gods' favour.'
Now the priest loudly urges them: 'Look, they're laid out
by cohorts in disgusting stupor. For shame!
270 Are these the men who dared besiege the Argive gates,
did these men watch our heroes?' He speaks, and draws his
    sword,
like lightning, with rapid killing strokes, flashes across
their lines. Who can number the dead, or name them?
He attacks – as if at random – backs and chests
275 and leaves a wake of groans stifled by helmets,
mingling departing spirits with their own life-blood.
Here lies one stretched abandoned on his bed, here one
yields late, and topples feebly armed onto his shield.
Here in company between drink and arms they lie,
280 here leaning on shields, just as ill-fated Sleep
tied them down, the last darkness overwhelms them.
A god is present. Armed Juno lifts a lunar torch
in her right hand to strengthen their resolve and show
where the bodies lie. Thiodamas feels her presence
285 but silently conceals his joy. Already his hand
slows, already his stroke weakens, and glutted
with success, his fury begins to diminish.
So a Caspian tigress, in slaughtering great bulls,
finds her rage appeased by huge amounts of blood,
290 and her jaws tire; fouled with thick gore, and her stripes
disfigured, she looks at her work, regretting
that hunger fails. So the seer wanders, exhausted
by slaughtering Thebans. He wants a hundred arms,
a hundred hands to fight with – now he tires of
295 squandered challenges to the enemy to rise.
    Elsewhere great Hercules' son destroys sleep-sodden
Sidonians, and elsewhere Actor; each leads on bloodstained track.
The darkening grass congeals, covered by pools of gore,
tents bow down under streams of blood, the ground steams,
300 and the breath of sleep becomes the gasp of death.
None of them lying there raised his eyes or his face.

The winged god[1] brooded over their fate with such darkness
that their eyes opened only as they lay dying.
Alert Ialmenus, now never to see the dawn,
had played his lyre to the last stars, singing the paean   305
of Thebes. The god pressed his weakened neck to the left,
and his head lay heedlessly against the lyre.
Agylleus thrust a sword through his chest and impaled
his right hand, ready-poised on the hollow lyre-shell,
his fingers quivering on the strings. The tables are   310
swept with a terrible liquid — juices mixed with blood
drip on every side, flow back into bowls and cup.
Wild Actor seizes Thamyris, who lies tangled
with his brother; Tagus stabs garlanded Echetlus
in the back; Danaus cuts off Hebrus' head: 315
Fate takes him unaware, his cheerful life flees down
to the dark, saved from the sorrows of wild Death.
Calpetus lay on the cold ground under the wheels
of his team, who cropped their native Theban grass, disturbed
by his snores. His drink-sodden mouth overflows, and wine   320
inflames his restless sleep. Here, the Inachian priest
slashes his throat — the wine spurts in a gush of blood,
blood cuts off his stertorous breath. Perhaps his stupor
prophesied, and in dismaying dreams he saw
Thiodamas and the desolation of Thebes.   325

   The fourth period of somnolent night had come,
when the dew has fallen and some stars' splendour fades,
and Bootes flees at the breath of a greater team.
Now their work slows, prescient Actor calls Thiodamas:
'The Argives have had enough unexpected joy.   330
I think almost none of this great army has escaped
savage slaughter, except a cowardly few
whose base instincts hid them beneath the flow of blood.
Place limits on success — harsh Thebes, too, has her gods,
and perhaps even now our protecting gods depart.'   335
He obeyed, raising his drenched hands towards the stars:

---

1. Sleep, often depicted in literature and art as winged.

'Phoebus, to you I dedicate these night-promised
victories; I sacrifice, uncleansed by water,
as fierce soldier and trusted priest at your tripods.
340 If I have not disgraced your commands, if I bore
your burden, come often, often constrain my mind.
Though now your prize is crude – shattered arms and soldiers'
     blood –
if, Argive Paean, I regain my ancestral home
and its beloved temples, demand this vow from me:
345 rich gifts and as many bulls for your sacred shine.'
He spoke, then recalled his joyous companions in arms.
    Among their number – by the will of Fate – have come
Calydon's Hopleus and Maenalian Dymas,
both beloved companions of their kings, whose deaths
350 make them scorn life. First Hopleus stirs the Arcadian:
'Is there no further office to your slaughtered king,[1]
whom birds and Theban dogs perhaps already tear?
What will you Arcadians take home? Think, when you go,
of meeting his stern mother, who demands his remains.
355 Tydeus still rages unburied in my heart –
though he had endured longer in the field than one
whose early cutting off is more worthy of tears.
We must go back to the dreadful battlefield
and search for them, even thrusting into Thebes.'
360 Dymas interrupted: 'I swear by the moving stars,
by the lost spirit of my king, like a god to me,
the same grief I feel, my prostrate mind has long sought
a helper, but now I shall lead the way.' He moves off,
and turning his sad face to the sky he speaks:
365 'Cynthian Diana, ruler of secret night,
if it be true your divinity can take three forms,[2]
and you can come down to the woods in changed guise,
now at least look down upon the one we search for,

---

1. The young king Parthenopaeus, whose death concludes the preceding book.
  2. As goddess of the moon, the hunt and the underworld (Hecate).

your forest companion, famous pupil and servant.'[1]
The goddess brings the chariot of her kind star down   370
to illuminate the corpses with her crescent.
The plain, and Thebes, and high Cithaeron appeared.
Thus, when Jupiter cracks the night sky with thunder,
the clouds part and at the flash the stars shine out,
and suddenly the whole world is revealed to the eyes.   375
Dymas catches the beam, and by the same light Hopleus
is thrilled to find Tydeus; rejoicing, they signal
across the night, and each lifts the weight to his back
as if his friend returned to life from a cruel death.
They do not dare either to speak, or to weep, for long;   380
cruel daylight lurks and the revealing dawn threatens.
They go silent with long steps through the gloomy quiet
and grieve as the growing light finishes the dark.

        Fate is hostile to duty, and fortune seldom
favours the brave. They feel themselves safe home,   385
their burdens lighten, when suddenly behind them
dust and a noise loom. Given orders to scout the night
and watchful camp, keen Amphion[2] presses his horsemen;
across the pathless plain he first sees something strange
(although light had not yet dispelled the shadows)   390
in the distance, corpses moving; nearing, he spots
the deception and shouts, 'Halt, whoever you are!'
But it's clear they are enemies – the unlucky
ones speed on, not afraid for themselves. He threatens death,
then flings his spear over them, aiming too high,   395
as though his grip were faulty. It lands by Dymas,
who happens to be in front, and he stops walking.
Courageous Aepytus, disdaining to waste his throw,
hits Hopleus in the back; the spear cuts through him
and pins Tydeus to him by a hanging limb.   400
Hopleus slid down, not yet forgetting his great
leader, and expires still holding him, and so

1. Parthenopaeus was the son of Diana's companion, Atalanta, and was furnished
   with quiver and arrows by the goddess herself (IV.256ff.).
2. This is the son of Amphion (X.787, 873) whose music built the walls of Thebes.

descends fortunate to the cruel shades, since
if the body was lost, he would never know.
405 Dymas sees this behind him, sees the group of soldiers,
and turns, uncertain whether to proceed with arms
or prayers; anger says fight, misfortune orders him
to pray and take no risk, but neither inspires faith.
Anger rejects prayer. He lays the sad corpse before him
410 and over his left arm twists the heavy tiger's hide
which by chance he had worn on his back. Now he
stands his ground, making his drawn sword a barrier;
he turns to confront all spears, to kill or be killed.
Alert as a lioness who protects her young
415 when hunting Numidians trap her in her fierce lair,
whose mind is torn, growling savage and pitiful –
her bite could smash through spears and sow confusion,
but love of her cubs overwhelms her cruel feelings,
and in the midst of her rage she looks around at them.
420 And now, although Amphion forbade violence,
they grab the young king's left hand and pull him along,
face upwards, by the hair. Too late a suppliant,
with lowered sword Dymas begs at last: 'Take him gently,
I pray you, by the cradle of lightning-born Bacchus,
425 by Ino's flight, by your Palaemon's tender years.
If by chance any of you delight in your children,
or fatherhood, give this youth a handful of dust
and a lowly pyre. Look! with upturned face he begs you.
Better leave me to sate the disgust of beasts and birds,
430 since I am the one who forced him to risk battle.'
'If,' says Amphion, 'you want so much to bury your king,
tell me the battle-plan of the timid Argives,
what intentions broken feeble men can have. Be quick,
and you may have life, and your leader's burial.'
435 The Arcadian shudders, then drives his sword hilt-deep
in his chest: 'Stricken Argos lacked only treason
and dishonour as her final catastrophe.
Nothing is worth this price, nor would he buy burial.'
So speaking, he throws himself, chest gouged open,

over the youth, and with his last breath murmurs,   440
'Let me be your sepulchre and your companion.'
So both the Aetolian and the renowned Arcadian
breathe out their noble souls in the long-sought embrace
of their kings, and their great hearts delight in death.

  Though my songs rise from a less distinguished lyre,   445
you are deathless, conquering the memory of years:
Euryalus shall not spurn your company,
and Trojan Nisus welcome your share of glory.[1]

  Fierce Amphion triumphs: he sends men back to inform
his king of the failed raid, taking the captured bodies;   450
then he outrages the trapped Pelasgians
by exhibiting their companions' severed heads.
Meanwhile, from the top of their wall, the Argives watch
Thiodamas return, and give their joy free rein.
When they see all the drawn swords and spears reddened   455
with recent slaughter, then fresh shouts fill the great sky,
and the soldiers hang greedily over the walls,
searching for their friends, like an expectant crowd
of nestlings who glimpse their mother flying back
and want to meet her, and hang open-mouthed from the rim   460
until with chiding wings their loving mother
saves them from tumbling with her soft protecting breast.
But as they recount their hidden deeds of mute Mars
and satisfy their friends with cheerful embraces,
they complain that Hopleus and Dymas are late.   465
Now Amphion, swift leader of the Theban squadron,
rides near, and when he sees the recent slaughter,
the earth writhing with uncounted bands whose people
gape in universal ruin, his own joy vanishes.
He shudders at the sight like a man struck by lightning   470
and under the weight of horror, he loses
his voice, sight, and strength. As he begins to groan,
his horse turns of its own accord, the squadron flees.

---

1. The poet alludes to the Euryalus and Nisus episode of Virgil's *Aeneid* (IX.314–
449), which his own Hopleus and Dymas episode 'rewrites'.

They had not reached the gates of Thebes, when already
475   the Argive army, exploiting the night's success,
pours onto the field, with their horses, across
gory weapons and limbs, rushes over ground fouled
with dead and dying. Heavy hooves crush the bodies, while
blood washes the wheels and impedes the hurrying troops.
480   The men find this road sweet, as if they proudly trampled
Sidonian homes in Thebes herself with bloody feet.
Capaneus exhorts them: 'Enough hidden courage.
Now let daylight witness a fine victory for us.
Go with me, men, raise dust openly and shout.
485   I, too, have prophetic omens for my right arm
and a terrifying frenzy when my sword is drawn.'
While keen Adrastus and Polyneices fire their men,
the now-saddened seer follows them. Closing on the walls
where Amphion is still describing the slaughter,
490   the Argives would have entered the ill-fated town,
had Megareus not shouted from the watch tower,
'The enemy are coming! Guards, shut the gates at once!'
Fear gives them the strength to close every door quickly
except the Ogygian gate, where Echion
495   is too slow to stop a band of rash Spartan youths
who break in and are cut down at the threshold:
Panopeus of Taygetus, Oebalus,
who swam rough Eurotas, and you, Alcidamas,
great among wrestlers, victor in the Nemean dust,
500   whose gauntlets were first fastened by Pollux;
dying, you gaze towards the vault of your shining teacher,
where the god responds, setting his averted star.
The Spartan forest and the waters which the feigned swan
made to sing and deceive the Laconian maid[1]
505   shall weep; Diana's nymphs will mourn at Amyclae;
and the mother who taught you the brave laws of war
will lament that you learned her precepts too well.

---

1. Leda, seduced by Jupiter disguised as a swan and made mother of Castor and
Pollux.

Thus Mars rages in the gateway of Echion.
Acron, thrusting his shoulders, and Ialmenides,
pressing with his powerful chest, manage at last   510
to bend back the bronze gate bars, as groaning bullocks
heave to break the long-unploughed soil of Pangaea.
Yet their efforts lose as much as they gain, trapping
enemies in but support out. Inside, Ormenus
falls; Argive Amyntor entreats with outstretched arms,   515
and pours out prayers, but is beheaded. His face falls
with his words, and a glorious collar drops
from his neck, through the wound onto the enemy sands.
Meanwhile the wall is breached, the first line of defence
fails; foot soldiers throng to the wall, but the horses   520
refuse to jump the deep trenches; shrinking from the drop,
they are amazed to be whipped on. Their whole instinct
is to retreat from the edge, spontaneously
they recoil against the reins. While some soldiers
uproot the defensive palisades, others   525
weaken the resisting gates and sweat to force back
the iron bars; they dislodge slabs from their places
with beams or ringing bronze; some exultantly
shoot flaming brands onto the roofs, while others sap
tower foundations, probing under their hollow shed.   530
    But from the tops of the walls, their only defence,
the Thebans regroup and hurl down blackened stakes,
bright steel darts, sling-shots that flame through the vacant sky,
and stones torn from the walls themselves onto the enemy.
The roof-tops pour down a fierce cloud and armed windows   535
vomit shrieking missiles. It is like a sudden storm
hovering, massing clouds above the dark hills
of Cape Malea or high Ceraunia,
which quickly swoops on ships. So Agenorean arms
overwhelm the Argive army, though no one turns   540
his face or chest away from the terrible shower
and they face the walls unflinching as if they saw
only their own weapons, oblivious of Death.
While Antheus' scythed chariot circles the walls

545 he is struck from above by an Ogygian spear
which knocks the reins from his hands and hurls his stunned limbs
back, but pins him by his greaves – a shocking scene of war:
the smoking wheels drag him behind in armour
and his spear ploughs a third furrow across the ground:
550 his flopping head raises a long wake of dust
and clearly marks a wide track left by his trailing hair.
　　Now the blaring trumpet dismays the city,
and its bitter sound breaks through the barricaded doors.
They divide the approaches and at each threshold
555 grim emblems hold suffering or joy that all will know.
Inside, the scene is frightful. Even Mars would take
no pleasure in it. Grief, Insanity, Panic,
and Flight, surrounded by unseeing shadows,
splinter the horror-crazed city with discord.
560 War appeared to have entered: strongholds swarm with movement,
streets are confused with shouting, the mind's eye discovers
steel and fire everywhere and submits to cruel chains.
Fear anticipates the future; already grief fills
houses and temples, throngs unresponsive altars,
565 all, of all ages, gripped by the same terror:
old men search omens, young men grow pale then burn,
quaking women make the halls echo with laments.
Trembling children cry without knowing the reason,
except that they are frightened by their mothers' cries.
570 Love and great danger make women put shame aside:
they hand spears to their men and stoke their anger,
they encourage them and rush forward with them,
pointing out their children and their ancestral gates.
So, when a plundering shepherd rouses the armed bees
575 from their chalky cave, the furious swarm rages,
encouraged by their own buzzing, and all fly
at the enemy's face, but soon, with failing wings,
they hug their golden home, grieve for their stolen honey,
and press the laboriously worked wax to their breasts.
580 　　The wavering crowd teems with conflicting opinions
which sow discontent: 'Let the brother surrender'

(no mutters, but in the open with loud shouts),
'surrender kingship!' Respect for the king has died
in the anxious: 'Let him fulfil the agreement,
and count his year, let him greet Theban gods and his   585
father's darkness, an unhappy exile. Why should I pay
my blood for the king's fraudulent, treacherous crime?'
or 'It is too late for good faith, better he conquers!'
Or a suppliant throng, weeping, begs Tiresias,
for the one consolation in difficult matters: 590
to know the future. He holds firm, suppressing
the gods' fatal word: 'Is this because our king
took my advice when I forbade this treacherous war?
Yet, unhappy Thebes, doomed to fall if I stand mute,
can I bear to hear you perish, or with blind eyes   595
swallow the misery of fire brought from Argos?
Duty, let me yield to you. Daughter, set the altar.
We'll ask the gods.' She works, and with skilful gaze describes
bloody flame-tips and double fire on the altar,
clear peaks rising from the middle of the blaze.   600
Now she shows to his wonderment a red thing –
a snake, obscurely spiralling and revolving,
then breaking, and so sheds light for her blind father.
For a long while he embraces the wreathed altar,
his face glowing, drinking the prophetic vapour.   605
His hair stands up in horror, a crazed white mane lifts
the fillets which weigh it down; his eyes seem reopened,
and long-lost colour seems returned to his cheeks.
Then words spring from his overpowering madness:
'Hear, guilty Thebans, the gods' final sacrifice –   610
for preservation offers, but the way is hard.
The dragon of Mars[1] demands a cruel offering.

---

1. The dragon killed by Cadmus, founder of Thebes. He sowed its teeth, whence
sprang a crop of armed men, which Cadmus set against each other. The five
survivors became the ancestors of the true Thebans or Spartoi ('Sown Men').
Creon and his two sons, Haemon and Menoeceus, are the only descendants of
pure blood of this original 'brood'. See Valerius, *Argonautica* VII.75 ff.

Victory comes only on this condition,
the last-born of the brood of dragon's teeth must fall:
615 fortunate he who leaves the light with such a promise.'
     Creon stands by the prophet's cruel altar,
still sharing only his countrymen's grief,
when the shock of recognition strikes him a hard blow,
like a spear piercing his chest. He realizes,
620 fainting, that it is Menoeceus who is meant.
What fear suggests to the anxious father must be true,
and ice penetrates his heart. So the Sicilian shore
might suffer the percussive surge of the Libyan sea.
Now Creon humbly clasps the knees, now holds the face
625 of the seer, whom Apollo's hastening command fills,
and vainly begs the prophesying voice for silence,
but inspired Rumour echoes through the shrines of Thebes.
     Now come, Clio, tell who stimulated the young man
to the joy of a glorious death (a desire men
630 never learn without divine cause), remember, since
you order the past, you preserve the centuries.
     Valour,[1] divine close companion of Jove's throne
(whose descents to earth, sent by omnipotent Jove
or choosing men able to bear her, are so rare),
635 now springs joyfully from the glittering sky.
Bright stars give way as she passes, even the fires
which she herself had installed through the heavens.
She alights, her face no distance from the aethereal,
so she disguises it as prophetic Manto,
640 hiding her divinity in order to inspire
full belief. She subdues her awesome gaze and force,
until only the soft shadow of her splendour
remains, and substitutes prophecy for the sword;
her robe undulates, and her fierce hair submits
645 to the laurel chaplet. Only her striving looks

---

1. In Latin *Virtus*, not simply an abstraction but a deity with temples and a college
   of priests in Rome.

and long stride betray her. Just so the Lydian wife[1]
laughed when Amphitryon's son shrugged off the lion's hide
to ruin luxurious robes on his back, and worked
spinning distaffs and wrecked timbrels with his right hand.

    Nor does she find you unworthy, Menoeceus,   650
as you battle before the tower of Dirce,
laying Argives low by the huge gate's unbarred door,
an equal to Haemon, descendant of Mars.
Although you were blood-brothers and shared in all,
you came first. Lifeless corpses piled up around you;   655
every spear hit home, no hit struck without killing.
Though Valour was not yet there, your mind, your right hand,
and your greedy weapons never rest. The raging Sphinx
which decorates your helmet seems endowed with blood,
and her figure grimaces from the spattered brass.   660
Now the goddess holds back his sword-arm as he fights:
'Great-hearted youth, Mars would know you indisputably
descended from the arms-bearing seed of Cadmus.
Cease this simple fight – more is owed your courage. Think!
The stars invoke you – send your spirit heavenward.   665
My father, possessed at the joyful altar, speaks
what Apollo urges through the fire and entrails:
one mortal in place of all our country's blood.
Report spreads the oracles and thrills Cadmus' people,
who, knowing you, know you will grasp this great destiny.   670
Go quickly, I beg, lest Haemon anticipate your chance.'
She speaks, and silently soothes his hesitating breast
with her right hand, and installs herself in his heart.
Swiftly as a pine ignited by lightning throws
the hostile flame from root to summit, the young man,   675
overwhelmed by the great power possessing his breast,
rouses his spirit to fall in love with death.
He watched her movement and appearance as she turned,
amazed at Manto rising skyward from the earth.

---

1. Omphale, queen of Lydia, with whom Hercules ('Amphitryon's son') fell in love. He
served her as a slave, wearing effeminate dress and performing women's duties.

680 'Whichever goddess you are called, I follow,
obeying immediately.' Even as he withdraws,
he stabs Agreus of Pylos, who stormed the wall.
Soldiers escort his weariness, the rejoicing mob
hails him as the source of peace, their preserver
685 and god, filling him with ardour for glory.
 Hastening along his way, at a breathless run,
he gains the walls, happy to have avoided
his unhappy parents, when his father stops him.
Each stands silent, unable to meet the other's eye.
690 Then his father asks, 'What pulls you from the fighting?
What do you prepare, my son, worse than battle –
tell one who begs to know why your glance is grim,
your pale face wears violence, why you avoid my gaze?
I see you know the oracle, but I beg you
695 by your years, mine, your mother's unhappy breasts,
not to believe the seer, my son. Would the gods deign
to enlighten a blind, old, impious man
whose punishment recalls terrible Oedipus?
What if the king reigns by treachery, fraud, and deceit,
700 and now in his desperate peril, is afraid
of our high standing and your pre-eminent courage?
Perhaps we mistake his words for the gods' words –
he pronounces! allow curbs to your hot spirit,
wait a little – hasty action leads to mistakes:
705 concede your parents this much. Thus in your turn
you may have grey temples, you may be a parent
and feel this fear. Do not rush to empty our house,
my valiant son. If other fathers – not your kin –
inspire you to feel for other families,
710 if you feel respect, first feel pity for your own.
This duty is true honour. That mere renown,
fickle as the breeze, fame which disappears with death.
I do not argue as a fearful parent. Go,
rejoin the fight, meet the Argive lines and waiting swords.
715 Let me delay you only to wash your throbbing wounds
with my tears and dry the flow of blood, before

I send you again, and yet again to battle,
Thebes' right choice.' Embracing his neck, Creon clings,
but no tears nor prayers can reach the gods' votive youth,
who obeys their prompting to comfort his father   720
and allay his fear with the right lie. 'You are deceived,
father, and miss my true fear. I am not troubled
by oracles or frenzied seers' fabrications –
let clever Tiresias chant for his daughter.
Though Apollo confronted me with wild prophecies   725
at his secret shrine, such vanities would not move me.
The grave case of my dear brother brings me back
eagerly to the city – Haemon groans, wounded
with Argive spear. It was hard to pull him back
from the dust between the lines – now Argos turns the tide –   730
but I delay – go, nurse his danger – tell the crowd
who bring him to be gentle – to move him lightly –
while I fetch Aetion, expert in closing wounds
and recalling the last flow of blood.' Breaking off,
he rushes away. Creon's confused emotions   735
sink his heart in black gloom. Doubting his duty,
he wavers, fear-torn, but Fate impels him to believe.

　　Meanwhile, in furious action, Capaneus scourges
the troops to the broken gates over the fighting plain,
horsemen and infantry, and chariots trampling   740
the corpses of their drivers. He weakens with rock
and hurtling stones the high turrets; he drives on
the horsemen, and steams in the bloodbath he raises.
Now, he whirls to sow new wounds with flying lead,
and now, arms extended, he spins a spear upwards   745
and no javelin reaches the roof-tops to fall back
without slaughtering its man, covered in blood.

　　Now the Argive army cannot believe Tydeus,
Hippomedon, their seer or the Arcadian slain:[1]
all his comrades' souls seem to unite in him,   750
so well he fills their roles. Not age, not dress or beauty

---

1. See lines 11–12 and 24–8 above.

move him; he punishes fighter and suppliant.
No one resists him or tests the chance of battle.
From the distance they shrink away from his fury,
755 the terrible sight of crest, helmet and weapons.
But reverent Menoeceus stands silently
at a well-chosen place on the walls, sublime
to see, his look more exultant than ever,
as if heaven-sent; he bares his head to be known,
760 looks down to the lines of men, and with a deep shout
turns all eyes on him and orders the fight to be still.
'Gods of arms, and you, Phoebus, who have granted me
this great death, give Thebes the joys which I have pledged
and bought prodigally with my blood. Roll back the war,
765 and hurl against captive Lerna her base remnants,
let their father Inachus recoil from them,
his dishonoured pupils, nursing their wounded backs.
But let my death ransom the Thebans' temples and fields,
homes, wives, and children; if your elected victim
770 has pleased you when I willingly accepted –
not with frightened ears – the seer's verdict, long before
incredulous Thebes, then reward Amphion's town
in my place, and beg my deceived father's pardon.'
He ends, his glorious soul already disdains
775 the body which regretfully holds it back,
and his flashing sword finds it and strikes it with one gash.
He splashes his blood on the tower, asperging the walls,
then throws himself onto the lines, sword still grasped,
trying to crush the grim Argives under his fall.
780 But Duty and Valour embrace him and bear
his body gently to the ground. His spirit long since
attends Jove, and demands his crown among the highest stars.
Now, joyfully, they bring in the hero's body,
recovered without labour as the Tantalids
785 willingly withdraw in respect, carried shoulder high
by young men in a long procession, and all acclaim
him above Cadmus and Amphion as their founder.
They cover his limbs with garlands and loose spring blossom,

then reverently lay him in his ancestral tomb;   790
praise done, they return to war. His anger exhausted,
the weeping father groans, the mother sobs at last,
'Was it as an expiation for cruel Thebes
that I nurtured your doomed life like a low-born mother,
noble boy? What crime inspired the gods to hate me?   795
No wallowing in monster-breeding union shames
my sons, nor have I, ill-starred, bred them grandchildren.
Does it matter? Jocasta keeps her children
and sees them reign, while I make grim offerings to war
to let Oedipus' sons exchange crowns. Oh, Thunderer,   800
does your work please you? But why do I blame the gods?
You, cruel Menoeceus, sped to crush your mother,
unhappiest of all. Who taught you to love Death?
What cursed madness stole your mind? What did I conceive,
how did I create children so different from myself?   805
It must be the dragon of Mars and the earth
which teemed with our freshly armed forebears which endowed
your breast with grim courage and too much of Mars.
Nothing from the mother. You raced willingly
into the sad shades of Death, despite reluctant Fate.   810
While I feared the Argives and Capaneus' spear,
it was this hand with the sword I foolishly gave it
I should have feared. See how he sheathed it in his throat,
deeper than a Danaan sword could have plunged.'

The unhappy woman would still be lamenting,   815
had her companions and servants not led her away
to her room. She sits, loathing consolation,
her nails scoring her cheeks, unseeing, unhearing,
her eyes fixed on the ground, both voice and mind gone.
She is like a wild tigress bereft of her cubs   820
who lies desolate in her Scythian cave,
licking their traces on the warm rock. Her rage gone,
the wild fierceness of her ravening mouth abates,
flocks and herds pass her safely; she lies staring blankly.
Where are they for whom her teats fill, the long-awaited, 825
for whom she accumulated abundant prey?

Thus far arms, horns, swords, and wounds — but now Capaneus
must be raised to fight hand to hand against the stars.
No more can I sing the poets' habitual song.
830 Helicon's groves must grant greater inspiration.
Dare with me, goddesses! Did his madness come
from the depths of night, did the Stygian sisters[1]
follow Capaneus' banner to snatch up arms
against Jove? or did valour burst its bounds?
835 or was it heedless lust for fame by glorious death?
or fatal success which lures men to nemesis?

Earthly battles seem worthless, and the heaped slaughter
wearies the hero, his right arm has exhausted
his own and Argive weapons; now he looks heavenwards,
840 with a grim look he measures the height of the walls,
and brings an upward path: countless the tree-bound rungs.
Terrible in the distance, he brandishes
an oak torch, burning with light, illuminating
his armour with its red glow. His shield blazes.
845 'My courage teaches me the way to enter Thebes,
by the tower slippery with Menoeceus' blood.
See the worth of sacrifice, and if Apollo lies.'
He speaks, ascending the walls — soon to be his —
exulting at every step. So the heavens once watched
850 the Giants mount towards the clouds when the impious earth
swelled to overlook the gods, before great Pelion
capped Ossa to threaten the trembling Thunderer.[2]

Then, aghast, with Fortune poised in the balance,
as if Bellona herself were coming on with torches
855 of blood to deal the city its final blow
from every roof they race to hurl great boulders,
and timbers, and whirl the strongest Balearic slings
(what hope was there in javelins or flying arrows?),

---

1. The Furies.
2. An allusion to the story of the attempt of the giant sons of Aloeus, Otus and
   Ephialtes, to climb from the earth to heaven by piling Mt Ossa on Mt Olympus
   and Mt Pelion on Mt Ossa. See also Seneca, *Trojan Women* 830.

a furious assault with bolts and rocks from engines.
Nothing turns him aside, not the rain of missiles,   860
from where he hangs in empty air, as securely
as if his firm step trod the ground. He presses on
through the hailing barrage, as if he were the flood,
a river testing the strength of an ancient bridge,
weakening the stones and pulling the beams away   865
with his incessant waters. He feels conquest close,
and with great violence and stronger surge,
the victor heaves the weakened pile with his swift flow
until its joints are all severed and he breathes free.

Outlined above the city, from its long-sought roofs,   870
he stood erect over the trembling town and sneered
at Thebes, in frightened shock at his huge shadow.
'Can these insignificant towers be Amphion's?
Did these docile walls follow the unwarlike song –
for shame! – in that ancient lying Theban legend?   875
Where is the glory in tumbling walls the soft lyre
summoned?' Instantly, he leaps to tear them down,
with fierce hand and foot on the keystones and lintels.
The arches fall, ceilings collapse on the stone columns.
He puts the dismembered rampart to new use,   880
throwing the broken pieces down on temple and house,
and smashes the city with the city's own walls.

Now the gods of Argos and of Thebes dispute
before Jove, who watches both sides impartially
as they confront each other with blazing anger   885
which he restrains. With a sidelong glance at his father,
Bacchus groans under his stepmother's watchful eye:
'Where is harsh treatment now, where is my cradle of flame,
and the lightning, the lightning?' Apollo laments
for the dwellings he endowed. Sadly Hercules weighs   890
Lerna against Thebes, and hesitates with drawn bow.
Danae's winged son[1] grieves for his mother's Argos.
Venus, afraid of her husband, withdraws weeping

---

1. Perseus.

247

for Harmonia's race, glaring at Mars in mute anger.
895   Bold Tritonia criticizes the gods of Thebes.
A silent Juno twists in quiet fury.
Yet none of this disturbs Jove's peace. Then Capaneus
is heard in the heavens, and all quarrelling ceases;
he shouts, 'Will no gods stand up for trembling Thebes?
900   Where are Bacchus and Alcides, coward sons
of this cursed soil? I scorn to challenge weaker gods!
Better you should come, Jupiter, a worthier
antagonist – look! I possess the ashes and tomb
of Semele! Now face me, fight with all your flame,
905   or do you bravely reserve thunder to frighten girls
and break the towers of your father-in-law, Cadmus?'
The gods groan with shock; Jove laughs at his insane words,
striking the mass of his sacred hair, and said,
'Can men still aspire after the Giants' defeat?
910   Must you, too, be struck down?' Around slow-acting Jove
the angry gods throng, demanding the avenging bolt.
His saddened wife no longer dares to obstruct Fate.
The heavenly palace thunders of its own accord,
before the sign is given, clouds gather with no wind
915   and storms appear, as if Iapetus had burst
his Stygian chains to overthrow Ischia
or Aetna and assault heaven. Though sky-dwellers
are ashamed to feel afraid, when they see the madman
stand in the centre of the turning world, and force
920   battle, they grow pale and mute at the thunderbolt.

    Above the Ogygian tower the heavens rumble,
the sky is hidden by mysterious darkness.
Capaneus still holds the walls he cannot see
and when the lightning shines through the bucking storm
925   shouts, 'Here are the fires that should be used against Thebes!
They will renew and rekindle my fading torch.'
As he speaks, driven with all Jove's force, the thunderbolt
overwhelms him. First his crest flies up to the clouds,
then his singed shield-boss drops, and the man's whole body
930   fulminates. From both lines squadrons fall back, fearing

where he may strike them with his burning body.
Bolt upright, he breathes his last and turns to the stars,
leaning his smoking chest upon the hated walls
to stop his fall, but his earthly limbs desert him
and release his life. Had they been a moment slower,   935
he could have hoped for another thunderbolt.

SILVAE

SELECTIONS

Translated by W. G. Shepherd

I.6

The First of December

Go, keep holiday far away,
Father Apollo, stern Pallas, you Muses:
We'll call you back on January first.
Saturn, your fetters all unloosed,[1]
5   December, loaded up with copious wine,
And laughing Mirth and salty Wit –
To me! I'll report the happy feast
Of cheerful Caesar's[2] vinous peace.

Scarce had Aurora stirred new day,
10   Already sweetmeats rained from the rope[3] –
Such the dews the east wind lavished:
The well-liked nuts from Pontic groves,
Dates from Idume's fertile heights,
Damsons that budded in godly Damascus,
15   And figs that parching Caunus ripened,
Fall without payment – plentiful plunder;

1. Saturn, enchained by Jupiter, was freed according to tradition during his festival, the Saturnalia, in December.
2. Domitian's.
3. A rope stretched across the amphitheatre, from which dainties were shaken on to the people.

Biscuits and melting gingerbread men,
Amerian apples and pears just ripe,
And laurel-cakes, and swelling dates
From bowered palms were showered down.   20
The Hyades and melted Pleiads
Don't swamp the earth with troubling storms
As winter hail from sunny skies
Then crushed the Roman theatre's throng.
Let Jupiter marshal clouds round the world   25
And menace with storm the widespread fields,
While Roman Jove[1] brings rains like these!

But see — another group that looks
Well dressed, distinctive, no less than those
Already seated, threads the throng.   30
These are carrying baskets of bread,
Dazzling napkins, and richer food;
Those pour out lavishly drowsy wine —
You'd think each one an Idaean waiter.[2]
Since, prosperous Sir, you feast the rows   35
Of those of the senior, graver sort,
And *all* citizens' families too,
Proud Price knows nothing about this day.
Antiquity, go, compare these times
With the age of gold, of Primeval Jove;   40
Wine did not flow so freely then,
Nor harvest pre-empt the tardy year.
One table feeds all ranks, children,
Women, senators, commons, knights:
Freedom remits respect of degree.   45
Indeed, even You — what god could find
Such leisure, vouchsafe so much? —
Attended with us the general banquet.
So now the poor, the rich — whoever —
Glory in being the Emperor's guests.   50

1. Domitian.
2. i.e. a Ganymede, the cup-bearer of Jupiter.

Amidst the din and novel profusion,
The pleasure of watching flies lightly by:
Untrained swordswomen take their stand,
Commence sub-standard mannish fights –
You'd think that Amazon platoons
Sweated by Don or outlandish Phasis.
Here swarms a bold array of dwarfs
Whose natural growth, abruptly stopped,
Has bound them for good in knotty lumps.
They deal out wounds in hand to hand fight
And threaten death – and with what fists!
Bloody Manhood and father Mars both laugh,
And cranes hovering for scattered spoils
Are aghast at these more dauntless thugs.
Now as the shades of night draw on,
Uproar keeps flowing what largess!
Enter girls! (reasonably priced):
We find here all that on the stage
Is praised for skill and pleases by looks.
Plump Lydian girls in a gaggle clap,
There Spanish cymbals jingle and clash,
There Syrians chatter together in droves,
And here show-business' lower orders,
And traders of matches for broken glass.
Amidst which suddenly drop from the sky
Innumerable birds – flamingoes from Nile,
Phasis pheasants, and guinea fowl which
Numidians cull in the humid south.
Captors lack: all here are glad to fill
Their tunics, adding still fresh winnings.
Countless voices are raised to heaven,
Extolling the Emperor's festive day,
Acclaiming their 'Lord'[1] with warm goodwill –
But this one liberty He banned.

55
60
65
70
75
80

---

1. A reference to Domitian's title of 'Lord and God' (*dominus et deus*).

Dusk was hardly surmounting the world,   85
When into the arena's thickest shade
Ball–lightning fell, surpassing the glitter
Of Ariadne's constellation.
The Pole shone out in fire, and allowed
Lawful nothing of darkling night.   90
Sluggish rest fled – and indolent Sleep,
Seeing this, went off to other cities.
Who can sing the entertainment, licensed mirth,
Social bond, the feasting free of cost,
And generous Lyaeus' streams of wine?   95
Bacchus, I wilt beneath you now,
And drag myself, late and drunk, to bed.

This feast shall continue throughout the years –
No age shall ever see it decay!
While father Tiber, the Latian hills,   100
And while Your Rome, and the Capitol You
Have restored, shall stand, shall remain.

IV.2

Thanksgiving to the Emperor Augustus Germanicus Domitianus

Virgil, who brought great Aeneas to Laurentian lands,
Praises the royal banquets of Sidonian Elissa;[1]
And Homer, who completed Ulysses' drawn out seafaring,
Paints in enduring verse the feasting of Alcinous:[2]
But I, on whom Caesar has now for the first time bestowed   5
The joy of a sacred dinner, to mount to my Prince's table,
How can my lyre make known my devotion, discharge

---

1. i.e. of Dido. The feast occurs at the end of *Aeneid* I (631ff.).
2. Described at *Odyssey* VIII.55ff.

My gratitude? Not even if Smyrna and Mantua[1] bound
My head with their fragrant laurels, could I utter
10 Adequate words. I seem to recline amidst the stars
With Jove and to take from Ganymede's outstretched hand
Immortal wine! I have let barren years go by,
And this is my earliest day, the threshold of life.
Is it You, the ruler of nations, the great father
15 Of the subject world, You hope of mankind, You care of gods,
Whom I behold? Is it then given to look on Your face
Amidst wine and food and right not to rise to my feet?

    Augustus' dwelling,[2] vast, famed not for a hundred pillars,
But as many as could support, were Atlas pardoned,
20 The skies and the gods! Jupiter's neighbouring palace[3]
Is stunned, the Powers rejoice that You inhabit
As fine a seat. No hurry to ascend the mighty skies:
The fabric spreads so wide; the extensive concourse's sweep,
More open than a plain, encloses massive volumes
25 Of air, is less than its Master only: He fills the house,
His mighty energy makes it rejoice. And here contend
Libyan mountain, and shining Ilian, and abundance
Of Chian and Syenite marbles, and that which competes
With sea-green Doris, and Lunan (enough to carry the columns).
30 Far upward yet the view: one's weary eyesight grasps
The roof and one deems it the golden ceiling of heaven.
Here, when Caesar has ordered it, Roman chiefs
And knightly bands at a thousand tables recline together:
Ceres, her robe girded up, and Bacchus work hard
35 To supply them. So bounteously spun the wheels of divine
Triptolemus; so Bacchus shaded the naked hills,
And sober farmlands, beneath the shoots of his vines.

    I had no leisure for food, the Moorish oaken board
Supported on ivory columns, the troops of girls in waiting,

---

1. Birthplace of Virgil, as Smyrna was the (reputed) birthplace of Homer.
2. What follows is a description of Domitian's newly built palace on the Palatine, the state rooms of which are now known as the *Domus Flavia*.
3. Jupiter's great temple on the Capitol in Rome.

So great was my desire to gaze at Him, at Him,   40
His tranquil countenance, His majesty serene
That tempered its rays, with modesty furling the flags
Of His estate. The grace He veiled shone nevertheless
In His visage, and even thus outlandish tribes
Of barbarian enemies would have known Him had they seen.   45
Just so does Mars recline in Rhodope's cool vale,
His horses unyoked; and so does Pollux, relaxed
After Spartan wrestling, dispose his well-oiled limbs;
So lies Bacchus by Ganges, while the Indians howl;
So mighty Hercules, returning after his awesome tasks,   50
Was pleased to lay his side on his lion-skin blanket.
Domitian, I speak of trifles, nothing to equal Your visage:
Such is heaven's king when he revisits Aethiopia's boards
And Ocean's bound and, features suffused with holy nectar,
Commands the Muses to sing their mystical hymns   55
And Apollo to celebrate the triumph at Phlegra.[1]

   May the gods grant (they are said often to attend to us
Lesser souls) that You shall surpass, twice and thrice over,
Your father's age![2] May You send Your appointed gods to
        heaven,[3]
Dedicate temples, and dwell in Rome! Often may You fling wide   60
The gates of the year, often greet Janus with new lictors,
Often renew the Capitol's garlanded competition!
The day when You vouchsafed to me the sacred blessings
Of your festal board, after long interval came at last
Like that when, beneath the hills of Trojan Alba, I sang   65
Now German battle array, now Dacian fights,
And on me Your hand placed Pallas' golden wreath.[4]

---

1. i.e. the victory of the Olympian gods over the giants.
2. Domitian's father and founder of the Flavian dynasty, Vespasian, lived from A.D.
   9 to 79.
3. Domitian 'deified' both his brother Titus and his niece Julia.
4. See V.3.225ff., where Statius again refers to his victory in one of the poetry
   contests organized by Domitian in his magnificent villa at Alba. The prize was a
   golden olive-wreath.

IV.9

Jocular Lines to Plotius Grypus

It was very funny, Grypus,
When you sent me a book for a book . . .
But even that may seem urbane
If now you send me something worthwhile:
5 To persevere in such jokes, Grypus, would be
Beyond a joke.
            Look, let's balance the books.
Mine was red, new paper,
A beautiful knob each end,[1] it cost
Me trouble plus ten bob. But yours,
10 Worm-eaten, rotting with mould,
Like a book soaked in cheap olive-oil,
Or wrapping Nile incense or pepper,
Or smelling of Byzantine fish –
Not even containing the speeches
15 You thundered when young to all three Forums[2]
Or the Hundred Judges,[3] before
Domitian gave you control
Of the biddable corn supply,
Put you in charge of all roads' staging posts –
20 But out of some wretched bookseller's box
Old Marcus Brutus's mouthings, price

---

1. At 'each end' of the stick of wood or ivory round which the papyrus 'paper' was rolled. The papyrus roll might be protected by a wrapper, often stained 'red'. Cf. above, Ovid, *Tristia* I.1.5ff.
2. The old 'Roman' forum and the two main imperial ones, the Forum of Caesar and that of Augustus. Courts of law were often held in the great buildings of the Forums.
3. The *Centumviri*, an important court of civil jurisdiction which usually sat in the Basilica Iulia in the old Roman Forum.

More or less one dud Caligula shilling[1] –
That's your gift.
          Was there a shortage
Of rag caps cobbled together
From worn-out cloaks, or scraps of papyrus,   25
Of Theban dates and Carian figs?
Nowhere a squash of plums,
Or figlets, packed in disposable wrappers?
No dried-out wicks, not cast-off
Onions' jackets? And not so much as an egg?   30
No fine grits and no coarse grain?
Nowhere the slimy 'home' of an arching snail
That wandered afar on Cinyphian plains?
No rancid bacon-fat or tasteless ham,
Lucanian sausage or leaden haggis?   35
No salt or butter or cheese,
Or cakes of green saltpetre,
Moscato wine (boiled, grapes and all),
Or must muddied with sugary lees?
How *could* you not give me smelly tapers,   40
Or a little knife, or a tiny notebook?
I ask you – couldn't you run to bottled grapes,
Or cheap crocks thrown on some wheel at Cumae?
Nor give a complete set – don't jump! –
Of plain white cups and pots?   45

                  Yet indeed, a fair dealer, your scales
    correct,
You weigh my measure precisely.
But if, half-dead, I get up
And bring you my morning greetings,
Must you greet me at *my* house?   50
Or you've cheered me up with an excellent dinner –
Do I owe you a similar feast?

---

1. A reference to the debasement of the coinage by the emperor Gaius, also called
  'Caligula' (reigned A.D. 37–41).

I'm angry with you, Grypus. Still, fare*well*.
Only don't, with your usual pleasantry,
55 Promptly send back jocular lines.

V.3

In Memory of His Father[1]

Father, grant me yourself from Elysian springs
A dour command of grieving song, the beat
Of an ominous lyre. It is not permitted to stir
The Delian caves or initiate Cirrha's accustomed work
5 Without you. Whatever Apollo lately ordained
In Corycian shade, or Bacchus upon Ismarian hills,
I have unlearned. Parnassus' woollen band has fled
My hair, I have been aghast at defunctive yew
Stealing among the ivy, the bays – unnatural! – parching.
10 Yet I, inspired, had set myself to extol the deeds
Of great-hearted kings, to equal in singing lofty Mars.[2]
Who makes my barren heart decay? And who, the Apollo
In me quenched, has drawn cold clouds before my lacking mind?
The goddesses stand dismayed about the seer, and sound
15 No pleasant music with fingers or voice. Their leader leans
Her head on her silent lyre, as after the rape of Orpheus[3]
She stood by Hebrus and gazed at the herds now deaf
And groves immobile since that song was taken away.

But you, whether, let go from the flesh, you reach
20 Up the steeps, review the shining tracts and bases of nature,

---

1. Statius' father, the teacher and poet, died perhaps some sixteen years (about A.D. 80) before this poem was published. There is added poignancy in the fact that the fifth book of *Silvae*, in which this poem occurs, was probably published after Statius' own death.

2. The reference is to *Thebaid* and (possibly) *Achilleid*.

3. Dismembered by Thracian Bacchants (see Virgil, *Georgic* IV.520ff.; Ovid, *Metamorphoses* XI.1ff.).

And find what is god, whence fire, what pathway leads
The sun, what lessens the moon, and what the cause that can
Restore her when waned, and you extend the bounds
Of famed Aratus; or whether, in Lethe's sequestered pastures,
By conclave of heroes and blessèd spirits, you,   25
Yourself no duller shade, attend upon ancient Homer and Hesiod,
Make music in turn and mix your song with theirs:
Supply a voice and talent, father, to my large grief.

For having thrice traversed the sky and thrice annulled
Her features, the moon has seen my sluggish, woeful vigils   30
Unsolaced by Art:[1] for since your pyre incarnadined
My face, and I gathered your ashes with streaming eyes,
My lowly craft is disesteemed. At first I hardly free
My mind for these things, and essay with drooping hands,
With flowing eyes, to rid my lassitude of silent care,   35
That leans upon the tomb in which you rest
And possess our acres, where after Aeneas' death
Starry Ascanius builded Alba upon the Latian hills,
Since he contemned the plains bedaubed with Phrygian blood,
His mischief-omened stepmother's[2] regal dowry.   40
Here I lament you – the breath of Sicanian crocuses
Does not exhale more gently, nor rare cinnamon gathered
By rich Sabaeans nor Arabia's fragrant harvest –
I lament in Pierian song; you deserve full measure
Of holy offerings: O accept the groans and pain   45
Of a son, and tears few fathers have ever received.

I wish it were my lot to tender an altar to your shade,
A work matching temples – to raise an airy fabric
Higher than Cyclopes' crags, or pyramids' daring masonry,
And to border your mound with a large grove!   50

1. The 'dramatic' context of this poem is thus three months after his father's death.
   Indeed the poem may have been written then and withheld from publication
   until after Statius' death.
2. The poet means Lavinia, the Italian princess, whose wedding with the Trojan
   Aeneas followed the latter's defeat of the Italian forces and 'united' both peoples
   – from which the Roman race evolved.

There I had surpassed the tribute of Anchises' tomb,
The Nemean grove, and the games for crippled Pelops.[1]
There no band of many Greeks would cleave the air
With Oebalus' discus, no sweat of horses would water
55 The ground, or the eroded track resound with hoof-beats:
Only Apollo's choir would be there; I would duly
Praise you, father, and bind on you the poet's leafy prize.
I myself, as priest of the shades and of your soul,
With wet eyes would lead a dirge, from which neither Cerberus
60 With all his mouths nor Orpheus' spells could turn you away.
And there, as I sang your character and deeds, perhaps
You had not rated mine lower than Homer's mighty speech,
And your fatherly kindness had even held me Virgil's equal.
Why does the mother who sits bereft by her son's still-tepid
        mound
65 Assail more than I the gods, and the Sisters'[2] brazen threads –
And why does she who observes her youthful husband's pyre
And wins through obstructing hands and the grabbing crowd,
With her blazing husband to die, if it be permitted?
Greater even than theirs, perhaps, does my reproach
70 Strike Tartarus and the gods: these obsequies even foreign eyes
May pity. Yes, not only Nature and Fatherhood
Have lent themselves to the grieving rite: you were snatched
From me at the threshold of your Fate, father, and under-
Went hard Tartarus in your prime. For Grecian Erigone
75 Did not bewail more scantly Icarius obliterated
By savage rustics' crime, than Andromache her son Astyanax
Dropped from the Phrygian tower. Indeed, Erigone stifled
Her sighs in a noose, but the other sank to serving,
After great Hector's funeral rites, a Thessalian husband.[3]

---

1. The references in lines 51–2 are to the tribute paid by Aeneas to his father
   Anchises in Virgil's *Aeneid* Book V, the funeral rites for Opheltes and the games
   in his honour in *Thebaid* VI, and the Olympic games. Pelops was supposed to
   have been buried at Olympia.
2. The three Fates (Clotho, Lachesis, Atropos).
3. Neoptolemus, also called Pyrrhus, son of Achilles, to whom Andromache,
   Hector's wife, was allotted after the fall of Troy: Seneca, *Trojan Women* 976.

I shall not bring to my father's pyre as tribute   80
The funeral music the swan transmits when surer of his doom;
Nor that with which the winged Tyrrhenian Sirens tempt
The sailors most sweetly from dismal cliffs; nor Philomela's
Groaning complaint, her lopped murmur, to her cruel sister:
Bards know these things too well. Who by the grave has not   85
Recounted all the Heliads'[1] boughs and their wept buds;
And Phrygian flint;[2] and him[3] who ventured against Apollo,
When Pallas rejoiced that the boxwood flute deceived his trust?

Let Pity, that has forgotten man, and Justice, recalled
To heaven, and Eloquence in twofold language lament,   90
And Pallas, and learnéd Apollo's Pierian escorts;
Those who draw out their epic verse in six-feet metre;
And those who find their toil and renown in the lyre,
Their lot in Arcadian tortoise-shell; and those world-wide
Whom arduous Wisdom numbers in sevenfold fame;[4]   95
Who have in awful buskins thundered the frenzies of kings,
And stars in the firmament turning their backs on our homes;
And those who gladly fine down their force with pleasant Thalia,
Or dock one pace from their heroic course.[5]
For your creative mind comprehended all wherever   100
The force of utterance opens the way, whether liking to bind
Its works in the Muses' measures or broadcast prose set loose
In emulation of storms' unbridled rhetoric.

    Reveal your face that was suddenly half-obliterated
With dust, Parthenope,[6] lay your hair a volcano's blast[7]   105

1. The sisters of Phaethon, who were turned into amber-dropping trees as they
   mourned him.
2. Niobe, turned into flint wet with tears.
3. Marsyas, defeated by Apollo and flayed alive. A river sprang from the tears of
   his mourners.
4. The Seven Sages.
5. In lines 92–9 the poet is referring to epic (92), lyric (93–4), prose (94–5), tragedy
   (96–7), comedy (98) and elegy (99).
6. Naples, where his father taught and Statius was born.
7. The explosion of Mt Vesuvius in A.D. 79.

Once buried, on your great foster-son's burial mound;
Than whom neither Athens' fortress nor learned Cyrene
Nor valiant Sparta bore anyone more excelling.[1]
If you had sprung from obscure stock, and lacked renown
110 Or good family, his citizenship would prove
You Greek and descended from Euboea by ancestral blood.
Each time he celebrated in praiseworthy verse
The Augustalia, he bent his head to you to receive the laurels,
Surpassing the speech of aged Nestor and that of king
115 Ulysses, and binding his hair in the semblance of both.

Yours was no degraded birth of obscure blood, your line
Was not inglorious, though expenses had straitened
Your parents' fortune: rich was the ceremony when Childhood
Enjoined your laying aside the proud-worn gold on your breast
120 And the purple-edged toga given to honour your birth.
Straightway at your entry the Muses favourably smiled,
And Apollo, even then inclined to me, dipped your small
Tortoise-shell lyre and steeped your mouth in the holy stream.
Nor is your fatherland's honour single, and your place of birth
125 Depends on uncertain contest between two regions. Hyele,
Acquired by Latian settlers, where the helmsman
Heavy with sleep fell from the poop and kept
His wretched vigil amidst the waves,[2] claims you by clan;
But then the greater Parthenope proves you hers by your life's
130 Long course: thus different cities with different births
Divide up Homer – and each proves right: yet he is not
Truly of all – a huge falsity's glory puffs up the vanquished.

And there where you commenced your years and greeted life,
You were straightway rushed to local contests, which grown men
135 Could hardly complete, so hot for praise, so bold of wit
Were you. The Euboean masses were stunned at your
Precocious song, and parents showed you to their sons.

---

1. From Cyrene came Callimachus, from Sparta Alcman.
2. The reference is to Palinurus, helmsman of Aeneas, who fell overboard on the
   final voyage from Sicily to Italy: see Virgil, *Aeneid* V.833ff.

Since then your voice has often contended and never lacked glory
In holy rites: less often green Therapnae applauded
Castor's successes in riding, his brother's in boxing.   140
You won with ease at home: what prowess yet to earn Greek
    prizes,
Shading your temples now with Pythian laurel, and now
With Nemean parsley, and now with Isthmian pine,[1]
When Victory, herself each time fatigued as though by age,
Never stole away your wreaths, or touched another's hair.   145

Hence parents trusted their hopes to you, and noble youths
Were ruled by your teaching and learned the customs and deeds
Of men of old: the fall of Troy; Ulysses' delay;
The power of Homer to rehearse swiftly in verse
The horses and fights of heroes; how Hesiod and Epicharmus   150
Enriched the godly countryfolk; by what system
Proceeds the flexile voice of Pindar's lyre; Ibycus,
Beseecher of birds; Alcman, performed by sombre Amyclae;
Warlike Stesichorus; heedless Sappho, who was not cowed
By Leucas, but undertook the heroic leap; all others   155
The lyre finds worthy. Yours the skill to expound
Callimachus' poems, crabbed Lycophron's hidden dens,
Intricate Sophron, and subtle Corinna's arcana.
But why do I speak of trifles? You were accustomed to bear
A yoke equal to Homer's, to match in prose his hexameters   160
And never to be outdistanced or outpaced.
What wonder they left their countries to seek for you:
Those whom Lucania sent; whom stern Daunia's furlongs;
Whom the homeland mourned by Venus, and region
Passed over by Hercules; whom the virgin sent   165
Who surveyed from Sorrento's heights the Tyrrhenian sea;
Whom the hill, known from Misenus' trumpet and oar,
By the nearer bay; whom Cyme, once long ago a stranger
To Ausonian household gods; and whom the gulf of Dicharchus

---

1. The references are to victories in the great poetry and music competitions of the
  Pythian games at Delphi, the Nemean games in the Argolid, and the Isthmian
  games at Corinth.

170 And shores of Baiae, where fire gasps intermixed amidst
Deep waters and smothered combustion preserves its lairs?
So, from all sides, peoples came to Avernus' crags,
To the Sibyl's murky cave, to inquire; and she would chant
Concerning the menaces of gods, the deeds of the Fates –
175 No vain prophet, although she played Apollo false.

And soon you train up Romulus' stock, our future chiefs,
And steadfastly lead them in their forefathers' tracks.
The Vestal torch's Dardanian pontiff throve
Under you, who hides the arcana of what Diomedes stole,[1]
180 Who learned from you the rite as a boy; you approved Mars'
    priests
And taught them the use of arms, and showed the augurs
The pure air of true prediction; and you may explicate
Cumae's oracle, why the hair of Phrygian priests is covered[2] –
The girded-up Luperci greatly dreaded your blows!

185 And now of that company one perhaps administers law
To Eastern peoples, another retrains Iberian tribes,
Another at Zeugma contains the Achaemenian Persians.
These curb rich Asiatic populations, those Pontus,
These with peaceable authority perfect the courts, and those
190 Keep our camps with loyal firmness: you are the source
Of their renown. Neither Nestor nor Phoenix, his untamed
Foster-son's mentor,[3] nor Chiron, who broke with different lore
Achilles' longing to hear the piercing trumpets and horns,
Would have contended with you in forming young men's spirits.

195 While you were busy thus, civil frenzy suddenly
Waved her torch upon the Tarpeian heights in Phlegraean
Fighting.[4] The Capitol glows with sacrilegious brands,

1. The Roman *pontifices*, 'pontiffs' or 'high-priests', had charge of the sacred fire in
   the Temple of Vesta and of the Palladium, stolen from Troy by Diomedes and
   Ulysses.
2. Priests of the Phrygian goddess Cybele wore small sacrificial caps.
3. i.e. Achilles' mentor.
4. The allusion is to the civil wars of A.D. 69, especially the fighting between the

And native Latin cohorts put on the fury of Gauls.
The flames had barely died down, nor that funeral pyre of gods
Subsided, when you, indefatigable, much swifter   200
Than the fires themselves, bitterly mourned with religious voice
The thunderbolts captured, gave solace for temples ruined.
The Roman chiefs and the gods' avenger, Caesar, marvelled;
And amidst the burning the gods' father, Jupiter, assented.

And lately you had it in mind to mourn in religious chant   205
Vesuvius' eruption, spending groans for our homeland's damage,
When Jupiter lifted the uprooted mountain from earth
To the stars and hurled it at large on the hapless cities.[1]

Me too, when I attempted the groves of song
And Boeotian vales, when I spoke of my descent from you,   210
The goddess admitted; for it was not only the stars, the ocean
And land you gave me, as by custom parents should,
But the lyre's glory, and you first taught me to speak
Unlike the people, and to hope for renown in my tomb.
What was your happiness when with my verse I gladdened   215
The Roman elders and you were a present witness of your own
Generosity! What confusion, alas, of joy with weeping,
Of a father's hopes and fears with modest rejoicing!
Indeed that day was yours, mine was not the greater glory!
Such is he who watches his youthful son in Olympic lists –   220
He smites harder, is struck more deeply beneath
His heart; it is more *him* the audience attend, and *him*
The Achaeans watch – while the choking dust clogs
His eyes, and he prays for death – provided the prize is won!

Alas for me that I bore on my brow only Alban leaves,   225
And only Ceres' wreath of Augustalian corn
Beneath your gaze! Your Trojan land at Alba
Had hardly contained you had you gained through me

Vitellian and Flavian troops in Rome. 'Phlegraean' means the fighting was like
that between the gods and the giants on the plains of Phlegra.

1. The eruption of A.D. 79 completely buried the cities of Pompeii, Herculaneum
and Stabiae on the bay of Naples.

A wreath presented by Caesar! What oaken vigour
230   Could such a day have given, and how relieved your age!
But mingled oak and olive leaves did not bind my head,
The honour hoped-for fled me.[1] How mildly you accepted
Jupiter's envious verdict! With you as my tutor, my *Thebaid*
Pressed hard the examples set by the classic bards;
235   You showed me how to spur on my chant, rehearse
The deeds of heroes, the modes of war and the setting
Of scenes. My path wanders within uncertain limits
Without you, my bereaved ship's sails are shrouded in mist.

Your ample familial love cherished not only me:
240   You were thus as husband too. You knew just one
Marriage-torch, one love. I cannot indeed disjoin my mother
From your pyre now cold: she feels and possesses you,
She sees you, each dawn and dusk she greets your tomb –
As with factitious fidelity other women cultivate
245   Dolour for Attis and Osiris,[2] and wail over alien graves.

Why should I describe your open but serious manner,
Your good faith, disdain of gold, your care for honour,
Love of truth; or again, when pleased to relax, how pleasant
Your conversation; your understanding that never aged?
250   For these merits, the gods' just providence has granted you
Renown and bounteous praise, no harsh reverse.

You were taken from us, father, in neither exiguous
Nor superfluous age, having threescore years and five –
But grief and loyalty will not let me enumerate thus,
255   O father, worthy to pass the bounds of Nestor's age,
And equal Priam's seniority, and likewise to see
Me too as old. But death's door was not harsh for you:
Your case was easy, no lingering egress consigned
Your frame to the waiting tomb in senile decay,

---

1. i.e. victory in the Capitoline contest (oak-wreath) to add to Statius' victory in the Alban contest (olive-wreath). See also IV.2.65ff.
2. The lamentation (for Attis and Osiris) which formed part of the cults of Cybele and Isis was well known.

But a dull torpor, and death that mimicked rest   260
Set you free, and bore you in counterfeit sleep to Tartarus.
How then I groaned – my band of friends saw with concern –
My mother saw, was relieved to recognize her child –
What lamentations I made! Forgive and indulge me, shades,
Father, I speak the truth: *you* would have done as much for *me*.   265

Happy he who embraced his father with empty arms:[1]
He would have liked to carry him off, though lodged
In Elysium, to bear him a second time through Grecian murk;
And when he strove with living steps to attempt
Tartarus, Hecate's ancient priestess[2] conducted him down.   270
A lesser cause[3] sent Orpheus' lyre to numbing Avernus;
Thus had Hercules wrought for Alcestis, Admetus' queen.
If one day brought back the shade of Protesilaus,[4] why,
Father, should your lyre, or mine, obtain by prayer
Nothing? Let it be lawful to touch my father's face,   275
Join hands – and then may come full rigour of any law!

But you, kings of the dead, and Ennean Juno,[5]
Since I pray to and laud you, call off the torch-bearing
Snake-haired Furies; let the gate-guard[6] bark with none
Of its mouths, let sequestered vales conceal the Centaurs   280
And Hydra's pack and Scylla's abortions, and let
The ultimate Ferryman,[7] the rabble dispersed, invite to the bank
The aged shade, and settle him gently upon the sward.
Go, faithful spirits and troops of Grecian poets,
Scatter Lethean garlands upon his illustrious soul;   285

1. Aeneas. The incident is related in *Aeneid* VI.700ff.
2. The Sibyl of Cumae.
3. To regain his lost wife, Eurydice.
4. He was allowed to return to his wife, Laodamia, 'for one day', in fact three hours.
5. Proserpina, abducted by Pluto from Enna in Sicily to become his wife and queen of the underworld.
6. Cerberus.
7. Charon.

Point out the grove, where no Fury intrudes, in which
Is a seeming day and the air is most like that of heaven.
Thence may you come where the better horn subdues
The malignant ivory,[1] and in dreamed pictures teach me,

290   As you were used to do. So the gentle nymph[2] ordained for
       Numa,
In the Arician cavern, the holy rites to be observed;
And so, the Ausonians believe, Scipio drew in dreams[3]
Filled full with Latian Jove; and Sulla too, with Apollo.[4]

V.4
To Sleep

Young Sleep, most gentle of gods, by what misdeed
Or mistake have I sadly deserved that I alone
Should lack your gifts? All flocks, wild beasts and birds
Are still; the billowing tree-tops evoke declining rest;

5   Turbid streams do not resound as they did; turbulent
Waters subside; sea leans on the land, is quiet.
Seven times now the returning moon has seen my sick
Eyes staring; each time the evening and morning stars
Have revisited me, Aurora has drawn past by my complaint

10   And pitied, and sprinkled me with her cool and dewy whip.
But how to last? – Not if the thousand eyes were mine
Which reverend Argus kept on changing watches,
And never stayed awake in *all* his body. Alas!
If anyone holds his girl through the long night,

15   With twining arms, and willingly rejects you, Sleep,

---

1. At the exit from the underworld are a gate of true dreams (made of horn) and one of false (made of ivory). In *Aeneid* VI.893ff. Aeneas leaves the underworld through the gate of false dreams.
2. Egeria, the nymph who instructed Numa Pompilius, the second king of Rome.
3. In the Temple of Jupiter on the Capitol, which he was accustomed to visit.
4. Under whose protection Sulla considered himself to be.

Then come – I don't demand that you bury and drown my eyes
With the force of your wings[1] – the happier crowd may pray
For that; touch me with your rod's extremest tip,[2]
It is enough, or cross me lightly on hovering feet.

1. Sleep is often represented in literature and art as winged – especially with wings
   on his temples. See *Thebaid* X.137ff.
2. Sleep sometimes carried a rod or bough 'dripping with the dew of Lethe', which
   he shook over a person's temples to induce sleep.

VALERIUS FLACCUS

INTRODUCTION

We lost a great deal recently in Valerius Flaccus.
Quintilian, *Institutio Oratoria* X.1.90

Quintilian's terse, moving obituary, written between A.D. 93 and 95, is the only external evidence for the life of Gaius Valerius Flaccus and provides the approximate date of its end. Some scholars have inferred from internal evidence (*Argonautica* I.5–7, VIII.239–42) that Valerius was a member of the board of priests in charge of the Sibylline books at Rome (*quindecimviri sacris faciundis*). If so he was neither poor nor without social position. What the internal evidence does show is that Valerius' epic *Argonautica* was probably begun *c.* A.D. 80 and was left unfinished in its eighth book (presumably at his death). *Argonautica* seems therefore to have been composed at almost exactly the same time as Statius' *Thebaid*, i.e. during the second decade following the civil wars and political and social convolution of A.D. 68–9 (for which see the introduction to Statius), and like *Thebaid* its response to the literary tradition and the contemporary world was to discourse on both. Like *Thebaid* too the initial challenge of Lucan was met by shifting the narrative subject matter from history to myth, while maintaining the contemporary focus of the Neronian poet's revolutionary epic. No less than Statius, Valerius used the epic form in part as critique of Flavian Rome.

Thebaid made civil war its central issue. *Argonautica* incorporates civil war into its narrative but places it within the framework of a myth of the birth of technology and the growth of civilization. It was one of the ancient world's most famous aetiological myths. The story of the voyage of the Thessalian ship *Argo* and Jason's quest for the Golden Fleece was in fact as old as Homer (*Odyssey* XII.70ff.) and had received its 'canonic' formulation in the third century B.C. Greek epic, *Argonautica*, of Apollonius of Rhodes, a poem which was itself adapted into Latin by the Roman neoteric poet Varro of Atax in the middle of the first century B.C. To Apollonius and (presumably) to Varro, whose work survives only in fragments, Valerius is much indebted. But his most important debt is to the specific deployment of the Argonautic myth by the Roman literary tradition from the late republic to Valerius' own day. From Catullus onwards major Roman poets (Virgil, *Georgic* I.136ff.; Tibullus, I.3.35ff.; Horace, *Odes* I.3; Ovid, *Metamorphoses* I.89ff.; Seneca, *Phaedra* 525ff.) had treated the invention of navigation as a sign of the end of the fabled Golden Age of pristine harmony between nature, man and god, the consequences of which were the loss of human innocence, the dissolution of familial bonds, the accelerated technological abuse of nature, the onset of greed, war, moral decadence and human suffering, the development of cities and the growth of civilization. Several poets (Catullus, Poem LXIV; Virgil, *Eclogue* IV.31ff., VI.42ff.; Horace, *Epode* XVI.57ff.; Seneca, *Medea* 301ff., 578ff.) had used the voyage of the *Argo* as paradigm of the initial stage of post-lapsarian decline, even creating the incoherent fiction of the Argonautic expedition as the first sea-voyage (so Catullus and Seneca, whom Valerius follows here in *Argonautica* I.1, V.472,660, etc.; see also Ovid, *Amores* II.11). The Argonautic and related myths had thus functioned in the Roman tradition as ingredients of a negative critique of the development of civilization. Virgil indeed explicitly connects the voyage with the 'original sin', *prisca fraus*, of Prometheus (*Eclogue* IV.31, VI.42), who made technology possible by stealing fire from the gods; and in both Virgil (*Eclogue* IV.12) and Catullus (LXIV.399) the voyage is presented as emblem and example of that human spiritual malaise which was to realize itself tragically in the Roman *scelus* or 'sin' of civil war. For Valerius' recent predecessor Seneca, on the 'slipper slope' of Roman power, the myth had functioned as image of the flawed morality and self-destructiveness of civilization itself. And Seneca too did not conceal the implications of his critique for Rome (*Medea* 364ff.).

Valerius' *Argonautica* thus gives epic form to what had become a
principal grammar of Roman civilization. And does so self-consci-
ously. The Roman tradition's deployment of the myth is signalled
throughout the poem, underscored and enriched by reference to
Lucan's damning text and its overt anxieties about contemporary
and future Rome. In this regard the epic's opening lines are pro-
grammatic:

> Seas first pierced by great sons of gods we sing
> And a fate/death-speaking ship which dared to hunt
> Scythian Phasis' bank and to burst through clashing rocks,
> And settled at last on fiery Olympus.

> (*Argonautica* I.1–4)

Allusions to Lucan in 'we sing' (*canimus, Argonautica* I.1, *Civil War*
I.2) and 'fate/death-speaking' (*fatidicam, Argonautica* I.2 – used in
the same initial position of Phoebus and his shrine at *Civil War*
V.70,147 but here transferred from Phoebus, addressed at I.5, to the
ship *Argo* itself), to Catullus and the Roman poetic tradition in
'dared' (*ausa, Argonautica* I.3 – a prominent motif in Catullus,
LXIV.6; Horace, *Odes* I.3.25ff.; Ovid, *Heroides* XII.13) and to the
first Argonautic ode of Seneca's *Medea* (301f.: 'dared', 'seas', 'first',
'ship', 'burst' – also 'pierced', *pervius*, at 372) declare the Roman
focus of the epic and its inheritance of a concern with the moral
and social problems of civilization.

In accordance with this programme Valerius 'Romanizes' the
myth through narrative and thematic emphasis, detail and innova-
tion. The first half of the epic, Books I–IV, deals with the back-
ground to the *Argo*'s voyage and narrates the journey from Iolcus
(modern Volos) in Thessaly to Colchis, a kingdom of the eastern
shore of the Euxine or Black Sea. The origin of the quest is
located in the Thessalian king Pelias' fear of his nephew, Jason,
whom he consequently plans to remove by sending him in search
of the Golden Fleece of the ram on which their kinsman Phrixus
flew to Colchis. (Phrixus' sister Helle fell from the ram into the
strait which became known as the Hellespont – the modern Dar-
danelles. Phrixus reached Colchis safely, where he married Chal-
ciope, a daughter of the Colchian king Aeetes.) The first book

relates Pelias' challenge, the building of the *Argo* and the departure of the heroes; while Books II–IV concern the (generally) violent experiences of the voyage itself. Throughout the four books attention is centred on the problems of absolute power, on war, civil dissension and the psychology of their operation. Extensive portraits are given of exemplary tyrannical figures such as Pelias, Laomedon and Amycus, king of Bebrycia (designated *tyranni* at I.30, 71, II.577, IV.751, etc.), in which the emphasis (interestingly) is not only upon the violence, arrogance, cruelty, rage, power-lust and treachery which define their tyrannical nature but upon the fear which motivates the actions of tyrant and subject alike (for the former see especially *Argonautica* I.26ff.). Narrative expansions (the Lemnian women's massacre of their menfolk in Book II, the tragic battle between the Argonauts and king Cyzicus in Book III), omissions (the incident of the Stymphalian birds related in Apollonius Rhodius II) and innovations (see especially the suicide of Jason's parents at the end of Book I) in the epic's first half reflect and sustain the aforementioned themes.

The second half of the epic, Books V – VIII, maintains and sharpens the focus on tyranny and civil war. The analysis of tyranny shifts to the Colchian king and father of Medea, Aeetes, referred to repeatedly as *tyrannus* (V.264, 319, 547, VI.16, etc.), who himself acknowledges the universal allurement of power (V.536: 'Thus all have the same lust for power'). Overt too and far more pronounced than in the earlier part of the epic is the concern with civil war, to which a whole book is given. For the Argonauts' arrival at Colchis in Book V is immediately followed by their participation (on Aeetes' side) in the civil war fought between the Colchian king and his brother Perses, the account of which occupies Book VI. The Argonauts are promised the Golden Fleece for their assistance, but in Book VII Aeetes reneges on his promise (VII.32ff.) and sets Jason the traditional tasks (to plough with the flame-breathing bulls, sow the teeth of Cadmus' snake and reap the metal harvest), which Aeetes' daughter Medea through her magic enables him to perform. Book VIII narrates Jason's capture of the Fleece, departure with Medea and marriage to her on the island of Peuce, and (after the Colchian fleet overtakes the fugitives) the drowning of Medea's former betrothed, Styrus. The text comes suddenly to a halt at VIII.467, but, though the epic is clearly unfinished, both the structure of the poem and the paucity of events requiring to be related have suggested to many that Book VIII is the final book.

At the level of narrative content the most innovative feature of the entire epic is Book VI, the detailed description of the civil war between Aeetes and his brother Perses, the background to which is provided in Book V (see especially V.263ff.). This seems to be entirely the invention of Valerius, who foreshadows this 'fraternal discord', *fraterna Erinys*, in the prophecy of Phineus in Book IV (IV.617). Modelled on the battle-books of Virgil's *Aeneid* (IX–XII), *Argonautica* VI not only gives substantial narrative realization to the epic's concern with civil war, but joins with the examination of tyranny and the dissolution of natural and familial bonds in these final books to reinforce the 'Roman' semiotics of the work. Other ingredients of Valerius' 'Romanization' of the myth include the use of Roman terminology throughout the epic (e.g. *patres*, 'fathers', used ubiquitously for senators), references to the evolution of Rome (I.558ff., II.573), allusions to Roman institutions, practices and places (e.g. II.245, 304f., III. 417–58, V.251, VI.55f., 410ff., VII. 83ff., 234, 635ff., VIII.243ff.) and to recent historical events (e.g. the eruption of Vesuvius, IV.507ff. – see also III.208f.). Worthy of special attention is the simile at *Argonautica* VI.402ff., where the destruction wreaked by a scythed chariot in the army to which it belongs is compared to the self-destructive violence of Roman legions engaged in civil war:

> Was as when savage Tisiphone stirs Roman
> Legions and their princes, whose lines glitter
> With the same spears and eagles. Their parents till
> The same fields; the same misfortunate Tiber
> Had sent its rural elite for wars not like these.

> (*Argonautica* VI.402–6)

The inversion of Virgil's famous simile at the end of *Georgic* I (511ff.), in which Rome's civil wars are the reality and the uncontrolled chariot is the image, clarifies the rules for reading Valerius' text. Behind myth lies history, behind fiction truth. As the opening lines of the epic had shown, the motivation of emperors and Argonauts are the same (I.7f., 76).

Relevant in this connection is Valerius' particular re-employment of the traditional divine machinery of epic, which differs markedly from that of Apollonius. The gods not only have a far greater role to play in Valerius' poem and exert a far greater control over human action, but they are also strongly 'Romanized'. Particular prominence in fact is given to the three great divinities of Rome's 'national' epic, *Aeneid*: Jupiter, Juno and Venus. In the first book of *Argonautica* (I.558ff.), as in the first book of *Aeneid* (I.257ff.), though less elaborately, Jupiter even prophesies the future power of Rome, and later in the epic, as in *Aeneid* X (100ff.), he settles the divine dispute over hostilities below (V.672ff.). Valerius' gods seem to function as they did in the Augustan epic not as Alexandrian ironic fictions but as images of the forces of history, their machinations and control serving to sharpen *Argonautica*'s focus on individual impotence within an inexorable movement towards civilization, self-destruction and death.

Several individuals are highlighted in this regard, none more poignantly than Medea, whose vain psychological and moral struggle is painstakingly delineated in Book VII, which has been chosen for inclusion in this volume. Book VII not only depicts Medea's emotional turbulence and conflict in the movement towards *fatum*, i.e. 'fate' and 'death', but emphasizes in a way far beyond what is to be found in Apollonius the divine manipulation of that emotion. Critics have remarked upon the way in which Medea's psychological turmoil and the dissolution of her ties to kin re-*present* Catullus' portrait of Ariadne in LXIV and Virgil's picture of Dido in the fourth *Aeneid*. But what are important to observe are the Roman implications of these allusions. Both Ariadne's distress and Dido's destruction had implications for contemporary Rome and it is no accident that the goddesses who shape Medea's behaviour were those responsible for Dido's downfall in the Augustan poem.

The essential innocence and vulnerability of Medea, rendered conspicuous through contrast with Medea's mythic history (known to both reader and narrator – VI.45ff.), are forcefully conveyed.

Valerius presents her not as the frightening witch of Ovid, *Metamorphoses* VII, nor as Seneca's irresistible force, but as both virgin and victim, locus of an intense emotional and moral struggle between passion for Jason and devotion to her father, driven to her doom by duplicitous gods. The narrative form and mode of *Argonautica* VII are indeed designed to highlight both the internal humanity of Medea and the impotence of that humanity in the face of historical and psychological forces. Book VII moves from Medea's broken, painful soliloquy (1–25) through the speech/action conflict between Aeetes and Jason (26–102), the increasing torment of Medea (103–52) and its divine manipulation (153–399), through the emotive scene between Jason and Medea in the grove of Hecate, Medea's magical assistance and Jason's pledge of love (400–538), into the book's climactic narrative in which Jason yokes the fiery bulls, sows the dragon's teeth and slays the armed crop which springs from them (539–653). It is a movement from the dramatic to the narrative mode, from internal, subjective epic to external, objective epic, underscored by the contrast between the narrator's address to Medea in Book VII's opening lines and his distant appraisal of Aeetes and Jason at the book's close (VII.653).

The psychological focus of Book VII impresses. In it human behaviour and emotion are precisely and abundantly observed. Contrast with the large-scale bloody narrative of Book VI highlights the book's interiority and humanistic force. Evident throughout is Valerius' sure dramatic sense, his ability to fit speech to psychology, psychology to situation and to charge them with dynamic life – the kind that advances action (see, e.g., the speeches of Medea, Aeetes and Jason at VII.1–100 and the great scene between Jason and Medea at VII.400ff.). Evident too is the narrative and descriptive power of Valerius' poetry, product of controlled verse-form and a mannered, neoclassical style – concise, spare utterance, redolent with ambiguity, yielding occasionally to baroque exuberance and hyperbole. Noteworthy is Valerius' deployment of the simile as visual punctuation, less frequent in dramatically intense scenes where the speeches themselves paragraph the action (nine similes in lines 1–538), plentiful in the climactic narrative (eight/nine similes in lines 539–653), the rapid, changing course of which is signalled by a mannered, almost *pointilliste* use of this device. Nor is the larger context ever distant. Rather, *Argonautica*'s psychological, dramatic and narrative power quickens its cultural force. As the epic's narrative and thematic *romanitas* attest, turbulent mythic events are realized in Valerius' poem not simply as turbulent mythic events but as images of a movement towards civilization, 'fate' and Rome. When it leaves Colchis, the *ratis fatidica*, Jason's 'fate/death-speaking ship', carries with it not simply Medea but Valerius' world.

A. J. B.

Further Reading

Boyle, A. J. (ed.), *The Imperial Muse: Flavian Epicist to Claudian* (Berwick, Victoria, 1990). Essays on Valerius and Flavian epic by M. A. Davis, P. Hardie, and D. McGuire.

Burck, E., 'Die *Argonautica* des Valerius Flaccus', in *idem* (ed.), *Das römische Epos* (Darmstadt 1979) 208–53.

Ehlers, W.-W., *Cai Valeri Flacci Setini Balbi Argonauticon Libri Octo* (Stuttgart 1980).

ARGONAUTICA

BOOK VII

Translated by Frederic Raphael and Kenneth McLeish

Dust takes you from the stranger's company,
The Thessalian; joy with Jason leaves.
Unfriendly dark engulfs you, lovesick girl.
You climb on flinching feet to lonely bed;
5 Shadows lend heat to feverish fantasies,
Set questions spinning in your sleepless head:
'What's wrong with me?' You know the pain,
Know not its cause. At last, from travail, truth
Is born. 'Oh, would it were not so! Why must
10 I lie so long awake? Until I saw
That strong, strong face, my nights were never so.
What, am I mad? Let oceans come between,
My heart goes out to him, and goes again.
Strange! When I think, I think of him alone.
Look, take the Fleece that cousin Phrixus owned:
15 That was your golden goal, you came for that.
Once gone, will you come back? Will my father,
The king, be offered reciprocity –
Haemonian sites to tour? O lucky crew,
Who dared high seas nor feared their captain's lead
20 This far! Now please, crew, captain, go. Begone!'
  She tosses in her bed, each corner tries.
Threshold pales; daystar wanes; new dawn alone
Refreshes that unsleeping love. Compare
How soft showers stiffen wilting wheat
25 Or happy breezes cool hunched oarsmen's backs.

Meanwhile, the Argonauts remember why
They came so far and in their eagerness,
Sure of reward, demand the Fleece. In vain,
The king denies them. Only Jason waits,
Patient. The sacrifice must burn before
The booty's shared. Eager, he stares ahead: 30
The Fleece, can it be there, lucking the court
With gold? He makes to speak. Too late. The king
Pre-empts him, leaping at him, gushing rage:
'Your world is not here, your shore, your throne!   35
What craziness compelled your hard sail here?
Was it family affection, love for me? Phrixus?
Some son-in-law! I would that he had drowned
With his sister! How happy I should be
Knowing no Greek today! No Pelias,
No Thessaly, no Greeklings. Who are they?
Cyanean rocks, pray, what – and where – are they?   40
So look, a stranger comes to Scythia:
Jason, with fifty louts, takes Asia!
For shame! One boatload faces down a king
And steals his treasure while he lives. Should I   45
Say help yourself, my lord? Should I fling wide
My groves, defeated? Should I scorn to fight?
What stops you pillaging our sacred shrines
Or snatching our daughters from their mothers' laps?
Do you have parents, homes? Or is that ship   50
Your all, suckling you with piracy, with storms?
Your own king – so you claim – cast you adrift,
Forbids you to return, since that ram's fleece
Is all he wants to have? Before he does,
We'll strip my Caucasus for planks and sail   55
Those seas to repossess our stolen pride;
Or Helle alive shall I resurgent see,
Whose funeral image, by my decree,
Stands duly crowned. [1] Yet if you will not go –

1. Kramer's supplement to the effect that the dead Helle would have to emerge
miraculously from the sea is adopted here.

If you're ashamed to sail empty-handed home,
60　If some force, more than mortal, ballasts that ship[1]
Of yours, I won't deny your quest. I make
Just one condition. This must you do first.
Before us lies the shaggy field of Mars,
Long years untilled, where fire-breathed bulls are slow
To acknowledge even royal ploughman's rights.
65　They more and more take licence from my age
And bellow, proud, in flame-tongued insolence.
So, Jason, stranger, strong-man, I challenge you.
Plough! Till my fields. As always, I'll supply
The seed – and when the crop's full grown, I'll yield
70　My harvest rights. Go, therefore. Sleep on it,
Consult your gods – and if you have the nerve,
Come back tomorrow with your sleeves rolled up!
Oh, which should I prefer: to see you crisped,
Fire blackened, or living long enough
75　To turn the sod and sow till champions
Spring up, the toothsome seed of Cadmus' snake,[2]
A metal crop to make the furrows flower?'
　　Aghast at this tirade, his daughter stares
At her savage king, then turns to Jason, pale
80　With fear, shaking lest, fool, he take the dare
And damn the odds. He, too, appalled stood there,
All surly rage, immobilized. Thus gapes
A steersman from Phoenicia, Tiber-bound,
Or some Levantine mate: blue sky above,
85　Lighthouse in view, when – crash! –
The haven's gone, gone calm Ausonia,
And raging whirlpools loom. So Jason stands
And ponders words to match the royal rant.
At last he speaks. 'Your tone was different once,'
90　He says. 'When Minyans armed themselves to fight
On your behalf, Aeetes, then you made

1. The *Argo* of course *is* a magical ship.
2. The serpent of Mars that Cadmus killed when founding Thebes. The first Thebans
　　(the 'Spartoi') sprang from its sown teeth. See Statius, *Thebaid* X.612ff.

Quite other promises. Turncoat, what tricks
Are these? I smell another Pelias,
Another sea to cross. Come, tyrants all,
Heap hatred on my head, and wild demands.
My hope is my right hand; I shall not fail.
Submissive ever, yet defiant too,   95
I ask but this: should that rank harvest's spears
O'erwhelm me – or tomorrow's furnace jaws –
Let word go hence to Pelias' vile ears:
Here died my men, and I, by you betrayed,
Who should have paid your debt, and seen me home.'   100
    He speaks, and hurries from that faithless hall,
Leaving father and daughter dumb. Medea stands
A-tremble, silent among her kin. She scans
The ground with teary eyes, then has to look.   105
She sees his parting back, not yet outdoors,
Love-graced with painful excellence. That neck,
Those shoulders! How can she forget him? Why
Does the house itself not up and after him?   110
As Io once stood trembling on the shore –
Afraid to take the plunge, afraid to stay,
Nagged by her Fury, Siren-called
By Pharian maids to swim the swelling sea –
So waits Medea, there beside the door.
Might not her father, even now, change smiles
For frowns? Might he not, e'en now, call Jason back?   115
    Alone, lovelorn, she cries her hero's name.
She hugs Chalciope (her sister), runs
All tongue-tied from the room, then hurries back.
'Tell me how Phrixus came to settle here,
How dragons snatched up Circe and flew away.'   120
Fond fool! She looks to her maids for comfort; none
Supplies. All smiles, she hurries in hope to hug
Her parents, to kiss her father's royal hand.
So lapdogs, cushioned, titbit-pampered, feel
The bite of madness, whimper through the halls,   125
Bewildered, before it's time to run and run.

There's no escape. Silky, herself she plies
The lash. 'You're mad! Why let him haunt you? Look,
He's gone, hull down. Now who are you to him?
130 Before he reaches home, your name's a blank.
Why must I care so much? What's it to me
If he wins, or loses and drowns all Greece in tears?
At least, if by the gods' decree his hour
Has come, let him die on an unknown shore!
135 Please, never here. They call him Phrixus' kin,
Blood of the starborne. Was not Chalciope
(Dear sister!) seen to weep for him? He swore
He came unwillingly, slave to destiny.
God grant him safe return. Let him not hate
140 My father, or know how hard I pray for him.'
   Her prayers all done, she falls back on the bed.
Will sleep relent, and grant her peace at last?
It brings her torment, sharper than before.
She dreams and writhes. Look: here her father kneels;
The stranger there; imploring, both. She wakes,
145 Starting in terror, sees her maids, her home,
Who but a moment since was roaming the towns
Of Thessaly. So did Orestes once,
Blinded by fear, fell Furies in his brain,
Snatch sword, hack wildly at his mother's hordes.
He struck himself with snaky, hissing lash;
Afire, in fancy, for his mother's death,
150 He tracked that tainted Spartan whore, in dreams
Put down divinities, then stumbled back
Dejected, to his sorry sister's arms.
   So, passion-tossed, Medea swoons – but still
She will not yield, will not admit her love.
155 Then Juno figures she'll no more play Chalci-
Ope (Medea's sister). No, that face and voice
No longer serve. Ruling her anger, up
She breezes to Olympus, where she tracks
Conspiring Venus, and remarks (with sighs),
160 'I know you've helped: she burns, she weeps, she raves –

But still unbending all my lures rejects.
Go down, I beg, and charge her with the love
She scorns from me. Make her hot to trot, make her take
The bait, depart her father's royal roof
And shield my darling Jason from all harm.   165
Black potions let her brew (she can, she can!),
To ensnare the sentry snake who, coil on coil
Circles the grove – there, look! – and guards the Fleece.
Just make him fall asleep, slump from his perch;
The rest the Furies and the girl can work.'   170
   Winged Cupid's mother answered, 'Lady, when
You first proposed to jumble all her mind,
With new emotion breach that virgin heart,
Did I refuse? No! My seductive sash
I straightway lent you – you alone! – whereby
The girl, reduced to tears, was bound to yield.   175
And now there's more? She needs me to strip away
Those cautious sighs, that two-faced modesty?
I'll do't! I'll hurl her into Jason's arms.
You send him – quick! – to bright Diana's shrine,
Where Medea and her coven, at dead of night,   180
Set torches blazing and dance for Hecate.
Do you blench at the Night-queen's name? Fear not.
My will be done. If she gets in my way,
She'll catch love's fever, run to serenade
Your hot-breathed bulls and – one, two, three – wind up   185
Mistaken for a cow!'
                  Queen Juno caught
Iris on the wing: 'Do as the lady says.
Prince Jason to the shrine. Quick as you can!'
Iris the Greeks, Medea Venus sought
While Juno on Mount Caucasus sat down,   190
Gazed at Aeaea's walls, in hope, in fear,
Wary as a mortal of the future tense.
   One Venus-glance (the city's in her sights)
And Medea falls again. Poor love! The pain,   195
The panting pain of it! She tumbles him,

The stranger, in her mind. Vain fantasies,
Although he's far away, make her cry out:
'Please God you packed some spell from Thessaly,
Your mother's or (woe, if she exist) your wife's!
I'm helpless, a woman – what can I do but weep?
Oh may I not be forced to watch your fate,
To keep my callused sister[1] company
Once more! He thinks that none here feels for him
Or has him in her heart! He hates us all,
Including me. Yet had I but the power,
The ashes that shall glue the baleful field,
The bones left by the bulls and greedy fire
I should compose and keep. It's right to love
A hero's ghost and cultivate his tomb.'

Speech done, here's Venus sitting on her bed!
All changed her godly lineaments: transformed,
Circe she seemed, the Titan's daughter, bright-
Dressed counterfeit, complete with magic wand.
Entranced, as if by slow, deceptive dream,
The girl's eyes stare, and then make out the great
King's sister. Innocent, with tears of joy,
She leapt to kiss the tricksy goddess' mouth,
First said 'At last, let's say at last, you're back
Among your own, cold Circe, whom dragons once
Took soaring hence! What happier shores kept you
From father's? Sailors here from Thessaly
Have come since you went hence. Here's Jason – oh
How much he had to dare, and dare in vain,
Before homesickness brought you back to us!'

Now Venus interrupts: 'I chose to go;
I went; that's that. Remember heaven's gifts.
The world is there for everyone, the gods
(Believe me) likewise. Home I'll call where'er
My sun comes up, or wanes; so have no mind
To fence me in this cold spot to suit your spite.

200

205

210

215

220

225

230

---

1. From the loss of her husband Phrixus.

How could the dreary Colchians have kept
Me here? How can they you? Ausonian Picus[1]
Has me for queen, whose pastures all are free
Of flaming bulls. I rule the Tuscan sea.
And what of you? Poor child! Do Black Sea tribes
Clamour to marry you? Dear god, what fierce
Hiberian or rough Gelonian   235
Will drag you (and others with you) to his bed?'
   Scorning this question, Medea made reply:
'Circe's great lesson I shall not forget,
Nor let some yokel herd me into bed.
Oh please, have no such fears on my account.   240
But since you can, oh, save me from much worse
Despair, dread fever's source. My mind's ablaze.
I'm desert-dry, sans rest, sans sleep, my dear.
Find me some pause, restore my mind, make day   245
And night discrete again! Cloak me in sleep
And touch my eyes with that composing wand!
Oh little mother, do me that much good!
I was better off alone. Marriage, life, all
Seem vile as those snakes rampant on your head.'   250
Weeping, she fell on unfair Venus' breast,
Contagion's pulse betrayed her secret fire.
   One Venus were they both. The goddess' kiss
Fused hate and love in shameless union.   255
She talks Medea round in casual tones
To happier things. 'Here,' she begins, 'cheer up!'
(The sobs persist.) 'While from Hesperian shores
This way gliding, a ship I spied all set   260
To slip from anchorage. What isle I know
Would care to lose that crew, though rich in men?
And one, I thought, made all the others plain
(I'd spotted him, this prince, from far away).
Assuming me your maid, he pounced and said: 265
"Have you some heart for those about to die,

---

1. In the commoner account, Picus, king of Italy, did not requite Circe's love and
she turned him into a woodpecker.

Who go to meet a fate we scarce deserve?
I beg you, take words, all salt with tears,
And pour their anguish in your mistress' ears.
My prayers I send, my hands I stretch to her.
The selfsame goddesses who pulled me through
A thousand fears have dumped me now; and she alone,
Medea, is my hope, if any hope there is.
Let her not destroy those she cannot see
Nor sentence us to anonymity.
Sad, no grateful debt can I here discharge,
But say this soul is hers, this body too,
Will she but save them. Pity, pity please!
Or should I . . ." He made to fall upon his sword.
I ran to you. Pray, fail him not. The man
So moved me, what he is and what he fears,
His question I hurried to put to you.
New glory you deserve, this suppliant
Whose fame your fame will dignify. I resign,
Who've spelt my name in notoriety.
Did not Hippodameia ease Pelops' task,
At last revolted by those severed heads
Her father's chariot rode vilely down?
If Ariadne her own brother could doom
To death, is it not right for you to help
Good men good deeds to do and Aeaean fields
Release to sweeter fruit? Damn Cadmus' crop
And damn those flaming, xenophobic bulls!'
    Medea, all twisted face and sullen-eyed,
Could scarce control her feelings and her fists.
The goddess would she strike, in furious shame.
Appalled, her ears she buries in her couch:
She will not hear. Dread shakes her bodily.
Where can she run? She's trapped, nowhere to turn!
If only the earth could cover her, and quick
Deliver her – please – from those fatal words.
The goddess beckons her to follow, leaves
The hall. So Bacchus once, his horns and crown

Fresh-gored with wine (or so the myth relates),
Left Pentheus drunk on godhead, snatching up
His mother's drag (not meant for males), her drum,
Her spear. All Pentheus now, Medea stands
Irresolute, afraid. She looks now here,   305
Now there. Who'll help her? Who'll advise? She can't . . .
She dare not . . . quit the palace gate. And yet . . .
Ungovernable passion, Jason doomed to die
And Venus' urgings billow in her breast.
What can she do? She sees herself, flint-hard,
Betray her father for a stranger, foresees
Her notoriety. She bores the gods   310
Above and nags at those below. Her hands
Are claws that punch the ground. She mutters prayers:
'O Hecate, Night-queen, Hades, help me die!
Bury with me the man who maddens me.   315
Pair me with Pelias, the stranger-king
Whose jealous rage sent Jason to this doom.'
Or should she use her spells to help the prince?
She will; she won't. She'd rather die with him
Than let her head be turned, for squalid love
Lavish her all on one she hardly knows.   320

    Then as she lies there, flung down on the bed,
Is it Venus comes teasing at the door?
Shame's caution overpowered and fresh impelled
By forces she cannot understand, she runs
To her secret den. Where is her strongest spell,   325
The formula to help the stranger prince?
Her trick doors spring apart, sigh dust from spells
Long spent. Before her lie her trophies, trawled
From the seabed, handed up from Hell, coaxed to Earth
From the horns of the blood-shot moon. 'You fool!'   330
She chides herself. 'Give up this madness. Death
Before dishonour. Choose!' So many deaths
Available! The quickest, quick! Let's go!
On the brink of death, she strives to summon up   335
Self-hate enough to drink. Unhappy day!

The light of life's too sweet – and sweeter far
There, on the threshold of eternity.
Appalled at her own passion, there she stands
And cries: 'How can you die, and lose the joys
340   Of youth? Not see the down of manhood grace
Your brother's cheeks! And Jason – Jason! –
How can you bear the thought that if you die
You're Jason's death as well? He kneels to you,
Relies on you, as when he first set foot
In Colchis. Father, why did you welcome him?
Why smile false smiles, shake hands with him, not set
345   Your monsters to kill him, right away? A fate –
Oh, I admit it – I too wished for him, then.
Dear Circe, Titan's daughter, give the word.
Lead on; I'll follow; let seasoned wisdom guide,
Green youth be guided.'
                              So she spoke, and fell
350   Once more to thoughts of Jason: care and dread,
Happy to live or die for him alone,
Whichever he decides. She prays again,
Begs Hecate to grant more drastic powers –
355   Her former magic's obsolete. To work!
She takes a herb, the deadliest she knows,
Grown on a ridge of Caucasus, sprung up
Long years ago, flower of Prometheus' blood,
When Zeus' vulture, liverish from its feast,
360   Dripped red from its cruel beak to wound the snow.
That plant no autumn knows, ne'er droops nor dies.
Forever green against the thunderbolt.
Erect, unplucked, it stood, till Hecate,
Her sickle tempered in fell Stygian pools,
365   Cropped from their craggy cairn those potent stalks,
A witch's harvest for her acolyte,
Plucked from the tortured Titan's giblets, high
On windy hill, by tenth moon's magic gleam.
Prometheus groaned, eyed Medea, hunched his limbs;
370   His chains quaked at the sickle's painful stroke.

So, trembling, witched with magic, Medea steps
Out to darkness to end her father's power.
The love-goddess greets her, takes her by the hand
And through the city guides her fearful steps.
When mother birds encourage short-winged chicks   375
To leap from the high nest, to launch themselves
And soar, the nestlings panic, loath to leave
The branch which is all they know. Medea feels
The same, tiptoeing with Venus through the town,   380
Shrinking at shadows, where silent houses loom.
They come to the city gate. She hesitates,
Stands gazing at Venus, then melts once more to tears.
'Does Jason really need me? Is it his voice,   385
Not guilty passion, calling me? And how
Can I serve, respect, a hero on his knees?'
     No answer comes to such inanities.
Now as Medea walks, dark echoes fill
The silence, hissing ancient spells. Fear falls.
Hill-spirits hide their faces. Rivers cringe.   390
Rocks cower. Stables, pastures, graveyards fill
With th'unearthly racket. Night, aghast, slows down
Her hours. Venus – her turn for fear! – hangs back.
They come to triple trees, the Night-queen's lair –   395
And Jason. Medea sees him, stops amazed.
Above them Iris soars – and Venus, too,
Slips from Medea's grasp and disappears.
So in the dark of night shepherd and flock   400
Share common panic; so in Hell's abyss
Blind, voiceless ghosts collide. Thus, in the midnight's grove,
Those two came on each other, all confused.
Aloof as firs they were, or cypresses,   405
Before the mad South Wind mates bough with bough.
     They stood there rapt, face to wordless face, as night
Rolled on its way. Oh, lift your eyes, and speak!
Say something, Jason, please! Speak now! Speak first!
The hero saw her fear, saw rolling tears,   410
Saw burning cheeks, saw misery, saw shame.

He spoke at last, and comforted her love.
'Well, do you bring bright hope?' he said.
'Do you pity my toils? Or will you, too, unkind,
Take pleasure in my death? Sweet girl, I beg,
415   Ape not your sire unspeakable! A face
As fair as yours should brook no hardening.
Is this due thanks, the proper recompense
For all I did? And justice? In your view?
Medea, answer me! Why must I fight
420   Such monstrous foes? Why does your father
Yearn so to see me pay such penalties?
Is it for Canthus, killed by some foreign spear?
Because Iphis (R.I.P.) died there, before
Your walls? Because those Scythians fought here?
425   He should have bid me go, and quit his realm
At once. Two-faced! He gave me hope and now
See how he keeps his promise! Die I can –
And so I shall, before I flinch from this,
Or whate'er he orders. I'll win that fleece!
430   You'll not be first to see me turn and run.'

     That's it! Her cue to speak. He looks to her.
She can't begin to make coherent sense,
She longs to spill her feelings, end to end,
435   But shame sits on her tongue. At last she lifts
Her eyes to his, and asks, 'What made you come,
Thessalian, to our land? Why turn to me?
You long to do so much – why can't you trust
440   Yourself? Had I but feared to quit the house,
Your life – and with it, mine – would have been the price.
Both doomed together. Where's kind Juno now,
Or that Tritonian girl? Amazing how
I alone respond to you when things go wrong!
445   A stranger princess! A babe in my own woods!
And yet, and yet . . . Your destiny trumps mine;
The suppliant I supply. Should Pelias
Again attempt your ruin, other trials
In other lands decree, don't trust your looks

To earn such help again!' Now from her breast
Titanian herbs and Circean potencies   450
She draws. She hesitates, then speaks again:
'But if you think your gods, or your own right arm,
Can still protect you, Jason, even now
I beg you: let me go, untainted, home.'   455
   Silence. Then quickly (stars were on the wane,
Boötes to the horizon's limit bent),
In tears – it hurt! – she gave him her store of spells,
Handed him her fatherland, her pride, her name.
   He held out eager hands, and took the lot.   460
Her innocence now gone beyond recall,
Passion ridden, never to blush again,
For every limb she chants her formula.
The hero's shield seven times is reinforced;
His spear gains weight and deadly quality.   465
The bulls, though distant, feel their fire die down.
'Now to it,' she says. 'This crested helmet take,
By Discord's deathly hand supplied! The ground
Once turned, pitch this amongst the crop, and straight
The serried ranks of warriors will warp in rage   470
Against each other. My father will cry out
And send hard looks my way.' Even as she spoke,
Her mind turned more and more towards the sea.
Already she imagined Jason's sails spread out,   475
Herself abandoned. Stabbed by sharp alarm,
She plucked the hero's hand and played his slave:
'Remember me – as I (oh, doubt it not!)
Shall remember you. Once you depart, pray tell,
Where shall I look for dawn? As time goes by,
I pray that you, somewhere, somehow, may think   480
Of me, recall the you you are today,
Your need of all my help, the girl I am!
Why have your eyes no tears to shed for me?
Soon shall I die at my angry father's hand:
I won't pretend. You've land, throne, happiness   485
Ahead of you. Your wife and children wait.

For me, betrayed, a traitor's death. Complain?
I'm happy, for Jason's sake, to lose the sun.'
　　The hero answered (since with silent spells
490　She'd fired his heart and hers with equal lust):
'How can you think that I could leave this land
And anywhere survive where you were not?
Betray me to the tyrant first; take back
Your spells. I'll none of them. What's life to me,
If you're not there? What means my fatherland,
Unless I see you clasped in its king's embrace –
My father's, Aeson's – while from afar all Greece
495　Your fleecy brilliance sees, and headlong runs
To the shore to greet you? Yes? Wife (!), say yes!
For by the power that awes the gods, in heaven,
In hell, by the stars whose course you bend at will,
500　By this hour, perilous to us both, I swear:
If ever I forget this night, and what
You did – for my sake leaving parents, home
And power – if ever I break my word to you,
May it avail me nothing to have escaped
505　The bulls and the earth-born army. Use your spells,
Your fires. In my own home, discomfort me!
If I betray you, bring me to my knees
With blackest magic. Lash me! Make me writhe!'
　　He spoke his own future pain. The Fury heard
510　Whose care is love abandoned – heard, and planned.
　　They stood awhile in silence, gazing at
The ground, blushing, darting quick glances, full
Of mischief, at each other, then looking down
515　Again. It was Medea's turn to speak.
'I promised to tell you all – and there's still more.
There's danger even when you've killed the bulls.
You've still to face the Guardian of the Fleece,
Monstrous, here on the Tree of Mars. Oh trust
520　In Hecate! Trust me! Trust our dark power!'
　　She spoke, and showed her hero what she meant.
She stirred the serpent, dozing in its coils,

Let it taste Jason's shadow. Hissing hard,
It coiled itself tighter round the Fleece, then reared   525
Its head, looping and lunging through the grove.
     'What is it? Medea, speak! What noise was that?'
Cried Jason, drawing his sword and shuddering.   530
She laughed, drew him aside and calmed the snake.
'It's father's final test, the last his rage
Devised for you. Oh Jason, nerve yourself
Once more! Let me see you scale this gnarled ash,   535
Its knots your ladder, till the restless coiled beast
You stamp to death! Then might I die for joy!'
So! Cloaked in waning night, she made for home,
Home to the palace before Night's shadows waned.

     Her father, meanwhile, drawn by empty hope,
Went down to the beach in the reddening dawn
To see how far away the Argonauts   540
Had sailed that night, to see if the sea was bare.
And as he stood there, gazing at the waves,
Arcadian Echion ran to him. 'My lord,
Our hero waits, there in the Field of Mars.
May it please you, send your bronze-hooved bulls to fight!'   545
     Hope winged Aeetes' heart. 'He took the dare!
Breathe fire, my bulls, and plough the field in flames!
Then let that Colchian yokel try his hand
At a harvest worth the reaping. Medea, come!
Your father calls! Rouse your serpent against the Greeks!   550
Let them die in that sacred grove, before the Fleece;
Let it feast my eyes, smeared red with bad Greek blood.'
     He spoke, and signed to his men to loose the bulls.
Some fetched the plough, while others, groaning, bent   555
To shoulder that dread seed, the dragon's teeth.
Jason stepped forward, thronged by Argonauts.
They cheered him on, gave him their best advice
And left him to face his fate. He stood awhile
Alone, like some migrating bird that strays   560
From the flock on a sunburned desert's edge
Or battles sleet and storm as it wings its way

Towards Riphaean crags where the winds are born.
Then, from the bull-pens, smoke and flame. Sea, land,
565 The shaggy slopes of Caucasus flash fire.
See! As when Jupiter, enraged, hurls flame
From heaven at mortals who have risked his rage,
570 The bulls charge: whirlwinds of flame, twin fires.
The Argonauts draw back. (Bold Idas, too,
Who late was lamenting that a woman's spells
Had kept him from the conflict, cowered down
575 And looked – unwillingly – Medea's way.)
     Not seeing Jason, the bulls charged up the field.
He ran towards them, waved his helmet plumes
And with his own hand beckoned the fire his way.
580 The first bull saw him, stopped in puzzlement,
Then changed its course and charged. So ocean waves
Hurl themselves headlong at high cliffs, and fall
Back broken. Twice, his nostrils snorting fire,
He runs on Jason, veiling him in smoke.
Each time the Colchian pirouettes aside,
585 Catching the flames on his enchanted shield
And dousing all their fury. Forth he puts
His hand, firm grips the horns, and twists. The bull
At first resists him, pushes hard against
590 Medea's magic, stands four square and tries
To toss him overhead and gore him. Then,
Exhausted, bellowing a deeper note, it drops
Its head and kneels. At once, beckoning to his crew
To bring the yoke, Jason muzzles its fiery jaws,
Then wrestles, dragging and being dragged,
595 Pressing hard against its flank, until the bull
Bends its neck at last and, trembling, takes the yoke.
     Medea meanwhile, fearful for Jason, tames
The second bull and leads him up the field,
Slowly. He shakes his head and grumbles threats.
She baffles him with cloud, and makes him kneel
At Jason's feet, crushed by the weight of his
600 Own rage. Straight Jason leaps on him, and rides

Him, hard, till all his fire is spent. Then on
With yoke, and plough, and up! He kicks his ribs
And goads him with a spear – as when Lapithes
Tamed Neptune's earth-born charger, bridled it   605
And rode it triumphantly on Ossa's slopes.[1]
  So Jason ploughed the plain, as easily
As farmers in Egypt furrow mud beside
The fertile Nile. He scatters dragon's teeth
In handfuls, sows new-tilled land with war.
Three times, as the ploughshare passes, trumpets blare   610
For battle, and warhorns echo from below.
The furrows heave, in labour with metal men.
An army sprouts in ranks across the plain.
Back to the Argonauts the hero goes.
He waits his moment, till the nearest row   615
Pokes necks, and heads, and nodding plumes
Above the ground. He leaps on them then, sword drawn,
And reaps them before their shoulders see the light.
Wherever gleaming corslets grow, or hands   620
Reach out for him from Mother Earth,
He slices them.
               But for each one he kills,
A thousand grow – as Hydra multiplied
Heads in that ancient myth, when Hercules,
Exhausted, heard and heeded Athene's voice
Advising fire. So Jason turns once more   625
To Medea's magic. He reaches up, undoes
His helmet-strap – and hesitates, for still
He'd rather, for valour, kill them one by one,
However many banners, trumpet-calls,
War-cries, they range against him. Then, they hurl   630
A storm of spears. With shaking hands he rips
The helmet (smeared with magic) from his head
And hurls it at them. Spears fall harmless down.

---

1. An allusion to Lapithes' taming of the first horse, which Neptune sent forth
from a chasm in the earth.

635 In Phrygia each year Cybele's tearful rage
  Cuts loose, unmans her acolytes; thus too
  Bellona her titivated eunuchs bleeds.
  Medea, their sudden equal, matches them,
  Sets man on man, brother at brother's throat.
  Deluded, each his Jason floors. One rage
640 Consumes them all. Aeetes strains to call
  The madmen back, but all at one fell stroke
  Are gone – one gulp, the earth has swallowed all.
   In lathered armour, straight to the river
645 Flew Aeson's son – like to some dusty Mars
  Plunging from Getic war to scorch the Hebrus
  With his bloody heat; like a Cyclops, furnace-black,
  Bolting the forge's glare to catch his breath
  In the Sicilian sea. Jason returns
  At last; his happy friends he can embrace,
650 But deigns not demand the liar king now keep
  The bond once volunteered. Nor, offered it,
  Would Jason take the fleece with loyal heart.
  No. Sullen, both men back away, all scowls.

SILIUS ITALICUS

INTRODUCTION

Punica, Silius' epic narrative of the second great war between Rome and Carthage (218–201 B.C.), is the longest extant poem in the Latin language. Its seventeen books comprise over twelve thousand lines. Often derided, it is a bold, important work. Valerius and Statius responded to Lucan's dismemberment of epic by reverting to the narrative mode and replacing the fatal glare of history with the symbolism of myth. Silius met Lucan half-way. He accepted Lucan's challenge to confront the past head-on but eschewed (rightly) Lucanesque style and theory, adopting a self-consciously Virgilian manner – related to but different from that of Valerius and Statius – for the epicizing of history. Lucan's banishment of the gods, performance rhetoric and narrative sparseness are rejected, as Silius saturates his text with the traditional devices of 'high epic': invocations of the Muse (e.g. I.3ff., III.222ff.), catalogues of forces (III.222–405, VIII.356–616), divine intervention and motivation (e.g. XII.605–728 in Selection V; XVII.522–604 in Selection VI), epic similes (e.g. III.535–9 in Selection II, XVII.487–90 in Selection VI), ecphrases (e.g. II.395–456, III.32–44), funeral games (XVI.275ff.), even a traditional Nekuia or Visit to the Underworld (XIII.385ff.) – unlike Lucan's untraditional one at the end of *Civil War* VI (570ff.). In a sense Silius is returning to the early Roman tradition, represented by the poets Naevius and Ennius (late third to early second century B.C.), of the epic mythologization of history. But he is doing so in the world after Lucan. And the insistent dialogue between *Punica* and both *Civil War* and Virgil's *Aeneid*, made conspicuous by Silius' choice of a period and course of events 'historically' intermediate between those addressed by his two predecessors, creates of the three poems an epic trilogy on the history of Rome – from its mythic foundation (*Aeneid*) through its republican zenith (*Punica*) to Rome's dismemberment by Caesar (*Civil War*).

Silius' subject was well chosen. The second Carthaginian or Punic war – often called after Carthage's brilliant general, Hannibal, the 'Hannibalic' war – was not only chronologically intermediate between the worlds of *Aeneid* and *Civil War* but represented something which Virgil and Lucan refer to but never depict: the Roman republic at its height. The war was a political, social and (to many) moral watershed of Roman history. Undoubtedly the Roman republic's greatest external crisis, the war produced many of Rome's finest heroes, paradigms of the values and valour of the Roman tradition at its best: Fabius Maximus, for example, fearless shepherd of the people (VII.123ff.), cautious, intelligent, forebearing, whose selfless wisdom was eulogized at the climactic point of Anchises' apocalypse in *Aeneid* VI (846); the compassionate and humane Marcellus (XIV.665ff.), who, unlike Aeneas in Virgil's great epic, fulfils Anchises' clemency ideal (*Aeneid* VI.853) in the hour of victory. But Rome's victory was also its defeat. It transformed the city into an imperial power, and began what many ancient historians saw (Polybius, Sallust, Livy, and the annalist Lucius Piso, for example – who differ however on the actual turning-point) as the moral and political decline of the second century B.C., which culminated in the death of the republic and the destruction of the very values which Rome's resistance to Hannibal displayed. *Punica* exploits the ambivalence of the Roman triumph. It highlights the courage, nobility, self-sacrifice, compassion and endurance of Rome in defeat but intimates also the self-seeking ambition (see the speech of Scipio Africanus at XVI.695–7) and vicious brutality (contrast the behaviour of Claudius Nero at XV.813ff. with that of Hannibal at XV.381ff.) which victory begins to promote. The poem points constantly in the direction of Lucan. Indeed the civil wars at the end of the republic are overtly predicted in the Sibyl's prophecy of Book XIII (864ff.). It is not accidental that *Punica*'s account of the Saguntine mass suicide (II.617ff.) alludes to Lucan's depiction of Roman self-slaughter (*Civil War* II.146ff.) and that Silius concludes the central triad of his poem (Books VIII–X), his account of defeated Rome's greatness at the battle of Cannae (216 B.C.), on a profoundly Lucanesque note:

> This was Rome then; if after your fall, Carthage,
> Rome's values were doomed to change, I'd rather you still stood.

(Punica X.657–8)

The second Punic war had been dealt with briefly by Ennius in his historical epic, *The Annals* (Books VII–IX), and at length in prose by the historian Livy, who devoted ten books of his *History of Rome from its Foundation* to its depiction (Books XXI–XXX), and on the latter Silius depends heavily for the historical details of his narrative. He depends on neither for the ideological structure of his epic. The centring of the narrative on the testing of Rome at Cannae (Books VIII–X) – an event which took place in the first three years of almost a twenty-year war – is not only a marked divergence from Livy (who with more chronological balance centres his account on Hannibal's failure to take Rome in 211 B.C. – Book XXVI) but part of a careful moral design aimed at underscoring the poem's major paradoxes: Rome's greatness in defeat, the ambivalence of her victory; Hannibal's defeat in victory, his pathos and moral stature in defeat. Thus the central triad itself is preceded by seven books devoted (primarily) to Hannibal's success and Rome's failures and followed by seven books devoted (primarily) to Hannibal's failures and Rome's successes. The military rise and fall of Hannibal are counterpointed by the military fall and rise of Rome. The first heptad, Books I–VII, directs itself to the origins of the war (in Dido's curse and Hannibal's oath: Selection I), Hannibal's capture of Saguntum in Spain (218 B.C.), his crossing of the Alps (218 B.C.: Selection II), his victories at the Ticinus, the Trebia (218 B.C.: Selection III) and Lake Trasimene (217 B.C.: Selection IV), the rising tide of Hannibal's success interrupted only slightly by the digression on Regulus and the moral lead given by Fabius Maximus (Books VI–VII). The second heptad, Books XI–XVII, recounts Hannibal's capture of Capua and the resultant enervation of the Carthaginian army, as it succumbs to the pleasures of luxury and wine; it details Hannibal's failures in Campania, his repulse from Rome (211 B.C.: Selection V), Roman victories in Sardinia, Campania (the recapture and punishment of Capua), Sicily, Spain, Umbria (at the Metaurus) and finally in Africa, where Scipio Africanus defeats Hannibal's forces in the decisive engagement at Zama (202 B.C.: Book XVII, Selection VI). The epic ends with a rich tableau of Scipio's triumphal procession at Rome in 201 B.C. Some critics have argued plausibly for a 2–3–2 partition in each heptad (Books I–II, III–V, VI–VII; Books XI–XII, XIII–XV, XVI–XVII), anticipating and recalling the central triad and underscoring the thematic counterpoint between different sections.

Punica's melancholic intimation of the perils of victory and the moral decline that attends success is no hackneyed exploitation of a rhetorical commonplace. It is the intellectual and moral verdict of a man who had witnessed as consul the fall of Nero and had himself supported one of the imperial candidates in the bloody upheaval of A.D. 69. What we know of Silius' life largely derives from others (especially the younger Pliny, *Letters* III.7). Tiberius Catius Asconius Silius Italicus was born in A.D. 25 or 26 (it is uncertain where) during the reign of Tiberius. Though he achieved early success as an orator in the law courts, he seems to have damaged his reputation during Nero's principate when he was believed to have brought prosecutions on his own initiative. Certainly he found favour with Nero, in whose final year (A.D. 68) he served as consul. In A.D. 69 he was involved with Vitellius, but the latter's replacement of Otho as emperor was soon followed by defeat at the hands of Vespasian, in whose principate (A.D. 69–79), however, Silius not only survived but served with distinction as governor of Asia (about A.D. 77). Silius then retired from public life to dedicate himself to writing and patronage. Immensely wealthy, he was a patron of the poet Martial (see *Epigrams* VII.63, VIII.66, etc.) and other literary figures, and made his house into a centre for literary conversation and debate, giving numerous readings of his own verse apparently to elicit critical appraisal. When he began to write *Punica* is not known, but he had certainly started it in the late A.D. 80s (see Martial, *Epigrams* IV.14, published in A.D. 89), although the finished poem was perhaps not published until the late 90s – probably after Domitian's death (A.D. 96). Silius did not long survive the completion of his text. In A.D. 100 or 101, having contracted an incurable illness, he starved himself to death in his house at Naples. His suicide placed him in fine literary company: Seneca, Petronius, most especially Lucan. But unlike *Civil War*, which killed its author (Lucan's suicide was compelled) and remained unfinished, *Punica* was finished and its author killed himself. In the end perhaps for Silius life and work were not to be separated.

As testimony to this perhaps: his veneration of Virgil. According to the younger Pliny (*Letters* III.7), Silius 'celebrated Virgil's birthday with more solemnity than his own and used to visit Virgil's tomb as if it were a temple'. This veneration is evident throughout the epic: in verse form, in language, in allusion. *Punica* I is programmatic in this regard. By presenting the Hannibalic war right from the start of the poem (I.81ff. in Selection I) as fulfilment of Dido's curse (*Aeneid* IV.622–9) and sequel to *Aeneid*'s epic action, Silius nominates *Punica*'s main subtext and intimates an extensive programme of intertextual reference. Thereafter language, theme, motif and situation are used to connect the two epics. Nomenclature included. Romans are called 'sons of Aeneas' (their first title at I.2), 'Laurentines', 'Dardanians', 'Trojans', etc.; Carthaginians are called 'Sidonians', 'Libyans', 'Tyrians', etc. – in order that the struggle between Rome and Carthage may be seen as originating in Aeneas' desertion of Dido and that the reader may draw appropriate comparisons between characters and episodes in Virgil's epic and in *Punica* itself. Situational allusions abound. At Book I.125ff. (Selection I), for example, the priestess' prophecy to the young Hannibal of the conflict to come echoes the Sibyl's prediction to Aeneas at *Aeneid* VI.83ff.; while the scene at Book XII.701ff. (Selection V), where Juno stops Hannibal's assault on Rome by revealing to him the Olympians guarding the city, recalls that at *Aeneid* II.589ff., where Venus shows Aeneas the same gods destroying Troy and persuades him to leave the city. Later in Book XII (744ff.) the description of the Romans pouring out of the city to inspect the deserted Carthaginian camp refers back to Troy's jubilation at the (feigned) departure of the Greeks at *Aeneid* II.26ff. In each

case situational similarities point up situational differences, the
ironies of history noted.

One irony merits special attention: Hannibal's prefiguration in,
and reversal of, Aeneas. The allusions to Aeneas in Books I and XII
noted above are part of an extensive series linking the Carthaginian
general to the Trojan hero. Hannibal's reception of the armour
and great shield at II.395–456, his confrontation with the temple
pictures at Liternum at VI.653–716, his reaction to the storm
which rises at XVII.236–89, and other scenes and episodes recall
and are modelled on famous encounters by Aeneas in Virgil's epic.
But although Hannibal dominates *Punica* as Aeneas does *Aeneid*,
his movement is the precise opposite of the Trojan hero's. Aeneas
moves from defeat to victory, from the model of Hector to that of
Achilles, from humanity to dehumanization; Hannibal moves from
victory to defeat, from the model of Achilles to that of Hector,
from suprahuman irresistibility to deluded vulnerability. Indeed at
Zama he plays Turnus (Selection VI, Book XVII.522ff.; cf. *Aeneid*
X.633ff.) to Scipio's Aeneas. At the same time, like Aeneas, he is
the cause of Roman greatness, generating Rome's finest moment
at Cannae and pressuring Rome to produce her own Hannibal,
Scipio Africanus. It is Scipio who gradually takes over the role of
the new Aeneas from Hannibal, visiting the underworld in a
manner that recalls both Odysseus and Aeneas himself and becom-
ing by the final book of the epic a 'Rhoeteian', i.e. Aeneas-like,
creator of corpses (XVII.486 in Selection VI). Of course, more lies
behind Hannibal than Virgil's epic hero – Statius' Capaneus, for
example, whose conflict with Jupiter in *Thebaid* X (827–936) is
echoed in Hannibal's own (*Punica* XII.605ff. in Selection V), but
most especially Lucan's Caesar, whose anti-Aeneas configuration
and individual war with the Roman state shape much of Silius'
presentation of Hannibal. In both *Civil War* and *Punica* the struggle
is essentially between the anti-Roman and Rome. In *Punica* the
anti-Roman generates Roman greatness, in *Civil War* he becomes
Rome itself. *Punica*'s multi-allusiveness has point. Silius uses it to
suggest the inevitability of Rome's dismemberment. Aeneas' rejec-
tion of Dido led to the anti-Aeneas onslaught and defeat and to
the generation of another Aeneas, Scipio, who opened the way for

the paradoxical Caesar, both anti-Aeneas and Aeneas, 'a Trojan descendant of grandsire Iulus' (*Punica* XIII.863f.). For Silius the death of the Roman republic and of the values for which at its finest moment it would stand were contained in its foundation.

The selections from *Punica* which follow trace the military rise and fall of Hannibal and the defeat but eventual triumph of Rome. They move from (I) Hannibal's oath sworn as a child in 237 B.C. at the shrine of Dido in Carthage and the priestess' aborted prophecy of his future, through (II) his crossing of the Alps in 218 B.C., (III) his defeat of the Romans at the river Trebia in 218 B.C. (where the Roman rout is balanced by the Achillean conflict between the father of Scipio Africanus and the river Trebia itself), (IV) his victory at Lake Trasimene in 217 B.C. (where the focus is on the selfless valour of the Volscian Bruttius), to (V) his repulse from Rome in 211 B.C. and (VI) his final defeat at Zama by the new Aeneas and replacement Hannibal, Scipio. The translation has endeavoured to reproduce something of the heroic simplicity, relaxed linguistic structure, and the descriptive, narrative, and psychological force of Silius' style (note especially Silius' representation of death in battle and of human panic and the skill with which he interweaves speech and narrative). Silius' use of the Latin hexameter, the standard metre for epic, is overtly Virgilianizing, but he forsakes his predecessor's verbal density and syntactic tautness in pursuit of a more Homeric, almost paratactic, highly perceptual mode. In this he differs signally from the baroque, luxuriant style of Statius and the mannerism of Valerius. But like them he has much to say about Flavian Rome. *Punica* projects itself as the central epic of the trilogy, *Aeneid*, *Punica*, *Civil War*, with specific purpose. Zama was the beginning of the end, as Scipio in Hades (and the reader) 'foresaw' (XIII.868ff.). Its inheritance was the worship of power. The irony of *Punica*'s final two lines, ostensibly addressed to Scipio, would not have been lost on a society whose leaders declared themselves gods:

> Rome truly tells no lie when she calls your stock divine,
> And names you child of the Capitoline thunderer.

> (*Punica* XVII.653–4)

A.J.B.

Further Reading

Ahl, F. M., Davis, M. A., Pomeroy, A., 'Silius Italicus', *Aufstieg und Niedergang der römischen Welt* 32.4 (1986) 2492–561.

Albrecht, M. von, *Silius Italicus: Freiheit und Gebundenheit römischer Epik* (Amsterdam 1964).

Boyle, A. J. (ed.), *The Imperial Muse: Flavian Epicist to Claudian* (Berwick, Victoria, 1990). Essays on Silius and Flavian epic by P. Hardie, D. McGuire and A. Pomeroy.

Delz, J. (ed.), *Silius Italicus: Punica* (Stuttgart 1987).

PUNICA

―――――

SELECTIONS

Translated by Marcus Wilson

I. Book I.81–139

Carthage, 237 B.C.[1]

At the city's heart stood the shrine to Dido's ghost –
Mother of Carthage. This place encircled by yews,
Buried beneath the mournful shade of pines, deprived
Of light, the Tyrians held in ancestral awe.
It was here, they say, the queen cast off the distress   85
Of her mortality. Cheerless stone effigies
Stand by, of Belus founder of the royal house,
And all Belus' line; Agenor pride of his race;
And Phoenix who gave the land its long-lasting name.[2]
With Sychaeus endlessly Dido sits at last,   90
At her feet the Trojan sword.[3] To Erebus' lord
And heaven's gods a hundred altars stand in rows.
Here in Stygian dress the priestess frees her hair
To call Acheron and Henna's Proserpina.
From the earth come groans; from the darkness horrible   95
Hissings erupt; on the altars fires flare unlit.

―――――

1. According to Silius this incident took place when Hannibal (born in late 247
   B.C.) was just ten years old (*Punica* XIII.744ff.). See also Livy XXI.1, where
   Hannibal is stated to be about nine years old.
2 i.e. of Phoenicia, the Roman name for the Carthaginians being *Poeni*, 'Punics'.
3. The sword of Aeneas, with which Dido had killed herself. See Virgil's *Aeneid*
   IV.646–7.

Dead souls stirred by incantation flit through the void
And from Dido's marble face perspiration drips.
To this shrine, called by his father comes Hannibal.
100   Hamilcar watches the boy's attitude and face:
Neither the shrieking Massylian priestess' rage
Nor the temple's bloodstained entrance, barbaric rites[1]
And flames that leap on hearing the chant turned him pale.
The father pats his son's head, kisses his son's cheeks,
105   Then whips up his son's feelings with a stirring speech:
'Unfairly the resurrected race of Troy wrongs
With treaties Cadmus' breed.[2] Should fate prevent my arm
Repelling this humiliation from our land,
Choose this, my son, as your glorious task. Start wars
110   To destroy the Laurentines. Make Etruscan youths
Shudder to see your dawning, and as you arise
Make mothers in Latium wish for childlessness.'
The boy, spurred by such promptings, repeats this harsh oath:
'With swords and flames, by sea and land, when I'm a man
115   The Romans I shall hunt. I shall revive Troy's doom.
No gods will deter me, no Mars-constraining pacts,
Not the towering Alps or sheer Tarpeian rock.
To this end I pledge my life, by our native Mars
And your shade, Queen Dido.' To triform Hecate[3]
120   A black victim is slain. In search of oracles
The priestess quickly opens up the breathing corpse
To catch the soul escaping entrails freshly bared.
And when by her ancient art she entered the mind

1. Perhaps a reference to the sacrifice of young children, common at Carthage (see *Punica* IV.765ff.).
2. The Carthaginians ('Cadmus' breed') resented the terms of peace imposed on them after the first Punic war (264–241 B.C.) by the Romans ('the resurrected race of Troy'). Carthage was forced to abandon Sicily and pay Rome a large indemnity over a period of ten years. Carthaginian ships were forbidden to enter Italian waters. In 238 B.C. Rome also annexed Sardinia and Corsica, previously Carthaginian possessions.
3. Hecate was a primitive goddess associated with the underworld, but also identified with the moon (Luna) and with Diana. Hence 'triform'.

Of divinity, as she'd sought, she spoke aloud:
'I see Aetolian fields vastly strewn with dead;[1]   125
I see lakes frothing red, warm with Idaean blood.
How massive the peaks that soar towards distant stars
Where your camp clings to the side of the highest cliff!
The army bursts from the mountains. City walls quail
And smoulder. All those lands stretched beneath western skies   130
Glow with Sidonian fire. Look! Thick with gore runs
The Po! Grim-faced in death on top of arms and men
Lies the third hero to honour Jove with choice spoils.[2]
But what's this? Clouds gather suddenly! A wild storm
Rampages. Fire flashing from the sky splits the air.   135
The gods prepare for great events. High heaven's court
Thunders. I see Jupiter at war.' Of fate's course
Juno barred further knowledge; at once the entrails
Fell silent, hiding the setbacks, the boundless toil.

II. Book III.477–556
The Alps, 218 B.C.

Memories of past struggles were expelled by fear
When Hannibal's troops descried the Alps imminent.
Hail and frost cloak the landscape endlessly in white
And lock in ice as old as time. Stiffened by cold   480
The tall mountain's sheer face meets rising Phoebus' rays,

1. A reference to the battle of Cannae in 216 B.C. (*Punica* VIII–X). Other incidents prophesied here are the battle of Lake Trasimene in 217 B.C. (*Punica* VI), Hannibal's crossing of the Alps in 218 B.C. (*Punica* III), his victories at the Ticinus and the Trebia, both tributaries of the Po, in 218 B.C. (*Punica* IV) and repulse from Rome in 211 B.C. (*Punica* XII), and the death of Marcellus in 208 B.C.

2. A reference to Marcus Claudius Marcellus, ambushed and killed by Carthaginian forces in 208 B.C. (*Punica* XV.334ff.), the year of his fourth consulship. 'Choice spoils' (*spolia opima*) were awarded to a Roman commander who fought and killed the leader of an enemy army. Marcellus had been only the third man in Roman history to achieve this honour, which he earned by slaying a Gallic king in 222 B.C.

Its glacial hardness unsoftened by his fire.
As far as Tartarus' pit – with its pallid realm
Of Underworld shades and stagnant pools of black swamp –
485 Lies beneath the earth does the ground rise through the air
Obtruding on the heavens with its silhouette.
Banished is summer's brilliance; spring never comes.
In these grim towers, guarding her permanent home,
Vile winter lives on her own. On all sides she makes
490 A turbulence of grey clouds and rain mixed with hail.
In the Alps all the squalls and tempests exercise
Boisterous dominion, mountains disappear
In mist and on high cliffs dizziness blurs the view.
Add Athos to Taurus, Mimas to Rhodope,
495 Othrys to Haemus and Ossa to Pelion:
The Alps would eclipse their collective magnitude.
First to invade these untouched heights was Hercules.
The gods saw him jolt the summits, burst through the clouds
And subjugate by brute force these crags undefiled
By human foot for aeons since the world began.
500 The soldiers slow their stride and trudge hesitantly,
Thinking they bear sinful arms into sacred space
In breach of nature's ban, and contend with the gods.
Not so their leader. No dread of the place, no Alps
Unsettle him. Irate at their spiritless hearts,
505 To revive their vigour he coaxes and exhorts:
'Shame! Tired of fortune and the gods' docility
Will you, battle-hardened and triumphant,[1] retreat
From snow-capped hills and surrender your arms to rocks?
Now, comrades, think now it's imperious Rome's walls
510 That you scale and Jove's lofty peak, the Capitol.
This work will shackle the Tiber and Italy!'
At once the army, inspired by the promised prize,
He guides up the slope. The track great Hercules beat
He bids his men desert and, marching over ground

1. Earlier this year Hannibal's army had completed the siege and capture of the town of Saguntum in Spain despite strong protests from Rome (*Punica* I–II).

Unexplored, discover their own path of ascent.   515
He breaks through impenetrable passes and first
To climb the steep scarp hails the column from above.
Where compacted frost encases the mountainside
And over white ridges the trail grows treacherous
He attacks with steel the opposing ice. Loose snow   520
Sucks men into its depths and from the pinnacle
An avalanche crashing down inundates the ranks.
At times Corus, his black wings bristling, lifts snowdrifts
And hurls them at their faces with his hostile blasts,
Or with a loud roar, storming wildly, snatches shields   525
From the soldiers' grasp and spinning them round and round
Whirls them with twisting flurries up amongst the clouds.
The further they go in their struggle to the top
Their task becomes more arduous. As one crest yields
The weary troops a course a greater crest is born;   530
They avoid glancing back at what their sweat and toil
Have surmounted, so alarming is the plunging
Drop that meets their gaze. A single view of white frost
Oppresses them as far as visibility
Lasts. Likewise the sailor who's left the welcome land   535
And floats becalmed in mid-ocean, his sails bereft
Of wind, his mast unstressed: a limitless expanse
Of water is his outlook. Wearily, to rest
His eyes confounded by the sea, he scans the sky.
    To these reverses and frustrations of terrain   540
Add the wild men who poke from crannies faces smeared
With filth, their hair matted stiff through ceaseless neglect.
Spilling from hollow caverns of eroded rock
This alpine tribe, vigorous by habit, agile
Over its thickets, well-known snow and wilderness,   545
Swarms down the mountain, surrounds the foe and attacks.
Now the landscape is transformed: here the snow is red,
Dyed with streaming blood; there the invincible ice
Yields little by little, melted by human gore.
Whenever their horses stamp the ground, their hard hooves,   550
Held fast by the perforated ice, become trapped.

A fall brings further hazards: they lose hands and feet
To frostbite; harsh numbness lops fractured arms and legs.
Twelve days, twelve savage nights of torment they endure
555   To reach the long-awaited summit. Then they rest
As their camp hovers high atop the precipice.

III. Book IV.525–703
The Trebia, 218 B.C.

525   Give me Maeonian Homer's resonant tongue,
Let father Phoebus grant my speech a hundred mouths –
The slaughter outstrips language, such was the consul's
Strength in arms, such was the Tyrian's frenzied wrath.[1]
Each leader killed a battle-hardened veteran
530   Right before his rival's eyes: the Libyan slew
Murranus; the Italian slew Phalantus.
Anxur had sent Murranus from her storm-tossed peak;
You, Phalantus, were sent from Lake Triton, revered
For her pure waters. When first his distinctive cloak
535   Marked out the consul, Cupencus blind in one eye,
The other ample for war, boldly threw his spear:
It stuck vibrating in the shield's rim. Anger seethed
In the consul's breast: 'Forfeit for your insolence
The light your brutish and disfigured face still meets.'
540   So saying, he hurled hard and straight his heavy spear
And the point passed through that hideous single eye.
No less ruthlessly raged the son of Hamilcar.
To him fell poor Varenus from Mevania
Clad in winter armour, for whom rich Fulginia
545   Ploughs her fertile plain and through open pasture-land

---

1. The 'consul' referred to here is Tiberius Sempronius Longus, whom Silius calls
Gracchus because of the connection between the Sempronii and the Gracchi. The
'Tyrian' is Hannibal.

The cool Clitumnus flows, colouring white the bulls.[1]
His care in raising victims for Tarpeian Jove
Was in vain, for the gods showed him no clemency.
The Spaniards are fast in attack, Moors faster still.
Here javelins, there Libyan spears, in dense clouds   550
Blanket the heavens, and quivering missiles hide
All the level ground as far as the river's banks.
The press of bodies denies the dead room to fall.
Allius the hunter from Argyripa brought
From the land of Daunus his crudely fashioned darts   555
And prancing native horse. He charged the enemy
Flinging light Apulian spears that found their marks.
The skin of a Samnite bear bristles on his chest;
His helmet is fortified with an old boar's tusks;
He spreads commotion as if chasing animals   560
On mount Garganus or through unfrequented woods.
From the left Mago saw him and at the same time
Savage Maharbal caught sight of him from the right,
Like two bears forced by hunger from opposite crags
To stalk the same bull quaking at the twofold threat,
Their frenzy disallowing a sharing of prey.   565
From two directions spears of Moorish yew-wood fly
Hissing and burst through both sides of Allius' chest.
In his heart's centre the spearheads met with a clang.
Which one killed him it was impossible to tell.

    The Romans lose formation, their standards scattered.   570
Hannibal drives the stragglers to the river's edge
And pressing hard seeks to drown them – a wretched death!
Then, prompted by Juno, ominous Trebia
Rouses its waves for a strange combat with tired men.
As they run, the deceptive ground subsides and sucks   575
Them down, where a mire of faithless mud devours them.
They can't struggle free or wrench their feet from the deep
Sticky clay; their legs are clogged in the sliding ooze,
Which binds them fast as the whole river bank dissolves,

1. The valley of the river Clitumnus in Umbria was famous for a breed of white
bull, often used for sacrifice at Roman triumphs.

580 Dumping them treacherously in the lurking swamp.
They scramble over the unstable shore, now one,
Now the next struggling in the shifting bog to find
A firm foothold on the inescapable slope.
They slip and with their own weight sink – buried alive.
585 One strong swimmer almost reaches safety. He strains
Stretching his body while his hand clutches the edge
Of the grass. As he drags himself from the morass
A well-aimed spear nails him to the sheer bank, transfixed.
Another, who's lost his weapons, clasps to his breast
590 His struggling opponent and drowns him while drowning.
Death takes a thousand forms. Ligus died on dry land,
But over the edge of the gliding stream his head
Dangled, drinking the bloody river in deep gulps.
From the main channel graceful Hirpinus swam clear
595 At last and, tired, called to his friends to lend a hand –
When the current carried a frantic, wounded horse
Into him and sank him beneath the swirling flood.
Their plight worsens. Suddenly they see elephants
With turrets on their backs driven into the waves;
600 They crash through the shadows like falling boulders torn
From high cliffs. Trebia learns new fears as their breasts
Break its flow and their bodies block its foaming course.
Perils test men. Up a steep ascent over rough
Terrain undaunted courage climbs towards renown.
605 Fibrenus, loath to squander death when it might win
Honour and fame, thinks, 'Never, Fortune, will you hide
My fate under water. I shall be prominent.
I'll show there's no creature on earth a Roman sword
Can't subdue, which a Tuscan lance can't penetrate.'
610 Rising, he thrusts his sharp point in one beast's right eye,
Then lets go so the shaft stays lodged in the deep wound.
With a terrible trumpeting the animal
Recoils from the gouging torment. It turns, throwing
Its rider, then lifts its bloodspattered head and flees.
615 Then they fire their arrows and cast their javelins,
Bolder now in hope of a kill. The vicious darts

Make one wound of its massive shoulders and vast flanks.
So many missiles lodged in its dark back and rump
That when its body shook, a large forest waved back
And forth. As they ran out of spears the elephant   620
Fell, damming the river with its enormous bulk.
    Look! Amidst these perils, into the Trebia
Remorseless Scipio,[1] though hampered by his wound,
Plunges, dealing death to countless antagonists.
Under the corpses, shields and helmets of the slain   625
The river is submerged, its waters lost to sight.
His spear kills Mazaeus, his sword Gestar. Then fell
Thelgon from Cyrene, Pelopian by race,
His open mouth pierced by a spear Scipio caught
As it floated by and flung at his face. The spear's   630
Long thin iron head buried itself in his throat.
His teeth, jarred by the blow, crunched on the wooden shaft.
Death brought no rest: his swollen limbs Trebia swept
Down to the Po and the Po down to the sea's surf.
You too, Thapsus, in death received no burial.   635
What profit now the home of the Hesperides
Or the groves tended by goddesses where the trees
Turn yellow, their branches heavy with golden fruit?[2]
Drawing water from its deepest pools, Trebia
Swells up and wildly hurls itself with all its might,
Urging on the whole flood. Frenzied waves and raucous   640
Whirlpools precede this fresh torrent's rumbling approach.
Sensing this, his anger inflamed, Scipio raged:[3]
'Traitorous Trebia, expect the punishment
You deserve! I'll scatter over Gaul's fields your stream

---

1. Publius Cornelius Scipio, consul in 218 B.C. and father of Scipio Africanus, who
defeated Hannibal at Zama in 202 B.C. (Selection VI). Publius had been wounded
in the previous battle at the river Ticinus, where he was rescued from death by
his young son (*Punica* IV.454–68).

2. Thapsus came from the far north-west of Africa, legendary site of the garden of
the Hesperides and its famous golden apples.

3. Scipio's fight with the river Trebia is modelled on that between Achilles and the
river Scamander in Homer's *Iliad* Book XXI.

645   Dismembered. I'll deprive you of the very name
       Of river. I'll choke your spring's source so you'll not touch
       Your banks or glide to the Po. What madness, poor wretch,
       Makes you suddenly a Sidonian river?'
       So he threatened. The surging ridge of water launched
650   Its strike. Above Scipio's shoulders the wave arched,
       Then crashed. Our leader stands erect, uses his weight
       Against the charging flood and checks it with his shield.
       To his rear a turbulent burst of gurgling froth
       Boils up, dampening with spray the top of his crest.
655   He can't wade or get a firm foothold, for the ground
       Slides at the rivergod's command. Strident and loud
       The torrent-battered rocks resound. Waves brawl, called out
       To their parent's war. The river has lost its banks.
       Raising his dripping hair and head wreathed with green weed
660   The rivergod speaks: 'Do you threaten haughtily
       To punish me and to blot out Trebia's name,
       In hatred of my kingdom? How many men killed
       By your hand do I bear? Crammed with shields and helmets
       From your victims I've lost my former bounds and course.
665   Look how my deep waters flow backwards red with blood!
       Restrain your arm. Go and assault the countryside!'
          Hidden by a cloud of dark mist, from a high hill
       Mulciber was watching with Venus at his side.
       Raising his hands to the sky Scipio complained:
670   'Ancient gods, whose favour stays Dardanian Rome,
       For this fate from the thick of battle recently[1]
       Did you save me? Do I seem unworthy of death
       At a brave man's hands? To the enemy, my son,
       And jeopardy restore me. Let a fighter's fate
675   Be mine to show my brother and Rome!' Venus groaned,
       Stirred by his words, and loosed her invincible spouse
       In all his searing strength against the stream. Fires spread
       Along the banks. The cool shade the river had reared
       Over long years is ravaged by the scorching heat.

---

1. At the battle of the Ticinus: see note on page 313.

All the thickets burn igniting the lofty groves 680
As victorious Vulcan crackles at full pelt.
Pines and alders blaze. The fir's foliage shrivels.
Birds which used to nest on the poplar's branching boughs
Take to the sky leaving their home, now a charred trunk.
Ravenous flames suck moisture from the river's depths 685
And devour it. The savage inferno's advance
Bakes the dried blood onto the banks. The rough earth splits
Apart all around tearing huge cracks in itself.
On Trebia's pools sit ash and soot in thick piles.
Father Eridanus[1] was astonished to see 690
His stream's eternal flow abruptly stop. A sad
Chorus of nymphs filled their caverns with shocked laments.
Three times Vulcan hurled his brands when the rivergod
Tried to raise his head from the steaming waves. Three times
The reeds caught fire and the god submerged, his hair singed. 695
At last his cries and entreaties obtained relief;
His plea was granted to flow in his former banks.
From the Trebia Scipio called his tired men
And, with Gracchus, withdrew to a fortified hill;
But Hannibal paid homage to the Trebia 700
As an ally, raising to it altars of turf,
Unaware of heaven's greater plans and the grief
You, Trasimene, held in store for Italy.

IV. Book VI.1–40

Lake Trasimene, 217 B.C.

The horses which Titan when discharged for the night
Had loosed in the Sea of Tartessus, he now yoked
On eastern shores and, like a new Phaethon, revealed
First the Chinese plucking fleeces from their silk trees,
Then soon exposed to view that gruesome butchery, 5

1. The river Po, of which the Trebia is a tributary.

The work of Mars gone mad: together arms and men
Lay intermixed with fallen steeds; lifeless hands cleaved
To the wounds of slain antagonists; all around
Were shields, crests and headless torsos; wedged in hard bone –
10   A broken sword; discernible too were the eyes
Of men almost dead looking up, not seeing sky;
Upon a grisly lake of blood-red frothing gore,
Bodies, never to be buried, undulating.
Italian valour endures despite defeat.
15   Beneath a massive pile of slaughtered men's remains
Bruttius stirs, his pierced flesh evidence of Mars'
Disfavour. Painfully he lifts his dismal head
Then crawls across the carnage, his strength faint, his limbs
Maimed. Born poor, lacking eloquence and noble blood,
20   He was a fierce swordsman. No other Volscian's
Name will live so long for courageous death. In youth,
His beard still immature, he'd wished to join the camp
And soon impressed shrewd Flaminius,[1] vanquisher
Of Celtic armies when the gods were more benign.[2]
25   Bruttius won honour and the sacred eagle's
Custody: this the glory that fostered his doom.
Knowing the battle was lost and death certain, feared
His standard would be spoil for Punic victory.
30   He sought to hide it meanwhile, trusting it to earth.
Hit by a sudden hail of spears, he rolled himself
Upon it, to bury it under his own corpse.
Then as the dawn dispelled night's Stygian shadows
His consciousness returned. Using a dead man's spear
35   He rises from the carcasses and stretching, propped,
Digs with his sword soil soft and yielding, blood-sodden.
He kneels; his hapless eagle's hidden effigy

1. Gaius Flaminius, consul of 217 B.C., who led the Roman army at Lake Trasimene. Silius describes the Roman defeat and Flaminius' death in *Punica* V.
2. In 223 B.C. Flaminius had attacked and defeated the Gauls across the Po, for which he was awarded a triumph.

He venerates, then pats the dirt with weary palms,
All spent. On the insubstantial air fell his last
Breath, to Tartarus his noble soul departing.   40

V. Book XII.538–752

Rome, 211 B.C.

Furiously along the banks stormed Hannibal,
Where chilly Anio's sulphurous waters glide
Towards father Tiber, smoothly and soundlessly.   540
There he fixed his standards and insolently camped.
His horse's hooves stamp on the water, flail the banks:
Ilia recoiled to her husband's sacred cave
In terror, and from the river all the nymphs fled.
Mothers through the city, as though the walls were razed,   545
Pacing madly back and forth, wander demented.
They shudder at mutilated apparitions
Of men butchered near malevolent Trebia
Or slow-running Ticinus. Past their anguished eyes
Drift bleeding shapes: Paulus, Gracchus, Flaminius.[1]   550
Crowds block the streets. With forbidding looks, senators,
Dignified, severe in wrath, check the mounting fear.
Behind helmets, at times, tears are shed silently:
What does Fortune threaten? What have the gods in store?
Young men assigned to the high defensive towers   555
Stand weighing in their hearts this humiliation,
That Rome aspires no higher than her own defence.
     The Punic leader gave his men, tired from their march,
Scarcely the hours of night for sleep. He stayed awake,
Averse to repose, thinking his life dispossessed   560
Of the time sleep steals. Soon, in resplendent armour

---

1. Roman generals killed during the war: Paulus (more commonly 'Paullus') at
Cannae in 216 B.C., Gracchus in Lucania in 212 B.C., Flaminius at Lake Trasimene
in 217 B.C.

Garbed, he joins his Numidians surging forwards,
And riding nimbly circles the horrified walls
Of a Rome unnerved by the clatter of hoof-beats.
565 Now he scans the best approaches; now bangs the gates
With truculent spear and savours the city's dread.
Now, from a high hill, leisurely he enters Rome
With his eyes, learning each part, each part's origin.
His gaze was probing, penetrating every
570 Nook, when from Capua still under Roman siege,
Like a mighty hurricane, up stormed Fulvius.[1]
Then to camp, leading his exultant cavalry,
Retired Hannibal, glutted with the sight of Rome.
From the sky darkness is expelled; with the sun's glow
575 Neptune reddens; Aurora brings back human toil.
Hannibal's camp, unbarred, discharges warriors.
His mount prances; his harangue rings out: 'By your fame
In war, comrades, and hands consecrated in blood,
Live up to yourselves! Let your violence in arms
580 Match Rome's nightmares! Rip apart this last obstacle
And you exhaust the world's stock of lands to subdue.
Ignore the Mars-begotten race's ancestry.
You'll take a city hordes of Gauls once occupied:[2]
Rome's used to being seized! On their high curule chairs
585 Perhaps the elders nobly awaiting their end
Follow precedent, preparing themselves to die.'
So the Punic leader spoke. No general's speech,
No special exhortation do the Romans need:
They see their mothers, their children, their parents' hands
590 Outstretched and faces drenched in tears. These are enough.
Women hold up infants whose wailing agitates
The soldiers' hearts. Some kiss the hands armed for killing.
Men are eager to stand before the walls close-ranked;

---

1. Quintus Fulvius Flaccus, consul of the previous year engaged in the blockade of
   Capua, which had revolted to Hannibal in 216 B.C. See *Punica* XI.129ff.
2. Hannibal alludes to the capture of Rome by invading Gauls *c.* 386 B.C. The
   story is told in Livy, Book V.

They look towards their families and choke back tears.
The hinges move; the gates open; the troops emerge   595
In a body, weapons ready. Over the walls
To the heavens rise the sounds of sobs, prayers, groans.
Loosening their hair, Roman matrons bare their breasts
And howl shrilly. Flying before the marching file
Goes Fulvius. 'You know,' he shouts, 'our Punic foes   600
Visit our homes and household gods reluctantly.
They've *fled* here from Capua's gates.' So he began.
Mighty rumblings in the gloomy sky distract him.
Thunder crashes and, from fast-massing cloud, storm breaks.
Jupiter, returning from Ethiopia,   605
Saw Hannibal threatening Romulus' ramparts
And, rousing the gods, despatched them to occupy
The seven hills and guard Rome's Dardanian homes.
He, aloft on the Tarpeian peak, mobilized
All his forces: vast clouds, winds, the fury of hail,   610
Lightning bolts, thunder, tempest and murky black rain.
The poles of the universe quaked. Darkness confined
The heavens as night's blinding robe enwrapped the land.
Storm attacks the enemy's eyes; they can't see Rome
Nearby concealed. Fires hurled at their ranks from the clouds 615
Scream through the air. Flames hiss around their arms and legs.
Notus, Boreas and swarthy-winged Africus,
Winds from every direction rush to engage
In battle, with the rage Jupiter's angry heart
Necessitates. A barrage of rainwaters falls
Interspersed with pitch-black whirlwinds, dirt-coloured squalls, 620
To envelop the neighbouring plains in deep flood
And frothing waves. From his hill's crest the king of gods
Raises his right arm and launches the thunderbolt
At Hannibal, who boldly stands his ground. It strikes
His shield. The point of Hannibal's spear wilts, molten;   625
As in a furnace, his fused sword disintegrates.
　　Sidonian Hannibal, his weapons destroyed,
Firmed his men's resolve. 'Aimless' he calls the fire sprung
From clouds, and 'meaningless' the roaring of the winds.

630 But his men are beaten; there's turmoil in the sky;
    The enemy's swords are hidden by mist and rain.
    So he orders retreat, then vents his sullen wrath:
    'One day's delay, Rome, you owe to wet, wintry gales.
    Tomorrow's better light will give no such reprieve,
635 Even should Jupiter himself descend to earth.'
    In frustration he gnashes his teeth as he speaks.
    Look! Clear, bright sunlight shines across a tranquil sky;
    The clouds are dispersed; a brilliance fills the purged air.
    Aeneas' Roman descendants sense Jupiter's
    Presence and, throwing down their weapons, stretch their hands
640 Towards the Capitol's peak in humility,
    Then festoon with festive laurel his hilltop shrine.
    The god's image, minutes before covered in sweat,
    Seems to smile. 'Grant, father, grant, greatest of all gods,
    That the Libyan be downed in battle by your
645 Thunderbolt. By no other hand can he be felled.'
    So they prayed, then remained quiet as Hesperus
    Obliterated the land with deepening dusk.
    He, in turn, gives way to Titan's stronger red glow,
    Which restores to mortals their tenancy of life.
650 Hannibal comes back. Nor do their quarters detain
    The Romans. Before the combatants drew their swords –
    When they stood apart no farther than is traversed
    By a well cast spear – the heavens' splendour was dimmed
    Suddenly; heavy gloom settled upon the field;
655 The day fled, and again for the fray Jupiter
    Armed. The winds hurtle into action; a thick bank
    Of rain-cloud, whirled by Auster, seethes. Jove's thunderclap
    Vibrates Taurus, Pindus, Atlas and Rhodope.[1]
    The pools of Erebus heard it. From the dark depths
660 Typhoeus recognized the sounds of cosmic strife.
    Slinging volleys of hailstones from swirling black clouds,
    Notus attacks Hannibal who, though he resists,
    Mouthing futile threats withdraws to his camp's shelter.

---

1. Greek mountain ranges.

Behind his barricade he'd put aside his arms,
When Olympus, beaming cheerily, turned serene.   665
A Thunderer so kind, you'd think, could not have used
Thunderbolts, nor thunder have vexed a sky so calm.
Hannibal perseveres. He denies Heaven's rage
Will thwart them again. Let their native bravery
Lend their hands vigour! Let Carthaginians cease   670
To think Rome's extermination sacrilegious!
Where were invincible Jupiter's bolts mislaid
When their swords strewed the Aetolian plain with dead
And the Tyrrhene lake overflowed with human blood?[1]
'If heaven's king,' he said, 'casts missiles from on high   675
To save Rome's walls, why – in such fuss – does he not crush
Me, his armed antagonist? Will strong winds and cold
Rout us? Recall that energy and stubbornness
Which, despite our elders' treaties and laws, impelled
You to start a new war.' Thus he inflamed their hearts,   680
Till Titan loosed from his steeds their foam-spattered reins.
Night did not allay his cares, nor sleep dare approach
His snarling face. With day returns his craziness:
He tells his nervous men to arm, then beats his shield
Deafeningly to counterfeit the heavens' din.   685
    Rome's Ausonian fathers had such confidence
In the gods, they'd sent from the city's gates at night
Reinforcements headed for Spanish Baetis' banks.[2]
That besieged men should be so heedless of himself,
So relaxed, makes more frantic Hannibal's assault.   690
As he charged towards the walls, Jupiter addressed
Troubled Juno, calming her fears with this advice:
'Sister and wife, dear to me, can't you discipline
This young Sidonian whose insolence admits
No bounds? He destroyed Saguntum, levelled the Alps,   695

---

1. The references are to the battles of Cannae and Lake Trasimene.
2. According to Livy XXVI.11 the Romans dispatched reinforcements for their
   army in Spain at the time that Hannibal's forces were camped within striking
   distance of the city.

Fettered sacred Eridanus' stream[1] and defiled
Our lakes.[2] Now is he proposing to smash his way
Into the *gods'* strongholds? Into the *gods'* abodes?
Stop the man! See how, calling for fire, he ignites
700　A conflagration to rival my thunderbolt!'
Saturn's daughter thanked her spouse then, deeply disturbed,
Flew down from the clouds and, taking Hannibal's hand,
Cried,[3] 'Where are you rushing, madman? You undertake
Battles beyond mortal competence!' She dispersed
705　The black mist to stand revealed in her true aspect.
'Your foes are not settlers from Troy or Laurentum.
I'll expel for a time the dimness from your eyes
And show you all. Look! Rising high into the air
Is the summit Parrhasian Evander called
710　The "Palatine". There lord Apollo bends his bow
And rattles his full quiver, warming up to fight.
See where the Aventine uplifts itself above
The hills close-by; Latona's virgin daughter[4] waves
Torches set alight in Phlegethon's burning stream,
715　And, avid of war, bares her arms in readiness.
See how Mars with his cruel weapons occupies
The field[5] which has his name. From this side Quirinus
Advances, from that Janus, each from his own hill[6]
Striding, arms in hand. But observe how storms and fire
720　Spout from the aegis almighty Jupiter shakes.
What flames erupt to nourish his ferocity!
Turn your face *this* way. Dare to see the Thunderer!
What lightning flashes from his eyes! What storms obey
His nod! What thundering as he tosses his head!
725　End this warfare fit for Titans. Yield to the gods!'

1. At the battles of the Ticinus and the Trebia.
2. Lake Trasimene is meant.
3. For the Virgilian allusions in this and the following scene see the Introduction to Silius above.
4. Diana, whose main temple was on the Aventine.
5. The Campus Martius.
6. The Quirinal and Janiculum, respectively.

So she spoke, then dragging back this man ignorant
Of restraint and peace, dazed by the gods' blazing limbs
And faces, she restored calm to heaven and earth.
He tells his men to move the standards and break camp.
Though he goes, he looks back and threatens to return.   730
At once the sky's bright lamp shone more resplendently;
Perfused with Phoebus' rays the blue daylight shimmered.

    Observing from afar Hannibal's withdrawal
And his standards dislodged, Romans on the walls trade
Glances silently. Gestures impart what none dare   735
Say aloud for lingering fear: they all suspect
A ruse, a trap, a sham retreat, the Punic mind.
In silence mothers kiss their small children. At length
The column receded from sight and with the source
Of terror gone, suspicions of deceit dissolved.   740
From all about they throng the sacred Capitol,
Embrace one another, combine in loud acclaim
Of Tarpeian Jove's triumph, and garland his shrine.
Now they throw open all the gates. Jubilant crowds
Rush here and there to savour unexpected joys.   745
They stare at places where Hannibal lately trod:
Here was pitched his tent; there he incited the troops
From his high platform. Where wild Garamantians,
Brutal Asturians and vicious Ammonites
Camped, Romans splash their bodies in the running stream.   750
They raise altars to the Anio-dwelling nymphs,
Purify the walls, then go home to festive Rome.

VI. Book XVII.481–617

Zama, 202 B.C.

Death comes in strange forms and contrasting images
In this grim fight: one lies flat, skewered by a sword;
Another moans woefully, his bones crushed by rocks;
Terror killed some in shame, from behind, as they fled;

485 Courage led others to confront Mars face to face.
Over heaps of corpses Rhoeteian Scipio[1]
Moves, aloft in his chariot like Mars himself
When by the cold Hebrus he melts the Getic snow
With hot-flowing blood, revelling in massacre,
While his war-chariot's wheels groan beneath their load

490 And crack the ice congealed by wintry Aquilo.
Fierily Scipio prowls the plain cutting down
Reputations for great valour. Men known world-wide
For slaughter are slain by his weapons near and far.
Those who ravaged your walls, Saguntum, and embarked

495 On wrongful war by your piteous destruction,
Those who stained with gore Trasimene and the Po
Where Phaethon plummeted, whose arrogance induced
Them to assault the home and throne of heaven's king[2]
In hope of spoil: all meet the same end, sacrificed

500 At close quarters. Those who claimed they unlocked the Alps
Barred to human tread, and so profaned the gods' haunts,
Surrender their souls. Terrified by consciousness
Of guilt, the rest run away more dead than alive.
So it is when Vulcan's baneful inferno spreads

505 From house to house and rapid-gusting winds excite
The soaring flames, sweeping them across the roof-tops:
Bewildered by sudden peril, the urban crowd

---

1. Scipio Africanus, son of Publius Cornelius Scipio who fought at the Trebia in
218 B.C. 'Rhoeteian' (= 'Trojan') recalls Aeneas in the final battle of *Aeneid* XII
(456).
2. The reference is to the Capitol in Rome.

Fills the streets. As in a captured town, panic rules.
    Weary of hunting fresh opponents here and there
And wasting time in easy struggles, Scipio   510
Decides to turn his full strength against Hannibal,
Cause of war and instigator of suffering.
While he alone remains, Carthage's walls might burn
And all the Punic army perish, yet Rome gain
Nothing. Should this one man fall, all their arms and men   515
Would not avail to save the Carthaginians.
Scipio scours the field seeking the enemy's
Leader, impatient to provoke the ultimate
Confrontation. He'd like all Italy to watch
The clash. Standing erect, in a harsh voice he taunts   520
Hannibal and challenges him to a new fight.
Juno heard his shouting and fearing its effect
On the Libyan general's unflinching ears
Created at once a likeness of Scipio,[1]
Its helmet crowned with a glittering plume. She adds   525
Scipio's shield and crest and on its shoulders sets
The bright cloak of high command. It has no substance
But his bold movements, his hostile manner, his gait.
Another empty illusion, a spurious
Steed, is fashioned for the warlike phantom to ride   530
Fleetly over distant parts to a fake showdown.
Before Hannibal's eyes Juno's false Scipio
Parades, eagerly brandishing his spear and sword.
Pleased to be facing Scipio at last, intent
On performing a mighty exploit, Hannibal   535
Speedily sets himself astride his horse and sends
His spear hurtling like the wind at his enemy.
The vision nimbly turns and flits behind the lines,
Flying from the field. Then sure of gaining his wish
And victory, Hannibal draws blood from his horse   540
With his iron spurs and shakes roughly the loose reins:

---

1. So at *Aeneid* X.633ff. Juno creates a likeness of Aeneas to draw Turnus away
from the battlefield.

'Where are you going? You forget this is our realm.
Libya holds no refuge for you, Scipio.'
So he speaks, and with drawn sword pursues the swift form.
545 It beguiles him into leaving the battlefield
Far behind, drawing him into remote country.
Suddenly the false image vanished into mist.
Hannibal's anger flared: 'What god hiding his true
Nature thwarts me? Why skulk behind this monstrous shape?
550 Does my glory exasperate the gods that much?
You god who aids Italy, whoever you are,
Your tricks will never save, never pluck from my grasp
My real adversary!' In a frenzy he turned
His lively steed and headed for the battlefield;
555 But seized by a violent fit the horse collapsed
And panted out its life, afflicted suddenly,
Through Juno's contrivance, by unforeseen disease.
Then he lost his temper. 'This is your treachery
Once more, gods! You don't fool me! I wish I'd been drowned,
560 Swallowed by the waves so the sea's crags marked my grave.[1]
For this doom was I saved? Around my standards men
Whom I led out to fight are being killed. I hear
Their cries and groans, though far away. I hear them call
Hannibal. What river of Tartarus will purge
565 Me of this guilt?' While venting these complaints he stared
At the sword he held, burning with passion for death.
Then Juno pitying the man adopts the form
Of a shepherd and, emerging from the trees' shade,
Hails him as he ponders his inglorious fate.
570 'What cause impels you to approach our woods in arms?
Do you want the bitter fight where great Hannibal's
Weapons subjugate what is left of Italy?
If you'd like to travel quickly, taking a short
Cut, I'll conduct you there by convenient paths.'
575 He agrees and loads the shepherd with promises

---

1. The reference is to the storm earlier in Book XVII (236ff.) which prevented
   Hannibal from returning to Italy and nearly sank his ship.

Of gifts; the senate of high Carthage, he explains,
And he himself will render splendid recompense.
As he bounds rapidly across the countryside,
Juno leads him in circles, recommends wrong tracks
And through disguise keeps him unwillingly secure.   580
      The soldiers of Carthage, abandoned and afraid,
See no Hannibal, nowhere their fierce general's
Famous warfare. Some think he's dead. Some think he's cursed
The battle, yielding to the gods' antipathy.
Over all the field Ausonian Scipio   585
Hounds and assails them. The towers of Carthage shake.
With her army repulsed, wavering fear infects
All Africa. Her men forget the fight and flee
Bewildered, filling far-flung shores with refugees.
Some scatter to Tartessus and the Spanish coast;   590
Some to Battus' home, Cyrene; some reach the Nile,
River of Lagus. Likewise, when Vesuvius
Conquered by obscure forces vomits to the stars
Fires nurtured over centuries, Vulcan's havoc
Spreads across land and sea: surprised Chinamen gape   595
At silk-fleeced trees turned white with Italian ash.
      Queen Juno brought weary Hannibal to a hill
Overlooking the sombre battlefield. His eyes
Took in the whole scene, the residue of defeat.
He'd seen the plain by Mount Garganus, Trebia's   600
Waters, the Tyrrhene lake and Phaethon's river Po
Smothered by Roman corpses; now his own men, slain,
Bestrew the landscape – a hideous spectacle.
Then Juno returned saddened to her home above.
Soon the enemy were near, coming up the hill;   605
Though alone, he spoke: 'Beneath my feet let the earth
Yawn open. On my head bring down the universe!
Never, Jupiter, will you erase Cannae's fame.
And you will lose your throne before the world forgets
The name and fears of Hannibal. Nor are you, Rome,   610
Safe from me. My country I survive. For desire
Of war with you, I will live. The battle you win;

Your enemy recedes: I'm pleased, I'm more than pleased
If mothers in Rome, if the land of Italy
615   Dread my return and know, deep in their hearts, no peace.'
He dashed off and, mingling with other fugitives,
Went into safe hiding on the high mountain slopes.

JUVENAL

INTRODUCTION

Decimus Junius Juvenalis, Martial's younger friend, has left little
biographical information about himself, except perhaps that he
took up writing late in life. There is a tradition that his equestrian
family haled from Aquinum, a town about seventy-five miles
south of Rome on the via Appia, and that he survived the emperor
Hadrian, who died in A.D. 138, when the poet would have been in
his early eighties. Suggestions that he was a Spaniard, that he was a
soldier in Britain or was exiled to Egypt must be regarded with
some scepticism. His writing career can be placed, with slightly
more confidence, within a span of A.D. 100 and 130, and his
rhetorical skills point to oratorical training and practice. But it
makes no matter when specifically the satires were composed or
given to the public, since Juvenal's idealized Golden Age of gener-
ous patronage combined with high civic and personal morality is
set in the far distant past and probably never existed. The political
and social stability of the Trajanic and Hadrianic periods induced
the poet to allege a real or pretended fear of retribution for any
outspokenness against contemporary scoundrels, and to go back to
the Julio-Claudian and Flavian dynasties – and even further back
in history – for his spectacular examples of vices among the ruling
classes and personal degradation among the lower orders.

The *Satires* present a coherent, if dark, universe, so oppressive
that only the literature of indignation can formulate a suitable
response to it. Like Persius and Martial, Juvenal regards the loftier
genres of epic and tragedy as mere escapist fustian. The first satire
presents his programme: to attack (1) ill-gotten inheritances and
unjustly acquired or ill-used wealth and the extravagances such as

gluttony and gambling that go with them; (2) the transgression of the natural boundaries of race, class, and gender; (3) the decadence of the higher social orders; (4) the dangerous and corrupt political atmosphere; (5) the vileness and violence of the female sex; and (6), not least, the abuses of the creaky patronage system. Because of the dangers, he will take his examples and warnings from history rather than contemporary events.

Satire II is an extended gloss on (3), attacking the immorality and hypocrisy of self-professed intellectuals, and *Satire* VII protests that a noble pedigree may hide utter degeneracy of one sort or another. (1) and (4) emerge in the portrait of Domitian's treason-hunting cabinet advising him on the proper disposition of a large and costly mullet. Extravagant dining habits are also the subject of *Satire* XI and financial greed the topic of XIV. The abuse of patronage (6) is sardonically treated in *Satire* IX through the *persona* of a pathic homosexual who has been scandalously used and then discarded by his rich 'friend'. The even more serious effects of the current system on the poor and on literature are described in *Satires* III, V and VIII.

Almost all of these topics are concretely exemplified in the monologue of Umbricius on the evils of living in Rome (*Satire* III) and all (and more) are used as whips to chastise the whole female sex in the infamous sixth satire, with particular vehemence being directed at Lady Chatterleys who turn to the lower orders for their pleasures and so demonstrate not only their insatiable sexuality but also their contempt for social decorum; see (2).

Against all these evils what has Juvenal to offer? A somewhat diluted Stoicism that situates true happiness and tranquillity in the pursuit of virtue alone (most fully expressed in *Satires* VIII and X), and an unshaken belief in traditional Roman values, if only they could be restored by the emperor perhaps or a nobility recalled to a sense of duty and fair play. The traditional system itself need not be questioned; only the times are out of joint. Juvenal is no revolutionary when it comes to the respective positions in the hierarchy of parasites and *rentiers*.

Satire X is perhaps the most universal of the satires and has found many admirers, not least Samuel Johnson, who imitated it closely and happily in *The Vanity of Human Wishes* (1749), although it has to be added that Juvenal's work as a whole left an indelible imprint on formal classical satire in English from Oldham through Dryden and Pope to Richard Churchill.

The poem parades the nature and consequences of human aspirations and hopes, whether for wealth, eloquence, civic power, military glory, longevity, or beauty. The force of composition, as often, lies in the powerful illustrations rather than in the basic message of Stoic freedom from ambition or passion and the calm acceptance of whatever befalls. The vivid presentations of Sejanus and Hannibal are carefully sketched until the *coup de grâce* is delivered with a crisp deflating statement like air being let out of a balloon. But the use of bathos is just one of the numerous rhetorical ploys that the satirist uses to achieve his dramatic effects.

Nevertheless the tenth satire is not necessarily his best in sustained artistic terms or for verbal brilliance. Other satires have been singled out by critics for their superior structure, such as the admittedly unsavoury *Satire* IX, or the emotional intensity of their bravura passages. These would surely include the atmospheric description in *Satire* VI of the empress Messalina stealing from Claudius' bed to faceless assignations in a low-class brothel or the vivid and detailed enumeration in *Satire* III – a poem often imitated by later metropolitan writers – of the physical perils of dawn-to-dawn life in the Roman capital.

A concentration on any individual satire also does an injustice to the obvious development of Juvenal's art. The satiric *persona* he adopts in *Satires* I to VI, the shrill and caustic voice of the indignant, but threatened, participant will modulate gradually into the unshockable and ironic confidant of *Satire* IX and then into the more mellow, reflective commentator of the later satires, whom nothing, however outlandish, seems overly to surprise. The verbal power is still there, but the energy and invention seems gradually to wane and with these the attention-holding directness of his miniature portraits and brief dramas.

The dramatic, pictorial nature of Juvenal's art at its peak has to be stressed, because we do not come to his work in search of a coherent philosophy or tightly knit and logical artistic structure.

His is the art of the orator who prefers a dazzling display of pyrotechnics or the loud squibs that will rivet our attention rather than a steady light that will guide us through an undergrowth of knotty ethical argument. Promises are not kept; trains of thought are derailed; and signals are crossed. That is why H. A. Mason can reasonably propose that Juvenal's unit of composition is the paragraph and our best guide to an understanding of his technique is a close study of Martial's satiric epigrams.

But this is only to stress once again that the great satirists are verbal artists first and moralists, or guides to conduct, second, if at all. It is to Juvenal's mastery of the extended and moving image, the pointed and quotable dictum, the subtle ironic touch and, above all, the sheer wit that one must look to appreciate him for what he is and then perhaps applaud Dryden's accolade: *he gives me more pleasure than I can bear.*

J.P.S.

Further Reading

Clausen, W. V., *D. Iuni Iuvenalis Saturarum Libri V* (Oxford 1959).

Coffey, M., *Roman Satire* (London 1976) 119–46.

Green, P., *Juvenal, The Sixteen Satires* (Harmondsworth 1967).

Highet, G., *Juvenal the Satirist* (Oxford 1954).

Mason, H. A., 'Is Juvenal a Classic?', in J. P. Sullivan (ed.), *Critical Essays on Roman Literature: Satire* (London 1963) 93–176.

SATIRES

SELECTIONS

Translated by Peter Green

Satire I

Must I *always* be stuck in the audience at these poetry-readings,
    never
Up on the platform myself, taking it out on Cordus
For the times he's bored me to death with ranting speeches
From that *Theseid*[1] of his? Is X to get off scot-free
After inflicting his farces on me, or Y his elegies? Is there
No recompense for whole days wasted on prolix
Versions of *Telephus*? And what about that *Orestes*[2] –   5
Each margin of the roll crammed solid, top and bottom,
More on the back, and *still* it wasn't finished!
I know all the mythical landscapes like my own back-room:
The grove of Mars, that cave near Aeolus' island
Belonging to Vulcan.[3] The stale themes are bellowed daily

1. Cordus is an unknown poet who supposedly has written a typical epic on the adventures of Theseus. Although epic writing was still regarded as the most prestigious literary form, its supposed irrelevance to real life was frequently criticized.
2. Telephus, king of the Mysians, was wounded and later healed by Achilles' spear; Orestes, son of Agamemnon, killed his mother, Clytemnestra, in revenge and was hunted by the Furies for the murder. Each was the subject of famous Greek tragedies and here they symbolize the high prestige enjoyed by mythological tragedy at Rome, another genre criticized by the satirists, perhaps wrongly, for its contemporary irrelevance.
3. Typical poetic motifs: the grove of Mars is perhaps to be located in Colchis; in it a serpent guarded the Golden Fleece; Vulcan's cave was on Hiera (*Volcano*) near

In rich patrons' colonnades, till their marble pillars
Crack with a surfeit of rhetoric. The plane-trees echo
10   Every old trope – what the winds are up to, whose ghosts
Aeacus[1] has on his hellish rack, from what far country
The other fellow is sneaking off with that golden sheepskin,
The monstrous size of those ash-trees the Centaurs used for spears:
You get the same stuff from them all, established poet
15   And raw beginner alike. I too have winced under the cane
And concocted 'Advice to Sulla'[2]: *Let the despot retire
Into private life, take a good long sleep,* and so on. When you find
Hordes of poets on each street-corner, it's misplaced kindness
To refrain from writing. The paper will still be wasted.
Why then have I chosen to drive my team down the track
20   Which great Lucilius[3] blazed? If you have the leisure to listen
Calmly and reasonably, I will enlighten you.
　　When a flabby eunuch marries, when well-born girls go crazy
For pig-sticking up-country, bare-breasted, spear in fist;
25   When the barber who rasped away at my youthful beard has risen
To challenge good society with his millions; when Crispinus[4] –
That Delta-bred house-slave, silt washed down by the Nile –
Now hitches his shoulders under Tyrian purple, airs
A thin gold ring in summer on his sweaty finger

Strongyle (*Stromboli*), home of Aeolus, god of the winds. They are part of the
highly volcanic Lipari islands, Aeolus' kingdom.

1. Judge of the dead; belittling allusions follow to Jason's quest for the Golden
Fleece (the subject of Valerius' *Argonautica*), the battle between the Centaurs and
the Thessalian tribe, the Lapiths.
2. A sneer at the pervasive rhetorical education which supposedly adversely affected
poetry. Typical exercises were the *suasoria*, a clever speech to persuade an in-
dividual or audience to follow some course of action, and the *controversia*, which
dealt ingeniously with some often fictitious legal or ethical problem. Again, the
remoteness from everyday life is the target of the criticism.
3. Gaius Lucilius (d. 102 B.C.) was credited with establishing satire as a literary
genre. His works were read and admired in imperial times for their abusive
political candour and verbal vitality.
4. Crispinus typifies the arrogant freedman who became prominent, rich, and
powerful in the imperial period. Like emancipated women, they were frequently
the objects of satire.

('My dear, I couldn't *bear* to wear my *heavier* jewels') –
Why then, it is harder *not* to be writing satires; for who   30
Could endure this monstrous city, however callous at heart,
And swallow his wrath? Look: here comes a brand-new litter,
Crammed with its corpulent owner, some chiselling advocate.
Who's next? An informer. He turned in his noble patron,
And soon he'll have gnawed away that favourite bone of his,
The aristocracy. Lesser informers dread him, grease   35
His palm with ample bribes, while the wives of trembling actors
Grease him the other way. Today we are elbowed aside
By men who earn legacies in bed, who rise to the top
Via that quickest, most popular route – the satisfied desires
Of some rich old matron. Each lover will get his cut,
A twelfth share in the estate, or eleven-twelfths, depending   40
On the size of his – services rendered. I suppose he deserves
Some recompense for all that sweat and exertion: he looks
As pale as the man who steps barefoot on a snake – or is waiting
His turn to declaim, at Lyons, in Caligula's competitions.[1]

   Need I tell you how anger burns in my heart when I see   45
The bystanders jostled back by a mob of bravos
Whose master has first debauched his ward, and later
Defrauded the boy as well? The courts condemned him,
But the verdict was a farce. Who cares for reputation
If he keeps his cash? A provincial governor, exiled
For extortion, boozes and feasts all day, basks cheerfully
In the wrathful eye of the Gods; it's still his province,
After winning the case against him, that feels the pinch.[2]   50
   Are not such themes well worthy of Horace's pen? Should I
Not attack them too? Must I stick to the usual round

---

1. The psychopathic emperor Caligula (A.D. 12–41) was supposed to have penalized
bad writers who entered his artistic competitions (here held at Lyons) by forcing
them to erase their unsuccessful compositions with their tongues or face a
ducking in the Rhône or a whipping.
2. An allusion to Marius Priscus, governor of Africa in A.D. 97–8, whose infamous
extortions were punished, according to Juvenal, only by a comfortable exile.
(Modern analogies need not be cited.)

Of Hercules' labours, what Diomede[1] did, the bellowing
Of that thingummy in the Labyrinth, or the tale of the flying
Carpenter, and how his son went splash in the sea?
55 Will *these* suffice in an age when each pimp of a husband
Takes gifts from his own wife's lover – if she is barred in law
From inheriting legacies[2] – and, while they paw each other,
Tactfully stares at the ceiling, or snores, wide awake, in his wine?
Will *these* suffice, when the young blade who has squandered
His family fortune on racing-stables still reckons to get
60 Command of a cohort? Just watch him lash his horses
Down the Flaminian Way like Achilles' charioteer,[3]
Reins bunched in one hand, showing off to his mistress
Who stands beside him, wrapped in his riding-cloak!
Don't you want to cram whole notebooks with scribbled
    invective
When you stand at the corner and see some forger carried past
65 On the necks of six porters, lounging back like Maecenas
In his open litter? A counterfeit seal, a will, a mere scrap
Of paper – these were enough to convert him to wealth and honour.
Do you see that distinguished lady? She has the perfect dose
70 For her husband – old wine with a dash of parching toad's blood.
Locusta's[4] a child to her; she trains her untutored neighbours
To ignore all unkind rumours, to stalk through angry crowds
With their black and bloated husbands before them on the hearse.
If you want to be someone today you must nerve yourself
For deeds that could earn you an island exile, or years in gaol.
Honesty's praised, but honest men freeze. Wealth springs from crime:

1. A Greek hero of the Trojan war. Reference to other typical epic or dramatic
   subjects follow: the Minotaur; and Daedalus and his son Icarus, who escaped
   from Crete by the invention of wings.
2. Restrictions on legacies were one form of social interventionist policy, used to
   punish adultery and encourage population growth, but here the allusion is to
   sharing the legacy with the spouse.
3. The via Flaminia ran from Rome to various towns in northern Italy. Achilles'
   charioteer was Automedon.
4. Notorious poisoner of the Neronian period. The poison referred to would be a
   form of bufotenin, a paralysing agent.

Landscape-gardens, palaces, furniture, antique silver –   75
Those cups embossed with prancing boats – all, all are tainted.
Who can sleep easy today? If your greedy daughter-in-law
Is not being seduced for cash, it'll be your bride: mere schoolboys
Are adulterers now. Though talent be wanting, yet
Indignation will drive me to verse, such as I – or any scribbler –   80
May still command. All human endeavours, men's prayers,
Fears, angers, pleasures, joys and pursuits, these make
The mixed mash of my verse.

                Since the days of the Flood,
When Deucalion[1] anchored his ship on a mountain peak
To search for a sign, the days when hard stones quivered
To living softness and warmth, and Pyrrha confronted
The first men with their naked mates, has there ever
Been so rich a crop of vices? When has the purse   87
Of greed yawned wider? When was gambling more frantic
Than it is today? Men face the table's hazards
Not with their purse but their strong-box open beside them.   90
Here you'll see notable battles, with the croupier for squire,
Holding stakes instead of a shield. Is it not plain lunacy
To lose ten thousand on a turn of the dice, yet grudge
A shirt to your shivering slave? Which of your grandfathers
Would have built himself so many country houses, or dined
Off seven courses, *alone*? Clients were guests in those days.   95
But now Roman citizens are reduced to scrambling
For a little basket of scraps on their patron's doorstep.[2]
He peers into each face first, scared stiff that some imposter
May give a false name and cheat him: you must be identified
Before you get your ration. The crier has his orders:
Each man to answer his name, nobility included –

1. Deucalion was the pagan Noah who, with his wife Pyrrha, survived the flood
   sent by Jupiter to wipe out the wickedness of mankind. The couple repopulated
   the earth by bringing stones to life.
2. The reference is to the daily *sportula* or basket of food distributed by a patron to
   any clients who cared to collect it. This archaic dole system no longer served any
   useful political purpose from the patron's point of view and so it became
   progressively less generous.

100   Oh yes, our Upper-Ten are scrounging with the rest.
      'The praetor first, then the tribune –' But a freedman blocks
      Their way. '*I* got here first,' he says, 'why shouldn't I keep
      My place? I don't give *that* for you. Oh, I know I'm foreign:
105   Look here, at my pierced ears, no use denying it – born
      Out East, on the Euphrates. But my five shops bring in
      Four hundred thousand, see? So I qualify for the gentry.
      What's in a senator's purple stripe, if true-blue nobles
      Are reduced to herding sheep up-country, while I have more
      Stashed away in the bank than any Imperial favourite?'
110   So let the Tribunes wait, and money reign supreme;
      Let the Johnny-come-lately, whose feet only yesterday were white
      With the chalk of the slave-market, flout this sacrosanct office!
      Why not? Though as yet, pernicious Cash, you lack
      A temple of your own, though we have raised no altars
      To Sovereign Gold (as already we worship Honour,
115   Peace, Victory, Virtue, or Concord – whose roosting storks
      Rattle and flap on the roof when you salute their nest),
      Still it is Wealth, not God, that compels our deepest reverence.
          When the Consul himself tots up, at the end of his year,
      What the dole is worth, how much it adds to his income, how
      Are we poor dependants to manage? Out of this pittance
      We must pay for decent clothes and shoes – not to mention our
          food
120   And the fuel for heating. But plenty who can afford
      A litter still queue up for their bob-a-day; some husbands
      Go the rounds with a sick or pregnant wife in tow,
      Or better (a well-known dodge) pretend she's there when she
          isn't,
      And claim for both, displaying a curtained, empty sedan.
125   'My Galla's in there,' he says. 'Come on, let us through! You
          doubt me?
      Galla! Put out your head, girl! I'm sorry, she must be asleep –
      No, don't disturb her, please –!'
                                        And so the day wears on
      With its prescribed routine, its fascinating round.
      Dole in pocket, we next attend my lord to the Forum;

Stare, bored, at all those statues – Apollo[1] beside the Law Courts
(He must be an expert by now) or that jumped-up Egyptian   130
Pasha who's had the nerve to gate-crash Triumph Row:
His effigy's only fit for pissing on – or worse.[2]
[Experienced clients follow their patron home again],
Hoping against hope for that dinner-invitation
Which never comes: worn out, they drift away to purchase
(Poor souls) their cabbage and kindling. But *he* meanwhile will
      loll
Alone at his guestless meal, wolfing the choicest produce   135
Of sea and woodland. These fellows will gobble up
Whole legacies at one course, off fine big antique tables:
Soon there won't be a parasite left. But who could stomach
Such measures in gourmands? What a grossly ravening maw   140
That man must have who dines off whole roast boar – a beast
Ordained for convivial feasting! But you'll pay the price
All too soon, my friend, when you undress and waddle
Into the bath, your belly still swollen with undigested
Peacock-meat – a lightning heart-attack, with no time
To make your final will. The story circulates   145
As a dinner-table joke, the latest thing. But no one
Cares about you. Your corpse is borne out to ironical
Cheers from your cheated friends. Posterity can add
No more, or worse, to our ways; our grandchildren will act
As we do, and share our desires. Today every vice
Has reached its ruinous zenith. So, satirist, hoist your sails,
Cram on every stitch of canvas! But where, you may ask,   150
Is a talent to match the theme? and where our outspoken
Ancestral bluntness, that wrote what burning passion dictated?
'Show me the man I dare not name,' Lucilius cried,
'What odds if the noble Consul forgive my libel or not?'

---

1. The Forum of Augustus, where legal proceedings took place, had a statue of
   Apollo.
2. The Pasha alluded to is thought to be Tiberius Julius Alexander, a Jewish convert
   who became prefect of Egypt in A.D. 66, and who was awarded a triumphal
   statue for helping the emperor Titus in the Jewish uprisings of A.D. 70.

155 But name an Imperial favourite,[1] and you will soon enough
    Blaze like those human torches, half-choked, half-grilled to
        death,[2]
    Those calcined corpses they drag with hooks from the arena,
    And leave a broad black trail behind them in the sand.
     But what, you may ask, about the man who has poisoned
    Three uncles with belladonna – are we to let *him* ride
    In his feather-bedded litter, and look down his nose at us?
160 Yes; and when he approaches, keep mum, clap a hand to your
        mouth –
    Just to say *That's the man* will brand you as an informer.
    It's safe enough to retell how Aeneas fought fierce Turnus;[3]
    No one's a penny the worse for Achilles' death, or the frantic
    Search for Hylas,[4] that time he tumbled in after his pitcher.
165 But when fiery Lucilius rages with satire's naked sword
    His hearers go red; their conscience is cold with crime,
    Their innards sweat at the thought of their secret guilt:
    Hence wrath and tears. So ponder these things in your mind
    Before the trumpet sounds. It's too late for a soldier
    To change his mind about fighting when he's armed in the battle-
        line.
170 For myself, I shall try my hand on the famous dead, whose ashes
    Rest beside the Latin and the Flaminian Ways.[5]

1. The imperial favourite is named by Juvenal as Ofonius Tigellinus, Nero's praetor-
   ian prefect in A.D. 62, who helped persecute Christians after the fire of Rome in
   A.D. 64.
2. A reference to the painful execution by the *tunica molesta*, papyrus smeared with
   pitch that was wrapped round the victim's body and set alight.
3. Aeneas, on arrival from Troy, had to fight the Italian tribes under the leadership
   of Turnus, king of the Rutulians. A graphic description of his death concludes
   Virgil's *Aeneid*.
4. Hylas was the beautiful boyfriend of Hercules, who accompanied him on the
   Argo in quest of the Golden Fleece. While looking for water on the island of
   Cios, he was pulled into a spring by the water-nymphs. Hercules left the
   expedition to search for him. The story is told in Valerius, *Argonautica* III–IV.
5. The via Latina runs south-east from Rome, the via Flaminia runs north; but all
   the main roads from the capital were lined with tombs.

Satire VI

During Saturn's reign I believe that Chastity still
Lingered on earth, and was seen for a while, when draughty
Caves were the only homes men had, hearth-fire and household
Gods, family and cattle all shut in darkness together.
Wives were different then – a far cry from Cynthia,   5
Or the girl who wept, red-eyed, for that sparrow's death.
Bred to the woods and mountains, they made their beds from
Dry leaves and straw, from the pelts of savage beasts
Caught prowling the neighbourhood. *Their* breasts gave suck
To big strong babies; often, indeed, they were shaggier   10
Than their acorn-belching husbands. In those days, when the
    world
Was young, and the sky bright-new still, men lived differently:
Offspring of oaks or rocks, clay-moulded, parentless.[1]
Some few traces, perhaps, of Chastity's ancient presence
Survived under Jove – but only while Jove remained   15
A beardless stripling, long before Greeks had learnt
To swear by the other man's head, or capital; when no one
Feared thieves in the cabbage-patch and orchard, when kitchen-
    gardens
Were still unwalled. Thereafter, by slow degrees,
Justice withdrew to heaven, and Chastity went with her,
Two sisters together, beating a common retreat.   20
   To bounce your neighbour's bed, my friend, to outrage
Matrimonial sanctity, is now an ancient and long-
Established tradition. All other crimes came later,
With the Age of Iron; but our first adulterers
Appeared in the Silver Era. And here you are in *this*
Day and age, getting yourself engaged,
Fixing up marriage-covenant,[2] dowry, betrothal-party;   25

1. Ancient speculation attributed the origins of mankind to trees, rocks, or earth
  (moulded by Prometheus).
2. Most Roman marriages involved contracts about the bride's dowry and property.

Any time now some high-class barber will start
Coiffeuring you for the wedding, before you know it the ring
Will be on her finger. Postumus, are you *really*
Taking a wife? You used to be sane enough – what
Fury's got into you, what snake has stung you up?
30 Why endure such bitch-tyranny when rope's available
By the fathom, when all those dizzying top-floor windows
Are open for you, when there are bridges handy
To jump from? Supposing none of these exits catches
Your fancy, isn't it better to sleep with a pretty boy?
35 Boys don't quarrel all night, or nag you for little presents
While they're on the job, or complain that you don't come
Up to their expectations, or demand more gasping passion.

But no: you staunchly uphold the Family Encouragement Act,[1]
A sweet little heir's your aim, though it means forgoing
All those pickings – fat pigeons, bearded mullet, the bait
40 Of the legacy-hunter's market.[2] Really, if *you* take a wife, I'll
Credit anything, friend. You were once the randiest
Hot-rod-about-town, you hid in more bedroom cupboards
Than a comedy juvenile lead.[3] Can this be the man now
Sticking his silly neck out for the matrimonial halter?
45 And as for your insistence on a wife with old-fashioned
Moral virtues – man, you need your blood-pressure checked,
     you're
Crazy, you're aiming over the moon. Find a chaste

1. Augustan legislation on marriage and family life (the *leges Iuliae* of 18 B.C. and the *lex Papia Poppaea* of A.D. 9) gave social and political privileges to those with three or more children and diminished the inheritance rights of the unmarried and childless.

2. Legacy hunting (*captatio*) is a frequent satiric topic. Flattery and gifts were used to get legacies from rich, preferably childless, old men and women. Will-making with the almost mandatory inclusion of relatives, friends and the emperor was more of a social institution in Roman than it is in modern times. Although legal disputes about wills in rich families continue, this has ceased to be a source of ridicule.

3. Bedroom farce was a common feature of Roman popular mimes, which revolved round such stock characters as the gullible old man, the fool, the bad wife and so on.

And modest bride, and well may you sacrifice
Your gilded heifer to Juno, well may you go down flat
And kiss the stones before the Tarpeian altar![1]
Few indeed are the girls with a ritual qualification
For the feast of the Corn-Goddess[2] – nine whole days' abstinence! –   50
Or whose fathers wouldn't prefer, if they could, to avoid
Such tainted filial kisses.[3] Hang wreaths on your doorposts,
Strew your threshold with ivy! Tell me, will Hiberina
Think one man enough? You'd find it much less trouble
To make her agree to being blinded in one eye.
But *you* maintain that a girl who's lived a secluded   55
Life on her father's estate, way out in the country,
Can keep a good reputation. Just put her down
In the sleepiest outback town you can think of – and if she behaves
As she did back home, then I'll believe in that country
Estate of yours. But don't tell me nothing ever
Came off in caves, or up mountains – are Jove and Mars *that*
    senile?

  Look around the arcades, try to pick out a woman   60
Who's worthy of your devotion. Check every tier of seats
At all the theatres in town: will they yield one single
Candidate you could love without a qualm? When pansy
Bathyllus dances Leda, all *fouettés* and *entrechats*,
Just watch the women. One can't control her bladder,
Another suddenly moans in drawn-out ecstasy   65
As though she was coming. Your country girl's all rapt
Attention, she's learning fast.
                     But when the theatrical
Season is over, the stage-props all packed away,

1. Juno was the goddess of marriage and the wedding ceremonies involved the sacrifice of appropriate animals. The Tarpeian altar refers to the Temple of Jupiter on the Capitol where Juno was also worshipped. Houses were traditionally garlanded for weddings.
2. The corn-goddess Ceres was an exceptionally chaste goddess; her all-female festival celebrating the first fruits was held in August.
3. The satirists, Martial and Juvenal, express strong feelings about the prevalence in Rome of oral sexual practices.

The playhouses closed and empty, in those summer
Dogdays when only the lawcourts go droning on,
Some women relieve their boredom by taking in
70 Low-down vaudeville farces – and their performers.
Look at that fellow who scored such a hit in the late-night
Show as Actaeon's mother,[1] camping it up like mad –
Poor Aelia's crazy about him. These are the women
Who'll pay out fancy prices for the chance to defibulate[2]
A counter-tenor, to ruin a concert performer's voice.
One has a kink for ham actors. Are you surprised? What else
75 Do you expect them to do? Go ape on a good book?
Marry a wife, and she'll make some flute-player
Or guitarist a father, not you. So when you erect
Long stands in the narrow streets, and hang your front-door
With outsize laurel wreaths, it's all to welcome an infant
80 Whose face, in that tortoiseshell cradle, under its canopy,
Recalls some armoured thug, some idol of the arena.
    When that senator's wife, Eppia, eloped with her fancy
        swordsman
To the land of the Nile, the Alexandrian stews,
Egypt itself cried out at Rome's monstrous morals.
85 Husband, family, sister, all were jettisoned, not
One single thought for her country; shamelessly she forsook
Her tearful children, as well as – this will really surprise you –
The public games, and her favourite matinée star.
Luxury-reared, cradled by Daddy in swansdown,
Brought up to frills and flounces, Eppia nevertheless
90 Made as light of the sea as she did of her reputation –
Not that our pampered ladies set any great store by *that*.
Boldly she faced this long and arduous voyage.
The chop and toss of Tuscan waters, the loud

1. Autonoe.
2. To remove the metal wire inserted through the prepuce to inhibit copulation,
which was regarded as detrimental to the singing voice.

Ionian swell. When a woman endures danger and hardship
In a good cause, her conscience clear, then chill   95
Terror ices her heart, her knees turn to water,
She can scarcely stand upright; but wicked audacity
Breeds its own fortitude. To go aboard ship is torture
Under a husband's orders: then the smell of the bilges
Is sickening, then the sky wheels dizzily around.
But a wife who's off with her lover suffers no qualms. The one   100
Pukes on her husband, the other sits down to a hearty
Meal with the crew, takes a turn round the quarter-deck,
Helps to haul on the sheets, and enjoys it.

                                           What was the youthful
Charm that so fired our senator's wife? What hooked her?
What did Eppia see in him to make her put up
With being labelled 'The Gladiatress'? Her poppet, her Sergius   105
Was no chicken, forty at least, with a dud arm that held promise
Of early retirement. Besides, his face looked a proper mess –
Helmet-scarred, a great wen on his nose, an unpleasant
Discharge from one constantly weeping eye. What of it?
He was a gladiator. That name makes all the breed   110
Seem handsomer than Adonis; this was what she preferred
To her children and her country, her sister, her husband: steel
Is what they all crave for. Yet this same Sergius,
Once pensioned off, would soon have bored her as much as her
    husband.

  Do such private scandals move you? Are you shocked by Eppia's
    deeds?
Then look at the God's rivals, hear what Claudius   115
Had to put up with. The minute she heard him snoring,
His wife – that whore-empress[1] – who dared to prefer the
    mattress
Of a stews to her couch in the Palace, called for her hooded
Night-cloak and hastened forth, alone or with a single
Maid to attend her. Then, her black hair hidden   120
Under an ash-blonde wig, she would make straight for her brothel,

---

1. Messalina.

With its odour of stale, warm bedclothes, its empty reserved cell.
Here she would strip off, showing her gilded nipples and
The belly that once housed a prince of the blood. Her door-sign
Bore a false name, Lycisca, 'The Wolf-girl'. A more than willing
125   Partner, she took on all comers, for cash, without a break.
Too soon, for her, the brothel-keeper dismissed
His girls. She stayed till the end, always the last to go,
Then trailed away sadly, still with a burning hard on,
130   Retiring exhausted, yet still far from satisfied, cheeks
Begrimed with lamp-smoke, filthy, carrying home
To her imperial couch the stink of the whorehouse.
    What point in mentioning spells, or aphrodisiac potions,
Or that lethal brew served up to stepsons? Sexual compulsion
135   Drives women to worse crimes: lust is their strongest motive.
    'Censennia's husband swears she's the perfect wife: why so?'
Because she brought him three million. In exchange he calls her
      chaste.
The shafts that waste him, the fires that burn him up
Have nothing to do with desire. That torch was lit
By cash; it was her dowry that fired those arrows,
140   And purchased her freedom. She can make come-hitherish signs
Or write billets-doux in front of her husband; your wealthy
Woman who marries a miser has widow's privileges.
    'Then why does Sertorius burn with passion for Bibula?'
When you get to the root of it, what he loves isn't his wife
But merely her face. When the first few wrinkles appear,
145   When her skin goes dry and slack, when her teeth begin
To blacken, when her eyes turn lustreless, then: 'Pack
Your bags!' his steward will tell her. 'Be off with you! You've
      become
A nasty bore, always blowing your nose. Be off,
And double quick: there's another wife due to arrive,
Without that eternal sniffle.' But now she's riding high,
She's the new princess, wheedling ranches and vineyards,
150   Prize sheep, herdsmen and all from her husband. Yet that's
      nothing:
She demands all his slave-boys, his field-gangs: if a neighbour

Owns any item they don't, it has to be purchased.
In wintertime,[1] when the arcades are crammed with
Canvas market-stalls, and the mural of Trader
Jason is blocked from view, armed sailors and all,
She goes on a shopping spree: huge crystal vases, outsize   155
Myrrh-jars[2] of finest agate, and lastly, a famous
Diamond ring, once worn by Queen Berenice –
Which adds to its price. (She had it from her brother,
That barbarous prince Agrippa, as a token
Of their incestuous love, in the land where kings
Observe the Sabbath barefoot, where – by long-established
Tradition – pigs are suffered to attain a ripe old age.)   160
   'Not one woman, out of so many, who meets your
     requirements?'
Assume one with beauty and charm, fertile, wealthy, her hall
A museum of old ancestral portraits, grant her
Virginity more stunning than all those dishevelled Sabine[3]
Maidens who stopped the fighting could raise between them,
Make her a *rara avis*, a black swan or the like – still   165
Who could stomach such wifely perfection? I'd far far sooner
Marry a penniless tart than take on that virtuous
Paragon Cornelia, Mother of Statesmen, so haughty,
So condescending a prig, her dowry weighted down
With famous triumphs. As far as I'm concerned
You can take your battle-honours – Hannibal, Syphax,   170
The whole Carthaginian myth – and get lost with them, madam.
   'Apollo, be merciful; Artemis, lay by your shafts,'
Amphion prayed. 'The children are not to blame –
Strike down their mother!' But Apollo, unheeding,
Drew back the bowstring. So Niobe lost, at one stroke,   175
Her quiverful and her husband – all through the fatuous pride

1. An allusion to the Saturnalia in December.
2. Myrrhine ware, made of polished and perfumed fluorspar or bluejohn, was
highly prized by the Romans.
3. Sabine women were regarded as models of old-fashioned chastity. They broke
up the battle between their Roman husbands and their own avenging kinfolk
after the Rape.

That made her boast she was nobler in her offspring
Than Leto – and more prolific than the white Alban sow.
  What beauty, what decorum are worth having thrown in your
      face
Day in day out? What pleasure remains in such rare
180 And lofty perfection, when pride of spirit has turned it
From honey to bitter aloes? What man is so besotted
That for half the day, or more, the wife he lauds to the skies
Doesn't give him cold shivers? Often it's trivial faults
185 That offend a husband most. What could be more repulsive
Than the way no modern girl will believe her looks
Are worth a damn till she's tarted up *à la grecque*?
Our provincial dollies ape Athenian fashion, it's smart
To chatter away in Greek – though what should make them blush
Is their slipshod Latin. All their emotions – fear,
Anger, happiness, anxiety, every inmost
190 Secret thought – find expression in Greek, they even
Make love Greek-style. It might be all right for schoolgirls
To behave this way; but when you're well over eighty,
195 And go round in public using such phrases as *Zoé*
Kai Psyché – 'My life, my soul!' – real bedroom language,
It's most unbecoming. Such naughty, caressing endearments
Have fingers, they'd start a twitch in any man's groin.
But don't go preening yourself, dear: even if your voice
Were softer and more seductive than any matinée idol's,
Your age is still scored on your face.
                            So, man, if you're not going
      to love
200 Your lawfully wedded spouse, why marry at all? Why waste
Good money on a reception, or those cakes handed out at the end
To your well-gorged guests, when the party's breaking up?
Why lose a salver of mint-new golden guineas –
205 Victory issues, too[1] – on the first-night bridal offering?

---

1. Gold victory coins (*aurei*) minted to celebrate Trajan's victories in Germany and
  Romania between A.D. 97 and 102. Gifts to a new bride from her husband were
  customary practice.

But if your mind is set, with uxorious obsession,
On one woman and one only, then bow your neck to the yoke
In voluntary servitude.
                    No woman spares any lover;
She may be on fire herself, but that doesn't lessen
Her gold-digging itch, her sadistic urges. So
The better you are as a man, the more desirable
Your husbandly virtues, the less you get out of your wife.   210
Want to give someone a present? Buy or sell property? *She*
Has the veto on all such transactions; she even controls
Your friendships: lifelong companions, visitors since boyhood,
May find the door slammed in their faces. Pimps and ring-masters,   215
The toughs of the arena – these, when they make their wills,
Have a free hand. But you are compelled to include
Two or three of her lovers amongst your legatees.
    'Crucify that slave!'
                    'But what is the slave's offence
To merit such punishment? Who has brought charges against   220
        him?
Where are the witnesses? You must hear his defence: no
Delay can be too long when a man's life is at stake.'
'So a slave's a *man* now, is he, you crackpot? All right, perhaps
He didn't do anything. This is still my wish, my command:
Warrant enough that I will it.'
                    So she imposes
Such whims on her husband. But soon enough she moves on
To another kingdom, switching establishments   225
Till her bridal veil's worn out; then, finally, back she comes
To the bed she scorned and abandoned, leaving behind her
A freshly garlanded house, the bridal hangings
Not yet removed, the boughs still green on the threshold.
Score up another husband: that makes eight
In under five years: it ought to go on her tombstone.[1]   230

---

1. The frequency of marriage and divorce in the late Roman republic and early
   empire may have been liberating for women but was highly offensive to the satir-
   ists.

While your mother-in-law still lives, domestic harmony
Is out of the question. She eggs her daughter on
To run through your capital and enjoy it. She gives advice
On the subtlest, least obvious way to answer billets-doux
From would-be seducers. It's she who hoodwinks or fixes
235 Your servants, she who takes to her bed when she's well,
Who lies tossing and turning under the sheets till the doctor
Makes his visit. Meanwhile, all hot impatience,
Hidden behind the scenes, her daughter's lover
Keeps mum, and pulls his wire. Do you really believe
Any mother will pass on a loftier set of morals
240 Than she learnt herself? Besides, it's profitable
For an old whore to bring up her daughter to the trade.

There's scarcely one court hearing in which the litigation
Wasn't set off by a woman. Defendant or plaintiff, if
She's not one she's the other, ready to deal with a brief
Single-handed, and full of advice to Counsel –
245 How to open his case, or present individual points.

And what about female athletes, with their purple
Track-suits, and wrestling in mud? Not to mention our lady-
        fencers –
We've all seen *them*, stabbing the stump with a foil,
Shield well advanced, going through the proper motions:
Just the right training needed to blow a matronly horn
250 At the Floral Festival[1] – unless they have higher ambitions,
And the goal of all their practice is the real arena.[2]
But then, what modesty can be looked for in some
Helmeted hoyden, a renegade from her sex,
Who thrives on masculine violence – yet would not prefer
To *be* a man, since the pleasure is so much less?
255 What a fine sight for some husband – *it might be you* – his wife's

---

1. The Floralia (28 April–3 May) was a licentious holiday celebrating the rites of
spring. Games, stage shows and exhibitions of naked prostitutes were featured.
As with all public shows, they opened with a flourish of trumpets.
2. Female gladiators were not uncommon and are documented in, for example,
Petronius and Martial. They still appeal to modern tastes, as in mud-wrestling.

Equipment put up at auction, baldric, armlet, plumes
And one odd shinguard! Or if the other style
Of fighting takes her fancy, imagine your delight when
The dear girl sells off her greaves! (And yet these same women
Have such delicate skins that even sheer silk chafes them;   260
They sweat in the finest chiffon.) Hark how she snorts
At each practice thrust, bowed down by the weight of her helmet;
See the big coarse puttees wrapped round her ample hams –
Then wait for the laugh, when she lays her weapons aside
And squats on the potty! Tell me, you noble ladies,
Scions of our great statesmen – Lepidus, blind Metellus,   265
Fabius the Guzzler[1] – what gladiator's woman
Ever rigged herself out like this, or sweated at fencing-drill?

    The bed that contains a wife is always hot with quarrels
And mutual bickering: sleep's the last thing you get there.
This is her battleground, her station for husband-baiting:
In bed she's worse than a tigress robbed of its young,   270
Bitching away, to stifle her own bad conscience,
About his boy-friends, or weeping over some way-out
Fictitious mistress. She keeps a copious flow
Of tears at the ready, awaiting her command,
For any situation: and you, poor worm, are agog,   275
Thinking this means she loves you, and kiss her tears away –
But if you raided her desk-drawers, the compromising letters,
The assignations you'd find that your green-eyed whorish
Wife has amassed! Suppose, though, you catch her in bed with
A slave, or some businessman? *Quick, quick, Quintilian,*   280
Find me a pat excuse, she prays. *I'm stuck*, says the Maestro,
You can get yourself out of this one.

                         And she does. 'We agreed long
    ago
To go our separate ways – you were at liberty
To do as you pleased, and I could have my fun on the side.
It cuts no ice with me if you bawl the house down –

---

1. Lepidus, Metellus, and Fabius are all typical representatives of distinguished
   Roman families.

I'm only human too.'
                 For sheer effrontery, nothing
Can beat a woman caught in the act; her very
285 Guilt adds fresh fire to her fury and indignation.
      What was it (you well may ask) that bred such monsters, how
Do they come about? In the old days poverty
Kept Latin women chaste: hard work, too little sleep,
These were the things that saved their humble homes from
      corruption –
290 Hands horny from carding fleeces, Hannibal at the gates,
Their menfolk standing to arms. Now we are suffering
The evils of too-long peace. Luxury, deadlier
Than any armed invader, lies like an incubus
Upon us still, avenging the world we brought to heel.
295 Since Roman poverty perished, no visitation
Of crime or lust has been spared us. Sybaris, Rhodes,
Miletus, shameless Tarentum, drunk and garlanded – all
Come pouring in upon our Seven Hills. But filthy
Lucre it was that first brought these loose foreign
Morals amongst us, enervating wealth that
Destroyed us, over the years, through shameless self-indulgence.
300   What conscience has Venus drunk? Our inebriated beauties
Can't tell head from tail at those midnight oyster suppers
When the best wine's laced with perfume, and tossed down neat
From a foaming conch-shell, while the dizzy ceiling
305 Spins round, and the tables dance, and each light shows double.
Why, you may ask yourself, does the notorious Maura
Sniff at the air in that knowing, derisive way
As she and her dear friend Tullia pass by the ancient altar
Of Chastity? and what is Tullia whispering to her?
Here, at night, they stagger out of their litters
310 And relieve themselves, pissing in long hard bursts
All over the Goddess's statue. Then, while the Moon
Looks down on their motions, they take turns to ride each other,
And finally go home. So you, next morning,
On your way to some great house, will splash through your wife's
      piddle.

Notorious, too, are the ritual mysteries
Of the Good Goddess,[1] when flute-music stirs the loins,
And frenzied women, devotees of Priapus,
Sweep along in procession, howling, tossing their hair,   315
Wine-flown, horn-crazy, burning with the desire
To get themselves laid. Hark at the way they whinny
In mounting lust, see that copious flow, the pure
And vintage wine of passion, that splashes their thighs!
Off goes Saufeia's wreath, she challenges the call-girls   320
To a contest of bumps and grinds, emerges victorious,
But herself is eclipsed in turn – an admiring loser –
By the liquid movements of Medullina's buttocks:
So the ladies, with a display of talent to match their birth,
Win all the prizes. No make-belief here, no pretence,
Each act is performed in earnest, and guaranteed
To warm the age-chilled balls of a Nestor or a Priam.   325
Delay breeds itching impatience, boosts the pure female
Urge, and from every side of the grotto a clamorous
Cry goes up, 'It's time! Let in the men!' Supposing
One lover's asleep, another is told to get dressed   330
And hustle along. If they draw a blank with their boy-friends
They rope in the slaves. If enough slaves cannot be found
The water-carrier's hired. If they can't track him down, either,
And men are in short supply, they're ready and willing
To cock their dish for a donkey. Would that our ancient ritual   335
(At least in its public aspect) was uncontaminated
By such malpractices! But every Moor and Hindu
Knows the identity of that 'lady'-harpist
Who brought a tool as long as both anti-Catonian
Pamphlets by Caesar[2] into the sanctuary where

1. The *Bona Dea* or *Fauna*, whose rituals totally excluded men; they were held at
   night in the house of the chief magistrate. In one notorious incident, Pompeia,
   wife of Julius Caesar, was in charge and Clodius in disguise gained surreptitious
   entry in pursuit of a lady friend.
2. Julius Caesar's political pamphlets against Cato (the *Anti-Catones*) were aimed to
   discredit him as a politician by accusing him of drunkenness and other personal
   vices.

340 All images of the other sex must be veiled, where even
A buckmouse, ball-conscious, beats an embarrassed retreat.
  Once, no man would have dared to make light of divine
    power,
Or sneer at the earthenware bowls, black pots, and brittle platters
Of Vatican clay that sufficed King Numa.[1] But nowadays
345 What altar does not attract its Clodius in drag?
O1   In every house where there's a practising Master
Of Obscene Arts installed – that occupational
Twitch in his right hand hints at unlimited prospects –
You'll find a disgusting crowd, camp if not actually queer.
They let these creatures defile their meals, admit them
O5 To the sacred family board. Glasses that should be broken
When La Courgette's drunk from them, or The Bearded
    Cowrie,[2]
Are washed up with the rest. The *lanista*[3] runs
A cleaner, more decent establishment than yours:
He quarters the fag targeteers and the armoured heavies
Well away from each other; net-throwers aren't required
To mess with convicted felons, nor are shoulder-guards
O10 And the light-armed fighter's trident found in the same cell.
Even the lowest riff-raff of the arena
Observe this rule; even in prison they chain them
With separate gangs. But the creatures your wife allows
To share your cup! A dyed blonde washed-up whore
O15 On the graveyard beat would gag at drinking from it,
Whatever the vintage. Yet these are the advisers
On whose say-so their mistress will marry – or suddenly
Decide to beat a retreat; with whom she relieves
Her flagging spirits, the boredom of daily existence;
Under whose expert guidance she learns to shimmy

1. Numa, an early legendary king of Rome, was regarded as an exemplar of strict
   Roman morality as promulgated through his laws. Associated with this was a
   very austere style of life, symbolized by pots made from clay from the Vatican
   hill, now close to St Peter's.
2. The names contain further allusions to oral sexuality.
3. The *lanista* was a manager and trainer of boxers and gladiators.

Her hips and pelvis. What other tricks she acquires   020
Only the teacher knows – and he's far from reliable
In every case. He may line his eyes with kohl,
And wear a yellow robe and a hairnet – but adultery
Is the end in view. The affected voice, the way
He poses, one arm akimbo, and scratches his bottom, shouldn't
Lull your suspicions. He'll be a champion performer   025
When he gets into bed, dropping the role of Thais
For that of the potent Triphallus.[1]

                      Hey there, *you*,
Who do you think you're fooling? Keep this masquerade
For those who believe it. I'll wager that you're one hundred
Per cent a man. It's a bet. So will you confess,
Or must the torturer rack the truth from your maids?
I know the advice my old friends would give – 'Lock her up   030
And bar the doors.' But who is to keep guard
Over the guards themselves? They get paid in common coin
To forget their mistress's randy little adventures;
Both sides have something to hide. Any sensible wife,
Planning ahead, will first turn the heat on them.   034

High and low alike, all women nowadays   349
Share the same lusts. The peasant trudging barefoot
Over black cobbles is no whit superior to
The lady who rides on the necks of tall Syrian porters.

   Ogulnia's mad on the Games. To see them she'll hire
Dresses, attendants, a carriage, a baby-sitter,
Cushions, lady companions, and a cute little blonde
To carry her messages. Yet whatever remains   355
Of the family plate, down to the very last salver,
She'll hand out as a present to some plausible athlete.
Many such women lack substance – yet poverty gives them
No sense of restraint, they don't observe the limits
Their resources impose. Men on the other hand   360
Sometimes at least show providence, plan for the future

---

1. Thais was a prototype of the expensive prostitute; Triphallus, i.e. with three
male organs, was a descriptive name of Priapus.

In a practical way, learn by the ant's example
To fear cold and hunger. But an extravagant woman
365   Never knows when she's overdrawn. None of them reckon
The cost of their pleasures, as though, when the strong-box was
     empty,
More money would grow there, the pile replenish itself.
    There are girls who adore unmanly eunuchs – so smooth,
So beardless to kiss, and no worry about abortions!
But the biggest thrill is one who was fully grown,
370   A lusty black-quilled male, before the surgeons
Went to work on his groin. Let the testicles ripen
And drop, fill out till they hang like two-pound weights;
Then what the surgeon chops will hurt nobody's trade but the
     barber's.
(Slave-dealers' boys are different: pathetically weak,
Ashamed of their empty bag, their lost little chickpeas.)
Look at that specimen – you could spot him a mile off.
Everyone knows him – displaying his well-endowed person
375   At the baths: Priapus might well be jealous. And yet
He's a eunuch. His mistress arranged it. So, let them sleep together –
Yet I wouldn't bet on a handsome, passionate youth
With his first beard sprouting to better *that* performance.
    If your wife has musical tastes, she'll make the professional
380   Singers come when she wants. She's forever handling
Their instruments, her bejewelled fingers sparkle
Over the lute, she practises scales with a vibrant
Quill once employed by some famous virtuoso –
It's her mascot, her solace, she lavishes kisses on it,
385   The darling object.
                A certain patrician lady,
Whose lutanist protégé was due to compete in
The Capitoline Festival,[1] made inquiry of Janus
And Vesta, offering wine and cakes, to find out
If her Pollio could aspire to the oakwreath prize

---

1. Reinstituted by Domitian in A.D. 86 in honour of Capitoline Jupiter, the festival
   featured competitions in poetry and music. See Statius, *Silvae* V. 3.231f.

For the best performance. What more could she have done
If her husband was sick, or the doctors shaking their heads
Over her little son? She stood there at the altar,   390
Thinking it no disgrace to veil her face on behalf of
This cheapjack twangler. She made the proper responses
In traditional form, and blanched as the lamb was opened.[1]
Tell me now, I beg you, most ancient of deities,
Old Father Janus, do such requests get answered? There must
Be time and to spare in heaven. From what I can see
You Gods have nothing on hand to keep you occupied.   395
One woman's mad on comedians, another's pushing some tragic
Ham of her choice: the diviner will soon get varicose veins.

    Yet a musical wife's not so bad as some presumptuous
Flat-chested busybody who rushes around the town
Gate-crashing all-male meetings, talking back straight-faced
To a uniformed general – *and* in her husband's presence.   400
She knows all the news of the world, what's cooking in Thrace
Or China, just what the stepmother did with her stepson
Behind closed doors, who's fallen in love, which gallant
Is all the rage. She'll tell you who got the widow   405
Pregnant, and in which month; she knows each woman's
Pillow-endearments, and all the positions she favours.
She's the first to spot any comet presaging trouble
For some eastern prince, in Armenia, maybe, or Parthia.
She's on to the latest gossip and rumours as soon as
They reach the city-gates, or invents her own, informing
Everyone she meets that Niphates[2] has overflowed
And is inundating whole countries – towns are cut off,   410
She says, and the land is sinking: flood and disaster!
    Yet even this is not so insufferable
As her habit, when woken up, of grabbing some poor-class
Neighbour and belting into him with a whip. If her precious

---

1. For the inspection of the entrails, which would reveal good or bad omens to the
   diviner (*haruspex*).
2. Niphates is a mountain of the Taurus range in south-east Asia Minor; it was not
   commonly mistaken for a river.

415 Sleep is broken by barking, 'Fetch me the cudgels,'
    She roars, 'and be quick about it!' The dog gets a thrashing,
    But its master gets one first. She's no joke to cross,
    And her face is a grisly fright. Not till the evening
    Does she visit the baths: only then are her oil-jars and
420 The rest of her clobber transferred there. First she works out
    With the weights and dumb-bells. Then, when her arms are
        aching,
    The masseur takes over, craftily slipping one hand
    Along her thigh, and tickling her up till she comes.
    Lastly she makes for the sweat-room. She loves to sit there
    Amid all that hubbub, perspiring. Meanwhile at home
    Her unfortunate guests are nearly dead with hunger.
425 At last she appears, all flushed, with a three-gallon thirst,
    Enough to empty the brimming jar at her feet
    Without assistance. She knocks back two straight pints
    On an empty stomach, to sharpen her appetite: then
    Throws it all up again, souses the floor with vomit
430 That flows in rivers across the terrazzo. She drinks
    And spews by turns, like some big snake that's tumbled
    Into a wine-vat, till her gilded jordan brims
    Right over with sour and vinous slops. Quite sickened,
    Eyes shut, her husband somehow holds down his bile.
      Worse still the well-read menace, who's hardly settled for
        dinner
435 Before she starts praising Virgil, making a moral case
    For Dido (death justifies all), comparing, evaluating
    Rival poets, Virgil and Homer suspended
    In opposite scales, weighed up one against the other.
    Critics surrender, academics are routed, all
    Fall silent, not a word from lawyer or auctioneer –
440 Or even another woman. Such a rattle of talk,
    You'd think all the pots and bells were being clashed together
    When the moon's in eclipse.[1] No need now for trumpets or brass:

---

1. An eclipse of the moon was traditionally associated with witchcraft, against
  which any loud din might be effective.

One woman can act, single-handed, as lunar midwife.
But wisdom imposes limits, even on virtue, and if
She's so determined to prove herself eloquent, learned,   445
She should hoist up her skirts and gird them above the knee,
Offer a pig to Silvanus (female worshippers banned) and
Scrub off the penny baths.[1] So avoid a dinner-partner
With an argumentative style, who hurls well-rounded
Syllogisms like slingshots, who has all history pat: 450
Choose someone rather who doesn't understand *all* she reads.
I hate these authority-citers, the sort who are always thumbing
Some standard grammatical treatise, whose every utterance
Observes all the laws of syntax, who with antiquarian zeal
Quote poets I've never heard of. Such matters are men's concern.   455
If she wants to correct someone's language, she can always
Start with her unlettered girl-friends. A husband should be
        allowed
His solecisms in peace.
                        There's nothing a woman
Baulks at, no action that gives her a twinge of conscience
Once she's put on her emerald choker, weighted down her ear-
        lobes
With vast pearl pendants. What's more insufferable   460
Than your well-heeled female? But earlier in the process
She presents a sight as funny as it's appalling,
Her features lost under a damp bread face-pack,
Or greasy with vanishing-cream that clings to her husband's
Lips when the poor man kisses her – though it's all
Wiped off for her lover. She takes no trouble about
The way she looks at home: those imported Indian   465
Scents and lotions she buys with a lover in mind.
First one layer, then the next: at last the contours emerge
Till she's almost recognizable. Now she freshens
Her complexion with asses' milk. (If her husband's posted
To the godforsaken North, a herd of she-asses   470

---

1. Silvanus, a god of the woodlands, was the object of an exclusively male cult.
   Imperial public baths charged women double what men paid.

Will travel with them.) But all these medicaments
And various treatments – not least the damp bread-poultice –
Make you wonder what's underneath, a face or an ulcer.
  It's revealing to study the details of such a woman's
475 Daily routine, to see how she occupies her time.
If her husband, the night before, has slept with his back to her,
      then
The wool-maid's had it, cosmeticians are stripped and flogged,
The litter-bearer's accused of coming late. One victim
Has rods broken over his back, another bears bloody stripes
From the whip, a third is lashed with a cat-o'-nine-tails:
480 Some women pay their floggers an annual salary.
While the punishment's carried out she'll be fixing her face,
Gossiping with her friends, giving expert consideration
To the width of the hem on some gold-embroidered robe –
Crack! Crack! – or skimming through the daily gazette;
Till at last, when the flogger's exhausted, she snaps, 'Get out!'
485 And for one day at least the judicial hearing is over.
Her household's governed with all the savagery
Of a Sicilian court.[1] If she's made some assignation
That she wants to look her best for, and is in a tearing hurry
Because she's late, and her lover's waiting for her
In the public gardens, or by the shrine (bordello
Might be a more accurate term) of Isis[2] – why then, the slave-girl
490 Arranging her coiffure will have her own hair torn out,
Poor creature, and the tunic ripped from her shoulders and
      breasts.
'Why isn't this curl in place?' the lady screams, and her rawhide
Lash inflicts chastisement for the offending ringlet.
But what was poor Psecas's crime? How could you blame an
      attendant
495 For the shape of your own nose? Another maid
Combs out the hair on her left side, twists it round the curlers;

----

1. Sicilian tyrants such as Phalaris of Acragas (mid fifth century B.C.), with his
   heated bronze bull, were notorious for their ingenious cruelties.
2. Temples of Isis were well-known rendezvous.

The consultative committee is reinforced by
An elderly lady's-maid inherited from Mama,
And now promoted from hairpins to the wool department. She
Takes the floor first, to be followed by her inferiors
In age and skill, as though some issue of reputation   500
Or life itself were at stake, so obsessionally they strive
In beauty's service. See the tall edifice
Rise up on her head in serried tiers and storeys![1]
See her heroic stature – at least, that is, from in front:
Her back view's less impressive, you'd think it belonged
To a different person. The effect is ultra-absurd
If she's lacking in inches, the sort who without stilettos   505
Resembles some sawn-off pygmy, who's forced to stand
On tiptoe for a kiss.
                        Meantime she completely
Ignores her husband, gives not a moment's thought
To all she costs him. She's less a wife than a neighbour –
Except when it comes to loathing his friends and slaves,   510
Or running up bills . . .
                        And now in comes a procession,
Devotees of the frenzied Bellona, and Cybele, Mother of Gods,
Led by a giant eunuch, the idol of his lesser
Companions in obscenity. Long ago, with a sherd,
He sliced off his genitals: now neither the howling rabble   515
Nor the kettledrums can outshriek him. His plebeian cheeks
Are framed in a Phrygian mitre.[2] With awesome utterance
He bids her beware of September[3] and its siroccos –
Unless, that is, she lays out a hundred eggs
For purificatory rites, and makes him a present
Of some old clothes, russet-coloured, so that any calamity,   520
However sudden or frightful, may pass into the garments –
A package-deal expiation, valid for twelve whole months.

1. This multi-tiered hairstyle was in fashion in the later years of the first century
   A.D.
2. An Asiatic hood, associated with exotic and decadent temperaments.
3. A dangerous month in Italy for fevers.

In winter she'll break the ice, descend into the river,
And thrice, before noon, let the eddies of Tiber close
525   Over her timorous head; then crawl out, naked, trembling,
And shuffle on bleeding knees, by way of penance,
Across the Field of Mars.[1] Indeed, if white Io so orders,
She'll make a pilgrimage to the ends of Egypt,
Fetch water from tropic Meroë for the aspersion
Of Isis's temple, that stands beside those ancient sheep-pens,
530   The public polling-booths. She believes that she's summoned
By the voice of the Lady herself – just the sort of rare
Mind and spirit, no doubt, that a god *would* choose to talk to
In the small hours! That's why high praise and special honours
Go to her dogheaded colleague, Anubis, who runs through the streets
With a shaven-pated crew dressed in linen robes, and mocks
535   The people's grief for Osiris. He it is who intercedes
For wives who fail to abstain from sex on the prescribed
And ritual days, exacting huge penalties
When the marriage-bed is polluted, or when the silver
Serpent[2] appears to nod. His tears and professional
540   Mutterings – after Osiris has been bribed with a fat goose[3]
And some sacrificial cake – will guarantee absolution.

     No sooner has *he* pushed off than a palsied Jewess,
Parking her haybox outside, comes round soliciting alms
In a breathy whisper. She knows, and can interpret,
The Laws of Jerusalem: a high-priestess-under-the-trees,
545   A faithful mediator of Heaven on earth. She too
Fills her palm, but more sparingly: Jews will sell you
Whatever dreams you like for a few small coppers.

550   Then there are fortune-tellers, Armenians, Syrians,
Who'll pry out the steaming lungs of a pigeon, predict
A young lover for the lady, or a good fat inheritance
From some childless millionaire. They'll probe a chicken's

---

1. See Glossary, under Campus Martius.
2. Serpents were associated with the cult of Isis.
3. Geese were a favourite sacrificial item in all Egyptian cults.

Bosom, unravel the guts of a puppy: sometimes
They even slaughter a child. The seer can always
Turn informer on his client.
                              Chaldaean astrologers
Will inspire more confidence: their every pronouncement
Is a straight tip, clients believe, from the oracular fountain
Of Ammon. (Now that Delphi has fallen silent   555
The human race is condemned to murky unknowing
Of what the future may bring.) The most successful
Have been exiled on several occasions – like you-know-who
With his venal friendship and rigged predictions, who settled
The hash of that great citizen dreaded by Otho . . .[1]

                                        . . . Nothing
Boosts your diviner's credit so much as a lengthy spell   560
In the glasshouse, with fetters jangling from either wrist:
No one believes in his powers unless he's dodged execution
By a hair's breadth, and contrived to get himself deported
To some Cycladic island like Seriphos,[2] and to escape
After lengthy privations. Your wife, your Tanaquil,
Is for ever consulting such folk. Why does her jaundice-ridden   565
Mother take so long dying? When will she see off
Her sister or her uncles? (She made all inquiries
About *you* some while back.) Will her present lover
Survive her? (What greater boon could she ask of the Gods?)
Yet she at least cannot tell what Saturn's gloomy   570
Conjunction portends,[3] or under which constellation
Venus is most propitious; which months bring loss, which gain.
When you meet such a woman, clutching her well-thumbed
Almanacs like a string of amber worry-beads,
Keep very clear of her. *She* isn't shopping around
For expert advice; she's an expert herself, the sort   575

1. i.e. Galba; Otho was urged to murder him by an Eastern astrologer.
2. Seriphos and similar islands in the Aegean Cyclades were common places of
   exile.
3. Saturn is an ill-omened planet (hence 'saturnine'), whereas Venus is associated
   with love and joy.

Who won't accompany her husband on an overseas posting –
Or even back home again – if the almanac forbids it.
When she wants to go out of town, a mile even, or less,
She computes a propitious time from her tables. If she rubs
One corner of her eye, and it itches, she must never
Put ointment on it without first consulting her horoscope; if
580   She is ill in bed, she will only take nourishment
At such times as Petosiris, the Egyptian, may recommend.
    Women of lower rank and fortune learn their futures
Down at the racecourse, from phrenologist or palmist,
With much smacking of lips against evil influences.
585   Rich ladies send out to hire their own tame Phrygian
Prophet, they skim off the cream of the star-gazers, or
Pick one of those wise old parties who neutralize thunderbolts:[1]
The Circus and the Embankment[2] preside over more
590   Plebeian destinies. Here, by the dolphin-columns[3]
And the public stands, old whores in their off-shoulder
Dresses and thin gold neck-chains come for advice –
Should they ditch the tavern-keeper? marry the rag-and-bone
        man?
Yet these at least endure the dangers of childbirth, all
Those nurturing chores which poverty lays upon them:
How often do gilded beds witness a lying-in
595   When we've so many sure-fire drugs for inducing sterility
Or killing an embryo child? Our skilled abortionists
Know all the answers. So cheer up, my poor friend,
And give her the dose yourself. Things might be worse – just
        suppose
She chose to stay pregnant, to swell her belly with frolicsome
600   Infants: you might become some piccaninny's Papa,
And find yourself making your will on behalf of a son and heir
Whose off-black face was better not seen by daylight.

---

1. A spot hit by a thunderbolt was ill-omened; its dangers were neutralized by
   Etruscan priets.
2. The banks of the Tiber.
3. Dolphin statues were used to count the laps in chariot racing.

I say nothing of spurious children, changelings picked up
Beside some filthy cistern, and passed off as nobly born –
False hopes, deluded prayers! – our future priesthood,
Our bluest patrician blood. Fortune by night   605
Is shameless, smiles on these naked babes, enfolds them
One and all in her bosom: then, for a private joke,
Deals them out to great families, loves and lavishes
Her care upon them, makes them her special favourites.

    Here comes a peddler of magic spells and Thessalian[1]   610
Philtres. With these any wife can so befuddle
Her husband's wits that he'll let her slipper his backside.
If you get mental blackouts, gross amnesia
About yesterday's doings, plain softening of the brain,
This is your trouble. Yet even these tricks can be endured
Provided you aren't driven raving mad by the kind   615
Of knock-out mixture Caesonia once brewed up
For her husband, Nero's uncle. When an Empress sets fashions
What women won't follow suit? Established certainties
Went up in flames then, mere anarchy ruled the world:
Had it been Juno herself who drove her husband crazy
The shock could have been no greater. Why, Agrippina's   620
Mushroom turned out less lethal: *that* only settled the hash
Of one old dotard, saw off his tremulous headpiece
And beslobbered, drooling chops to some nether heaven. But
Caesonia's potion brought fire and sword and the rack,
Mowed down Senate and burghers in one mangled, bloody heap: 625
Such was the cost of one philtre, a single poisoner.

    Wives loathe a concubine's offspring. Let no man cavil
Or call such hatred abnormal: to murder your step-son
Is an old-established tradition, perfectly right and proper.
But wards with rich portions should have a well-developed
Sense of self-preservation. Trust none of the dishes at dinner: 630
Those pies are steaming-black with the poison Mummy put there.
Whatever she offers you, make sure another person
Tries it out first: let your shrinking tutor sample

---

1. Thessaly was traditionally notorious for the practice of the black arts.

Each cup you're poured. Do you think this is melodrama?
635   Am I making the whole thing up, careless of precedents, mouthing
Long-winded bombast in the old Sophoclean[1] manner
That's quite out of place here under Italian skies?
How I wish that it *was* all nonsense! But listen to Pontia's
Too-willing confession: 'I did it, I admit I gave aconite
To my children. Yes, they were poisoned, that's obvious –
640   But *I* was the one who killed them.'
                              'What, you viper,
    Two at one meal? The brutality of it! *Two*
You did away with?'
                    'Indeed; and if there'd been seven
I'd have polished *them* off, too.'
                          Whatever the tragic poets
Tell us about Medea and Procne may well have happened:
645   I won't dispute that. Such women were monsters of daring
In their own day – but not from the lust for cash.
We find it less freakish when wrath provides the incentive
For a woman's crimes, when whitehot passion whirls her
650   Headlong, like some boulder that's carried away by a landslide,
What *I* can't stand is the calculating woman
Who plans her crimes in cold blood. Our wives sit and watch
Alcestis undertaking to die in her husband's stead:
If they had a similar chance, *they'd* gladly sacrifice
Their husband's life for their lapdog's. Take a morning stroll,
655   You'll meet Danaids galore; an Eriphyle
Or Clytemnestra turns up in every street. The only
Difference is this: whereas Clytemnestra used
A clumsy great double-axe, nowadays an ounce of toad's lung
660   Is just as effective. But cold steel may have a comeback
If our modern Agamemnons take a hint from old Mithridates,
And sample the pharmacopeia till they're proof against every drug.

---

1. Representing the high style of Greek tragedy in general.

Satire X

Search every land, from Cadiz to the dawn-streaked shores
Of Ganges, and you'll find few men who can distinguish
A false from a worthwhile objective, or slash their way through
The fogs of deception. Since when were our fears or desires   5
Ever dictated by reason? What project goes so smoothly
That you never regret the idea, let alone its realization?
What you ask for, you get. The Gods aren't fussy, they're willing
To blast you, root and branch, on request. It's universal,
This self-destructive urge, in civilian and soldier
Alike. The gift of the gab, a torrential facility,   10
Has proved fatal to so many; so has excessive reliance
On muscle and physical beef.[1] But more are strangulated
By the capital they amass with such expense of spirit,
Those bloated fortunes that dwarf any normal inheritance,
Till they look like some puny dolphin beside a British whale.
So during the Reign of Terror, at Nero's command,   15
Longinus was banished, Seneca – grown too wealthy –
Lost his magnificent gardens, storm-troopers besieged
Lateranus' ancestral mansion. Garrets are very seldom
The object of military raids. When you go on a night journey,   20
Though you may have only a few small treasures with you,
You'll take every stirring shadow, each moonlit reed
For a sword or a cudgel. But the empty-handed
Traveller whistles his way past any highwayman.

   The most popular, urgent prayer, well-known in every temple,
Is for wealth. *Increase my holdings, please make my deposit account* 25
The largest in town! But you'll never find yourself drinking
Belladonna from pottery cups. The time you should worry is
      when
You're clutching a jewelled goblet, when your bubbly gleams
      with gold.

---

1. An allusion to the athlete Milo of Croton, who was eaten alive by wolves while
   trying to split open a tree with his bare hands.

They had a point – don't you agree? – those two old philosophers:
One of them helpless with laughter whenever he set foot
30 Outside his house, the other a weeping fountain.
The cutting, dismissive sneer comes easily to us all –
But wherever did Heraclitus tap such an eye-brimming
Reservoir of tears? Democritus' sides shook non-stop,
Though the cities *he* knew had none of our modern trappings –
35 Togas bordered or striped with purple, sedans, the tribunal,
The rods and axes. Suppose he had seen the praetor[1]
Borne in his lofty carriage through the midst of the dusty
Circus, and wearing full ceremonial dress –
The tunic with palm-leaves, the heavy Tyrian toga
Draped in great folds round his shoulders; a crown so enormous
40 That no neck can bear its weight, and instead it's carried
By a sweating public slave, who, to stop the Consul
Getting above himself, rides in the carriage beside him.
Then there's the ivory staff, crowned with an eagle,
A posse of trumpeters, the imposing procession
45 Of white-robed citizens marching so dutifully beside
His bridle-rein, retainers whose friendship was bought
With the meal-ticket stashed in their wallets. Democritus long ago
Found occasion for laughter in all human intercourse,
And his wisdom reveals that the greatest men, those destined
To set the highest examples, may still be born
50 In a land with a sluggish climate, a country of muttonheads.[2]
The cares of the crowd he derided no less than their pleasures,
Their griefs, too, on occasion: if Fortune was threatening,
'*Up you*,' he'd say, and give her the vulgar finger. So
If our current petitions are pointless – destructive, even –
55 What *should* we ask for, what message leave on the knees of the
        Gods?
Some men are overthrown by the envy their great power

---

1. What follows is a detailed description of a Roman triumphal procession, which
   ended up in the Circus.
2. Abdera, Democritus' native town, like Kerry and other places, was a butt for
   jokes about the stupidity of its inhabitants.

Arouses; it's that long and illustrious list of honours
That sinks them. The ropes are heaved, down come the statues,
Axes demolish their chariot-wheels, the unoffending   60
Legs of their horses are broken. And now the fire
Roars up in the furnace, now flames hiss under the bellows:
The head of the people's darling glows red-hot, great Sejanus
Crackles and melts. That face only yesterday ranked
Second in all the world. Now it's so much scrap-metal,
To be turned into jugs and basins, frying-pans, chamber-pots.
Hang wreaths on your doors, lead a big white sacrificial   65
Bull to the Capitol! They're dragging Sejanus along
By a hook, in public. Everyone cheers. 'Just look at that
Ugly stuck-up face,' they say. 'Believe me, I never
Cared for the fellow.' 'But what was his crime? Who brought
The charges, who gave evidence? How did they prove him   70
     guilty?'
'Nothing like that: a long and wordy letter arrived
From Capri.' 'Fair enough: you need say no more.'
                                                    And what
Of the commons? They follow fortune as always, and detest
The victims, the failures. If a little Etruscan luck
Had rubbed off on Sejanus, if the doddering Emperor   75
Had been struck down out of the blue, this identical rabble
Would now be proclaiming that carcase an equal successor
To Augustus. But nowadays, with no vote to sell, their motto
Is 'Couldn't care less'. Time was when their plebiscite elected
Generals, Heads of State, commanders of legions: but now
They've pulled in their horns, there's only two things that concern 80
     them:
Bread and the Games.
                            'I hear that many are to be purged.'
'That's right, they're turning the heat on, and no mistake.'
                                                            'My
     friend
Bruttidius looked somewhat pale when I met him in town just
     now –
Our slighted Ajax, I fear, is out for blood: disloyal

85　Heads will roll.'
　　　　　　　'Come on, then, quickly, down to the river –
Boot Caesar's foe in the ribs while his corpse is still on show.'
'Yes, and make our slaves watch us – eyewitnesses can't deny it,
Can't drag their wretched masters into court at a rope's end.'
That's how they talked of Sejanus, such was the private gossip
90　After his death. Would you really choose to be courted as
He was? To own his wealth? To hand out official appointments –
Consulships, army commands? To be known as the 'protector'
Of an Imperial recluse squatting on Capri's narrow
Rocks with his fortune-tellers? You'd certainly enjoy
95　Having the Guards Brigade and the Household Cavalry
At your beck and call, and a barracks with you as Commandant.
Why not? Even those who lack the murderer's instinct
Would like to be licensed to kill. Yet what fame or prosperity
Are worth having if they bring you no less disaster than joy?
Would you rather assume the mantle of the wretch who's being
　　　dragged
100　Through the streets today, or lord it over some sleepy
Rural backwater, an out-at-elbows official
Inspecting weights, giving orders for the destruction
Of short-measure pint-pots? Admit, then, that Sejanus
Had no idea what to pray for. His interminable pursuit
105　Of excessive wealth and honours built up a towering
Edifice, storey by storey, so that his final downfall
Was that degree greater, the crash more catastrophic.
Take men like Pompey or Crassus – and that other tyrant
Who cowed Rome's citizens, brought them under the lash:
110　What proved their downfall? Lust for ultimate power
Pursued without scruple – and the malice of Heaven
That granted ambition's prayers. Battle and slaughter
See most kings off; few tyrants die in their beds.
114　　　Eloquence, that's what they're after, all of them: even the
　　　schoolboy
　　– With one small houseslave to carry his satchel behind him,
And only a penny to spare for an offering to Minerva –
Spends all his holidays praying that one day *he'll* become

370

As good – and successful – as Cicero, or Demosthenes. And yet
Both of these perished because of their eloquence, both
Were destroyed by their own overflowing and copious talent.
That talent alone cost Cicero his severed head and hand: 120
What third-rate advocate's blood ever stained the rostra?
O fortunate Roman State, born in my great Consulate –
Had he always spoken thus, he could have laughed Antony's
Swords to scorn. I prefer such ridiculous verses
To you, supreme and immortal Second Philippic.[1] And then   125
Violent, too, was the end of Demosthenes, who held
All Athens spellbound with his torrential oratory
In the crowded theatre. Under an evil-fated star
He was born, and the Gods were against him, that ardent boy
Whom his father – swart and bleary with working red-hot ore –   130
Sent away from the coals and the pincers, the grime of the smithy,
The sword-forging anvil, to learn the rhetorician's trade.

   Consider the spoils of war, those trophies hung on tree-trunks –
A breastplate, a shattered helmet, one cheekpiece dangling,
A yoke shorn of its pole, a defeated trireme's   135
Flagstaff or figurehead, the miserable frieze of prisoners
On a triumphal arch – such things are coveted
As the zenith of human achievement. These are the prizes
For which every commander, Greek, barbarian, Roman,
Has always striven; for them he'll endure toil
And danger. The thirst for glory by far outstrips the   140
Pursuit of virtue. Who would embrace poor Virtue naked
Without the rewards she bestows? Yet countries have come to
      ruin
Not once, but many times, through the vainglory of a few
Who lusted for power, who wanted a title that would cling
To the stones set over their ashes – though a barren
Fig-tree's rude strength will suffice to crack the stone asunder,   145
Seeing that sepulchres, too, have their allotted fate.

---

1. The longest and most virulent speech which Cicero composed against Antony
   in 44 B.C. Named after Demosthenes' abusive speeches against Philip of Mace-
   don.

Put Hannibal in the scales: how many pounds will that peerless
General mark up today? This is the man for whom Africa
Was too small a continent, though it stretched from the surf-beaten
Ocean shores of Morocco east to the steamy Nile,
150 To Ethiopian tribesmen – and new elephants' habitats.
Now Spain swells his empire, now he surmounts
The Pyrenees. Nature throws in his path
High Alpine passes, blizzards of snow: but he splits
The very rocks asunder, moves mountains – with vinegar.
155 Now Italy is his, yet still he forces on:
'We have accomplished nothing,' he cries, ''till we have stormed
The gates of Rome, till our Carthaginian standard
Is set in the City's heart.'
                              A fine sight it must have been,
Fit subject for caricature, the one-eyed commander
Perched on his monstrous beast! Alas, alas for glory,
What an end was here: the defeat, the ignominious
160 Flight into exile, everyone crowding to see
The once-mighty Hannibal turned humble hanger-on,
Sitting outside the door of a petty Eastern despot
Till His Majesty deign to awake. No sword, no spear,
No battle-flung stone was to snuff the fiery spirit
165 That once had wrecked a world: those crushing defeats,
Those rivers of spilt blood were all wiped out by a
Ring, a poisoned ring. On, on, you madman, drive
Over your savage Alps, to thrill young schoolboys
And supply a theme for speech-day recitations!
      One globe seemed all too small for the youthful Alexander:
Miserably he chafed at this world's narrow confines
170 As though pent on some rocky islet. Yet when he entered
Brick-walled Babylon, a coffin was measure enough
To contain him. Death alone reveals the puny dimensions
Of our human frame. A fleet, we are told, once sailed
175 Through Athos (the lies those old Greek historians
Got away with!), the sea was spanned with a bridge of boats
And chariots drove across it: deep streams and rivers
Were drunk dry by the Persians at breakfast-time. (The rest

You can hear when some tame poet, sweating under the armpits,
Gives his wine-flown recital.) Here was a barbarian
Monarch[1] who flogged the winds with a rigour they'd never   180
   known
In Aeolus' prison-house, who clapped chains on Poseidon
And thought it an act of mercy, no doubt, to spare the God
A branding as well: what God would serve *this* master?
But mark his return from Salamis – the single unescorted   185
Vessel, the blood-red sea, the prow slow-thrusting
Through shoals of corpses. Such was the price he paid
For that long-cherished dream of glory and conquest.
  '*Grant us a long life, Jupiter, O grant us many years!*'
In the bloom of youth it's this which, pale with anxiety,
You pray for, and this alone. Yet how grisly, how unrelenting   190
Are longevity's ills! Look first at your face, you'll see an ugly
And shapeless caricature of its former self: your skin
Has become a scaly hide, you're all chapfallen, the wrinkles
Scored down your cheeks now make you resemble nothing so
   much
As some elderly female baboon in darkest Africa.   195
Young men are all individuals. A will have better looks
Or brains than B, while B will beat A on muscle;
But old men all look alike, all share the same bald pate,
Their noses all drip like an infant's, their voices tremble
As much as their limbs, they mumble their bread with toothless   200
Gums. It's a wretched life for them, they become a burden
To their wives, their children, themselves; the noblest and best of
   them
Become so loathsome a sight that even legacy-hunters
Turn queasy. Their taste-buds are ruined, they get scant pleasure
From food or wine, sex lies in long oblivion –
Or if they try, it's hopeless: though they labour all night long   205
At that limp and shrivelled object, limp it remains.
What can the future hold for these impotent dodderers?
Nothing very exciting. Sex is a pretty dead loss –

---

1. Xerxes, king of Persia, who invaded Greece in 480 B.C.

The old tag's true – when desire outruns performance.
210   Other senses deteriorate: take hearing, for instance.
How can the deaf appreciate music? The standard
Of the performance eludes them: a top-line soloist,
Massed choirs in their golden robes, all mean less than nothing.
What does it matter to *them* where they sit in the concert-hall
When a brass band blowing its guts out is barely audible?
215 The slave who announces the time, or a visitor, must bawl
At the top of his lungs before they take in the message.
     The blood runs thin with age too; now nothing but fever
Can warm that frigid hulk, while diseases of every type
Assault it by battalions. (If you asked me their names
220 I'd find it less trouble to list all Oppia's lovers,
The number of patients Doc Themison kills each autumn,
The partners that X, the wards that Y has defrauded,
The times tall Maura goes down in a day, the pupils
225 Hamillus has off; I could sooner list all the country-houses
Owned by the barber who shaved me when I was a lad.)
One has an arthritic hip, another sciatica,
Lumbago plagues a third, while the totally sightless
Envy the one-eyed. Here's a fellow whose jaws would open
230 Wide, once long ago, at the prospect of dinner – but now
Those leaden lips must mumble the tit-bits another hand
Feeds to him; when he gapes today, he's like a baby
Swallow that sees its mother approaching, her beak
Well-crammed with grubs. But worse than all bodily ills
Is the senescent mind. Men forget what their own servants
235 Are called, they can't recognize yesterday's host at dinner,
Or, finally, the children they begot and brought up. A heartless
Codicil to the will disinherits their flesh and blood,
And the whole estate is entailed to some whore, whose expert
          mouth
– After years in that narrow archway – earns her a rich reward.
240   If he keeps his wits intact, though, a further ordeal awaits
The old man: he'll have to bury his sons, he'll witness
His dear wife's end, and his brother's, he'll see the urns
Filled with his sisters' ashes. Such are the penalties

If you live to a ripe old age – perpetual grief,
Black mourning, a world of sorrow, ever-recurrent   245
Family bereavements to haunt your declining years.
Nestor, the King of Pylos, if we can trust great Homer,
Lived longer than any creature save the proverbial crow –
Happy, no doubt, to have postponed his death for so many
Generations of men, to have sampled the new-made wine   250
So many times, to have passed beyond his hundredth year.
But wait a moment – just look at the way he went on
About Fate's decrees, and his too-long threat of life, while
The funeral flames were licking up round his son,
His Antilochus: look how he asked all his fellow-mourners the
    reason
He'd survived till now, what crime he'd ever committed
To deserve such longevity. So Peleus, mourning the dead   255
Achilles; and so his father at Odysseus the seafarer's passing.[1]
If Priam had died at a different time, before
The building of those ships for Paris's reckless venture,
He might have gone down to the shades while Troy still stood,
    with
Magnificent obsequies – his coffin shouldered
By Hector and Hector's brothers, while Ilion's womanhood   260
Wept, and Cassandra keened, and Polyxena rent her garments.
So what did length of days bring him? He saw his world   265
In ruins, saw its destruction by fire and the sword;
Then put off his crown, took arms, and – a dotard, but a soldier –
Fell before Jove's high altar, like some ancient ox
Turned off from the plough, whose stringy neck is severed   270
By his master's knife. This at least was a manly death:
But Hecuba lived on, stark crazy, grinning and barking
Like a mad dog.
                I'll pass over Mithridates
And Croesus (warned by the wise and eloquent Solon
To beware of his final years): let our own countrymen   275
Provide an example. What else brought great Marius

1. Laertes.

To exile and prison, to an outlaw's life in the marshes,
To begging his bread through the streets of conquered Carthage?
But suppose he'd expired at the climax of his triumphal
280 Procession, after parading those hordes of captured Teutons,[1]
Just as he stepped from his chariot – what more fortunate
Paragon, men would say, had Rome, or the world, to show?
Pompey's Campanian fever came as a providential
Blessing in disguise; but the public prayers of so many
285 Cities prevailed. Rome's destiny, and his own,
Kept him alive for defeat and decapitation – a fate
Such as not even Catiline or his fellow-conspirators
Suffered: at least they died whole, without mutilation.

290 When a doting mother passes the shrine of Venus, she'll whisper
One prayer for her sons, and another – louder, more fanciful –
For her daughters to have good looks. 'And what's wrong with *that*?'
She'll ask you. 'Didn't Latona rejoice in Diana's beauty?'
Perhaps; but the fate of Lucretia should warn us against our urge
To pray for a face like hers; Virginia would be happy
295 To take on poor Rutila's hump, to give Rutila best. A handsome
Son keeps his wretched parents in constant anxiety:
Good looks and decent behaviour too seldom are found
In the same person. However old-fashioned his background,
However strict the morality on which he was brought up –
And even if Nature, with generous, kindly hand has
300 Turned him out a pure-minded, modestly blushing
Youth (and what greater gift, being more powerful
Than any solicitous guardian, could she bestow?) –
Manliness still is denied him. A seducer will not scruple
305 To lay out lavish bribes, corrupt the boy's very parents:
Cash always wins in the end. But no misshapen
Stripling was ever unsexed by a tyrant in his castle,
No Nero would ever rape a clubfooted adolescent –
Much less one with hump, pot-belly, or scrofula.

310 So you're proud of your handsome son? Fair enough – but
don't ever forget

1. A reference to Marius' defeat of the Germanic invaders in 102 and 101 B.C.

The extra hazards that face him. He'll become a notorious
Layer of other men's wives, always scared that some husband's
Hot on his tail for revenge. He'll have no better luck
Than Mars did, he can't expect to steer clear of the toils for ever –
And sometimes an outraged cuckold will go far beyond   315
All legal sanctions, will horsewhip his rival to ribbons,
Stick a knife in his heart, or a mullet up his backside.[1]
Maybe the first time your dream-boy goes with a married
Woman he'll really love her. But when she gets in the habit
Of giving him little presents, it won't be long before
He's become the perfect gigolo, taking them all for their eye-   320
    teeth –
And remember, there's nothing these women won't do to satisfy
Their ever-moist groins: they've just one obsession – sex.
'But what's wrong with good looks if you're chaste?' Try out *that*
    question
On Hippolytus or Bellerophon: did stern self-restraint   325
Benefit *them*? The women whose love they'd spurned,
Phaedra and Sthenoboea, both hot with shame, flared up
And lashed themselves into a fury. Pure feminine ruthlessness
Thrives best on hatred and guilt.

                                What advice, do you suppose,
Should one give the young man[2] whom Caesar's wife is   330
    determined
To marry? This blue-blooded sprig of the higher nobility –
Wonderfully handsome, too – is raped and doomed by one glance
From Messalina's eyes. She sits there, waiting for him,
Veiled as a bride, while their marriage-bed is prepared
In the public gardens. A big traditional dowry   335
Will be handed over, the ceremony witnessed in due form,
The omens taken. Did you think these were secret doings
Known only to intimate friends? But the lady's determined
On a proper, official wedding. So what's your decision? If

---

1. An allusion to a traditional punishment for adulterers. A spiny fish or a radish
   might be used for this.
2. Gaius Silius.

You refuse her commands, you'll die before lighting-up time;
340 If you do the deed, you'll get a brief respite, until
Your liaison is so well known that it reaches the Emperor's ears:
He'll be the last to learn of this family scandal. Till then
Better do what you're told, if a few more days' existence
Matter that much. But whichever you reckon the quicker
345 And easier way, your lily neck still gets the chop.
    Is there nothing worth praying for, then? If you want my
       advice,
Let the Gods themselves determine what's most appropriate
For mankind, and what best suits our various circumstances.
They'll give us the things we need, not those we want: a man
350 Is dearer to them than he is to himself. Led helpless
By irrational impulse and powerful desires
We ask for marriage and children. But the Gods alone know
What they'll be like, our future wives and offspring!
Still, if you must have something to pray for, if you
355 Insist on offering up the entrails and consecrated
Sausages from a white pigling in every shrine, then ask
For [a sound mind in a sound body,][1] a valiant heart
Without fear of death, that reckons longevity
The least among Nature's gifts, that's strong to endure
360 All kinds of toil, that's untainted by lust and anger,
That prefers the sorrows and labours of Hercules to all
Sardanapalus' downy cushions and women and junketings.
What I've shown you, you can find by yourself: there's one
Path, and one only, to a life of peace – through virtue.
365 Fortune has no divinity, could we but see it: it's we,
We ourselves, who make her a goddess, and set her in the
       heavens.[2]

---

1. An interpolation deleted by M. D. Reeve.
2. The worship of *Tyche* or Fortune, Lady Luck, by ordinary people was widespread
   in the sprawling and unpredictable cosmopolitan world of Alexander and his
   successors. Virtue or Pleasure were the guides of the more sophisticated.

MINOR POETS

INTRODUCTION

Besides the major poetic talents which have survived from the
early imperial period, there are a number of minor (or non-canoni-
cal) writers who deserve representation in these pages. Some of
them do little more than provide evidence of the continuing liter-
ary activity particularly noticeable in the reigns of Nero and the
Flavians. All of these emperors were, in their different ways and
for different motives, generous patrons of literary men as well as
other artistic professionals, not least architects.

The economic matrix of imperial literature is not our concern
here except in so far as it was conducive to the general encourage-
ment of the arts among the upper classes. Amateurs have a short
wind and administrators and politicians little enough time, and so
it was fortunate, and then again perhaps no coincidence, that the
writing of epigrams – or, more properly, short poems – was so
popular. Critical respectability for the cultivation of the genre
could be found in the poetic theory of Callimachus, a superb
epigrammatist himself, who seemed to champion the less ambitious
genres of poetry, defending therefore by implication the craft of
the miniaturist, as against the vast canvases and paint pots
demanded by epic and drama. But there was hardly need of such
justifications. Catullus' achievement, for one, was firmly esta-
blished as an esteemed Roman model with a variety of metres.
For those who needed Greek precedents, the popular *Garlands* (or
anthologies of epigrams) put together by Meleager of Gadara (*c.*
90 B.C.) and, more recently, by Philippus of Thessalonica in the
reign of Caligula or Claudius were there for inspiration and even
creative translation.

The younger Pliny, however, is perhaps more representative of contemporary attitudes to this respectably established and wide-spread avocation. He says in a letter to his friend Fuscus (*Epistles* VII.9) that he uses this form of unambitious composition for relaxation. These short poems become the receptacles of his affections and his hostilities, of his anger, pity, and wit, and as records of everyday life whether public or private. To justify his enthusiasm, he gives a long list of distinguished upper-class versifiers, which includes Cicero, Brutus, Seneca, and even Julius Caesar and Augustus (*Epistles* V.3.4–6). The popular and delightful little poem to his Soul by the Emperor Hadrian had no doubt illustrious predecessors.

Pliny's own verse efforts are lost, but there are a number of examples that survive to represent the tradition which Pliny defends so heatedly. The supreme master of the form was of course Martial, but he stands quite apart from the other practitioners for his sheer dedication and successful mastery of the genre (if it can be called that) in most of its manifestations. But there are other practitioners such as Seneca and Petronius, whose high reputations depend on other works, but who also at times found the fashionable form congenial or suitable for their literary purposes.

Over seventy epigrams are attributed to Seneca in our sources. Whether those printed below are authentic examples of Seneca's talents in this area is open to dispute, but at least they represent the tradition of the short occasional poem. Whether written by Seneca, or perhaps a well-placed friend of his in Claudius' court, they fit the baroque and epigrammatic style favoured by some contemporary writers. The topics may be traditional or philosophic, as in the poem on Time, or inspired by current circumstances or events (as with the epigrams on Corsica, Seneca's place of exile between A.D. 41 and 49), or inspired by their setting in a larger work, such as the extract taken from *Apocolocyntosis*.

Not surprisingly, Seneca's contemporary and rival at the court of Nero, Petronius Arbiter, was also an accomplished hand in the production of light occasional verse. Tacitus reports that he regaled himself on his deathbed in A.D. 66 with readings of them in order to meet his enforced end in the insouciant style of the cultivated Epicurean (*Annals* XVI.18). Some of the short poems transmitted under his name to posterity in the large collection we call the *Latin Anthology* may be *ben trovato* rather than genuine specimens of his talent. But the style and spirit of many of them are reminiscent of the short *ad hoc* verse compositions that are woven into the fabric of his picaresque, but highly literary, novel, *Satyricon*. (This, like Seneca's *Apocolocyntosis*, the short satire written to ridicule the recently demised emperor Claudius, is an instance of Menippean satire, a narrative *mélange* of prose and verse which had been adopted by the Romans from the Greek exemplars.)

These varied examples of short poems composed around the first century A.D. would not prepare the modern reader for the strange and anonymous collection of poems on one single, and singular, subject: the phallic garden-god Priapus. This collection is known as the *Priapea* (or the *Corpus Priapeorum*). It has been variously dated to the Neronian or Flavian period (A.D. 54–96) and also to the opening decades of the second century A.D.

There were a number of Greek and Roman poems of varying antiquity and scope on Priapus, who had slowly lost over the centuries his powerful cult status in his original home at Lampsacus in Asia Minor and become assimilated, like Bacchus, to other Italian fertility gods, Faunus and Mutunus. Through this tradition, he had become an amusing literary character as well as a slightly ridiculous, ithyphallic guardian of orchards and plots, a crudely carved scarecrow to ward off evil in general and deter young thieves in particular from stealing fruit. His large phallus, with the unselective sexual drives naturally attributed to it, made him both a sexual symbol and also a comic figure given different roles accordingly to the playfulness of the authors who chose him as a topic – and these include Tibullus, Horace, and supposedly Virgil, as well as Martial. But none of these will prepare the modern reader for this monothematic corpus, devoted entirely to the description, conversations, comminations, and obscene jokes and puns of Priapus. The poems themselves are short and often witty or ingenious, generally taking the form of warning inscriptions to be affixed to the wooden or stone statue of the god.

The *Priapea* come at the end of a long Greek epigrammatic tradition that had adapted itself comfortably to the Roman tradition of epigram. But there were other Greek literary currents, not least from Alexandrian literary theory and practice, that continued to influence Roman literature long after the first impact of Callimacheanism on the Catullan circle, the later elegists, and then the Augustan poets. Not the least influential was didactic poetry, which went back to Hesiod, but, since to the ancients almost all literature was fundamentally didactic, it developed its own momentum in the Alexandrian period through the production of versified handbooks on such subjects as meteorological phenomena, agriculture, and even the cures for snakebite and poisons. The tradition continued in Roman literature often via translations of Greek works. But it is a mistake to equate these with our modern popularizations of science. These didactic works were seen as a *poetic* challenge and some of the results, such as Lucretius' *On the Nature of Things* and Virgil's *Georgics*, are literary masterpieces of the first order.

Marcus Manilius, who lived during the reigns of Augustus and Tiberius, has been compared to Ovid for his individual style, his ingenious treatment of his material and, above all, for his verbal concision and point. Like Lucretius, Manilius left us, in his *Astronomica*, a scintillating *tour de force*, a triumph of poetic talent against astronomical odds, as it were. His subject, at first sight, appears almost intractable, nothing less than a technical description of contemporary astrological knowledge of the signs of the Zodiac and the other heavenly phenomena that affect human destiny. He begins in Book I with a survey of the heavenly sphere and the Stoic view of the origins of the universe. The scientific description of astrological influence occupy the remaining books, but they are interspersed with fascinating digressions on myth and history to lighten the technical load. The passage printed in this section, which deals with the ineluctable influence of the heavens and fate on everyday affairs and also famous personages and events, is remarkable for the concise and rarely unjust summaries of complex events in Greek and Roman history.

Most of the examples of minor or non-canonical verse so far discussed have behind them a poetic that derives largely from Alexandria, however transmuted. But early imperial literature, it should be remembered, embraced Menippean satire and *Priapea* as well as epigram, pastoral, epic, and drama. The *Fables* of Phaedrus should be assimilated to this literary strain, since they go back for their roots to the humble tradition of the folk tale and the implicitly satirical beast fable. The literary polish and sophistication imparted to them by Phaedrus does not entirely conceal their basic subversive character.

The possible perils involved in literary endeavour under the early empire are well illustrated by this writer's case. Phaedrus was, he tells us, a freedman of Augustus, having been born in Thessaly in the Roman province of Macedonia. He began publishing his collections of fables, written in Latin but following the tradition of Aesop, under Tiberius, and he survived into the reign of Claudius, despite the fact that his moralistic and allegorical writings, according to his own account, had gravely offended the powerful praetorian prefect, Aelius Sejanus, who took him to court.

Although Phaedrus never received the respect he hoped for from his socially superior literary contemporaries, his five innovative collections of engaging and pellucid Aesopian animal stories, each capped with a moral, enjoyed belated popularity in late antiquity and in the medieval period. Couched in a flexible iambic metre, his brief narratives, not all of which are concerned with animals, are lively and generally comprehensible, while displaying a typical taste for neat antithesis in the exposition of his popular philosophy. His main social concerns are the abuse of power and the struggle between the weak and the strong, as in the pessimistic fable of the wolf and the lamb (translated here). There is a subtle satiric note in his work, as might be expected from its origins, and he shares with some Roman satirists a misogynistic strain exemplified in his retelling of the story of the Widow of Ephesus, as well as a dislike for informers (witness the moral of the first fable in this collection) and a generally gloomy view of contemporary civic life.

Phaedrus' fables, even if most of the material goes back to the collection attributed to another ex-slave, Aesop, represents exceptionally the voice of the lower orders in Rome and he was perhaps naïve in expecting recognition from his ideologically unsympathetic fellow writers. In the prologue to the Third Book, he claims that the fable was invented to allow slaves to express covertly what the fear of punishment deterred him from speaking aloud; his sympathy for the lower classes under any political system is voiced in the fables of the wolf who refused to lead a dog's life and the donkey who regarded a change of master as irrelevant, provided he did not have to do double the work.

J. P. S.

Further Reading

Buecheler, F., and Reise, A. (eds.), *Anthologia Latina*, Part I (Leipzig 1894; Amsterdam 1964).

Cox, A., 'Didactic Poetry', in J. Higginbotham (ed.), *Greek and Latin Literature: A Comparative Study* (London 1969) 124–61.

Currie, H. MacL., 'Phaedrus the Fabulist', *Aufstieg und Niedergang der römischen Welt II* 32.1 (1984) 497–513.

Goold, G. P., *Manilius: Astronomica* (London and Cambridge 1977). Text and translation.

O'Connor, E., *Symbolum Salacitatis: A Study of the God Priapus as a Literary Character* (Frankfurt am Main 1989).

Parker, W. H. (ed. and trans.), *Priapea: Poems for a Phallic God* (London 1988).

Perry, B. E., *Babrius and Phaedrus* (Cambridge, Mass., 1965).

PHAEDRUS TO HADRIAN

SELECTIONS

Translated by Various Hands

I. PHAEDRUS

Fables I.1
The Wolf and the Lamb

A wolf and lamb had come to the same little brook
to slacken their sharp thirst. Wolf took
his place to drink upstream; much farther south
stood Lamb. Aroused to hunger then, Wolf's wicked mouth
impelled him to invent a case for injury.
Addressing Lamb, the robber said: 'Why have you made me   5
with your licking drink a turbid water?' Terrified,
the fleecy one gave answer; Lamb replied:
'How could I do what you complain of, Wolf? From *you*
the water flows to reach *my* lips': an answer true
and unimpeachable. So next Wolf claims   10
an insult. 'You called me dirty names
six months ago,' he said. 'I am not six months old,'
was Lamb's reply. 'Your *father* mocked me then. I'll hold
you culpable,' said Wolf. So snatching him,
Wolf tore Lamb, unjustly slaughtered, limb from limb.
Composed, this allegory, as a monument
to those who on false charges crush the innocent.   15

EUGENE O'CONNOR

Appendix Perottina XV
The Widow and the Soldier or:
The Measure of a Woman's Inconstancy and Lust

There was a woman who had lost her husband
for years cherished, and laid his body
in a sepulchre. Since she could nowise be torn from him
but consumed her life in mourning in the tomb,
5   she gained a reputation as a spotless wife.
Meantime, men caught plundering Jove's temple
were nailed to crosses for their crime against the god.
To prevent removal of their bodies, guards were posted
10 next door to the tomb in which the widow had immured herself.
A guard once, by thirst goaded, asked
a midnight drink of water from the servant then, by chance,
attending to her mistress as she went to sleep. For she
had kept her vigil long, her lantern trimmed, still burning.
15 The tomb's door, slightly open, let the soldier peer in
to behold a woman of no common beauty.
His corrupt soul was straightway set on fire,
His lust burned gradually beyond all shame.
20 A thousand stratagems he cleverly devised
to see more of the widow. She, captivated
by this daily custom, bit by bit surrendered to the stranger.
Soon a tighter bond held her heart fast. While he,
25 the guard, kept constant lover's vigil in the tomb,
the crosses' body count fell short by one. Terrified,
the soldier asked the woman what to do and she – chaste
      matron! –
saying, 'Not to worry!', gave him to crucify instead
her husband's corpse. The dead man paid the penalty
the living owed for his neglect of duty.
30 Thus did infamy usurp the place of fame.

EUGENE O'CONNOR

II. MANILIUS

Astronomica IV.1–118

Why do we in worries waste our lives, and torture
ourselves with fear and blind desires? Why do we,
made old by endless cares, squander our days
in searching and, contented with no limit to our prayers,
plead always that we'll do our living soon, but never do?   5
Why is each man poorer for his goods, still wanting more,
not counting what he owns, but praying for
what he lacks? Why do we, though nature asks but little
for herself, heap up through our desires
a great pile, poised to topple, buy luxuries with our gains   10
and with luxurious living acquire plunder – of ourselves?
Is the greatest boon of wealth to squander wealth?

   Set free your minds, mortals, and relieve your cares
and of complaints, so many and superfluous, rid your lives.
Fate rules the world, all things are governed by strict laws,
and every life, however long, is marked for death, its hour   15
precisely fixed. As soon as we are born, we start to die:
each end derives from a beginning.
Fate is the source of wealth and kingdoms and, more common,
poverty: all creatures are endowed with given skills and characters,
vices, virtues, losses, gains. No man can rid himself   20
of his allotment, or take what he's denied, or with his prayers
entice unwilling fortune or escape when fortune threatens:
each has his lot to bear. If fate did not decree
the laws of life and death, would the flames have fled
before Aeneas; would Troy, in its destruction, have been victorious 25
in one man's safety?[1] Would the she-wolf of Mars

---

1. Romans professed that Rome was Troy reborn and Aeneas its spiritual founder
   in order to claim a longer historical record and (sometimes – see the Introduction
   to Seneca, above) to justify their empire as the work of destiny.

have suckled the brothers left to die?[1] Would Rome have grown
from simple huts; would the shepherds have brought the rites
of thunder to the Capitol?[2] Would Jove have been shut up within
30   his citadel, and the whole world conquered
by a conquered people? Would Mucius,[3] the fire extinguished
by his blood, have returned to Rome in triumph? Would
    Horatius[4]
alone have saved at once the city and the bridge from attacking
weapons; Cloelia voided the truce? Would three brothers
lie dead at the feet of one courageous man?[5]
35   No army gained such victory: Rome, though destined to rule
the world, depended on a single hero and lay helpless.
Why mention Cannae and the weapons close to the city walls;
Varro renowned for flight, Fabius for delay? And how, after
40   the battle, Trasimene, at your lakes, defeated Carthage donned
the yoke even when she could have conquered? And how
    Hannibal,
thinking we had him trapped, paid for his nation's fall by
an ignominious death?[6] Add the Latian battle lines
and Rome like a body at war with her own limbs;[7]
45   the Cimbrian helpless in the face of Marius, and Marius

---

1. Romulus and Remus, the builders of the city of Rome, were exposed to die by Amulius, king of Alba Longa, his niece, Rhea Silvia, having conceived them through Mars. They were saved by a she-wolf and returned to assassinate their usurper uncle.
2. An allusion to Rome's supposed pastoral origins and the primacy in Roman religion of the worship of Capitoline Jupiter, here in the cult of Jupiter the Thunderer.
3. Mucius Scaevola.
4. Horatius Cocles.
5. Another Horatius who unaided slew three Alban brothers, the Curiatii, in combat.
6. Hannibal, seeking refuge at the court of Prusias of Bithynia, committed suicide to avoid extradition to Rome. On Hannibal, Trasimene and the Punic war see Silius' *Punica*, above.
7. Allusions to the Social War of 91–88 B.C., when the Italian allies rebelled against Rome to redress their grievances.

helpless in his cell; so often a consul,
then an exile, and a consul yet again – a fortune rivalling
the fall of Africa – his march on Rome, from the levelled stones
of Carthage, is something fortune
never would bestow had fate not granted it.
Magnus,[1] who would think that, after conquering Mithridates,   50
recovering the seas, and after three triumphal marches,
your reward for victories throughout the world – when you
could style yourself another Magnus – you would perish
on Egyptian shores, and that charred bits of shipwrecked timber
would supply your coffin, and fragments of a cast-up prow   55
your funeral pyre? Who, without the nod of fate,
could suffer such change? Even that man born of heaven[2]
and to the sky returned – although he had put down civil conflict
with success and brooked the laws of peace – he still could not
avoid the wounds so many times predicted.
Before the Senate's gaze he grasped in his right hand   60
the listed names of the conspirators and with his blood
erased them, to have the fates prevail.
What should I count of cities overthrown and ruined realms,
Croesus lying on his pyre, on the shore the trunk of Priam,
denied the pyre of Troy? What tell of Xerxes, who lost more ships   65
than in a storm at sea? What of that man born of slaves
made king of Rome?[3] What of the fire rescued from fires
and the flame that ravaged temples retreating from a man?[4]
    How many deaths invade the bodies of the sound, how many
        deaths
again retire from their gains and wander through the funeral fires!   70

1. Magnus, i.e. Pompey the Great. See Lucan, *Civil War* V, above.
2. The man born of heaven is Julius Caesar, who claimed descent from the goddess
   Venus. His policy of clemency towards his opponents led to his assassination.
   There were numerous predictions of his death and he was familiar with all the con-
   spirators.
3. Servius Tullius, sixth king of Rome (*c.* 550 B.C.), was reputedly the son of a maid-
   servant.
4. Lucius Caecilius Metellus rescued the sacred fire of Rome, when the Temple of
   Vesta was burning down.

Some borne off to burial have come back
from the very tomb itself: to these a double life is given,
others winning barely one. See how a trifling disease proves fatal,
a more acute alleviated. The arts of healing yield,
75 and science fails; care harms, neglect improves:
often delay gives pause to pain. Food kills
and poison spares.

   Sons fall short of fathers or surpass their parents, yet retain
their own identity. Fortunes rise with one, slip from another.
80 One man burns with passion: he can swim across the sea
and topple Troy.[1] Another turns his mind to framing laws.
See now, sons destroy their fathers, fathers murder sons.
Armed brothers meet to deal wounds on each other.[2]
This war is not men's doing: they are compelled to action,
85 driven both to suffer punishment and mangled limbs.
Not every age gives birth to Decii[3] or a Camillus, or Cato,
his mind still undefeated in defeat.
Though matter enough and more exists to make them,
it proves reluctant from the laws of fate. Not always the poor
90 receive the shorter years of life. The fates cannot be bought
even with vast wealth; instead fate claims a victim
from a lofty manse, assigns the rich man's pyre
and builds his tomb.

   How great a kingdom this, that gives command to kings!
Even virtue proves calamitous, while guilt prospers; with bad
      plans
95 come rewards, and prudence fails. Fortune does not probe
a case's merit or escort the worthy: a careless vagabond,
she roams among men. High and low to her are equal.

---

1. Paris' voyage to Sparta and the elopement with Helen was the spark that led to
   the destruction of Troy.
2. A reference to the great tragic houses of Mycenae and Thebes with their inter-
   necine and generational strife exemplified by Oedipus killing his father Laius, his
   sons, Eteocles and Polyneices, killing each other.
3. There were several early Roman heroes named Decius Mus, who performed
   notable, often self-sacrificing, deeds in battle while defending their city against
   various enemies in the fourth and third centuries B.C.

Surely there is something else that guides and rules us,
something greater, bringing to men's affairs its own laws,
assigning to its children length of years and turns   100
of fortune. It often mixes human limbs and animals'.
Yet not from any seed comes such an issue, for what have we in
   common
with the brutes? What adulterer's sin breeds monsters?
It is the stars assume new shapes, and heaven interbreeds.   105
Why, in the end, if it does not exist, is the ordering of fate
time honoured? Why do men prophesy all that
will happen at a certain time? And yet this reasoning
is not in haste to counsel crime or to cheat virtue of
virtue's rich reward. Death–dealing herbs are no less hated   110
though they grow not from choice but from appointed seeds:
no less thanks are given to pleasing foods,
which nature's bounty gives, no wish of theirs.
And so for human merits let the glory grow
because they owe their plaudits to the sky; in turns, we must   115
   despise
the guilty all the more, since they were born for blame
and punishment. It matters not whence crime comes down,
it must be called a crime. This too is fated (and my theme),
that I expound on fate.

EUGENE O'CONNOR

III. SENECA

Latin Anthology 232

Voracious Time, uprooting all, consumes it.
  Time disturbs, holding nothing long.
From shores athirst a sea retreats; streams dwindle;
  Mountains' sides slip; their high peaks fall.
Why speak of trivia? The sky's fair dome will   5
  blaze, the flames bursting in a flash!

Thus all is death's. That end's no penalty, but
law. One day here will be no world.

MARCUS WILSON

Latin Anthology 237

O barbarous Corsica,[1] locked in by crags,
Rugged and vast where endless deserts stretch,
Fall brings no fruit, and summertime no crops,
No Attic olives bend the winter's branch;
From rainy spring no new births lure a smile,
And no grass grows on this ill-omened earth;
No bread, no taste of water, no fire in hearth:
Only two things – the exiled and exile.

J. P. SULLIVAN

Latin Anthology 408

'Flee every friendship and live': a greater truth
  Than 'Flee the friendship of kings.'
My fate is proof: struck down by the mighty,[2]
  Deserted by the weak. Watch the mob.
All my colleagues fled the crack of thunder,
  Deserted the house before it fell.
Go now and flee only kings! Life's lesson:
  Live for yourself. You'll die for yourself.

A. J. BOYLE

---

1. The Mediterranean island to which Seneca was exiled by the emperor Claudius
   for eight years (A.D. 41–9).
2. A reference to Seneca's banishment.

Latin Anthology 422

Britannia, free from foes and foreign kings,
Set far-distant from our world,
Happy in adversity, crushed by luck,
We and you will now share Caesar.[1]

A. J. BOYLE

Apocolocyntosis 4[2]

This said, she twirled the thread on an ugly spool,
Cut from the imperial line one doddering life.
But Lachesis, locks looped, with tresses dressed,
Pierian crown of laurel on forehead and hair,
Takes from the snowy fleece the bright white yarn,   5
Shaping with happy touch; new colours now dawn.
The sisters look at their work in awed surmise,
To see cheap wool turn into a mass of gold.
The Ages of Gold spin out in a lovely line.
No limits are set. They tease the favoured fleece,   10
Filling their hands in joy, so sweet their task.
As if by itself, the work went on, with ease;
Softly the threads turn on to the twirling spool –
Tithonus? his aeons – Nestor? his years surpassed.
Phoebus is by to assist and the decades to come   15
Gladden his heart, so he helps with a song,
Now plucking the strings, now happily passing the wool.
He keeps them to work with his song, beguiling their labour,
No praise too much for his lyre, his brotherly songs.
Their hands spin more than they used; and the work he salutes   20

1. Claudius, whose general Aulus Plautius conquered south-east Britain in A.D. 43
   and made it into a Roman province.
2. A poetic description of Claudius' death and the accession of Nero.

Surpasses the lot of a man. 'Stint not, o ye Fates!'
Says Apollo. 'Let him surpass by far a mortal span,
Image of me in looks and beauty as well,
In song and voice no less. To a weary folk
He brings glad times, to muted law a tongue.
Like the Morning Star, setting the stars to flight,
Like the Evening Star, rising with the star's return,
As the shining Sun, whenso the ruddy Dawn,
The shades of night dispersed, brings back the day,
Looks on the world and starts his chariot off:
So Caesar comes, so Nero appears to Rome,
His bright face fired with gentle radiance,
His neck all beauty under his flowing hair.'

J. P. SULLIVAN

25

30

IV. PETRONIUS

Latin Anthology 479

Beauty is not enough; who wishes to be fair
Must not content herself with average care.
Talk, be witty and smile to show your wit –
If Nature's unaided, nothing comes of it.
Art is Beauty's aid, her finest dress:
Beauty, if scornful, dies of nakedness.

J. P. SULLIVAN

5

Latin Anthology 698

My bed was soft, the early night was bliss.
My drowsy eyes surrender – Love broke my rest
And shook me by the hair in wild protest.
Nails ripped my flesh. 'To waste a night like this!

You're mine,' he said. 'You broke a thousand hearts,   5
Can you, hard-hearted, lie alone and rest?'
I leap from bed, barefoot and barely dressed;
I try each road, but all roads are false starts.
I run, but hate to go or to retreat,
Then stand ashamed to halt, so late abroad.   10
No song of birds, no watchdog even roared,
No human voice, no bustle in the streets.
Alone of all, I fear my bed and sleep:
At your command, great Love, your watch I keep.

J. P. SULLIVAN

Latin Anthology 699

Long may our hearts, Nealce, guard that night,
When first you came to me as I lay still;
The bed, its guardian spirit, the silent light –
They saw your soft submission to my will.
So come, let us endure, though youth has passed,   5
And use those years that have so short a stay.
Justice and Law allow old loves to last:
Make our quick love go not so quick away.

J. P. SULLIVAN

Latin Anthology 700

Coition's brief, a nasty cheat,
Such loving ends in quick disgust.
So let us not, like brutes in heat,
Blindly rush to slake our lust.
For so love wanes, a dying flame;   5
Let me just lie with you and kiss –
No pain in this, in this no shame –

Unending play, like this, like this.
This has, does, and will long delight,
Forever beginning, no end in sight.

J. P. SULLIVAN

V. THE PRIAPEAN CORPUS

II

I ask you to witness, Priapus,
these risqué verses, material more fit
for bathrooms than for bookstalls:
no *magnum opus*, no
'Sing to me, Muses.' Warned off
from this place, all virgins.
So how dare I bring down
the chaste sisters, their Pierian
meadows untouched, to Priapus' prick?
Therefore, whatever their worth, please accept
in good faith these graffiti I've leisurely scrawled
on the walls of your temple, Priapus.

EUGENE O'CONNOR

IX

To your question: why are my private parts
not covered? My reply is: deities don't conceal
their weapons. The king of the sky
brandishes his thunderbolt openly,
the seas' lord includes the trident
among his regalia.
Mars won't hide his sword, his symbol of power,
the spear of Pallas is not tucked within

the warm folds of her cloak.
Does it shame Phoebus to carry his golden arrows?
Does Diana blush to flex her bow?
Does Hercules conceal his knotty cudgel,
Mercury his wand? Who's seen Bacchus
drape his graceful thyrsus,
Cupid dim his lighted torch?
Don't rebuke me, then, for exposing my phallus.
With it I'm armed,
without it I'm nothing.

10

EUGENE O'CONNOR

XXV

Having left behind its cutting
in the forest, stripped of its leaves,
this phallic sceptre, longed for
by wanton ladies, hand-held
(and lovingly) by kings
and moistened by the lips
of queenly queers, this sceptre
will, with its whole length,
invade the thief's posterior
and be thrust inside
clean to the scrotal bag and
tuft of pubic hair.

5

EUGENE O'CONNOR

XXVI

Romans, I appeal to you,
for there's no end in sight
of wanton molestation

of Priapus every night
by a pack of sex-starved females,
so I beg you, operate,
and amputate my penis
or it soon may be too late.
5   More randy than spring sparrows,
the neighbours' girls and wives
will cause my cock to rupture –
so get ready with the knives!
I'm nearly dead already,
exhausted, sick and pale,
10   who once could bugger brawny thieves,
was ruddy, fit and hale.
I'm sure I've got consumption –
my prognosis isn't good:
I fall to fits of coughing
till my spittle's bright with blood.

EUGENE O'CONNOR

LI

What business, this? What reason should we give
for the vast inrush of thieves into our garden,
especially when each victim pays the price
of forceful penetration, more than once,
between his curving buttocks?
5   My figs are hardly preferable to my neighbours',
nor my grapes the sort that blond Arete gathers,
my pears and apples are not nourished by Picenan groves –
why pick them at the price of so much peril?
10   I've got no plums more tawny than new wax, no sorb
that calms the cramps of diarrhoea,
no filbert of the kind called *Abellana*,
or almond glowing with its roseate flower.

I cannot boast of cabbages or beets in quantities   15
unmatched by other gardens, or leeks thick at the base.
I can't believe that anyone would come to steal
my pumpkins full of seeds, the basil, or the cucumbers
that lie along the ground, the dwarf lettuces,
the bitter onions or garlic heads; he wouldn't come   20
to take away by night the randy colewart,
fragrant mint or rue for medicine.
Though my patch boasts all these things, the gardens
neighbouring mine contain no fewer.
All these aside, you come here, wanton thieves, to 'get it' 25
from me: hither to my all too obvious punishment you fly.
The very thing that threatens is the lure.

EUGENE O'CONNOR

LXI

Bailiff, why your useless plaints about
my being sterile now two seasons, I who
was once a fruitful apple tree?
It's not the weight of years, as you suppose,
not pelting hail; no late frost pinched   5
the buds just emerging from the twigs.
I can't complain of gales or rain or drought,
no starling harmed me, no rapacious jackdaw,   10
coot, aged crow or thirsting raven –
but because I bear on straining limbs
the rotten verses of a rotten poet.

EUGENE O'CONNOR

VI. HADRIAN

The Emperor Hadrian to his Soul

Little soul so sleek and smiling
Flesh's friend and guest also
Where departing will you wander
Growing paler now and languid
And not joking as you used to?

STEVIE SMITH

LITERARY CHRONOLOGY

───

(b. = born; d. = died; m. = married)

Political Events		Literary Events
Augustus consul (XI). Conspiracy of Caepio and Murena. Second 'Augustan Settlement' with proconsular command and tribunician powers. Marcellus d.	23 B.C.	Horace, *Odes* I–III, published.
Augustus in Greece and Asia Minor.	22	
Agrippa and Julia m.	21	
Restoration of standards by Parthians. Temple of Mars Ultor begun.	20	Horace, *Epistles* I, published; Ovid, *Amores* (1st edn).
Agrippa pacifies Spain.	19	Virgil d. (21 Sept.); Tibullus d.
Agrippa co-regent. Augustan Marriage Ordinances: *Leges Iuliae*.	18	Virgil, *Aeneid*, published; Propertius d. (?).
Ludi Saeculares: Centennial Games. Adoption of Gaius and Lucius.	17	Horace, *Carmen Saeculare*, published.
Tiberius and Drusus on Danube. Agrippa visits Jerusalem.	15	
Tiberius consul. Uprising in Thrace. Theatre of Marcellus dedicated.	13	Horace, *Odes* IV, *Epistles* II, published.
Agrippa d. Augustus Pontifex. Temple of Vesta on Palatine dedicated. Tiberius in Pannonia; Drusus in Germany.	12	Horace, *Ars Poetica*, published (?).
Tiberius and Julia m.	11	
Drusus d. *Ara Pacis Augustae* dedicated.	9	
Imperial Census held.	8	Horace, Maecenas d.
Tiberius' triumph over Sugambri	7	

Political Events		Literary Events
Tiberius given tribunician power; retires to Rhodes.	6	
Augustus consul (XIII) and *pater patriae*. Julia exiled. Temple of Mars Ultor dedicated in Forum of Augustus.	2	Ovid, *Amores* (2nd edn), published.
	I	Ovid, *Ars Amatoria*, published. Seneca b. (?) at Cordova.
C. Caesar in Syria.	A.D. I	Ovid, *Remedia Amoris*, published.
	1–8	Ovid, *Fasti; Metamorphoses*.
Lucius Caesar d. Tiberius returns from Rhodes.	2	
Gaius Caesar d. Tiberius adopted by Augustus; Germanicus adopted by Tiberius; commands in Germany.	4	
Tiberius at Elbe.	5	
Revolts in Pannonia and Illyricum; Judaea becomes a province.	6	
Pannonia subdued.	8	Ovid exiled to Tomis. *Metamorphoses* completed.
	9–12	Ovid, *Tristia* I–V, published.
Augustan Marriage Ordinances: *Lex Papia Poppaea*. Dalmatia subdued. Varius defeated in Germany. Temple of Concord dedicated to *Concordia Augusta*.	9	
	12–20	Manilius, *Astronomica*.
Tiberius' triumph over Illyria.	12	
Tiberius co-regent.	13	Ovid, *Epistulae Ex Ponto* I–III, published.
Augustus d. (19 Aug.). Reign of Tiberius (–37). Sejanus praetorian prefect. Revolt of legions in Pannonia and Germany. Germanicus crosses Rhine.	14	
Germanicus invades lower Germany.	15	
	16	Ovid, *Epistulae Ex Ponto* IV, published.

Political Events		Literary Events
Revolt of Tacfarinas in Africa. Germanicus' triumph; command in eastern provinces.	17	Livy, Ovid (?) d.
Germanicus (consul) in Asia Minor and Syria; visits Egypt.	18	
Jews expelled from Rome. Germanicus d. (10 Oct.).	19	
Trial and suicide of Cn. Piso.	20	
Tiberius consul (IV) with Drusus. Revolt of Julius Florus in Gaul.	21	
Praetorian Camp built in Rome.	21–2	
Drusus d. (14 Sept.).	23	
Tacfarinas d.	24	
	25	Cremutius Cordus, historian, d.
	25–6	Silius Italicus b.
	25–40	Phaedrus, *Fables* I–IV.
Thrace revolts. Pontius Pilate governor of Judaea.	26	
Tiberius withdraws to Capri.	27	
Livia d. Elder Agrippina exiled.	29	
Nerva b.	30	Velleius Paterculus, *Historiae Romanae*, published.
Sejanus (consul) with Tiberius (V) d. Macro praetorian prefect.	31	
Agrippina d.	33	
	34	Persius b. (Volaterrae).
	37–41	Elder Seneca, *Controversiae, Suasoriae*.
Tiberius d. (16 Mar.) Temple of Divus Augustus dedicated. Reign of Gaius, 'Caligula' (–41), Nero b. (15 Dec., Anzio).	37	
Lepidus and Gaetulicus d. Julia and Agrippina exiled.	39	Lucan b. (Cordova).
Cn. Domitius Ahenobarbus d. Octavia b. Judaean riots.	40	Martial b. (Bílbilis). *Garland of Philippus* published (?).

Political Events		Literary Events
Caligula d. (24 Jan.). Reign of Claudius (-54). Britannicus b. (Mar.).	41	Seneca exiled to Corsica; *Ad Marciam* published.
Dalmatian revolt.	42	Seneca, *Ad Helviam*, published.
Aulus Plautius invades Britain.	43	Seneca, *Ad Polybium*, published.
	44-9	Seneca, *Epigrammata de Exilio*, published. Plutarch b.
Claudius' triumph over Britain. Judaea province once more.	44	
	45-8	Statius b. (?) at Naples. Seneca, *De Ira* I-II.
Ludi Saeculares. Claudius censor.	47	
Messalina d.	48	Seneca, *De Constantia Sapientis*, published.
	49-52	Seneca, *De Ira* III.
	49-65	Seneca, *Tragedies* (?).
Claudius m. Agrippina. Seneca recalled to tutor Nero; praetor.	49	
Nero adopted by Claudius.	50	Phaedrus d. (?); *Fables* V, published (?).
Burrus praetorian prefect; Vespasian consul.	51	
Gallio proconsul in Achaea.	51-2	
Nero m. Octavia. Parthians reoccupy Armenia.	53	
Claudius d. (13 Oct.). Reign of Nero (-68). Parthian War begins.	54	Seneca, *Apocolocyntosis* (Dec.?).
Britannicus d.; Nero consul and *pater patriae*; Pallas dismissed; Agrippina out of power. Corbulo attacks Parthians.	55	*Commentarii* of Agrippina (Jan.); Seneca, *De Clementia* (or 56). Juvenal b. (?); Tacitus b. (?).
Seneca consul.	56	
Nero orders participation of senators and knights in games.	57	Seneca, *De Beneficiis*, published.
Poppaea mistress of Nero. Corbulo captures Artaxata.	58	Columella, *De Arboribus, Laus Pisonis*, published; Calpurnius Siculus, *Eclogues* (?).
	58-65	Lucillius, *Epigrams*, published (?).

Political Events		Literary Events
Agrippina d. (Mar.); Nero's literary circle founded; *Ludi Iuvenales; Augustiani* formed.	59	Seneca, *De Vita Beata*, published; Nero, *Attis* and shorter poems, published.
Puteoli *colonia Claudia Neronensis; Neronia* I. Festus governor of Judaea; Corbulo governor of Syria.	60	Columella, *De Re Rustica* (60–64?); Nero performs *Attis*; begins *Troica*; Lucan, *Civil War* (60–65); *Carm. Einsied*; Persius, *Satires* (60–62); younger Pliny b. (Como).
Nero's gymnasium built. Revolt of Iceni under Boudicca.	61	Annaeus Cornutus, *Epitome of Greek Theology* (?); Seneca, *De Tranquillitate Animi.*
Burrus d.; Tigellinus, Faenius Rufus praetorian prefects; Seneca retires; Octavia divorced, exiled, and d.; Nero m. Poppaea. T. Petronius Niger suffect consul (May–Aug.); joins Nero's literary circle (*arbiter elegantiae*).	62	Seneca, *De Otio*; Persius d. (Nov.). Nicarchus, *Epigrams*, published (?).
Nero's daughter Claudia Augusta b. and d.; end of Parthian war and revolt in Britain.	63	Seneca, *Quaestiones Naturales* (63–4); *De Providentia*; Persius, *Satires*, published.
Nero on stage at Naples; fire of Rome (18 July); persecution of Christians; *Domus Aurea* begun. Gessius Florus governor of Judaea.	64	Petronius, *Satyricon* (64–6); Seneca, *Epistulae Morales* (64–5); Lucan banned from publication; Nero's *Troica* finished.
Neronia II. Pisonian conspiracy (Apr.); Piso, Faenius Rufus, etc. d.; Musonius Rufus exiled; Poppaea d.	65	Elder Pliny, *Dubius Sermo; Studiosi* published; Lucan, Seneca d.; Martial arrives in Rome; finds patron in Lucan's widow, Argentaria Polla.
Thrasea Paetus, Barea Soranus, Scribonius Rufus d.; Helvidius Priscus exiled. Nero m. Statilia Messalina; conspiracy of Vinicianus; Nero departs for Greece (Sept.–early Oct.). Revolt in Palestine.	66	Petronius d.
	66–75	Curiatius Maternus, *Domitius, Medea, Cato*, and *Thyestes*.
Vespasian fights Jewish revolt (Feb.). Corbulo d. Nero's triumphant tour of Greece: at Corinth (Nov.); Nero returns to Italy (Dec.).	67	Josephus surrenders to Vespasian.

Political Events		Literary Events
Silius Italicus consul; revolt of Vindex (Mar.); Galba in arms against Nero (Apr.); Verginius defeats Vindex at Vesontium (May); Nero d. (9 June). Galba becomes emperor.	68	
Galba d. (15 Jan.); succeeded by Otho, Vitellius, Vespasian as emperor; Dacians attack Moesia. Sack of Cremona (Oct.) and capture of Rome by Vespasian's forces. Reign of Vespasian (–79).	69	Nero's *cantica* performed for Vitellius; Cluvius Rufus, *History of Nero's Reign* (?); pseudo-Senecan *Octavia* published (late 68–early 69).
Vespasian arrives in Rome (summer); destruction of Jerusalem (Sept.); Gallic revolt.	70	
Nerva, Vespasian consuls. Titus returns from the East. Temple of Janus closed. Colosseum begun. Astrologers and philosophers exiled. Temple of Capitoline Jupiter restored.	71	
Vespasian, Titus censors. Flavius Caesar b.	73–4	
Agrippa II, Berenice in Rome. Invasion of Armenia by Alani. Temple of Peace and Library completed.	75	Josephus, *Bellum Iudaicum*, published (?).
Hadrian b.	76	
Agricola governor of Britain (–85).	78	Pliny, *Natural History*, published.
Vespasian d. (24 June). Reign of Titus (–81). Eruption of Vesuvius (24 Aug.); destruction of Pompeii and Herculaneum.	79	Elder Pliny d.
Colosseum dedicated (June). Fire in Rome; destruction of Capitoline Temple.	80	Martial, *De Spectaculis* (Sept.); Statius begins *Thebaid* (?); Valerius Flaccus begins *Argonautica* (?). Epistle of Hebrews, Gospels of Matthew and Luke (–90?).
Titus d. (13 Sept.). Reign of Domitian (–96) (consul VII–XVII). Agricola in N. Britain.	81	

Political Events		Literary Events
Restored Capitoline Temple dedicated; Domitia made Augusta.	82	
Domitian's triumph over Chatti; takes cognomen Germanicus (autumn); Agricola's victory at Mons Graupius in Britain. Execution of three Vestals.	83	Statius' pantomime *Agave* with Paris; Paris the dancer d.
	84–5	Martial, *Xenia and Apophoreta*, published (Dec.).
Recall of Agricola from Britain.	84	
Dacian king Decebalus defeats Oppius Sabinus in Moesia; expulsion of philosophers from Rome; Domitian *censor perpetuus*.	85	Statius, *De Bello Germanico*, published. *Apocalypse* of John (–90?).
Decebalus defeats Fuscus (summer).	86	Martial, *Epigrams* I, published. Capitoline Games instituted by Domitian (summer). Collinus wins prize for Latin poetry.
	86–7	Martial, *Epigrams* II, published.
	87–8	Martial, *Epigrams* III, published.
Plot against Domitian; Julia d. (or 89).	87	
Defeat of Dacians at Tapae; legislation on client's doles (*sportulae*). *Ludi Saeculares*: Centennial Games (Sept.).	88	Quintilian retires; begins *Institutio Oratoria*; Silius begins *Punica* (?).
Rebellion of L. Antonius Saturninus (Jan.); Domitian's triumph over Chatti and Dacians; military pay raised; Vestinus d.	89	Martial, *Epigrams* IV, published (Dec.).
Execution of Cornelia, chief Vestal; laws against adultery and castration reinforced; expulsion of philosophers and astrologers.	90	Martial, *Epigrams* V, published (autumn); Statius' father d.; Capitoline Games. Johannine Epistles; Gospel of John (?).
Equestrian statue of Domitian dedicated.	91	Stella m. Violentilla; Martial, *Epigrams* VI, published (summer–autumn); Martial seriously ill; Curiatius Maternus d.; Statius, *Thebaid*, published (or 92).

Political Events		Literary Events
Domitian in Pannonia; second expulsion of philosophers from Rome. Capitolium, Forum of Nerva, *divorum porticus*, Iseum, Serapeum, *horrea pipatoria*, Palatine palaces, Temple of Vespasian, Minerva Chalcidica dedicated; Odeum completed.	92	Martial, *Epigrams* VII, published (Dec.); Valerius Flaccus d., *Argonautica* published (92–5).
	93–4	Martial, *Epigrams* I–VII, edited and reissued (?); Josephus, *Jewish Antiquities*, published.
Stella praetor; Agricola d. (23 Aug.); Pliny praetor; successfully prosecutes Baebius Massa.	93	
L. Silius Decianus consul.	94	Martial, *Epigrams* VIII, published (autumn); Statius, *Silvae* I–III, published; Capitoline Games (Statius fails to win prize); Martial, *Epigrams* IX, published (Dec.?).
Plot against Domitian; Flavia Domitilla exiled; T. Flavius Clemens and Acilius Glabrio d. (atheism); persecution of Christians; expulsion of philosophers from Italy.	95	Martial, *Epigrams* X, first edition published (Dec.); Statius, *Silvae* IV, published (summer–autumn); Quintilian, *Institutio Oratoria*, published.
Assassination of Domitian by wife and Parthenius (18 Sept.). Reign of Nerva (–98).	96	Martial, *Epigrams* XI, published (Dec.); Statius d. (spring); Statius, *Achilleis*, published.
Parthenius killed by mutinous praetorians; *lex agraria* for land distribution; Forum of Nerva dedicated (?); Trajan adopted by Nerva.	97	Martial, *Select Epigrams* (X and XI) to Nerva, published; Statius, *Silvae* V, published.
Nerva d. (Jan. 28). Reign of Trajan (–117).	98	Pliny granted *ius trium liberorum* by Trajan; Tacitus, *Germania, Agricola*, published; Martial, *Epigrams* X second edition, published; Silius Italicus, *Punica*, published (?).
Trajan returns to Rome.	99	
Trajan consul (III); Pliny consul	100	Pliny, *Panegyricus*; Fronto b.; Silius Italicus d. (or 101).
Trajan on Danube for Dacian campaign.	101	Tacitus, *Dialogus*, published.

Political Events		Literary Events
Trajan 'Dacicus' celebrates triumph over Dacians. Licinius Sura consul.	102	Martial, *Epigrams* XII first edition, published (Jan. ?).
	102–4	Martial d. (?).
	103	Frontinus d. (?).
	104	Martial, *Epigrams* XII (second edition), published.
Trajan's second Dacian war (June); Sarmizegethusa stormed; defeat and suicide of Decebalus; Dacia becomes a Roman province; Arabia annexed.	105–6	
	107	Pliny, *Epistles* I–III (97–102), published.
	108	Pliny, *Epistles* IV–VII (103–7), published.
Final victory over Dacians; monument to Mars Ultor dedicated at Adamclisi.	109	Tacitus, *Histories*, published.
	110	Pliny, *Epistles* VIII–IX (108–9), published.
Pliny governor of Bithynia.	111	
Forum of Trajan dedicated (Jan.).	112	Pliny, *Epistles* X, published; Juvenal, *Satires* I, published (?); Pliny d. (?).
Armenia and Mesopotamia annexed.	114	
Jewish revolt in Cyrene; spreads to Egypt and Cyprus.	115–16	
	115	Dio of Prusa d.
	116	Juvenal, *Satires* II, published.
Trajan d. (9 Aug.). Reign of Hadrian (–138).	117	Aelius Aristides b.; Juvenal, *Satires* III, published.
Hadrian in Rome (9 July).	118	
	120	Juvenal, *Satires* IV, published. Tacitus (?), Epictetus d. Lucian d. Tacitus, *Annals*, published (?).
Hadrian in western provinces; M. Aurelius b. (26 Apr.).	121	Suetonius, *Lives of the Caesars*, published.
Hadrian visits Britain.	122	

LITERARY CHRONOLOGY

Political Events		Literary Events
	123	Plutarch d. (?) Apuleius b. (?).
Hadrian in Asia Minor.	124	Juvenal, *Satires* V, published.
Hadrian in Athens.	129	Galen b.
Hadrian founds Antinoöpolis in Egypt; Aelia Capitolina on site of Jerusalem.	130	Second Epistle of Peter (?).
Jewish revolt under Simon Bar Cochba.	131	
Alani invade Parthia. Antoninus proconsul of Asia.	134	
Hadrian defeats Jews. Temple of Venus and Rome dedicated.	135	
Hadrian adopts L. Aelius (Caesar).	136	
Aelius Caesar d. (1 Jan.); Antoninus (Pius) adopted co-regent (25 Feb.); Hadrian d. (10 July). Reign of Antoninus (−161).	138	
Mausoleum of Hadrian dedicated.	139	
Marcus Aurelius consul (I).	140	Juvenal d. (?).
Fronto consul.	143	
Temple of Divus Hadrianus dedicated.	145	
900th anniversary of founding of Rome.	148	

GLOSSARY

———

The following glossary lists names predominantly in their Latinate forms. Graecized spellings (e.g. 'Bromios' for 'Bromius') are not listed separately.

ACCIUS: Latin tragic poet, 170–85 B.C; author of *Bacchae*, based on Euripides' play of that name.

ACHAEANS: Inhabitants of the province of Achaea in the northern part of the Peloponnese; Greeks in general.

ACHAEMENIAN: From Achaemenes, the ancestor of the old Persian kings. His name is the eponym of the Achaemenians, another appellation for the Persians.

ACHERON: A river of the underworld.

ACHILLES: Son of Peleus, king of Thessaly, and of Thetis, a sea-nymph. He is the hero of Homer's *Iliad* and the leader of the Myrmidons. His love for Patroclus was famous.

ACTAEON: Hunter who accidentally saw Diana naked and was turned into a stag to be torn to pieces by his own hounds. His mother was Autonoe, daughter of Cadmus, who helped to dismember Pentheus in the Bacchic rites at Thebes.

ACTIUM: Promontory on the Ambracian gulf in north-western Greece; site of the decisive naval battle in 31 B.C. in which Octavian defeated Antony, becoming unchallenged ruler of Rome. The victory in effect ended the Roman republic. See AUGUSTUS; CLEOPATRA.

ADMETUS: Mythical king of Pherae in Thessaly and the husband of Alcestis.

ADONIS: Young and beautiful lover of Venus; he was killed by a boar and the anemone sprang from his blood. The death and resurrection of Adonis (or Tammuz) was the focus of a popular eastern cult for women.

ADRASTUS: King of Argos, one of the famous 'Seven' who fought against Thebes to support Polyneices' claim on its throne.

AEACIDES: Descendant of Aeacus.

AEACIUS: Descendant of Aeacus.

AEACUS: King of Aegina; grandfather of Achilles; later a judge of the dead.

AEAEA: The land of Colchis.

AEETES: King of Colchis, father of Medea.

AENEAS: Trojan hero, son of Venus and Anchises, and legendary ancestor of the Roman people. His journey from Troy to Italy and the war that ensued are the subject of Virgil's epic poem *Aeneid*.

AEOLUS: Mythical divine king of the Aeolian islands (Lipara?), between Italy and Sicily; he controlled the winds, which he kept pent up in a mountain except when he unleashed them (by request) to help or hinder such heroes as Ulysses or Aeneas.

AESON: King of Thessaly, father of Jason, who drank a fatal draught of bull's blood when it seemed that the Argonauts were lost.

AETNA: See ETNA.

AETOLIA: A region of north-western Greece associated with the Homeric hero Diomedes and famous for the Calydonian boar hunt. In Silius Italicus' *Punica* it refers to Apulia, a region of southern Italy also associated with Diomedes.

AFRICUS: The south-west wind.

AGAMEMNON: Son of Atreus, king of Mycenae (or Argos), and leader of the Greek expedition to Troy. Victorious in the Trojan war, he returned home only to be murdered by his wife Clytemnestra and her lover Aegisthus.

AGE OF GOLD: See GOLDEN AGE.

AGENOR: Father of Cadmus and an ancestor of Dido. 'Agenorean' is sometimes used instead of 'Theban'.

AGRIPPA: (1) Victorious admiral at Actium and major supporter of Augustus (Octavian); (2) Agrippa II (b. A.D. 27/28), Jewish king, brother of Berenice.

AGRIPPINA: the younger, A.D. 15–59; mother of Nero by Domitius Ahenobarbus, she married in A.D. 49 the eccentric Claudius, whom she was generally believed to have poisoned with mushrooms.

AJAX: Famous Greek warrior of the Trojan war and a tower of strength to the army. Maddened because he was passed over in the contest for the arms of Achilles, he tried to slaughter the Greek leaders.

ALBA LONGA: Mother city of Rome founded *c.* 1152 B.C. by Ascanius, situated in the hills south of Rome. Statius was awarded a prize in the annual contest of poetry held by Domitian in honour of Minerva at his villa near the original site of Alba.

ALCESTIS: Wife of Admetus, king of Pherae in Thessaly. Alcestis sacrificed her own life for Admetus, but was afterwards brought back from the underworld by Hercules and restored to her husband.

ALCIDES: Hercules, from his family connection with Alcaeus, father of Amphitryon.

ALCINOUS: King of the mythical Phaeacians who entertained Ulysses as a guest during his wanderings.

ALCMAN: Lyric poet who flourished in Sparta during the second half of the seventh century B.C.

ALCMENE: Mother of Hercules by Jupiter, who had visited her disguised as her absent husband Amphitryon.

ALEXANDER: III of Macedon, the Great, 356–323 B.C.; conquered Greece, Persia and most of the Middle East, penetrating even into India. His meteoric career ended the Greek city state, hellenized the East, and introduced the concept of the supranational state. His untimely death in Babylon split up his hastily acquired empire and paved the way for Rome's conquests.

ALEXANDRIA: City built by Alexander the Great on the north coast of Egypt. It became a centre of learning under the Ptolemies.

ALLIUS: In *Punica*, an Italian warrior fighting against the Carthaginians at the battle of the river Trebia in 218 B.C.

ALTHAEA: Wife of Oeneus, king of Calydon, and mother of Meleager. When Meleager slew her brothers during a boar-hunt, she took revenge by burning the firebrand on which his life depended.

AMAZON: One of a mythical race of female warriors whose right breasts were removed in childhood in order to enable them to handle the bow more easily in battle.

AMBRACIA: Corinthian colony in Epirus, near the Gulf of Ambracia and the Ionian Sea; modern Arta.

AMERIAN: Belonging to Ameria, an ancient town in southern Umbria. The town was known for its pears and apples.

AMMON: Egyptian god identified with Zeus and Jupiter, whose temple in the oasis of Siwa in the Libyan desert was the seat of a famous oracle.

AMMONITE: Person associated with Ammon.

AMPHIARAUS: Priest and prophet of Argos, one of the 'Seven'.

AMPHION: Son of Antiope and Jupiter. He built the walls of Thebes by drawing the stones after him with the music of his lyre. He was the husband of Niobe. Their (sole surviving) son was also named 'Amphion'.

AMPHITRYON: Earthly father of Hercules, his divine, 'true' father being Jupiter. See also ALCMENE.

AMYCLAE: Town in Laconia famous for its temple and Colossus of Apollo; Helen's birthplace.

ANCHIALUS: Town on the west coast of the Black Sea, south of Tomis.

ANCHISES: Father of Aeneas, who bore him upon his shoulders from Troy.

ANDROMACHE: Wife of Hector and mother of Astyanax. After the death of her husband and fall of Troy, she became a slave to Pyrrhus (also called Neoptolemus), son of Achilles.

ANIO: Tributary of the river Tiber.

ANTENOR: Trojan elder and counsellor; the post-war foundations of several cities are attributed to him.

ANTIOPE: Mythical Theban heroine, mother by Jupiter of Amphion and Zethus, who killed her tormentors; also a play by Pacuvius.

ANTONY: Marcus Antonius ('Mark Antony'), c. 82–30 B.C.; Julius Caesar's chief lieutenant in the civil war with Pompey. He joined with Octavian and Lepidus to form the second triumvirate (43 B.C.) and together with Octavian defeated Caesar's assassins at the battle of Philippi (42 B.C.). He was himself defeated by Octavian at Actium in 31 B.C. See CLEOPATRA and ACTIUM.

ANUBIS: Dog-headed attendant of the Egyptian Isis and her husband Osiris.

ANXUR: Ancient town in Latium, later called Tarracina.

APENNINE(S): Mountain range that runs north–south down Italy.

APICIUS: Extravagant gourmet (fl. A.D. 20), who produced a cookery book and committed suicide when his income could no longer support his customary style of life.

APOLLO: God of music, poetry, prophecy, healing, and archery; son of Jupiter and Latona, brother of Diana. He was sometimes identified with the sun. Also called Phoebus.

APULIA: Region in south-east Italy, immediately north of Calabria.

AQUILO: North wind.

ARATUS: Greek poet from Cilicia who flourished during the first half of the third century B.C. He was the author of an astronomical poem entitled Phaenomena.

ARCADIA: Mountainous area of central Peloponnese; often associated with an idyllic pastoral environment and with Pan; hence 'Arcadian'.

ARETE: Literally 'virtue', the name of a female slave in the Priapean Corpus.

ARGIVE: Of Argos. 'Argives' are citizens of Argos, sometimes Greeks generally.

ARGO: Speech-endowed ship that carried the Argonauts to recover the Golden Fleece.

ARGOS: Principal city of the eastern Peloponnese; sometimes serves as the capital of Agamemnon's kingdom. In *Thebaid* it is ruled over by Adrastus.

ARGUS: Hundred-eyed giant who was set to watch Io after Jupiter metamorphosed her into a heifer. After Mercury killed him at the command of Jupiter, Juno placed his hundred eyes in the tail of the peacock.

ARGYRIPA: Town in Apulia, later called Arpi.

ARIADNE: Daughter of Minos, king of Crete. She helped Theseus to slay her brother, the Minotaur, and escape from the labyrinth. Deserted by him, she became the bride of Bacchus (Dionysus).

ARICIA: Ancient town in Latium near Alba Longa.

ARMENIA: Mountainous country of Asia, east of Euphrates; a Roman protectorate, it became part of the province of Cappadocia.

ASCANIUS: Son of Aeneas. He was king of Lavinium and founder of Alba Longa.

ASSARACUS: King of Troy; son of Tros and grandfather of Anchises.

ASTURIA: Region of northern Spain; its inhabitants were renowned for their intransigence.

ASTYANAX: Son of Hector and Andromache. He was thrown from a tower by Ulysses during the destruction of Troy. In Seneca's *Trojan Women* he leaps from the tower 'of his own will'.

ATHENA: See PALLAS.

ATHENS: Most famous city in Greece; its eponymous goddess and patron was Pallas Athena.

ATHOS: Mountainous headland giving its name to the eastern promontory of the Chalcidice, through which Xerxes cut a canal for his troops invading Greece in 483–481 B.C.

ATLAS: Originally a Titan, then also the name of his mountain in North Africa. Either the guardian of the pillars of heaven (Homer, *Odyssey* 1.53) or the bearer of the sky upon his shoulders (Hesiod, *Theogony* 517).

ATREUS: Son of Pelops and brother of Thyestes, whose children he served up to him at a feast. A frequent subject for tragedy.

ATRIDAE: Sons of Atreus, viz. Agamemnon and Menelaus.

ATTIS: Emasculated devotee (or consort) of the goddess Cybele; subject of compositions by Catullus and Nero. See CYBELE.

ATTIUS: See LABEO.

AUGUR: A diviner at Rome who made known the future by observing the flight of birds, the feeding of sacred fowl, the appearance of mammals, and unusual natural phenomena.

AUGUSTALIA: Quinquennial celebration held at Naples on 12 October in commemoration of the day on which Augustus returned triumphantly to Rome. A wreath of corn ears was awarded to the victorious poet at the festival.

AUGUSTUS: Gaius Octavius, 63 B.C.–A.D. 14; heir to Julius Caesar, he emerged from the bloody civil wars of the last years of the republic after the battle of Actium in 31 B.C. to establish the principate and create the Roman empire as it would survive until A.D. 476. His early patronage of literature and the arts gave way to increasing autocracy and the banishment of Ovid.

AULIS: Boeotian sea-port, the fabled jumping-off point for the Greek invasion of Troy.

AURORA: Goddess of the dawn.

AUSONIA: Lower Italy or a poetic name for Italy itself; hence 'Ausonian'.

AUSTER: South wind.

AUTONOE: Daughter of Cadmus; mother of Actaeon; she participated in the dismemberment of Pentheus in the Bacchic rites. See ACTAEON.

AVENTINE: One of Rome's seven hills.

AVERNUS: A lake the ancients considered to be near the entrance to the underworld.

BACCHANTS: Ecstatic devotees of Bacchus.

BACCHUS: Son of Jupiter and Semele; god of vegetation, wine, poets, and inspiration. He forcibly imposed his cult in Thebes. The Theban Bacchants associated him with Apollo at Delphi.

BAETIS: River in southern Spain, now called Guadalquivir.

BAIAE: Small suburb in Campania near Naples; a favourite resort of the Romans on account of its warm baths and pleasant situation.

BASSARID: A Maenad, female devotee of Bacchus.

BASSUS: See CAESIUS.

BATHYLLUS: Famous pantomime and sensuous ballet dancer of the Augustan times. The popular solo ballets generally had mythological, often erotic, themes, such as the seduction of Leda, mother of Helen, by Jupiter in the form of a swan.

BATTUS: Founder of Cyrene. The poet Callimachus claimed descent from him.

BEAR: Name of two constellations: the Great Bear (Arcturus) and the Lesser Bear.

BELLEROPHON: Falsely accused of making sexual advances to the wife of Proetus, he was sent to kill the monster Chimaera, which he did with the aid of the winged horse, Pegasus. His name cleared, he became the king of Lycia.

BELLONA: Native Roman war goddess who was later assimilated to, or associated with, Cybele. Her devotees were also self-castrated.

BELUS: Founder of Dido's royal line.

BERECYNTHUS: A mountain or stronghold in Asia Minor, associated with Cybele.

BERENICE: Jewish princess, mistress of the future emperor Titus (A.D. 39–81); she resided in Rome for a time around A.D. 75.

BESSA: A city of Locris in central Greece.

BESSIAN: Associated with the Bessi, marauding people of the Haemus mountains in north-eastern Thrace.

BESTIUS: Name of an extravagant wastrel in Horace, a greedy heir in Persius.

BÍLBILIS: Rich, strategic Celtiberian town in north-eastern Spain; near Calatayud in Aragón; birthplace of Martial.

BOEOTIA: A district in central Greece; its most famous son was Hesiod.

BOÖTES: The northern constellation of 'The Wagoner'.

BOREAS: North wind.

BOSP(H)ORUS: 'Ox-ford'. (1) Narrow Thracian strait between the Black Sea and the Sea of Marmora, dividing Asia from Europe; (2) Cimmerian Bosphorus, the Straits of Kerch, between the Black Sea and the Sea of Azov.

BOTERDUS: Area of modern Campiel, close to Bílbilis.

BOVILLAE: First small town south from Rome on the Appian Way near Aricia, where there was a hill; the traditional haunt of beggars.

BRINDISI: Brundisium, the best harbour on the lower east coast of Italy; the regular port for crossing to Greece.

BRISEIS: Achilles' captive and concubine; taken and later restored by Agamemnon in Homer's *Iliad*.

BROMIUS: Another appellation of Bacchus (= 'the Noisy One').

BRUTTIUM: Region of southern point of Italy; its inhabitants were the 'Bruttii'.

BRUTTIUS: Roman standard-bearer who died of his wounds after the battle of Lake Trasimene in 217 B.C.

BRUTUS: (1) Lucius Junius, 'The Liberator'; one of the first consuls after he had expelled the Etruscan tyrants from Rome in 510 B.C.; (2) Marcus Junius, assassin of Julius Caesar; defeated at the battle of Philippi (42 B.C.) by Mark Antony and Octavian. Both were symbols of political freedom.

BUSIRIS: Egyptian king and son of Neptune, who slew all foreigners until he was killed by Hercules.

BYZANTINE: Belonging to Byzantium.

BYZANTIUM: City in Thrace on the Bosp(h)orus, once Constantinople, now Istanbul.

CADMEAN: Theban, after Cadmus, founder of the city.

CADMUS: Son of Agenor, king of ancient Tyre. He founded Thebes by sowing the teeth of the dragon of Mars which he had killed and setting against each other the crop of armed men which resulted. The five survivors were the ancestors of the true Thebans, the Spartoi, or 'Sown Men'. In *Punica* 'Cadmus' breed' refers to Carthaginians because of their association with Phoenicia.

CAELIAN: One of Rome's seven hills.

CAESAR: (I) Gaius Julius, 100–44 B.C.; soldier and statesman, who after his conquest of Gaul defeated the senatorial forces under Pompey and Cato in a bitter civil war and made himself master of Rome. He was assassinated on the Ides of March 44 B.C. He is the central figure in Lucan's epic, *Civil War*. (2) Normal appellation of the emperor, beginning with the first emperor Augustus, the adopted son of Julius Caesar.

CAESIUS BASSUS: Distinguished lyric poet (*fl.* A.D. 60) who became Persius' friend and later editor.

CAESONIA: Milonia, a wife (A.D. 38) of the emperor Caligula. She supposedly kept his affections through love potions which affected his rationality.

CALABRIA: The flat south-eastern 'heel' of Italy; nowadays its south-western promontory.

CALCHAS: Leading priest and prophet of the Greeks at Troy.

CALIGULA: Gaius Caesar, A.D. 12–41; emperor from A.D. 37 to 41 who became increasingly autocratic as his personality became more unstable. His brutality and oppression led to his assassination in January A.D. 41. The name, 'Little Boot', was given him by the troops in Germany.

CALLIMACHUS: Influential Alexandrian poet (*c.* 305–240 B.C.), grammarian, and critic, whose works include *Aetia* (the 'Origins'), a long poem on the origins of places, names and rituals, *Hecale*, a mini-epic, and *Hymns*.

CALYDNAE: The Sporades in the eastern Aegean.

CALYDON: Settlement in Aetolia, north-western Greece; centre of the famous myth of the boar hunt.

CAMILLUS: Marcus Furius, saviour of Rome from the Gauls *c.* 386 B.C.;

victor over Veii, the Aequi and the Volscians. Regarded as the second founder of Rome. He was 'dictator' five times and a conciliatory statesman in the struggle between patricians and plebeians.

CAMPANIA: Area of western central Italy bounded by the Apennines and the Tyrrhenian Sea, and by Latium and the Sorrento peninsula. Its towns include Capua, Naples, Baiae, Pompeii and Puteoli.

CAMPUS MARTIUS: The Field of Mars, a large area on the bank of the Tiber, studded with temples, colonnades, theatres, gymnasia, and running tracks. A popular meeting place for business, athletics, and religious and social gatherings.

CANNAE: Village in Apulia, scene of Hannibal's greatest victory over the Romans in 216 B.C.

CANTHUS: Argonaut, son of Abas, who was killed in Libya.

CAPANEUS: Argive hero, one of the 'Seven' who fought against Thebes to support Polyneices' claim on its throne.

CAPITOL: Most important of Rome's seven hills. Built on it was a citadel and temple of Jupiter.

CAPITOLINE FESTIVAL: Five-yearly celebration instituted in A.D. 86 by the emperor Domitian and consisting of poetic, mimic, and athletic contests; the prizes given were oak-leaf crowns and sums of money.

CAPPADOCIAN: Type of untrustworthy, unintelligent slave from Asia Minor used for heavy work.

CAPRI (or CAPREAE): Resort island in Roman times also. The ruins of Tiberius' villa, in which the emperor spent the latter part of his life, are still there.

CAPUA: Chief city of Campania which went over to Hannibal after the battle of Cannae in 216 B.C.

CARIAN: Pertaining to Caria, a province in Asia Minor south of Lydia.

CARTHAGE: City of North Africa founded and ruled in legend by Dido. It became the chief rival to Rome's power in the Mediterranean and was Rome's enemy in the three Punic wars, of which the second is the subject of Silius Italicus' *Punica*.

CARYSTOS: Prominent town on the south-western promontory of Euboea, known for its marble quarries.

CASSANDRA: Daughter of Priam, virgin priestess of Apollo, who had loved her and had given her the power of prophecy but caused her always to be disbelieved. She became the captive mistress of Agamemnon and was killed by Clytemnestra.

CASTALIA: Nymph of the Castalian spring (of poetic inspiration) at the foot of Mt Parnassus. The fountain was sacred to Apollo and the Muses.

CASTOR: Son of the Spartan king Tyndareus (or Jupiter), and brother of Pollux. Castor and Pollux, the Heavenly Twins, were identified with the constellation Gemini, which served as a guide to sailors at sea.

CATILINE: Lucius Sergius, d. 62 B.C.; aristocrat with frustrated political ambitions who took up the cause of the people and attempted a revolution against the state during Cicero's consulship. His forces were defeated and he himself executed. His co-conspirators included such men as Lentulus and Cethegus and such women as Sempronia.

CATO: (1) The elder, 234–149 B.C.; conservative, moralizing statesman, best known for his hostility to Carthage; (2) The younger, 95–46 B.C.; staunch and moralistic republican who committed suicide rather than surrender to Caesar in the civil war. Both were symbols of Roman puritanical conservatism. See BRUTUS.

CATULLUS: Gaius Valerius, c. 84–54 B.C.; Roman lyric poet, notorious for his liaison with Lesbia.

CATULUS: Quintus Lutatius, aristocratic statesman (consul 102 B.C.), who used his Germanic spoils to build a famous portico on the Capitoline.

CAUCASUS: Range of mountains between the Black and Caspian Seas; scene of Prometheus' punishment.

CAUNUS: Ancient town on the coast of Caria well known for its figs.

CELTIBERIAN: Racial combination of Celts and native Iberians, who dominated north-east Spain.

CENTAUR: One of a race of half-equine, half-human creatures who lived in the wooded mountians of Thessaly; known for their unbridled passions.

CEPHALENIA: Largest of the islands in the Ionian Sea off western Greece.

CERAUNIA: Mountains on the east coast of Epirus in north-western Greece.

CERBERUS: Monstrous three-headed dog that guarded the entrance to the underworld.

CERES: Goddess of agriculture, mother of Proserpina.

CHALCIOPE: Daughter of Aeetes, sister of Medea, and widow of Phrixus.

CHALCIS: Town in Euboea, the crossing point from Aulis on the Greek mainland.

CHARON: Ferryman of the underworld, who conveyed the shades of the dead across the river Styx.

CHASTITY: *Pudicitia*, who together with Justice (*Astraea*) left the earth in the later years of Jupiter's governance of the world.

CHIAN: Belonging to Chios, an island in the Aegean Sea famous for its marble, fine cloth, wine, corn and figs.

CHIRON: Centaur famous for his knowledge of archery, music, plants, medicine, and divination. He served as the tutor of such heroes as Jason, Achilles, and Aesculapius.

CHRYSIPPUS: Prominent Stoic logician, *c.* 280–207 B.C. His logical paradox, *Sorites*, or the Heap, which turned on the definition of an unquantified mass, was famous.

CICERO, Marcus Tullius, 106–43 B.C.; Roman orator and statesman who revolutionized Roman prose. Of provincial origins, he was a political moderate who fought the trend towards autocracy. His speeches against Mark Antony, *Philippics*, led to his proscription and execution. Among his mediocre attempts at poetry the most notorious was a long poem on his own consulship.

CIMBRI: See MARIUS.

CINYPHIAN: Belonging to the fruitful region in Libya through which flowed the river Cinyps.

CIRCE: Daughter of Helius and Persa, the divine enchantress of the island of Aeaea, who kept Ulysses on her island for a year and bore him Telegonus (or Agrius). In *Argonautica* she is sister of Aeetes, king of Colchis, and claims to have escaped to live in Italy with King Picus.

CIRRHA: Ancient town near Delphi in Phocis, often used for Delphi itself.

CITHAERON: Mountain of Boeotia, overlooking Thebes. Used for orgiastic revelry by Bacchic worshippers. Oedipus was exposed here as an infant.

CLASHING ROCKS: See SYMPLEGADES.

CLEANTHES: Leading Stoic philosopher (*fl.* 250 B.C.) who centred ethics around disinterestedness and inner virtue.

CLEOPATRA: VII, queen of Egypt, lover of Julius Caesar and Mark Antony, whom she aided in the struggle against Octavian. After Actium, her hopes disappointed, she committed suicide (30 B.C.).

CLIO: Muse of history.

CLITUMNUS: River in the region of central Italy called Umbria.

CLOELIA: Roman hostage of the besieging Etruscans, who violated the warring armies' agreement by escaping across the Tiber. She was handed back, but freed by Porsenna for her bravery.

CLYTEMNESTRA: With her lover Aegisthus, she slew her husband, Agamemnon, in the bath with an axe on his return from the Trojan war.

COLCHIS: Kingdom east of the Black Sea; home of Aeetes and Medea.

CONSUL: One of the two chief officers of the Roman state, originally elected annually. During the republic the consuls were the supreme civil and military magistrates of Rome. The office retained its prestige under the empire but lost most of its power.

CORINNA: Famous fifth century B.C. Greek lyric poetess of Tanagra; also the name of Ovid's poetic 'mistress'.

CORNELIA: (1) Daughter of Scipio Africanus (*fl.* 160 B.C.), famous for her morality and intelligence; mother of the Gracchi, a pair of revolutionary tribunes of the people, who were assassinated by reactionary senatorial mobs; (2) Daughter of Metellus Scipio and fourth wife of Pompey, whom she married in 52 B.C. After Pharsalus she accompanied him to Egypt where she saw him murdered.

CORNUTUS: Lucius Annaeus; literary critic, Stoic philosopher, and teacher of rhetoric (*fl.* A.D. 55); a friend of Persius, he was exiled by Nero. Perhaps the author of the tragedy *Octavia*.

CORUS: North-west wind.

CORYCIAN: Belonging to the fabled Corycian mountain cave on Parnassus. A district in Cilicia which produced saffron.

COTYS: King of Thrace, who supplied the republic with five hundred cavalrymen led by his son.

CRASSUS: Marcus Licinius, d. 53 B.C.; initially a conservative republican financier of enormous wealth and some military ability; ambitious for more political power, he joined Pompey and Julius Caesar in the first triumvirate. Hoping to rival their military reputations, he took on the Parthians who defeated and killed him at Carrhae.

CRATINUS: Politically controversial writer of Old Comedy (*fl.* 430 B.C.).

CREON: Ex-regent of Thebes, in succession to Oedipus, who was both his brother-in-law and nephew. Father of Haemon and Menoeceus.

CRETE: Largest island in the eastern Mediterranean; the prehistoric centre of Minoan civilization, it generated the myths of King Minos, Pasiphae, the Minotaur, Daedalus, the Labyrinth, and Ariadne.

CROESUS: Last king of Lydia (*c.* 560–546 B.C.) and sympathetic towards the Greeks; his wealth was proverbial, but he was overthrown and almost executed by the Persian king, Cyrus, whose friend he may have become, unless the story of his suicide is found more plausible.

CUMAE: Ancient colony of the Chalcidians on the coast near Naples, celebrated on account of its Sibyl. The cheapest pottery came from Cumae.

CUPENCUS: One-eyed warrior fighting on the Carthaginian side at the battle of the Trebia.

CUPID: Son of Venus; usually a smiling winged infant armed with a bow and arrows, which when shot inspired love and desire.

CURETES: Ancient inhabitants of Crete who worshipped Jupiter, having protected him in his infancy.

CURIA: Senate-house or the Senate itself.

CURIO: Gaius Scribonius; two prominent politicians, father and son, in the period of the first triumvirate. The father opposed Caesar, the son eventually supported him and became an important Caesarian commander in the war with Pompey. He was killed in Africa, fighting Juba (Lucan, *Civil War* IV).

CURIUS: Manius Dentatus, consul 290 B.C.; victorious general and Roman symbol of moral severity.

CURULE CHAIR: Official chair of Roman consuls, praetors and curule aediles.

CYANEAN ROCKS: See SYMPLEGADES.

CYBELE: Orgiastic Anatolian mother-goddess, associated with Mt Ida and Mt Dindymus and Phrygia in general; her cult was officially introduced into Rome around 205 B.C. and it was celebrated 15–28 March. Her consort was Attis and her priests were the castrated Galli.

CYCLOPS: (1) One-eyed smiths who worked for Vulcan under Mt Etna; (2) Gigantic, one-eyed Sicilian shepherds, the most famous being Polyphemus.

CYCNUS: (1) Son of Neptune, distinguished for his magic and white hair; killed by Achilles, he was turned into a swan; (2) Son of Ares and a brigand, who was killed by Hercules.

CYDONEA: City on the north coast of Crete; hence 'Cydonian'.

CYME: City in north-western Asia Minor; also alternative form of CUMAE.

CYNIC: Unkempt philosopher who mocked social conventions as based on hypocrisy and the avoidance of truth.

CYNOSSEMA: 'The dog's tomb'. See HECUBA.

CYNTHIA: Mistress of Propertius, the love poet; associated by Juvenal with Lesbia, lover of Catullus, who wrote a poem on the death of her pet sparrow. Name for Diana – see CYNTHIAN.

CYNTHIAN: Epithet of Apollo and Diana, who were born on Mt Cynthus on the island of Delos.

CYRENE: Important town in north-western Libya.

DACIA: Roman province from A.D 100 to 270, comprising mainly the area of Transylvania and part of Romania.

DALMATIA: Roman province on the upper east coast of the Adriatic, home of fierce Illyrian tribesmen.

DAMASCUS: Ancient capital of Coelesyria on the Chrysorrhoas river.

DANAAN: Often used for 'Argive' or 'Greek'. Danaus was the founder of Argos.

DANAE: Mother of the hero Perseus (killer of the Gorgon Medusa) by Jupiter, who had appeared to her as a shower of gold.

DANAI: 'Greeks'. See DANAAN.

DANAIDS: The fifty daughters of the Egyptian king Danaus, almost all of whom slew their husbands, the children of Egyptus, on their wedding night.

DARDANIA: Poetic name for Troy.

DARDANIAN or DARDAN: Pertaining to the famed city of Troy founded by Dardanus near the Hellespont in north-western Asia Minor; often used for 'Trojan', sometimes (*Punica*) even for 'Roman' because of Rome's 'descent' from Trojan Aeneas.

DARDANUS: Founder of Troy.

DAUNIA: Poetic for Apulia, a province in southern Italy.

DAUNUS: Legendary king of Apulia.

DEIOTARUS: An astute ruler of Galatia, ally of the republic until Pharsalia.

DELIAN: Belonging to Delos, a small island in the Aegean Sea, the birth-place of Apollo and Diana.

DELPHI: Cult centre of Apollo and the most famous oracle in the ancient world. It was situated in Phocis in central Greece.

DEMOCRITUS: of Abdera, *c.* 460–370 B.C.; founder of the materialist Atom-ist school of philosophy; he was later known as 'the Laughing Philoso-pher'.

DEMOSTHENES: Athenian orator, 384–322 B.C.; son of an arms manufac-turer, he made his name prosecuting his own guardians for embezzle-ment before becoming politically active. His policies were nationalistic, directed mainly against Philip of Macedon and his Greek allies, and best expressed in his famous *Philippics* (351 B.C. and later). Condemned to death by the Athenians, he committed suicide.

DIANA: Virgin goddess of the hunt, the moon, and childbirth.

DICAEARCHUS: Distinguished late fourth-century B.C. philosopher, biogra-pher, and geographer who lived most of his life in Sparta.

DICTATOR: Exceptional Roman supreme office, filled only in times of national emergency.

DICTE: Mountain in Crete.

DIDO: Legendary founder and queen of Carthage. Her abandonment by Aeneas and suicide are narrated by Virgil in *Aeneid* IV.

DIOMEDES: (1) One of the greatest warriors at Troy who helped Ulysses steal the Palladium, the sacred image of Pallas, on which the fortunes of the city depended; (2) A Thracian king who fed his horses on human flesh. He was killed by Hercules.

DIONE: Mother of Venus.

DIONYSUS: Greek name of Bacchus, the god of wine and poets.

DIRCE: Spring near Thebes which gave its name to one of the seven gates of the city.

DIS: Divine lord of the underworld and the dead; known also as Hades and Pluto.

DISCORDIA: Goddess of strife, daughter of Jupiter and Juno.

DON: The river Tanais, usually considered as the boundary between Europe and Asia.

DORIS: Daughter of Oceanus and Tethys, and sister and wife of Nereus; used by metonymy for the sea.

DYMAS: Devoted squire of Parthenopaeus; committed suicide when trapped during an attempt to bring his chief's body off the battlefield.

ECHION: (1) Argonaut, son of Hermes, born in Arcadia; (2) One of the warriors who sprang up from the sowing of the dragon's teeth by Cadmus, king of Tyre.

ECHO: Love-sick nymph who faded away into a repetitive voice.

EETION: King of Thebes in Cilicia and father of Andromache. He was killed by Achilles.

EGERIA: One of four prophetic Italian nymphs, the Camenae, later the Italian Muses; honoured as the 'wife' and adviser of Numa.

ELEUSIS: Important Attic town near Athens, famed for its mysteries celebrating Ceres (Demeter) and Proserpina (Persephone).

ELIS: Region of north-western Peloponnese, containing the great shrine of Olympia.

ELISSA: Another name for Dido, the founder of Carthage.

ELISSO: Town on the border of Illyria and Epirus.

ELYSIAN: Of or belonging to Elysium.

ELYSIUM: The abode of the blessed in the underworld, in whose fields the heroic dead followed patterns of earthly life.

ENDYMION: Youth beloved by the moon-goddess Selene, who spent his immortal life in sleep.

ENISPE: Place in Arcadia (central Peloponnese).

ENNA: Ancient city in central Sicily with a famous temple of Ceres. It was from here that Pluto carried off Proserpina.

ENNIUS: Quintus, 239–169 B.C.; revered Roman tragedian and epic poet, whose *Annals* chronicled the rise of Rome and influenced Virgil's *Aeneid*. He supposedly believed that he had been Homer and a peacock in former lives.

EPICHARMUS: Sicilian writer of comedy active in the early fifth century B.C.

EPIRUS: An area of north-western Greece (now part of Albania), known for its powerful king Pyrrhus (319–272 B.C.), the oracle at Dodona, and the battle of Actium (31 B.C.). It is the setting for most of Lucan, *Civil War* V.

EREBUS: The underworld.

ERIDANUS: Mythical name for the river Po.

ERIGONE: Daughter of Icarius who hanged herself through grief for her father's death.

ERINYS: Any of the three persecuting Furies.

ERIPHYLE: Wife of Amphiaraus who was bribed by a necklace to send her husband on the ill-fated mission of the Seven against Thebes, from which he did not return.

ETEOCLES: King of Thebes, son of Oedipus, and noted for his self-confident tyrannical violence. He refused to adhere to the agreement to reign in alternate years with his brother Polyneices and died in mortal combat with him.

ETNA: The great volcano in Sicily, under which the Cyclopes forged the thunderbolts of Jupiter.

ETRURIA: District north of Rome.

ETRUSCAN: Associated with, or an inhabitant of, Etruria.

EUBOEA: Large island in the Aegean Sea off the east coast of central Greece; hence 'Euboean'.

EUHOE: A Bacchic cry.

EURIPUS: Fast-flowing channel separating Euboea from Boeotia.

EUROTAS: River running through Sparta and Laconia.

EURYALUS: Young friend of the Trojan warrior Nisus in Virgil's *Aeneid*. The pair figure in a famous episode when they attempt unsuccessfully to carry a message through the enemy lines to Aeneas (*Aeneid* IX. 176–502).

EVANDER: Arcadian king, in Roman legend, who established a settlement in the place where Rome was later founded. In Virgil's *Aeneid* he is an ally of Aeneas.

FABIUS: Quintus Maximus Cunctator, consul 215, 214, 209 B.C.; he was the master of delaying tactics to wear down the invading Carthaginian forces of Hannibal.

FABRICIUS: Gaius Luscinus, consul 282, 278 B.C.; victorious general, and a Roman symbol of austerity.

FALERNIAN: One of the best of the Roman wines, produced in northern Campania.

FATES: The *Parcae*, three sisters who determined the length of a man's life, conceived of as a thread of varying length; see LACHESIS.

FAUNUS: Native Italian god of field, flock, and village.

FIBRENUS: In *Punica* he is a soldier fighting on the Roman side at the battle of the river Trebia.

FLAMINIAN WAY: the arterial road leading from Rome to northern Italy.

FLAMINIUS: Gaius, consul 223, 220, 217 B.C.; commander at Lake Trasimene (217 B.C.), where he perished.

FLORA: Italian goddess of flowers.

FULGINA: Town of the eastern Italian region of Umbria.

FULVIUS: Q. Fulvius Flaccus, consul 212, 209 B.C.

FURIES: Spirits who avenged bloodshed; they carried out the curse pronounced on criminals, tortured the guilty with the pangs of conscience, or inflicted famines and plagues.

GALLI: (1) Tribesmen of Gaul; (2) Eunuch priests of Cybele.

GANGES: River in northern India.

GANYMEDE: Handsome son of Laomedon who was carried by Jupiter's eagle from Mt Ida to heaven to serve as cup-bearer to Jupiter and the Olympians in place of Hebe.

GARAMANTIANS: Tribesmen from the eastern Sahara.

GARGANUS: Mountain in Apulia.

GAUL (TRANSALPINE): Country occupied by the Gauls. It included much of northern Italy as well as modern France.

GAURUS: Unpleasant poetic acquaintance of Martial. Also a mountain near Naples; hence a possible allusion to the poet Statius.

GELONIANS: Scythians who lived near the river Don.

GENUSUS: River (modern name Tjerma or Skumbi) in Illyria.

GERYON: Three-headed king of Hesperia, the plundering of whose magnificent oxen on Erytheia was one of Hercules' tasks.

GESTAR: Carthaginian warrior at the battle of the Trebia in *Punica*.

GETAE: Thracian tribe around the lower Danube.

GETIC: Associated with the Getae.

GIANTS: Monstrous offspring of Earth, who engaged in an epic battle with the Olympian gods and were defeated. Often grouped with them are the sons of Aloeus, Otus and Ephialtes, who tried to climb from earth to heaven by piling Mt Ossa on Mt Olympus and Mt Pelion on Mt Ossa.

GLYCON: A tragic actor.

GOLDEN AGE: The primal era under Saturn of innocence, peace, and harmony between man, god, and nature which preceded the rise of cities, commerce, and war. See Virgil, *Eclogue* IV. The restoration of the Golden Age by a new emperor became a propaganda motif in the Augustan and early imperial period.

GONOESSA: A place near Sicyon in the Peloponnese.

GORGONS: Three mythical monsters, girded with snakes and having wings, brazen claws and enormous teeth. The most famous was Medusa, whose face could turn men to stone. She was killed by Perseus with divine help.

GORTYN: Important ancient town in southern central Crete. Famous for its early legal code, it became the Roman capital of the province.

GRACCHUS: (1) Ti. Sempronius Longus, consul 218 B.C., one of the Roman commanders at the battle of the Trebia; (2) Ti. Sempronius, consul 215, 213 B.C.; trapped and killed by the Carthaginians in 212 B.C. See also CORNELIA.

HADES: God of the underworld; also known as Dis or Pluto.

HAEMON: Menoeceus' elder brother in the Theban cycle of myth.

HAEMONIAN: Thessalian, from Mt Haemus in Thrace.

HAEMUS: Mountain range in northern Thrace.

HAMILCAR BARCA: Carthaginian general in the first Punic war (264–241 B.C.) and subsequently in Spain; father of Hannibal.

HANNIBAL: Leader of the Carthaginian invasion of Italy in the second Punic war (218–201 B.C.), and the central figure in Silius Italicus' *Punica*.

HAPSUS: River (modern name Crevata) in Illyria which flows into the Ionian Sea.

HARMONIA: Wife of Cadmus and daughter of Venus and Mars.

HARPIES: Fierce, winged monsters, with faces of women and the bodies of vultures. They left a stench, snatched and defiled the food of their victims, serving as ministers of divine vengeance and punishing criminals.

HEBRUS: Principal river in Thrace, the large territory to the north-east of Greece, now the Maritza.

HECATE: Goddess of the moon and the underworld, and of magic and witchcraft, often represented with three heads; daughter of Perses and Asteria, sister of Latona. Identified with Diana, Luna, and Proserpina, she presided over enchantments and conjurations, and was particularly associated with the underworld.

HECTOR: Son of Priam and Hecuba, husband of Andromache, and the bravest warrior among the Trojans in Homer's *Iliad*. He finally fought Achilles, who slew him and dragged his corpse thrice round Troy. His body was ransomed by his father, Priam; his funeral concludes Homer's epic.

HECUBA: Wife of Priam and mother of numerous Trojan heroes and heroines. In her grief over Greek brutality and the loss of her children, she was turned first into a barking dog and then into a rock, which became known as 'the Dog's Tomb' (Cynossema), a promontory near the Hellespont and the site of an Athenian naval victory in 411 B.C..

HELEN: Daughter of Jupiter and Leda and wife of Menelaus; sometimes called 'Tyndaris' after Tyndareus, Leda's husband and her reputed father. She was carried off to Troy by Paris, who had been promised the most beautiful woman in the world as a reward for judging Venus superior in beauty to Juno and Minerva. The abduction precipitated the Trojan war.

HELENUS: Trojan warrior and prophet; son of Priam. Spared by the Greeks, he settled in Epirus, married Andromache, and entertained Aeneas on his way to Italy.

HELIADS: Daughters of Sol (Helios) and sisters of Phaethon, for whom they wept until they were transmuted into poplars (or alders).

HELICON: Mountain in Boeotia in mainland Greece, inhabited by the Muses; it became a symbol of poetic inspiration.

HELLE: Daughter of Athamas and Nephele, sister of Phrixus. She fled with Phrixus from their jealous stepmother Ino on a ram with a golden fleece to Colchis, but was drowned in the strait thereafter called Hellespont, 'the sea of Helle', in her memory.

HELLESPONT: Modern name, the Dardanelles.

HENNA: See ENNA.

HERACLITUS: Of Ephesus, *fl. c.* 500 B.C.; enigmatic philosopher who described the universe in terms of conflicting and then unifying opposites, with fire as the active principle. He was regarded as a forerunner of the Stoics. His dictum, 'Everything flows', may have given him the reputation for tears, but he is supposed to have had a melancholy disposition.

HERCULES: Son of Jupiter and Alcmene; a hero of incredible strength who was deified for his mighty achievements. His Twelve Labours were performed either out of duty to Eurystheus of Argos or as a penance imposed by Delphi to expiate his killing of his children in a fit of madness. He had close connections with both Thebes (his birthplace) and Argos and was responsible for an early sack of Troy, killing Priam's father Laomedon but sparing the boy Priam.

HERMAPHRODITUS: Son of Hermes and Aphrodite; he became half-man and half-woman through bathing in the fountain of the nymph Salmacis whose uniting with him was responsible for his epicene form; see SALMACIS.

HERMIONE: Daughter of Helen and Menelaus.

HESIOD: Greek poet of Boeotia, who flourished around 700 B.C. His most famous works were *Theogony* and *Works and Days*.

HESPERIA: The western land, often used in Roman verse for Italy.

HESPERIDES: Keepers of the legendary golden apples in the far west.

HESPERUS: The evening star (Venus).

HIPPODAMIA: Daughter of King Oenomaus, whose chariot had its axles loosened to prevent him winning the race against her suitor, Pelops.

HIPPOLYTUS: Son of Theseus by the Amazon Queen Antiope (or Hippolyte), and a devotee of hunting and Diana. His rejection of the love of his stepmother, Phaedra, led to the deaths of both of them. He was later identified with the Italian rustic god, Virbius.

HIPPOMEDON: Argive warrior killed in the river Ismenos outside Thebes; one of the 'Seven'.

HIRPINUS: A warrior fighting on the Roman side at the battle of the Trebia.

HOMER: Eighth-century Greek poet who was author of *Iliad* and *Odyssey* and who is regarded as the founder of the epic tradition. He was reputed to have been blind and born in Chios or on the Ionian mainland.

HOPLEUS: Loyal squire of Tydeus, killed by Thebans while attempting to recover his chief's body.

HORATIUS COCLES: Roman soldier who held off single-handed the Etruscan army of Lars Porsenna, until a vital bridge was destroyed.

HYADES: 'The Raining Ones'. Seven (according to some accounts, five) daughters of Atlas and sisters of the Pleiades; they wept themselves to death when their brother Hylas was killed hunting, after which they were translated to the heavens as the constellation comprising the head of Taurus. The constellation's morning rising and setting were associated with rainy weather. See PLEIADES.

HYBLA: Town famous for its honey, situated on the southern slopes of Mt Etna in Sicily, the birthplace of pastoral poetry.

HYDRA: Nine-headed water-serpent killed by Hercules near the Lernean Lake, although it grew fresh heads when one was cut off, until the stumps were cauterized (on Athena's advice).

HYELE: Town on the coast of Lucania, later known as Velia.

HYLAS: Handsome young lover of Hercules who was snatched away by water nymphs on the coast of Mysia. His disappearance prompted Hercules to abandon the Argonauts.

HYMEN: Roman god of marriage.

IAPETUS: A Titan, son of Heaven and Earth, hurled into Tartarus by Jupiter; father of Prometheus and Epimetheus.

IBERIA: Spain; hence 'Iberian'.

IBYCUS: Greek lyric poet of Rhegium in the sixth century B.C.; celebrated on account of the flock of cranes which he called upon to witness and avenge his murder at the hands of some thieves.

ICARIUS: King of Sparta, who received Bacchus hospitably when he came to Attica and was given the vine.

ICARUS: Son of Daedalus who, in escaping with his father from Crete, flew too near the sun, which melted the wax structure of his wings. Where he fell to his death – between the islands of Samos and Icaria – was called the Icarian Sea.

IDA: Mountain near Troy.

IDAEAN: A poetical equivalent for 'Trojan'.

IDAS: One of the Argonauts, husband of Marpessa.

IDUME: See PALESTINE.

ILIA: Rhea Silvia, daughter of Numitor and the mother by Mars of Romulus and Remus. Roman poets tell how she threw herself into the Anio, or Tiber, and was taken by the river-god to be his wife.

ILIAN: Belonging to Ilium (Troy).

ILIUM: Troy.

ILLYRIA (or ILLYRICUM): Country bordering the Aegean Sea, corresponding to the modern Albania and south-western Jugoslavia.

IMBROS: Small island in the Aegean Sea near Samothrace and Lemnos.

INACHUS: River-god and first king of Argos. Hence the Argives are sometimes called 'Inachian'.

INARIME: Pithecusa, volcanic island off the Campanian coast, now Ischia.

INO: Sister of Semele, mother of Palaemon and daughter of Cadmus, the founder of Thebes.

IO: Daughter of Inachus, seduced by Jupiter, who turned her into a heifer to avoid suspicion. Tormented by a gadfly sent in jealousy by Juno, she wandered the world until she returned to Egypt and became a woman once again. Her Egyptian connections facilitated her assimilation to Isis.

IOLCUS: City in northern Thessaly, sheltered by Mt Pelion, and home of the Argonaut Jason; modern Volos.

IONIA: Central west coast of Asia Minor. Colonized around the eighth century by Athens and other Greek cities, it developed a high degree of culture, despite pressure from its barbarian neighbours.

IPHIGENIA: Daughter of Agamemnon; sacrificed by her father to get favourable winds for the Greek expedition against Troy. According to other accounts, she was rescued by Diana (Artemis) and made her priestess among the Tauri (in modern Crimea).

IPHIS: Argonaut, son of Sthenelaus, who was killed fighting the troops of Aeetes.

IRIS: Rainbow-goddess, daughter of Thaumas, and messenger of the gods.

ISCHIA: See INARIME.

ISMARIAN: Pertaining to Mt Ismarus in Thrace (therefore often = 'Thracian').

ISMENOS: River flowing past Thebes.

ITHACA: Island in the Adriatic Sea, off the west coast of Greece, the centre of Ulysses' kingdom.

JANUS: Old Roman god of the gate, and so of beginnings (hence January); he was typically represented with two faces, one in front and one behind.

JASON: Leader of the Argonauts on the quest for the Golden Fleece. His adventures decorated a famous colonnade, the *porticus* of Agrippa, in the Campus Martius at Rome.

JOCASTA: Wife and mother of Oedipus and mother of his children, Eteocles, Polyneices, Antigone and Ismene. According to some accounts she killed herself on discovering that she was Oedipus' mother; according to other accounts (e.g. Statius' *Thebaid*) she lived to witness the mutual fratricide of her sons.

JOVE: See JUPITER.

JUBA: Arrogant client king of Numidia, who sided with the senate against Julius Caesar and was granted control also of Libya. After the battle of Thapsus (46 B.C.) he committed suicide.

JULIA: Daughter of Julius Caesar and wife of Pompey, to whom she was devoted. She died in childbirth.

JUNO: A daughter of Saturn, wife of Jove, and queen of heaven; in *Punica* a supporter of the Carthaginians and Hannibal.

JUPITER: The Roman sky god, king of the Olympian gods.

JUSTICE: Astraea or Nemesis, who left the earth with Chastity (*Pudicitia*) in the later years of the Silver Age, when mankind had deteriorated from the primal innocence of the Golden Age.

KALENDS: The first day of the Roman month.

LABEO: Attius, unpolished translator of Homer and contemporary of Persius.

LABIENUS: Titus, Caesarian lieutenant in the Gallic campaign, who supported the senatorial cause in the civil war. He was killed at the battle of Munda.

LACHESIS: One of the Fates, who decided on the length of life for each individual; see FATES.

LACONIA: South-eastern part of the Peloponnese in which Sparta is situated; 'Laconian' is often used for 'Spartan'.

LAERTES: In Homer's *Odyssey*, retired king of Ithaca and father of Ulysses (Odysseus).

LAGUS: A king of Egypt, its first Macedonian pharaoh.

LAIS: Name of two celebrated courtesans of Corinth, one in the fifth, one in the fourth centuries B.C. They were paradigms of the expensive, high-class prostitute and subjects of various anecdotes.

LAMPSACUS: City on the Hellespont.

LAODAMIA: Young bride of Protesilaus, the first man killed in the Trojan war. After his death the gods allowed her to see him again for three hours. She then took her own life.

LAPITHES: Ancestor of the Lapithae, a Thessalian tribe, renowned for their horsemanship and constant warfare with the centaurs.

LAR(ES): Household god that provided the centre of Roman family worship; generally depicted as a young man dancing. Tutelar deity, often of a house.

LATERANUS (Plautius): Rich senator, implicated in a plot against Nero and forced to kill himself in A.D. 65.

LATIAN: Belonging to Latium, a district of central Italy.

LATIUM: Region of Italy in which Rome is situated. Its inhabitants, the *Latini*, gave their name to the Latin language.

LATONA: Mother of Apollo and Diana.

LAURENTINES: Inhabitants of Laurentum or Latium in general. Supporters of Aeneas; used for 'Romans' in *Punica*.

LAURENTUM: City in Latium, ruled by King Latinus; hence 'Laurentian'.

LEDA: Wife of Tyndareus, king of Lacedaemon. She was seduced by

Jupiter disguised as a swan and became, through the two fathers, mother of the Dioscuri, Castor and Pollux, and of Helen of Troy and Clytemnestra.

LENTULUS: (1) Spinther, Publius Cornelius, consul in 57 B.C.; friend of Cicero; executed by Caesar after Pharsalus; (2) Crus, Lucius Cornelius, consul 49 B.C.; fought on the senatorial side in the civil war; slain in Egypt after escaping from Pharsalus.

LERNA: Small settlement near Argos, sometimes used as another term for Argos. The killing of the many-headed Hydra at Lerna was one of Hercules' Labours.

LESBIA: Catullus' married mistress; usually identified with Clodia Metelli. She had a famous pet sparrow.

LESBOS: Largest island off Asia Minor, not far from Troy; famed for its culture, it boasted Sappho and Alcaeus among its poets.

LETHE: The river of Forgetfulness in the underworld from which the shades drank and became unconscious of the past. A standard symbol for death.

LETO: A Titaness, and mother by Jupiter of Apollo and Diana – but only after months of harassment by Juno, who allowed no land to harbour her. She gave birth on the island of Delos.

LEUCAS: Island in the Ionian Sea off the west coast of mainland Greece.

LIBYA: Coast district of North Africa, west of Egypt, which includes the city of Carthage; North Africa generally.

LIBYAN: Associated with Libya. In *Punica*, the 'Libyan' is Hannibal.

LICTORS: Attendants of magistrates whose main functions were to carry out arrests and summons.

LIGURIA: Area of northern Italy and southern France, stretching from the Rhône to the Arno and inland to the south of the river Po.

LONGINUS: Cassius; famous jurist who was exiled by Nero in A.D. 66 on suspicion of treason.

LUCANIA: District in southern Italy; hence 'Lucanian'.

LUCILIUS: Gaius, *c.* 180–*c.* 102 B.C.; first great Roman satirist of the republic, much imitated, except for his political frankness, by Persius and Juvenal.

LUCRETIA: Legendary Roman heroine, wife of Brutus the Liberator; her rape by Sextus Tarquin in 510 B.C. led to the expulsion of the Etruscan kings from Rome and the establishment of Rome as a republic. She became a symbol of old-fashioned Roman chastity.

LUNA: Town in northern Etruria near the modern Carrara on the Gulf of Spezia.

LUNAN: The white marble of Carrara.

LUPERCI: Priests of Lycean Pan. In the festival of the Lupercalia (March) they ran through Rome half-naked, striking women with goatskins to induce fertility.

LUPUS: Cornelius Lentus; consul in 156 B.C. and target of Lucilius' satire.

LYAEUS: Another name for Bacchus.

LYCOPHRON: Grammarian and tragedian of Chalcis in the early third century B.C. who moved to Alexandria where he composed the obscure poem *Alexandra*.

LYDIA: Region of western Asia Minor. Ruled by King Croesus in the sixth century B.C., it later became part of the Persian empire.

MACEDONIA: A kingdom between the Balkans and Greece, adjacent to Thessaly and the battlefield of Pharsalus. It became an international power under Philip and Alexander in the fourth century B.C.

MAENAD: Ecstatic devotee of Bacchus.

MAENALUS: Mountain range in Arcadia.

MAEONIA: Another name for the area in Asia Minor known as Lydia.

MAEOTIS: Sea of Azov.

MAGNA MATER: The great Phrygian Mother-Goddess, whose acolytes castrated themselves. See CYBELE.

MAGNUS: 'The Great', a title given to Pompey by Sulla and Lucan's favourite term for him.

MAGO: In *Punica* a Carthaginian warrior at the battle of the Trebia.

MAHARBAL: In *Punica* a Carthaginian warrior at the battle of the Trebia.

MALEA: Southernmost promontory of Greece, notorious for rough weather.

MANIUS: A typical name for a beggar or nondescript.

MANTO: Daughter of Tiresias, his principal assistant.

MANTUA: City on the Mincius river near which the poet Virgil was born.

MARCELLUS: Marcus Claudius, consul 222, 214, 210, 208 B.C.; one of the great Roman generals in the war against Hannibal, especially in Sicily where he captured the city of Syracuse. He was ambushed and killed by the enemy in 208 B.C.

MARIUS: Gaius, *c.* 157–86 B.C.; Roman general who through military achievements in Spain, against King Jugurtha in Africa and against the Celtic Cimbri in upper Italy (102–101 B.C.), became for a time an important political figure (consul seven times between 107 and 86 B.C.). His new model army, recruited partly from the lower classes, became an instrument for future military coups. His political feud with Sulla, marked by failures, exile, a flight to Carthage, and successes, prompted the first of the republic's civil wars. He died of ill health before he could consolidate his temporary ascendancy in Rome.

MARS: God of war and father of Romulus, the founder of Rome. The 'dragon/snake of Mars' was the monster slain by Cadmus at the founding of Thebes.

MASSILIA: Modern Marseilles; an early and prosperous mercantile town on the coast of southern Gaul, long allied with Rome.

MASSYLIA: Region of Numidia occupied by the people known as Massylians.

MATERNUS: Curiatius, *fl.* A.D.. 75; senatorial dramatist; author of a *Cato* and a *Thyestes*; possibly executed for political subversion.

MAVORS: Mars, the war god.

MAZAEUS: In *Punica* a Carthaginian warrior at the battle of the Trebia.

MEDEA: Tragic heroine who, for love, helped the Argonaut Jason in his quest for the Golden Fleece. When he rejected her for a princess of Corinth, she killed both the princess and her own children in revenge.

MEGARA: Greek city on the Saronic Gulf.

MELICERTES: A sea deity; the younger son of Ino, the sea-goddess.

MEMNON: Son of Aurora, the dawn-goddess, and an ally of Troy.

MENANDER: Most famous writer of New Comedy, *c.* 342–290 B.C.. His light plays and Roman adaptations of them were popular in early republican times.

MENELAUS: Younger brother of Agamemnon; husband of Helen; and a commander in the Trojan war.

MENOECEUS: Younger son of Creon; sacrificed himself voluntarily when Teiresias revealed that Menoeceus' death would allow Thebes to survive.

MERCURY: God of travellers, boundaries, unexpected treasure trove, merchants, and thieves; the guide of souls to the underworld.

MEROE: Large island of the Nile in Ethiopia on which stood a famous temple of Isis.

MESEMBRIA: City on the west coast of the Black Sea, south of Tomis.

MESSALINA: Notoriously unfaithful wife of the emperor Claudius; mother of his son, Britannicus, who was poisoned during the second year of Nero's reign (A.D. 55).

METTUS: Latin general of Alba Longa who broke his word to Rome. As a punishment, he was tied to two chariots and torn apart.

MEVANIA: City in the central Italian region of Umbria.

MILETUS: Prominent city in Ionia, on the coast of Asia Minor; known for its educated courtesans and its free-wheeling life style, symbolized in the Milesian Tales.

MILO: Of Croton, *c.* 525 B.C.; multiple victor in the Olympic games, who could carry a bull. Trying to complete the splitting of a tree, he was trapped and eaten by wolves.

MIMALLONEAN: Macedonian adjective for Maenads.

MIMAS: Mountain in Ionia.

MINERVA: Virgin goddess of arts and wisdom, and so of schoolboys, who paid their fees on or around the Festival of Minerva (19 March). Identified with Pallas Athena. See PALLAS.

MINYANS: The Argonauts, so-called after Minyas, the original king of the Boeotian tribe from whom most of the Argonauts claimed descent.

MISENUS: Trumpeter of Aeneas who, after a jealous Triton drowned him, was buried at Misenum, whence the town received its name.

MITHRIDATES: VI, 120–63 B.C.; king of Pontus, who waged war successfully against the Romans, but was finally defeated by Pompey. Immune to poison because of his prophylactic precautions (or 'mithridates'), he had himself killed by a guard's sword.

MOTHONE: Town in eastern Thessaly.

MUCIUS SCAEVOLA: (1) Legendary Roman hero who, failing to assassinate Porsenna, the Etruscan king besieging Rome, held his left hand in a fire to prove Roman endurance; (2) Consul in 117 B.C.; a prominent lawyer and politician, he was derided by Lucilius.

MULCIBER: Another name for Vulcan, the god of fire, husband of Venus.

MURRANUS: In *Punica* a warrior fighting on the Roman side at the battle of the Trebia.

MUSES: The nine goddesses of the liberal arts.

MYCENAE: Prehistoric town in the Argive plain; centre of Mycenaean civilization. In myth, it was the kingdom of Atreus and Agamemnon and the leading participant in the expedition against Troy.

MYSIA: An area in north-western Asia Minor which included the Troad. Its mythical king Telephus plays a part in the Trojan cycle.

MYTILENE: Important city on the east coast of Lesbos and capital of the island.

NAIAD: Nymph of fresh water streams, lakes, and fountains.

NEMEA: Important city in the eastern Peloponnese near which Hercules slew the Nemean lion as one of his Labours and established the Nemean games.

NEPTUNE: The Olympian ruler of the seas, sharing universal power with

Jupiter and Pluto. His symbol was the trident. He helped build Troy and persecuted Ulysses for the blinding of his son, the Cyclops Polyphemus.

NEREID: Sea-nymph born of Doris and Nereus.

NEREUS: A god of the sea, father of the Nereids.

NERITOS: Mountain on Ithaca, wrongly thought by Seneca to be an island.

NERO: Claudius Caesar, emperor, A.D. 54–68. Famous for his interest in the arts and his persecution of Christians. Hero of Seneca's *Apocolocyntosis*, he was the villain in *Octavia* and in the eyes of posterity.

NESTOR: Mythical king of Pylos who contributed his experience and his sons to the war against Troy. Celebrated among the heroes of Troy for his wisdom, eloquence and longevity.

NILE: Largest Egyptian river, which became a Roman symbol of the exotic and decadent.

NIOBE: Daughter of Tantalus who had twelve children by Amphion and boasted she was the equal of Leto, mother of Apollo and Artemis. The two gods killed her children for her presumption and Niobe turned into a rock. According to some accounts a son, Amphion, survived.

NISUS: See EURYALUS.

NOTUS: South wind.

NUMA: Second king of Rome (715–673 B.C.), a law-maker, who taught the values of peace.

NUMIDIA: Region of North Africa, now eastern Algeria; hence 'Numidian'.

NYMPHAEUM: (1) Promontory less than three miles from Elisso, on the border between Illyricum and Epirus; (2) Grotto or shrine honouring the nymphs of a locality.

OCEAN: The great sea that encompasses the known land-masses.

OCTAVIA: Nero's first wife, daughter of Claudius and Messalina; executed in A.D. 62. Also an anonymous historical drama, published in A.D. 69, and still extant, about her life and death.

ODESSOS: City of Lower Moesia on the Black Sea.

ODYSSEUS: See ULYSSES.

OEBALUS: Early king of Sparta; also the founder of Tarentum.

OEDIPUS: King of Thebes. An oracle foretold that he would kill his royal father, Laius, and sleep with his mother, Jocasta. Abandoned to die, he was adopted by the Corinthian royal family, whom he left, hoping to frustrate the prophecy, but in fact he killed Laius and, for saving Thebes from the Sphinx, he was made king with his mother as queen, by whom he begot four children (Eteocles, Polyneices, Antigone, and Ismene). When the truth was revealed, he put out his eyes and abdicated his throne to Creon. His story was a frequent theme in tragedy and epic. See JOCASTA.

OETA: Mountain range in north-eastern Greece between Thessaly and Aetolia.

OGYGIAN: From Ogyges, another mythic founder and king of Thebes. Sometimes used to denote Thebans.

OLENOS: Town in Achaea.

OLYMPUS: Mountain in Thessaly and the highest in Greece, traditionally regarded as the home of the gods or the heavens.

OMPHALE: Queen of Lydia, with whom Hercules fell in love and for whom he served as a slave, wearing effeminate dress and jewellery and performing women's duties.

OREAD: Mountain nymph.

ORESTES: Son of Agamemnon and Clytemnestra, who murdered her husband after he returned from Troy. Orestes avenged his death at the bidding of Apollo by slaying his mother and was pursued by the Furies, until he was acquitted in a trial presided over by Athena.

ORPHEUS: Famed singer and musician of Thrace who, after the death of his wife Eurydice, went to the underworld, where he so charmed Pluto with his singing that she was allowed to leave. However, he lost her on turning to look back at her just before arriving in the upper world, thus breaking his pledge to Pluto. He was the reputed founder of the Orphic religion.

OSIRIS: Egyptian god of the underworld who was identified with Bacchus; consort of Isis, he was associated with fertility. When he was killed and dismembered, Isis searched for his remains.

OSSA: High mountain in Thessaly on which the centaurs once lived. It was piled on Pelion by the Giants to assault Mt Olympus.

OTHRYS: Mountain in Thessaly.

PACUVIUS: Roman dramatist, 220–c. 130 B.C.; wrote tragedies, e.g. *Antiope*, using historical and mythical themes.

PAEAN: A name of Apollo, as god of healing.

PAGASAE: Sea-port in Thessaly where the Argo was built and to which it returned.

PALAEMON: Son of Ino, taken with her when in a fit of madness she jumped into the sea at Corinth.

PALAESTE: Sea-port in Epirus.

PALAMEDES: A cunning Greek warrior at Troy, son of Nauplius; his death was contrived by Ulysses.

PALATINE: One of the seven hills of Rome. It overlooked the Roman Forum and was the site of the main imperial residence from Augustus onwards.

PALES: Country god and goddess who protected herds and flocks. Their festival was the *Parilia* (21 April).

PALLAS: A title of the Greek Athena (Roman Minerva), patron goddess of Athens, protectress of civilized life and goddess of war, wisdom and agriculture, especially the cultivation of the olive.

PAN: God of woods and shepherds, protector of sheep, inventor of the shepherd's pipe, consisting of several reeds of different lengths.

PANGAEA: Mountain in Thrace.

PARIS: Trojan hero, son of Priam, whose abduction of Helen precipitated the Trojan War. See HELEN.

PARNASSUS: Famous high mountain in central Greece, overlooking Delphi. It was sacred to Apollo, the home of the Muses, and a haunt of the Bacchants.

PARRHASIA: Town of Arcadia in southern Greece from where Evander led his people to settle what was later to be the site of Rome.

PARRHASIAN: Associated with the Arcadian town and with Evander; then with the Palatine palaces because of their connection with Evander. Sometimes used for 'Arcadian'.

PARTHENOPAEUS: Arcadian warrior; the youngest and most handsome of the 'Seven' against Thebes, whose fate is described at length in *Thebaid*.

PARTHENOPE: One of the Sirens who threw herself into the sea when Ulysses passed by their island; the name was applied to the city of Naples.

PARTHIA: Unconquered kingdom on the Roman frontiers in Asia Minor; perceived as a constant military threat, the Parthians figured frequently in Roman historical poetry.

PATROCLUS: Greek hero in Homer's *Iliad*, Achilles' companion and great friend.

PAULLUS: L. Aemilius, consul 219, 216 B.C.; Roman general who died at the battle of Cannae.

PEDIUS (POPLICOLA): Defence lawyer who appears in Horace's *Satires*. In Persius, *Satire* I, he is a character defending himself against a charge of theft.

PEGASUS: Winged horse of Bellerophon; a blow of its hoof uncovered the spring Hippocrene, sacred to the Muses.

PELASGI: Ancient inhabitants of the northern Aegean; hence Greeks, Argives, and certain early Italian tribesmen.

PELASGIAN: Generally, 'Argive' or 'Greek'.

PELEUS: Father of Achilles and husband of the sea-goddess Thetis.

PELIAN: From or belonging to Mt Pelion.

PELIAS: Thessalian king who usurped the crown of his brother, Neleus; fearing his nephew Jason he sent him on the quest for the Golden Fleece. Medea tricked his daughters into killing him.

PELION: Mountain in Thessaly.

PELOPIAN: Connected with Pelops or the Peloponnese.

PELOPS: Son of Tantalus, he was slain and his flesh cooked by his father as a dish for the gods, whereupon he was restored to life by Jupiter, who gave him an ivory shoulder in place of the one eaten by Ceres. He wooed and won Hippodamia. His children were Atreus and Thyestes. The southern part of Greece (the Peloponnese, 'the island of Pelops') was named after him.

PENELOPE: Daughter of Icarius and Periboea, and wife of Ulysses. She was a model of chastity and devotion to her husband.

PENTHESILEA: Amazon queen; slain by Achilles in battle round Troy.

PENTHEUS: King of Thebes; in resisting the Bacchic religion, he was induced by the god to don female clothing and was torn to pieces by his mother Agave and her fellow Bacchants.

PERSAEA(N): Connected with Perse, mother of Circe and Aeetes; magical.

PERSE: An Oceanid, wife of Apollo, by whom she was mother of Circe and Aeetes.

PERSEIS: See CIRCE.

PERSEUS: Son of Danae by Jupiter. He was given winged sandals by Mercury. Among his triumphs were the fetching of the head of the Gorgon Medusa and the rescue of Andromeda.

PETOSIRIS: Supposedly an Egyptian priest who helped establish the fundamental principles of astrology. A handbook on the subject, written about 150 B.C., circulated under his name.

PHAEDRA: Daughter of King Minos of Crete and Pasiphae; wife of Theseus. She fell in love with her stepson, Hippolytus; angered by his repulse, she accused him to his father of making sexual advances. Hippolytus was cursed by his father and killed; Phaedra committed suicide (either after Hippolytus' death or at the time of her false accusation). See HIPPOLYTUS.

PHAET(H)ON: Hero who was permitted to drive the chariot of his father, the Sun, but was unable to control the reins and, struck by Jupiter's thunderbolt, fell to his death in the river Po (Eridanus).

PHALANTUS: In *Punica* a warrior on the Carthaginian side at the battle of the Trebia.

PHARIAN: Egyptian.

PHARIS: Town in the Peloponnese south of Sparta.

PHAROS: Island with a famous lighthouse off Alexandria; a symbol of Egypt.

PHARSALIA: Thessalian district around Pharsalus.

PHARSALUS: Town in Thessaly near which Caesar defeated Pompey in the decisive battle of 48 B.C..

PHASIS: River in Colchis, a kingdom in Asia south-east of the Black Sea.

PHILIPPI: City in Macedonia famous for the battle (42 B.C.) in which the assassins of Julius Caesar, Brutus and Cassius, were defeated by Mark Antony and Octavian.

PHILOMELA: Daughter of Pandion, king of Athens and sister of Procne; she was violated by Tereus, her brother-in-law, and eventually turned into a nightingale. See PROCNE.

PHLEGETHON: Burning river of the underworld.

PHLEGRA: Otherwise Pallene, the westernmost peninsula of Chalcidice in north-eastern Greece where the gods defeated the giants.

PHOCIS: Region of Delphi in central Greece between Locris and Boeotia. It was sometimes confused with Phocaea, the Ionian mother-city of Massilia.

PHOEBAS: Priestess or prophetess of Apollo, often used of the Delphic or Cumaean Sibyl or of Cassandra.

PHOEBUS: Epithet of Apollo.

PHOENIX: (1) Son of Amyntor, he was given by Peleus to Achilles to act as his tutor and companion in the Trojan war; (2) Son of Agenor.

PHOLOE: A mountain in Thessaly.

PHRIXUS: Son of Athamas and Nephele, who escaped on a ram with a golden fleece, to Colchis, where he sacrificed the ram and married Chalciope, daughter of the Colchian king, Aeetes. See HELLE; CHALCIOPE.

PHRYGIA: Region of north-western Asia Minor; hence 'Phrygian'.

PHTHIA: City in Thessaly, birthplace of Achilles.

PICENAN: Of Picenum, a fertile region of east-central Italy.

PICUS: Early king of Italy, a prophet beloved by Circe, who turned him into a woodpecker when he rejected her.

PIERIAN: Sacred to the muses, poetic.

PINDAR: Distinguished Greek lyric poet of Thebes who flourished during the first half of the fifth century B.C.

PINDUS: Mountain in Thessaly.

PIRITHOUS: Friend of Theseus, king of Athens. He accompanied Theseus in an unsuccessful venture to carry off Proserpina from the lower world.

PISA: District in Elis around Olympia.

PLATEA: Small town near Bílbilis in north-eastern Spain; modern Castejón de las Armas.

PLEIADES: Seven daughters of Atlas and Pleione, pursued fruitlessly by Orion; thence the constellation of the Seven Stars whose rising was a sign of rainy weather. See HYADES.

PLEURON: Town in southern Aetolia.

PO: Chief river of Italy.

POLLUX: Twin brother of Castor; son of Tyndareus or Jupiter.

POLYDAMAS: Trojan hero and counsellor.

POLYNEICES: Theban prince, son of Oedipus, who fought his brother Eteocles for the right to reign in Thebes in alternate years; one of the 'Seven'.

POLYPHEMUS: One-eyed Cyclops, son of Neptune. He was blinded by Ulysses, who was then hounded by Neptune for the deed.

POLYXENA: Daughter of Hecuba and Priam, sacrificed to the spirit of Achilles.

POMONA: Goddess of fruit.

POMPEY: Gnaeus Pompeius Magnus, 'the Great', 106–48 B.C.; republican general who served Sulla and then the Senate with great military successes in Spain, Africa, and the Middle East (over Mithridates). His uneasy alliance with Julius Caesar in the first triumvirate broke down and he became the Senate's military leader against the would-be autocrat. Defeated at Pharsalus, he fled to Egypt, where he was assassinated by Pothinus and burnt on the Egyptian coast. His famous stone theatre was built in 55 B.C.; according to the elder Pliny it held 40,000 spectators. Many prefer a figure of 10,000.

PONTIA: Woman in the reign of Nero who was accused of poisoning her own children; she later committed suicide.

PONTIC: see PONTUS.

PONTUS: The Black Sea; sometimes the region around the Black Sea. Also a region in Asia Minor between Bithynia and Armenia, which became a Roman province in A.D 64.

PORCIA: Wife of Brutus, the assassin of Julius Caesar, who committed suicide on learning of her husband's death.

PORSENNA: Lars, of Clusium, who besieged Rome in order to restore the exiled Tarquin the Proud.

POSEIDON: Greek name of Neptune.

POTHINUS: Eunuch regent of Egypt in 48 B.C. He had Pompey killed and was in turn executed by Caesar for conspiring against him.

PRIAM: Famed king of Troy during its war with the Greeks and father of numerous Trojan heroes and heroines including Hector, Paris, Polyxena, and Cassandra; his wife was Hecuba. He was slain during the sack of Troy as he sought refuge at the altar of Jupiter in his palace. He was a symbol of longevity and tragedy.

PRIAPUS: Ithyphallic god of sexuality and fertility (his symbol was the erect phallus and the sickle); also the protector of gardens, in which his statue, normally of wood, was placed to warn off thieves. He was the subject of many Latin poems and a standard symbol of lust and male potency.

PROCNE: Wife of Tereus, the Thracian king, to whom she served up his son, Itys, in revenge for the rape of her sister Philomela; she metamorphosed into a swallow.

PROMETHEUS: A Titan who defied Jupiter to help men by stealing fire from heaven. He was punished by crucifixion to a crag in the Caucasus, where a vulture daily devoured his liver.

PROPONTIS: Sea of Marmora.

PROSERPINA: Daughter of Ceres and Jupiter. Pluto seized her as she was gathering flowers in a Sicilian meadow and carried her away to the underworld to be his wife.

PROTESILAUS: Son of Iphiclus and leader of the Thessalians against Troy. He was celebrated as the first man killed in the Trojan war. See LAODAMIA.

PROTHOUS: Greek hero at Troy; commander of the Magnetes.

PTOLEMY: XIII, boy-king of Egypt, Cleopatra's brother.

PUNIC: Carthaginian.

PYLADES: Son of King Strophius, famous as the friend of Orestes.

PYLOS: Mycenaean town on the west coast of the Peloponnese; the Messenian kingdom of Nestor, the aged Homeric hero.

PYRRHA: Wife of Deucalion. The two were the only survivors of the great flood sent by Jupiter. They repopulated the world by throwing stones behind them.

PYTHIAN: See PYTHON.

PYTHON: Dragon, offspring of Earth (Gaea), that guarded the oracle of Delphi until slain by Apollo, who then took control of the sanctuary. Hence Apollo is called 'Pythian' and his Delphic priestess 'Pythia'.

QUINTILIAN: Marcus Fabius (b. Calgurris), *c.* A.D. 35–98; like Martial, Lucan, and the Senecas, a Spaniard; he was the first professor of rhetoric to receive an imperial salary. A friend of Martial.

QUIRINUS: Roman deity often identified with Romulus.

RHAMNUS: Attic deme famous for its statue of Nemesis.

RHASCYPOLIS: Thracian tribal chief who provided the republicans with two hundred cavalrymen; Caesar commends his bravery in his commentary.

RHESUS: King of Thrace, who brought supernatural horses to aid Troy; they were taken by Ulysses.

RHIP(H)AEAN: Fabulous mountains in the extreme north; Scythian.

RHODES: Large island off the south-west coast of Asia Minor, famous for pure air, seafaring, rhetoric and the Colossus; home of Sol or Helios (the Sun) and thus associated with Apollo; honoured for contributing to the Roman republican navy.

RHODOPE: Mountain (range) in Thrace.

RHOETE(I)AN: Poetical adjective for 'Trojan'.

RHOETEUM: Small town in the Troad.

ROME: Principal Italian city; capital of the empire.

ROMULUS: Mythical founder and first king of Rome.

RUTILA: Representative figure in Juvenal of an early Latin tribe, who stood for plain living and moral decency.

RUTULIAN: Belonging to the Rutuli, the Latin nation of Turnus, which dwelt south of Rome.

SABAEAN: Belonging to Saba, a large city in Arabia, famous for its frankincense and myrrh.

SABINE: Territory north-east of Rome, whose population had been quickly absorbed into the Roman state; Horace had a farm there.

SADALAS: Son of Cotys.

SAGUNTUM: City in Spain, the fall of which to the Carthaginians precipitated the second Punic war.

SALAMIS: Island in the Saronic gulf a few miles east of Athens, which controlled it for most of its history. In its waters the Persian fleet was soundly defeated in 480 B.C. Its most famous mythical hero was Ajax, son of its king Telamon, and a tower of strength to the Greeks at Troy.

SALMACIS: Spring at Halicarnassus, which turned bathers into hermaphrodites; the nymph of the spring; hence 'Salmacian'.

SAMNITE: Belonging to Samnium, a region situated roughly in the middle of Italy.

SAMOS: Island off the west coast of Asia Minor.

SAMOTHRACE: Island to the west of Troy near the Dardanelles.

SAPPHO: Famous Greek poetess born in Mytilene on the island of Lesbos; she flourished in the first half of the sixth century B.C..

SARDANAPALUS: Last and most decadent of the Assyrian kings; faced with a revolt, he fought bravely, but finally, besieged in his capital Nineveh, he immolated himself with his wives and possessions, c. 876 B.C. He became a symbol of an extravagant style of living.

SARMATIA: Slavic nation extending from the Vistula to the Don, corresponding to modern Russia and Poland; later moving to the Danube.

SASO(N): Island off the coast of Illyria.

SATURN: Mythical king of Italy, then an early Italian god of agriculture, who was later identified with the Greek Kronos (hence the father of Jupiter and Juno). He ruled in Italy during the Golden Age. 'Saturn's daughter' denotes Juno.

SATURNALIA: Cheerful winter festival celebrated 17–19 December, when it was customary to give gifts.

SATURNIAN: Epithet of Juno, sister-wife of Jupiter.

SAUROMATIANS: See SARMATIA.

SCAEVOLA: See MUCIUS.

SCARPHE: A city of Locris in central Greece.

SCIPIO: (1) Publius Cornelius, consul 218 B.C.; commander of the Roman forces at the battle of the Trebia, he was killed in Spain in 211 B.C.; father of Scipio Africanus. (2) Africanus, consul 205, 194 B.C.; distinguished Roman general who eventually defeated Hannibal and the Carthaginians in the second Punic war (218–201 B.C.) at the battle of Zama.

SCORPUS: Famous charioteer of Martial's time.

SCYLLA: (1) Famous rock opposite Charybdis between Italy and Sicily inhabited by a sea-monster (daughter of Phorcys) of the same name, who preyed on sailors passing through the Sicilian straits; (2) Princess of Megara who betrayed her father Nisus for love of Minos, the Cretan invader. Rejected by him for her treachery, she was transformed into a bird. The two Scyllas are often confused.

SCYROS: Island in the Aegean off Euboea, where the bones of Theseus were supposedly discovered.

SCYTHIA: Area in northern Europe and Asia stretching from the Black Sea and inhabited by nomadic tribes.

SEJANUS: L. Aelius, d. A.D. 31; of distinguished Etruscan origins, he quickly rose to power as Prefect of the Praetorian Guard under Tiberius and ruled Rome in the emperor's absence after A.D. 27. His ruthlessness made him many enemies; their influence with Tiberius suddenly toppled him on charges of treason and he was executed.

SEMELE: Daughter of Cadmus, the founder of Thebes, and mother of the god Bacchus by Jupiter. Angry at her husband's infidelity, Juno persuaded Semele to request Jupiter to visit her in all his might. She was killed by the fire of his thunderbolt.

SERES: Roman name for the Chinese.

SIBYL: Female prophetess, variously located. The most famous was the Cumaean Sibyl, who inhabited a cave at Cumae from the time of Aeneas. Apollo granted her request for immortality, but, when she spurned his advances, he refused to grant her eternal youth, after which she withered away in old age. The Sibylline books, containing prophecies relevant to Rome, were kept in the temple of Apollo on the Palatine and consulted in times of national crisis.

SICANIAN: Belonging to the Sicanians, inhabitants of Sicily.

SICILY: Large triangular island by the toe of Italy. It was colonized by the Greeks.

SIDON: Ancient Phoenician city, mother-city of Tyre, from which Dido came to Carthage.

SIDONIAN: Connected with Sidon. Thebans are sometimes referred to as 'Sidonian' because of the Phoenician origins of the city's founder Cadmus. In *Punica* 'Sidonian' is equivalent to 'Carthaginian'.

SIDRA: See SYRTES.

SIGEAN: Connected with Sigeum; hence 'Trojan'.

SIGEUM: Town and promontory in the Troad.

SILVANUS: Roman god of woods and wilderness.

SINON: Greek who persuaded the Trojans to admit the Wooden Horse, containing the Greek Chieftains.

SIRENS: Birds with the faces of virgins who dwelled on the south coast of Italy. With their sweet songs, they lulled ashore those who sailed by and then killed them.

SMYRNA: Coastal city in Ionia celebrated as the birthplace of Homer.

SOLON: Athenian poet and statesman, *fl.* 600 B.C. His conservative reforms of the Athenian constitution alleviated debt and redistributed power between the underprivileged, the merchant classes, and the landed aristocracy. He was accepted as one of the Seven Sages.

SOPHRON: Fifth-century B.C. Syracusan composer of mimes.

SORRENTO: Coastal town in Campania on the southern tip of the bay of Naples.

SPARTA: Important Greek state in southern Peloponnese, famous for its military strength and the martial qualities of its citizens. It was once ruled by Menelaus and his wife Helen.

SPHINX: Legendary monster terrorizing the area round Thebes until Oedipus solved her riddle, whereupon she destroyed herself. As a reward Oedipus was offered the throne of Thebes and marriage to the queen.

STELLA: L. Arruntius consul A.D. 101; closely connected to Domitian, and a good patron of Martial and Statius.

STESICHORUS: Early sixth-century B.C. Greek lyric poet of Himera.

STHENOBOEA: Wife of Proetus who fell in love with Bellerophon; being rejected, she accused him of making advances to her, which prompted Proetus to send him on a lethal errand. Like Potiphar's wife and Phaedra, she became a symbol of the rejected and vengeful woman.

STRYMON: River dividing Thrace and Macedon.

STYGIAN: Often used to mean 'of the underworld', after its main river, the Styx.

STYX: Chief river of the underworld. By it the gods swore their 'greatest and most dread oath'.

SUBURA: The commercial and red-light district between the Esquiline and Viminal Hills; the social centre of Rome.

SULLA: Lucius Cornelius, 131–78 B.C.; famous Roman general and dictator.

SURA: Lucius Licinius, consul A.D. 97, 102, 107; Spaniard; governor of Germany; patron of Martial.

SYBARIS: Greek town in southern Italy; once a powerful state, it became a byword for sybaritic luxury.

SYCHAEUS: Husband of Dido who died before she met Aeneas.

SYENITE: The granite of Syene, a town in southern Upper Egypt.

SYMPLEGADES: The Clashing, or Cyanean, Rocks, famous as the passage taken by the Argonauts on their journey to Colchis to seize the Golden Fleece.

SYPHAX: Numidian prince, ally of the Carthaginians, who was defeated by Scipio Africanus in 203 B.C..

SYRTES: Treacherous shoal off the coast of North Africa, now the Gulf of Sidra.

TAENARUS: Promontory in Laconia in the southern Peloponnese, where a cave supposedly led down to the underworld.

TAGUS: Gold-bearing river in Spain, the modern rio Tajo.

TANAIS: River to the west of Scythia; modern name, the Don.

TANAQUIL: Fortune-telling Etruscan wife of Tarquinius Priscus, the fifth king of Rome (*c.* 600 B.C.).

TANTALIDS: Descendants of Tantalus, son of Jupiter and father of Pelops, often used to denote 'Argives'.

TARENTUM: Greek town on the 'heel' of Italy (Calabria); well known as one of the ancient world's fleshpots.

TARPEIAN: Connected with the Vestal Virgin, Tarpeia, who betrayed the citadel to the Sabines. She was buried and commemorated on the Capitol, to which 'Tarpeian' often refers. From the 'Tarpeian Rock' on the Capitol criminals were thrown.

TARQUIN: Tarquinius Superbus, 'the Proud'; Etruscan (and last) king of Rome; expelled in 510 B.C.

TARTARUS: Bottommost pit of Hell; the grimmest part of the underworld, where the souls of the wicked were consigned for punishment.

TARTESSUS: Ancient town on the south coast of Spain, west of Gibraltar.

TAURUS: Mountain in south-eastern Asia Minor.

TAYGETUS: Mountain range to the west of Sparta.

TEIRESIAS: See TIRESIAS.

TELEMACHUS: Son of Ulysses.

TELEPHUS: King of Mysia, son of Hercules. His wound from Achilles' spear could be cured only by its rust.

TEMPE: Beautiful river valley in Thessaly between Mts Ossa and Olympus.

TEREUS: Mythical Thracian king, married to Procne, who raped his sister-in-law Philomela; he was turned into a hoopoe. Frequent subject of mythological melodrama.

TETHYS: Sea-goddess, wife of Oceanus; in general, the sea.

THAIS: Famous Athenian courtesan whose name, frequently borrowed by other prostitutes, later became (like Lais) a synonym for an expensive call-girl.

THALIA (THALEA): Muse of comedy and pastoral; sometimes of lyric poetry.

THAPSUS: In *Punica*, a warrior fighting on the Carthaginian side at the battle of the Trebia.

THAUMANTIAS(N): Iris, daughter of Thaumas, a sea-god; messenger of the gods and goddess of the rainbow.

THEBES: Capital city of Boeotia, founded by Cadmus.

THELGON: In *Punica*, a warrior fighting on the Carthaginian side at the battle of the Trebia.

THEMIS: Greek goddess of justice (also called Astraea). A Titaness, she is said to have ceded her oracle at Delphi to Apollo peacefully.

THERAPNAE: Small town in Laconia associated (like Amyclae) with the birth of the Dioscuri and Helen.

THESEUS: Fabled king of Athens, son of Aegeus or Neptune, husband of Ariadne and later Phaedra, father of Hippolytus by the Amazon Antiope (or Hippolyte). Famous for his slaying of the Minotaur and subsequent escape from the Labyrinth. See also PIRITHOUS.

THESSALY: Large district of northern Greece, famous for its heroes and horses.

THETIS: Sea-goddess, daughter of Nereus, who was destined to bear a son greater than his father, and so she constituted a threat to Jupiter and Neptune. She was married off to Peleus, to whom she bore Achilles.

THIODAMAS: Argive augur who replaced Amphiaraus as the army's priest.

THOAS: King of the Taurians. He wanted Orestes and his friend Pylades to be sacrificed.

THRACE: Territory stretching from the Danube to the Hellespont and from Byzantium to the Strymon; its tribes were regarded as wild and primitive.

THUNDERER: Jupiter or Jove, the Roman sky-god, whose symbol was the thunderbolt.

THYESTES: Tyrant of Mycenae who was given his sons to eat by his brother Atreus.

THYRSUS: Symbol of Bacchus and his followers; a staff tipped with a pine cone.

TIBER: River that flows through the city of Rome.

TICINUS: River in the far north of Italy and location of a battle in the second Punic war.

TIGRIS: River of south-western Asia which flows into the Persian Gulf.

TIRESIAS: Old blind prophet of Thebes; was transformed into a woman for nine years.

TIRYNTHIAN: Adjective applied to Hercules, native son of Tiryns, or to the town itself.

TISIPHONE: One of the three Furies.

TITAN: Sun-god, Sol (Helios), who was of Titan descent; often identified with Apollo.

TITANIAN: Related to the Titans, the first race of gods; possessing magical powers.

TITANS: Generation of gods ruled by Kronos who were forcibly replaced by Jupiter and the Olympians.

TITARESSUS: Thessalian river running into the Peneus and said to have its source in the Styx.

TITHONUS: Trojan prince loved by the goddess of the dawn. He was granted immortality without youth and became a symbol of decrepit old age.

TOMIS: Town of Moesia on the west coast of the Black Sea. It is famous as the place to which Augustus exiled the poet Ovid.

TRACHIS: Thessalian town at the foot of Mt Oeta; cf. Sophocles' *Women of Trachis*.

TRASIMENE: Lake in Etruria and site of a battle in the second Punic war (217 B.C.).

TREBIA: A river in upper Italy, by which a battle was fought in the second Punic war (218 B.C.).

TRICCE: City in western Thessaly.

TRIPTOLEMUS: Culture hero associated with Eleusis near Athens. He was taught the arts of agriculture by the goddess Ceres (Demeter) and passed them on to mankind.

TRITON: (1) River, with lake, in North Africa, flowing into the Syrtis; (2) Minor sea-deity attending on Neptune.

TRITONIA: Epithet of Minerva, goddess of artistic creativity, from the story of her first visit to earth at Lake Tritonis in North Africa.

TROEZEN: Town at the end of the Argolid peninsula in the Peloponnese; birthplace of Theseus.

TROY: Celebrated city in north-western Asia Minor plundered and destroyed by the Greeks. Aeneas escaped to establish a new race in Italy and a reborn Troy.

TURNUS: Youthful king of the Rutulians, who made war on Aeneas and was slain by him.

TUSCAN: Etruscan.

TYDEUS: Argive chieftain killed just before *Thebaid* X opens; one of the 'Seven'.

TYNDAREUS: King of Sparta and husband of Leda; father (real or putative) of Castor, Pollux, Clytemnestra and Helen.

TYNDARIS: Daughter of Tyndareus; a description used of Clytemnestra, but most especially of Helen.

TYPHO(N): Son of, or another name for, Typhoeus.

TYPHOEUS: Primeval monster or giant, who struggled for supremacy, but was subdued by Jupiter's lightning bolts and buried under Mt Etna in Sicily.

TYRE: Major maritime and commercial city of Phoenicia from which Carthage was colonized.

TYRIANS: Inhabitants of Tyre. Thebans and Carthaginians are sometimes called 'Tyrians' because their cities' founders were Phoenicians. .

TYRRHENE: Etruscan.

TYRRHENIAN SEA: Sea between Corsica, Sardinia and Italy.

ULYSSES: King of Ithaca who was pre-eminent among the Greek heroes at Troy for his cunning and eloquence. Through the device of the Wooden Horse he contrived Troy's fall.

VARENUS: In *Punica*, a warrior fighting on the Roman side at the battle of the Trebia.

VARRO: Gaius Terentius; consul in command of the Roman forces at Cannae.

VEII: Important Etruscan city north of Rome; captured by Camillus in 396 B.C.

VENUS: Roman goddess of sexual love (corresponding to the Greek Aphrodite), mother of Aeneas and Cupid, and protectress of Rome. The emperor Augustus and the Julian family claimed descent from her through Aeneas' son, Iulus.

VESTA: Roman goddess of the hearth and of the city; her cult, with the care of the undying flame, was served by the Vestal virgins.

VESTAL: Pertaining or belonging to the Vestal virgins who guarded the sacred fire that burned in the temple of Vesta.

VESUVIUS: Famous volcano in Campania near the bay of Naples that erupted on 24 August A.D. 79, burying Pompeii, Herculaneum and Stabiae.

VIOLENTILLA: Mistress and later wife of Stella; herself a poet.

VIRBIUS: Italian hero worshipped at Aricia; he was identified with the Greek hero Hippolytus.

VIRGIL: P. Vergilius Maro, celebrated Roman poet born near Mantua in 70 B.C. His major works were *Eclogues*, *Georgics* and *Aeneid*.

VIRGINIA: Legendary heroine, who was stabbed to death by her centurion father to save her from the immoral machinations of the decemvir Appius Claudius. Her death signalled the return to non-tyrannical government.

VOLSCIANS: Tribe of Latium in central Italy, conquered by the Romans in the fifth century B.C.

VULCAN: God of fire and technology; married to Venus, and cuckolded by Mars.

XANTHUS: River near Troy.

XERXES: King of Persia, who twice invaded Greece, but was defeated by the Greeks in the sea battle at Salamis (480 B.C.) and lost even more of his ships on his retreat home.

ZACYNTHUS: Island in the Ionian Sea, off the coast of Elis.

ZAMA: Town in Numidia and site of the decisive, final battle in the second Punic war.

ZEUGMA: Town in Syria on the Euphrates river. Its name 'junction' signified its importance as a border post and as the crossroads of various trade routes.

FOR THE BEST IN PAPERBACKS, LOOK FOR THE 🐧

In every corner of the world, on every subject under the sun, Penguin represents quality and variety – the very best in publishing today.

For complete information about books available from Penguin – including Puffins, Penguin Classics and Arkana – and how to order them, write to us at the appropriate address below. Please note that for copyright reasons the selection of books varies from country to country.

In the United Kingdom: Please write to *Dept E.P., Penguin Books Ltd, Harmondsworth, Middlesex, UB7 0DA*.

If you have any difficulty in obtaining a title, please send your order with the correct money, plus ten per cent for postage and packaging, to *PO Box No 11, West Drayton, Middlesex*

In the United States: Please write to *Dept BA, Penguin, 299 Murray Hill Parkway, East Rutherford, New Jersey 07073*

In Canada: Please write to *Penguin Books Canada Ltd, 2801 John Street, Markham, Ontario L3R 1B4*

In Australia: Please write to the *Marketing Department, Penguin Books Australia Ltd, P.O. Box 257, Ringwood, Victoria 3134*

In New Zealand: Please write to the *Marketing Department, Penguin Books (NZ) Ltd, Private Bag, Takapuna, Auckland 9*

In India: Please write to *Penguin Overseas Ltd, 706 Eros Apartments, 56 Nehru Place, New Delhi, 110019*

In the Netherlands: Please write to *Penguin Books Netherlands B.V., Postbus 195, NL–1380AD Weesp*

In West Germany: Please write to *Penguin Books Ltd, Friedrichstrasse 10–12, D–6000 Frankfurt/Main 1*

In Spain: Please write to *Alhambra Longman S.A., Fernandez de la Hoz 9, E–28010 Madrid*

In Italy: Please write to *Penguin Italia s.r.l., Via Como 4, I-20096 Pioltello (Milano)*

In France: Please write to *Penguin Books Ltd, 39 Rue de Montmorency, F-75003 Paris*

In Japan: Please write to *Longman Penguin Japan Co Ltd, Yamaguchi Building, 2–12–9 Kanda Jimbocho, Chiyoda-Ku, Tokyo 101*